W9-AVC-714

THE
LAST FLIGHT

THE
LAST FLIGHT

A NOVEL

GREGORY P. LIEFER

YUCCA

Copyright © 2016 by Gregory P. Liefer

All rights reserved. No part of this book may be reproduced in any manner without the express written consent of the publisher, except in the case of brief excerpts in critical reviews or articles. All inquiries should be addressed to Yucca Publishing, 307 West 36th Street, 11th Floor, New York, NY 10018.

Yucca Publishing books may be purchased in bulk at special discounts for sales promotion, corporate gifts, fund-raising, or educational purposes. Special editions can also be created to specifications. For details, contact the Special Sales Department, Yucca Publishing, 307 West 36th Street, 11th Floor, New York, NY 10018 or yucca@skyhorsepublishing.com.

Yucca Publishing® is an imprint of Skyhorse Publishing, Inc.®, a Delaware corporation.

Visit our website at www.yuccapub.com.

10 9 8 7 6 5 4 3 2 1

Library of Congress Cataloging-in-Publication Data is available on file.

Jacket design by Haresh R. Makwana of HRM Graphics
Jacket photograph by Adamcain62 courtesy of Wikipedia

Print ISBN: 978-1-63158-097-0
Ebook ISBN: 978-1-63158-098-7

Printed in the United States of America

THE
LAST FLIGHT

PROLOGUE

South Vietnam
July 1972

Death hung in the air thick as humidity from the monsoon rains. There was no odor, taste, or feel in the wind, only a heightened sense of foreboding, knowing evil was there, unseen, waiting for an opportunity.

The four crewmen aboard the low flying helicopter were no strangers to death. Not anymore. Death was a constant companion, an invisible shadow lurking over their shoulder, reminding them of their mortality.

For some men in battle, dying was an act of fate, a roll of the dice, or chance encounter, and for others a predetermined destiny unalterable by choice or events. A strong warrior dealt with death by choosing to ignore the surrounding darkness, accept the inevitable, and use the inherent fear as an advantage. The weakest let the thought of impending doom slowly eat away at their soul, amplifying the anxiety to an inescapable paranoia until the paranoia became worse than the enemy.

That morning, a silencing overcast hovered over the jungle's thick canopy, disturbed only by the sound of the lone helicopter skirting the high trees, the dark silhouette scarcely noticeable against a dense background of rain-soaked forest. Downwash from the spinning rotors shook the branches as a trail of swirling vapor quickly faded behind.

The surrounding landscape, with fingers of mist hanging beneath the clouds, was beautiful yet ominous. Days of heavy downpour had cleansed the odor of old undergrowth and decay, enhancing the fresh, sweeter smell of lush foliage and masking any threats within.

Sounds of the engine echoed off the hills, dulled by the thick humidity so the helicopter's position was barely discernible.

The two pilots sat in the cockpit scanning ahead for a break in the weather, their faces strained with intensity below the brow of their helmets. Their vision was sharp and focused, synchronized with anxious reflexes for a quick reaction on the controls. In spite of their ages, the dangers of battle were not foreign to them. Death and destruction was an almost daily experience.

The door gunners in back gazed intently out the sides of the helicopter, their eyes conditioned for signs of movement. Poised in the open doors with hands resting on their M-60 machine guns and fingers close to the trigger, they were ready for a fight.

Viet Cong and North Vietnamese regulars controlled the area near the Laotian border. Encountering hostile fire was a very real possibility. Enemy soldiers were more emboldened to shoot at a passing helicopter when the weather helped conceal their position, delaying a reaction from far more powerful aircraft. Retaliatory firepower from the Americans was deadly but was on the decline. For the Viet Cong and North Vietnamese, the long war was nearing a successful end. Shooting down another helicopter would only make the coming victory more gratifying.

Gil Connor flew the helicopter from the right seat. He had a two-day's growth of stubble, more noticeable from the contrast with his sun-darkened skin. His lean frame easily stretched across the cockpit, with his shoulders and head protruding above the side armor plating. Blue eyes, as hard as tempered steel, reflected his physical toughness and determination. Only twenty-four years old, he was on his second tour in South Vietnam.

"You got us on the map?"

In the opposite seat, Fred "Mac" McClellan stared intently between the map unfolded on his legs and the outside terrain. A tuft of dark hair was stuck against his forehead beneath his helmet, matching the thick mustache and heavily tanned face. He was busy keeping the map oriented with the helicopter's heading, holding his finger on their position as they maneuvered over the jungle. They were off course. The territory was new for both of them, but he wasn't concerned. Like Connor, he was young and experienced beyond his age.

"Yeah, I got us." He spoke without shifting his gaze. "Right in the middle of Indian Country. Sure hope the bad guys aren't expecting us in this weather."

"Shit, Mister McClellan," the door gunner, Jimmy Stanton, boasted over the open mike, "we're ready. No different than shooting squirrels back on the farm in Iowa."

"Yeah, except squirrels can't fight back," Mac added with indifference.

Jimmy smirked and shifted position behind his machine gun. "Not the squirrels where I'm from, Mister McClellan. They're big and mean."

"You want big and mean?" Pedro Hernandez asked from the opposite gunner's position. "We hunt rats in the projects of South Chicago. They can hold you down while they chew on your flesh."

The door gunners were positioned across from each other beside the open cargo doors. Stanton was on the left, facing out at a forward angle and sitting back from the drizzle, one arm resting on the breach of his machine gun and his legs braced against the gun mount. He was thin and wore a two-piece flight suit with the sleeves rolled up above his forearms. The helmet appeared too big for his head and a smoldering cigarette dangled from his lips. He kept his eyes on the jungle, a thin smile on his blemished face.

Hernandez was more subdued. Older and soft spoken, his expression was more brooding, accentuated by his thick eyebrows and dark complexion. He wore the same style coffee colored flight suit and sat beside his gun in an almost identical position. Heavier than Stanton, but quick and agile, he was one of the best marksman in the company.

"Stay alert back there," Connor said over the intercom. His voice was stern, yet reassuring at the same time.

Hernandez glanced over his shoulder and nodded toward Stanton before replying. "Okay, sir. Nothing moving so far. How far we out?"

Connor looked at Mac, who answered for him. "Fifteen, twenty minutes if we go direct. But that's not happening in this weather."

"We'll get there," Connor added. "You see anything, tell us immediately."

"Roger. We're ready."

"Yeah, we're ready Mister Connor. Those gooks will think twice when us farm boys start firing." Stanton grinned at his own comment, knowing Pedro had never set foot on a farm.

Hernandez was used to Stanton's bluster. Over the past several months, he learned to tolerate his demeanor, along with being grateful for his shooting skills, which nearly matched his own. Spotting and firing on the enemy was critical. The safety of the helicopter often depended on their timely accuracy.

Hernandez was determined to survive his tour in Vietnam. Ensuring Stanton was at the top of his game was one way to make it happen. Being assigned as a member of Connor's crew was another. Connor had a reputation as a maverick, but his flying skill was unmatched. He seemed adept at surviving the worst situations.

The visibility decreased to a few hundred yards as Connor followed an overflowing creek along a low drainage, forcing him to slow the helicopter and increasing the chance of becoming a target. He was about to turn around when Mac suddenly pointed through the windshield.

"Over there. Looks like an opening."

Connor saw the contrast of lighter haze at the same time and banked the helicopter before Mac finished speaking. In less than a minute they were there, only to realize the opening was just a thin patch of clouds with some brief sunlight filtering through. Too close to the higher terrain, it was what pilots negatively referred to as a sucker hole. Connor reluctantly turned back toward the center of the valley.

"At least this weather is keeping the VC's head down," Mac said as he glanced back inside. "Don't imagine they enjoy this rain any more than we do."

Connor made a slight adjustment with the control stick between his legs, altering course a few degrees. "Maybe, or they're using the weather to their advantage."

Poor flying conditions made it impossible for the Air Force to strike enemy positions accurately. The North Vietnamese were cunning and determined. Thirty years of war had taught them to exploit every advantage.

Mac nodded his head. He knew Connor was right. "I guess we'll find out soon enough, if we can get there. At least nothing is happening here."

Light drizzle, joined by heavier but sporadic rain showers, continued pelting the windshield. A narrow space cleared by the wiper blades provided the only relief. Navigation was difficult and keeping the helicopter over the desired route was impossible.

Both pilots scanned intently ahead, searching for a clear passage. Connor was taut against the seat, bent forward slightly for a better view through the Plexiglas. His face was haggard from lack of sleep, hiding his rugged good looks, but his eyes remained sharp and focused, intent on the perils he knew were ahead.

The mission was in jeopardy. For close to an hour, they had been flying only a few feet above the jungle, trying to stay out of the clouds and somehow reach the extraction point. Staying in the low valleys was the best option, but the varying directions were taking them further off course. Finding a way through the weather was becoming less likely and fuel for the return leg was decreasing with each passing minute.

Sporadic breaks in the overcast were visible for a few seconds, only to close again from the shifting air currents as quickly as they appeared.

The temporary patches of blue sky were enticing. They were also dangerous, baiting Connor toward terrain hiding on the other side.

Passage over the smaller ridges was almost as hazardous. When the helicopter managed to sneak through, the next valley would be no different, and in a short time the clouds would close in behind, completely masking the hills. A quicker route was needed or they would have to abort.

Heavier rain began falling again. Once more Connor slowed and followed the only route available, forcing the helicopter further away from their destination. The crew searched and hoped for another option.

Ten miles away, near a wide river basin, a special operations assault team was converging on a clearing of waist-high elephant grass, surrounded by high jungle and bamboo. The soldiers of the Long Range Reconnaissance Patrol, or LRRP, had been on the move for the past seven days, monitoring enemy movements and setting ambushes. They were now on the run. A battalion of North Vietnamese was in close pursuit, trying to head off the six-man patrol before they reached the extraction point.

The team had radioed for an emergency extraction the night before. They were told a rescue helicopter would be sent first thing in the morning, weather permitting. The forecast wasn't good. Their only options were to dig in and fight or keep running and hope they could lose the enemy in the jungle. Neither option had much chance of success. One of the men was seriously wounded. The team was near exhaustion, and their ammunition supply was dwindling rapidly.

Connor kept the helicopter only feet above the dense forest. The valley ahead looked no different from the one before, filled with the same dark jungle and falling rain. He maneuvered the helicopter over the middle of the basin, only turning to avoid lower clouds or high trees along their flight path. The moving wiper blades made seeing obstacles even harder. Twice the skids brushed against protruding limbs, forcing him to reduce speed. Visibility was shrinking and the narrow gap below the overcast was almost nonexistent.

The needle on the fuel gauge seemed to drop faster with each passing minute. Connor flew as if they were in a giant maze, turning one way, then another, each time being drawn further away from their destination or being forced to turn back by a wall of clouds. He became frustrated, knowing they were the LRRP team's only hope.

Connor was ten months into his second tour. The mission schedule was winding down, and he looked forward to returning home. Death had become routine for him. He was no longer shocked by the horrors of war and the lack of emotion was beginning to affect his subconscious. Suppressing his emotions was a daily occurrence, at least while he was awake. The dead only haunted him in his dreams.

Thoughts of his family were pushed aside for fear they would distract him. His survival depended on staying focused. Only at night and when he wasn't preoccupied with flying did he think of his wife and kids. His last thoughts were always of them before drifting into a restless sleep. They gave him strength to awaken another morning.

Two weeks remained on Mac's tour before he returned stateside. With so few days remaining, flying another combat mission wasn't a requirement, but he volunteered anyway. He and Connor were good friends, both seasoned pilots who had flown together before. When the assigned copilot for the mission became ill, Mac readily took his place. He knew what was at stake and relished the thought of flying with his friend one more time.

"Mac, you still have us on the map?" Connor's calm voice hid his concern.

"I won't get us lost," Mac answered. "Running out of fuel is a bigger concern."

He ran a finger along the sides of his mustache then stretched his neck from side to side. "Damn. I still show us about ten miles out."

Connor hesitated a moment, looking out his side window before banking hard to the right, reversing course. "We need to try something else."

Mac's face remained expressionless except for a slightly raised eyebrow. He knew Connor would push as far as they could without giving

7

up. He was confident in his friend's ability and his own, but their diminishing fuel was a concern.

"You want to fill me in, Gil?"

"We won't make the extraction dodging this shit weather. There was another thin break in the overcast about a mile back, right in the middle of the valley. If the opening's still there, we can try to climb through and get above this scud."

Mac looked down at his map, then back at Connor. "Okay, but what then? We still need a clear hole to get back down. Unless you want to abort and head back to base. I'm tired of poking around in this crap."

"And abandon the LRRP team?"

"I don't want to any more than you, but we might not have a choice." Mac looked at Connor with a steady gaze, his voice blunt with concern.

The fuel gauge was nearing the turnaround point. They had a half hour to find the landing zone, pick up the reconnaissance team, and fly direct to the nearest refueling site. Counting on the weather to cooperate seemed a foolish gamble, but giving up was something neither of them wanted to consider.

Connor had already weighed the options. "I think my plan will work. If we can't find a large hole near the extraction point, we'll head back and refuel. Maybe the weather will improve by then."

His last statement sounded hollow. They all knew the reconnaissance team didn't have a chance without them arriving soon. Six brave men would be killed or captured if they aborted the mission.

The weather, as if hearing their predicament, suddenly changed. A break materialized in the overcast and Connor pulled back sharply on the cyclic, climbing rapidly through the narrow opening, too small even for the helicopter. The abrupt maneuver was a calculated risk, one he was willing to take.

The rotors caught the vaporous mass of air, pulling the cloud closer around the helicopter. The visibility faded into nothingness, with only the flight instruments guiding Connor on the controls. Edgy voices in back announced a loss of all outside references.

Mac spoke without emotion as he watched the gauges. "Heading looks good. Another thousand feet and we'll be above the hills."

Connor fought a brief sense of vertigo and kept the helicopter in a steady climb through the overcast. Any attempt to turn or descend now could be fatal.

Two minutes and nearly four thousand feet later, the helicopter broke clear of the cloud layer. A blanket of pillowed cotton stretched below as far as they could see. The only acknowledgment was Mac's brief smile, cut short by Connor's calm voice.

"Get the FAC on the radio. Ask him if he can see any breaks we can descend through in his area."

Radio contact with the FAC had been sporadic. High terrain interfered with communication close to the ground. At their present altitude, the signal would be loud and clear.

The FAC, short for Forward Air Controller, was flying a small twin-engine Cessna somewhere over the jungle near the extraction point. He, or another one like him, had been in radio contact with the LRRP team for the previous twelve hours.

Mac pressed his transmit button, first noting the time on the clock. He figured the river basin would take them a little over seven minutes to reach. Their fuel reserve would be stretched to the limit.

The FAC responded immediately, his slight Texas drawl scratchy after several hours in the air. He explained the team was already in position on the west side of the landing zone and taking sporadic fire. A large enemy force was close behind.

Connor pulled in maximum torque, increasing airspeed to the red line. "Jimmy, Pedro, keep a sharp look out. I need a hole to descend through in a few minutes. If we get through the overcast, stay alert on the guns. The LZ is going to be hot."

Both door gunners acknowledged. A devout Catholic, Pedro gave the sign of the cross and said a silent prayer. Jimmy rubbed his good luck charm, a piece of shrapnel retrieved from the seat frame on his first mission, now fastened as a piece of jewelry around his neck.

Five minutes passed before they were over the eastern edge of the wide river basin. There was no discernible difference in weather. Clouds effectively masked the lower terrain, obscuring any visible reference.

"Dancer Eight, we're nearing your location. Do not have you in sight. Any breaks visible in the overcast, over?" Mac waited for a response with his hand on the radio selector.

"Negative, Windrunner. I'm at seven point five, well above you. Are you receiving Bootlegger?"

Bootlegger was the LRRP team's call sign. They were using a tactical frequency and the helicopter's FM radio had been picking up static transmissions since climbing through the overcast. The chatter became clearer with each passing mile.

"Affirmative, Dancer. If we can find a way down, I'll talk to them directly." Mac was looking ahead to where the FAC should be circling. He pointed when he saw a flash of sunlight off the metal wing.

"We have you in sight now. Estimate two minutes to your location."

"Roger that, Windrunner." The steady hum of the Cessna's engines could be heard in the background. "Still no breaks visible . . . wait! I have a small opening out my left wing," the FAC continued. "The river is directly below. I'm turning toward the opening now."

Connor watched the Cessna change course and turned the helicopter in the same direction. "This is it guys. We've got enough fuel for one try."

Mac gave Connor a thumbs up and informed Dancer of their intentions. The FAC acknowledged and relayed to Bootlegger. Sounds of weapon fire were noticeable over the patrol's radio.

The hole in the clouds was the size of a football field, just big enough for what he intended. Connor dove through in a tight spiral, keeping his orientation over the muddy river until the helicopter was barely above the trees along the riverbank. He leveled and turned on the heading Mac gave him, searching the jungle.

"Dancer, we're through. We'll talk with Bootlegger direct."

Mac felt an adrenaline rush as they neared the LZ. He could feel his heart pounding. Connor was no different. The intensity in each of their expressions was obvious.

"Bootlegger, we're a mile out. What's your status?" There was no immediate response and Connor exchanged a worried look with Mac.

"Bootlegger, do you copy, over?"

Mac was about to try again when a different voice answered.

"This is Bootlegger. The LZ is hot! I repeat, the LZ is hot! Land as close to the smoke as you can. Popping green smoke now. Do you confirm?"

They saw the smoke billowing near the edge of the jungle. Connor turned the helicopter away for a few seconds before banking hard over a small drainage, shielding their path into the LZ. He followed the rising terrain in a shallow climb, staying a leg's length above the jungle canopy.

The sound of the beating rotor blades gave away their position in advance. Small arms fire erupted from a narrow ridge below the clearing. Heavy caliber tracers joined in, barely missing behind the tail boom as the helicopter cleared the trees. Jimmy immediately returned fire from the left side, raking the perimeter where muzzle flashes were visible. He stopped firing short of the swirling smoke, unable to see the position of the recon team.

"Mac, stay on the controls with me. Watch the gauges. I'm going in hot."

"I'm with you. Power looks good," Mac replied. The pitch in his voice was higher with anticipation.

Connor brought the helicopter in fast. At the last second he flared and kicked in left pedal, swinging the nose so both M-60s could concentrate forward on the area of enemy fire. He landed with a slight jolt as Pedro opened up from his side.

Mac quickly moved his hands from the controls and grabbed a short-barreled assault rifle he kept by his seat, sticking the muzzle out the window and firing a series of short bursts. He felt vulnerable on the ground. The small caliber weapon wasn't as effective as the heavier machine guns in back, but helping with suppressive fire was better than doing nothing.

Three hurrying figures in camouflage fatigues emerged from the smoke. The one in front carried another soldier across his shoulders, struggling with the weight. His face was heavy with exhaustion, streaked with sweat and camouflage paint, and his wet uniform was slick with mud. Ammo pouches and a smoke grenade hung from the straps of his web gear.

The arms of the carried soldier dangled lifelessly toward the ground. His fatigue shirt was open, soaked with blood, his eyes unmoving.

Immediately behind, the other two soldiers supported each other as they hurried toward the helicopter. Both were wounded. One limped with a bandaged thigh and the other had a bloody arm hanging weakly at his side. Half-empty rucksacks bounced on their backs as they moved. An assault rifle was slung around one man's neck and the other was carrying an identical weapon in his hand.

All three reached the helicopter about the same time. The unmoving soldier's body was quickly laid on the floor against the rear seats. He was dead. The others took up position on each side of the helicopter and began laying down return fire.

Connor counted the seconds. Twenty had passed since landing and the wait was taking too long. The helicopter could be damaged by enemy fire any moment. He silently cursed the delay but refused to leave even as rounds began pelting the fuselage. Three successive *thwacks,* distinguishable above the whine of the engine and the rattle of automatic fire, reverberated with a hollow echo.

"Keep firing. They're zeroing in on us."

Connor's voice was surprisingly calm, hiding the urge to yell over the intercom. He checked the engine gauges, relieved they were showing normal indications. His breathing quickening between each burst as he listened to the steady fire from the gunners.

The last two soldiers emerged from the dissipating smoke thirty yards away. They were running and firing behind them at the same time. The closest carried a radio with the antenna hooked over his shoulder. He turned long enough to fire a grenade through the green haze before running even harder. Only a few feet behind, the other man fired rapid bursts from an M-60 machine gun cradled at his side. A belt of ammo was draped over one arm with the metal links extending up and around his neck. The barrel glowed from the heat, steam rising from the metal surface.

Mac stopped firing, afraid he might hit the soldiers when the M-60s in back became silent.

"Pedro's hit." The voice was Jimmy's, higher pitched and without the usual bravado.

Connor turned in his seat, knowing what he would see and cursed. "Jimmy, get back on the gun!"

Stanton hesitated, not with fear, but with concern for his friend.

"Get back on the gun, now!" Connor ordered. "The others will take care of him."

Pedro's gun was already firing again as one of the recon soldiers took his place. Jimmy joined in a second later.

More rounds hit the helicopter. On the edge of the tree line, a squad of enemy soldiers emerged and ran toward them, firing wildly.

Mac saw them and reloaded. "Jimmy! A hundred yards out on the tree line, your side. Redirect your fire!"

Jimmy's gun jammed as he shifted in the doorway. He hurried to clear the weapon but kept looking up toward the approaching enemy. Only Mac's and the recon soldier's smaller automatics were firing in their direction. The rounds seemed to have no effect.

Suddenly, two bright flashes erupted directly in front of the enemy soldiers. They dove for the ground, seeking protection from the new threat.

Just then, a voice broke over the radio. "Looks like you boys could use some help." The FAC sounded jubilant as his small Cessna swooped in over the clearing before banking hard left over the jungle. "I've got a few more white phosphorous rockets that might keep their heads in the dirt."

Connor answered immediately. "Put them on the same target. Buy us another minute and the drinks are on me."

"Got them in sight, Windrunner. I'm coming in low and fast from your seven o'clock. Sure as hell hope this ruse works again."

The marker rockets, nonfatal but frightening all the same, hit in the middle of the enemy combatants, seconds before the Cessna roared over their heads.

The soldiers stayed glued to the ground, unaware the rockets were virtually harmless against troops in the open.

"Yeehaw! That should tighten their assholes. I suggest you boys get out of Dodge before the rest of the Injuns show up."

A dirty haze billowed from the minor explosions and spread with the breeze as the last two members of the LRRP team reached the helicopter. The first dove inside, rolling to the opposite door where he continued firing. The last was pulled in by the others and began yelling. "Go, go! We're all clear."

Connor was already pulling in power. Some of the team popped smoke canisters and tossed them as far as they could out the sides. Thick colors of red and yellow mixed with the last of the green, providing a psychedelic display of swirling fog that helped mask their position.

The enemy, now congregated in large numbers around the LZ, began firing blindly at the sound of the departing helicopter. The smoke shielded the location but also prevented the door gunners from returning accurate fire.

In seconds the haze dissipated in the swirling wind from the rotor blades. Connor swung the tail sharply, dumping the nose and accelerating a few feet above the wet grass. He pulled back at the last moment to clear the trees, not wanting the helicopter silhouetted against the sky longer than necessary.

"Dancer, we're clear, departing north. We sure appreciate that rocket run. Perfect timing."

"Don't mention it, partner. I was getting bored doing circles. Glad I could help."

The North Vietnamese were familiar with the tactics used by the American military. The enemy commander knew a helicopter would be used for extracting the reconnaissance patrol. Once his forces closed on the LZ, he directed troops around the perimeter to set up an ambush position.

They were assembling a heavy caliber machine gun when the helicopter arrived. A minute later the weapon aimed low and missed as the silhouette rose over the trees. Only a last second burst was possible before the helicopter completely disappeared off the side of the hill.

The gun crew cursed themselves for not being faster, convinced by the fading sound of the engine that their bullets had been ineffective. Most of the bullets only sliced through air, but three managed to hit their target. One round embedded in the protective armor around Mac's seat. Another passed through the small Plexiglas side-window before exiting out the windshield. The third was far more deadly.

The metal-jacketed bullet deflected off the doorframe and splintered, penetrating Mac's helmet above his left temple. He slumped forward. A stream of blood rolled down his forehead and nose, staining his shirt. Only the shoulder harness stopped him from falling against the controls.

Connor saw his friend shift noticeably forward. He thought Mac was reaching for something before realizing the movement was involuntary.

"Mac's hit! Jimmy, pull his seat back. See if you can help him."

Reaching over with his left hand, Connor tried pulling Mac into a sitting position. He couldn't move him. "Mac, can you hear me? Mac? Goddamn it! Shit! Stay with me. Stay with me, buddy."

There was no response. Jimmy pulled the seat back on the rails and pulled Mac's helmet off. A quarter size hole of broken scalp was visible. His head was bleeding profusely and his eyes were glazed, but he was alive.

"He's breathing but not conscious. Man, he's hurt bad," Jimmy announced anxiously.

Connor's methodical training took over. He held back his anger, fighting emotions of remorse and blame for letting Mac come along on the mission. He took several deep breaths before advising Dancer of their status, letting him know their fuel situation, the number of injured, and their intention to proceed direct to the nearest hospital.

He asked Dancer to relay the information and thanked him again, but the words were barren. Completing the mission, the adrenaline rush, the euphoria of invincibility—they were all meaningless. He suppressed his emotion, but the guilt was there, lingering and festering, eating deeper into his gut.

The FAC was unaware of the personal turmoil in the helicopter. As far as he was concerned, the mission was a success, although at a price. There was always a price. Still, he was satisfied. There would be more to come, of that he was sure.

Dancer climbed through the overcast and leveled at seven thousand feet. He was hungry after several hours in the air. He enjoyed a pinch of chewing tobacco now and then to suppress his hunger, but after repeatedly spilling his spit cup he decided to leave the habit on the ground.

Instead, he reached into a bright olive-green helmet bag beside his seat, retrieving a candy bar. The wrapper was wadded and tossed aside, hitting the corner of his helmet bag. Sewn on the pocket of the bag was a unit insignia in the shape of a shield. Depicted on the shield were a small airplane above a jungle landscape and an apparition of an angel with open wings. The word *Guardians* was stitched in white above contrasting colors of green, gold, and maroon, framed by the name 56th Support Squadron around the bottom.

The FAC consumed the candy bar in a few, quick bites before wiping his mouth. He reached forward and tuned the navigation receiver, then made a slight turn correction to maintain course.

He smiled. "Time to put the horse in the barn." The words were a local expression he picked up as a kid in West Texas. In thirty minutes he would be drinking a cold beer at the officer's club.

Connor didn't waste time looking for a hole to climb through. Not with Mac's condition and the other wounded on board. He flew over the center of the river before pulling up in steep, direct climb through the clouds. They emerged into the bright sunlight, and he turned and headed away from the border, a place where the war wasn't even supposed to exist.

No one spoke during the flight back, each of them absorbed with personal relief and regret. Thoughts of home would come later, in solitude, when memories of battle and blood and lost friends could be pushed aside, if only for a moment.

Twenty minutes later they touched down. Mac was dead. The head injury was too severe. He died in transit, a faint wheeze of air his only goodbye before passing away. His body was carefully covered with a poncho and positioned beside the dead recon soldier.

Three of the five surviving team members were wounded, as well as Pedro. His injury was enough for an early ticket home. The bullet tore a jagged hole in his upper thigh, damaging muscle tissue and barely missing a major artery. A thick scar and lingering limp would be a permanent reminder of the war.

Connor sat in the helicopter after the blades coasted to a stop. Stanton and the soldiers left after the wounded and dead had been evacuated by medical personnel. No words were necessary. They respected his desire to be alone.

A light rain began to fall again. He thought of all the past missions, of fallen friends, and blood and fear and crippled bodies, of better times, and finally of his family back home. He rested with his head against the seat, eyes open, staring into the emptiness of a lead sky.

CHAPTER ONE

Alaska
August 2005

The twin-engine commuter plane lifted off the small runway, using almost all the distance before slowly raising its nose skyward. Painted white with a thin maroon stripe along the fuselage, the aircraft ascended in a slow turn to the northwest. In the distance lay the snow-capped peaks of the Alaska Range.

Noise from the turboprop engines quickly subsided, leaving only a fading silhouette visible in the morning light. In a short time the outline was completely gone, lost against a background of lavender sky.

A crew of two pilots and a full load of nineteen passengers and cargo, including two sled dogs, were on board. Departure from the Gulkana Airport was exactly on time. Arrival at the Fairbanks International Airport, two hundred miles away, was estimated at fifty minutes after takeoff.

Captain Scott Sanders, thirty-two years old, medium height with almond colored hair and a receding hairline, sat in the left cockpit seat. He was content with allowing his energetic first officer to fly the aircraft.

Sanders had been piloting twin-engine commuters with Northern Mountain Air for nearly five years. Another three years were spent flying single-engine bush planes. After eight years of flying, he had finally accumulated enough flight hours to be considered by one of the major airlines. He had been anxious for over a week, waiting for a response to any of his recently submitted resumes.

First Officer Ken Illiamin was new with the company. His prior experience consisted of mostly charter flights for a small air service. In his mid-twenties, tall and lanky with a thin face, he had a propensity for telling stories. His comedic talent aside, he eventually planned to establish his own flying business. Alaska's expanding economy and proposed gas pipeline were strong enticements. A lucrative aviation career was a realistic goal he was determined to fulfill.

In the cabin, four of the passengers were young girls, twelve to fourteen years of age, returning home after placing second in a regional swimming tournament. They were busy chatting and gesturing out the windows at the passing scenery.

All the girls except one appeared to have stepped from the pages of a teen magazine. Expensive clothes and makeup were attempts at appearing older than their actual age. The youngest was the most mature. She wore no makeup, and her clothes were fashionable yet modest. Freckles and a ponytail portrayed a subtle innocence only partially hiding the wisdom of someone much older.

The girls were accompanied by their swimming coach, a slender, waxy-haired woman in her late twenties, wearing a light blue jogging outfit with the team name stenciled on the jacket. Athletic and plain looking, she conveyed an air of self-importance disguising an inner frailty.

Across the aisle, a petite, middle-aged woman was returning from a visit with her sister. Attractive with a friendly disposition, her warm eyes and pleasant smile always put people at ease. Auburn hair, tinted to hide the sprigs of silver, was styled below her ears. A retired teacher, she had been widowed for several years.

Two men situated in the middle of the cabin were looking forward to a two-week hunting expedition. Close friends since childhood, the taller of the two was a rancher from central Idaho and the other a biologist with Idaho Fish and Game. The guided hunt was a joint endeavor after years of planning and long conversations convincing their skeptical wives of the necessity.

Nine of the remaining passengers were tourists from a cruise ship docked at the Port of Valdez, a couple hours' drive south of the Gulkana Airport. Most were elderly retirees enthusiastic about the scenic flight north to Fairbanks.

All seemed to be enjoying themselves, except for a couple on vacation at the urging of the wife. Their marriage and upscale lifestyle were in disarray. For the husband, there were other priorities. Unfortunately for the wife, she wasn't one of them. Brokering trades in the stock market, making money and occasional infidelities were his primary focus. He treated his wife like a tarnished trophy, a reminder of a past conquest kept on the mantel for his ego. Overweight and diabetic, he was in poor health.

In the last row, an older man with thinning hair and narrow eyes leaned against the window, ignoring the inane conversations around him. His face was bearded and weathered, as tough as dried-out leather. He appeared uncomfortable, continually stretching and bending his legs while flipping pages of an in-flight magazine.

Mining had been his main occupation before starting a side business raising sled dogs. The enterprise began purely by chance after acquiring a pair of malamute-wolf hybrids for payment of a past debt. Two of the prized animals were kenneled in the cargo compartment.

His great nephew, a tough lad of eighteen, sat next to him. The old man was the lad's only family after his mother died when he was twelve. The boy wasn't planning on a return flight, intending instead to seek employment in Fairbanks—a detail he hadn't shared with his elderly uncle. Working all day on an isolated homestead was not a life he wished to continue.

The air was smooth as the two turboprop engines pulled the modern commuter plane to a speed of nearly three hundred miles an hour. A pale blue sky, brightened by the morning sun, stretched across the horizon. High mountains, gleaming in reflective light, rose in a jagged line in the distance. Off the port wing, an approaching mass of frontal clouds was barely visible.

The forecast was for good flying conditions. Light winds, unlimited visibility and high, scattered clouds were the same as every day for the past week. A large weather system was moving in from the west, bringing worsening conditions, but it wasn't expected to arrive until later in the morning. The plane's passengers expected to be safely on the ground by then, at home or enjoying the sites of Alaska's second largest city.

CHAPTER TWO

The intensity of the rising sun cast a blinding reflection through the mirror of the parked car. The tired soldier behind the wheel squinted and turned his head, as if awakened from a troubling dream.

Gil Connor sighed with a reserved finality. Lost in a void of uncertainty only moments before, he concluded today would be different. Today he would do what was necessary, without approval, without remorse and without consequence, for tomorrow might be too late.

As Connor shifted his gaze to the rearview mirror, studying his reflection, he grimaced at how haggard he appeared. His face was creased with age, etched in a constant frown, and his short-cropped hair was stained with the color of granite. The rest of his body was worn and tired, the once lean frame now heavier and sagging. More than three decades of flying and a multitude of injuries had taken their toll.

He should have retired years ago, but circumstances guided him down a different path. He hung on to a waning career, dismissing the thought of a sedentary life in the civilian world as unappealing. Flying and the military were the only things holding his life together. For him, there was nothing else to look forward to.

At least he believed the thought to be true until he learned death was beating at the door. Disease was eating away at his body, killing him from the inside. After three combat tours, two helicopter crashes, twenty thousand hours of flying, and a multitude of lesser injuries, he figured cancer was fate's way of getting even. There was a time he almost thought he was invincible. Not that he wanted to be. On many occasions he wished providence had provided a quick ending.

Connor had experienced more than his share of pain. He carried the physical scars along with the emotional trauma. Shrapnel wounds dotted his legs and a three-inch scar marked where a bullet cut through his shoulder. Healed bones and damaged tissue still flashed an occasional sting of remembrance.

Some would say he was lucky, and maybe he was, at least physically. None of the injuries were debilitating in a permanent sense, except for haunting memories of how they occurred. War had a way of doing that to a man. The sight, smell, and fear of death are never forgotten.

Nightmares and flashes of recollection were the worst, consuming him through the years, bit by bit, even if they weren't always visible. He hid the emotional scars well, his hard demeanor casting a protective shell around the fragile core inside.

He was certain today would be different. He didn't know how, exactly, only that today he would face his demons for the last time.

Less than thirty minutes earlier, Connor sat in a sterile hospital room, listening to a man barely half his age list his options. The doctor described with clinical analysis, devoid of emotion, how the tests revealed a spreading malignancy. "The outcome might be prolonged with proper treatment," he explained, "possibly extending your life expectancy a few months longer."

The doctor failed to mention the certainty of a lengthy hospitalization, with limited hope and only misery for company. Remaining bedridden in a losing struggle against inevitable deterioration was a process Connor was determined to avoid.

"Of course, there is always the hope of a new medical breakthrough extending your life even further," the doctor reasoned. "Cancer is a numbing realization. I'll schedule you for counseling if you'd like?"

The doctor sat on a stool in front of a cluttered desk, studying his notes and speaking without making eye contact. "As the cancer progresses and accelerates, drugs can alleviate the pain. Over the next couple of months, you can still be productive. Unfortunately, not as a pilot." The doctor cleared his throat. "In the long term . . . well, even modern medicine will ultimately fail. I'm sorry. I know you want me to be up front with you."

Connor nodded then glanced out the window at the lush grass and trees, vibrant with life. He wondered if he could fly at least once more, just to say goodbye.

"There is always hope and prayer, if you're so inclined," the doctor continued. His voice sounded vacant, without belief.

Connor turned and focused back on the doctor, thinking how ironic the comment was in suggesting science might not be the answer. Perhaps the advice was a way of reassuring him there was still hope. But was there really? Religion had never been a strong focus in his life, and any connection was lost long ago.

Connor shut the doctor's voice from his thoughts, allowing only a brief stare of acknowledgment. His mind was on other things as he stood, scraping the chair noisily across the tiled floor. He ignored the doctor's startled expression and turned toward the door, abruptly pulling it open before exiting the room. Halfway down the corridor, he heard his name being called and kept walking.

The diagnosis was a stinging realization for Connor. He returned to his car and sat in a daze, contemplating the end. He was not entirely surprised. Shortness of breath and increased pain had plagued him for months. He ignored the symptoms at first, convincing himself they were a result of age and old injuries. In the back of his mind, he had suspected something worse.

Only when the escalating symptoms began interfering with his performance in the cockpit did he reluctantly seek medical assistance. Tests detected a malignancy intertwined around nerves and vertebra in his spine. Further analysis showed abnormalities in his lungs and a growth near his brain stem. The disease was spreading.

The potential success of treating tumors in his lungs was encouraging. Removing tumors from the spine and brain was far less optimistic. Modern medicine hadn't reached that level of sophistication, at least not to the point a patient could survive. Connor didn't intend to die clinging to false hope or waiting for the inevitable.

Through life's challenges, Connor became convinced faith was dependent on one's actions. He wanted nothing to do with a lengthy and bedridden illness, whether at the mercy of science or God. He would take his chances alone, as he always did, and find a way to end the suffering on his terms.

In a way, his acceptance of the disease was a call to action, only requiring a short period of contemplation. Connor was determined to go out with more than a whimper. Dying with a multitude of tubes and wires attached, unable to function or communicate until the last breath escaped his body, was an option he was unwilling to accept.

Perhaps the recurrence of a dream the night before, after years of absence, was somehow a premonition. The loss of his beautiful, young daughter still haunted Connor. The recollection never completely went away. At times he found a release for his emotions in fits of tears and anger but only when alone.

Connor often displayed a temperament of apathy that few understood. He knew he could never let the memories of his daughter or his guilt completely disappear. He never wanted to. Soon, maybe, they could be together again, dad and his little girl. The life he let slip away and the one he would never forgive himself for losing.

The day so long ago began innocently enough. He was with his family in a relaxing setting on a pristine lake. Connor and three-year-old Tara were spending time together after his return from a second tour in Vietnam. They were boating while his wife and fourteen-month-old son remained ashore. Tara was as excited about going fishing with her dad as he was having her along. At the age of three, anything new was a big adventure, and he relished the chance to teach her about the outdoors, just as his father had done with him.

"Cutie pie," as he often called her, always made Connor happy. Her big almond eyes and brilliant smile could charm the hardest soul. Tara always greeted him by running into his arms and giving him a big hug, speaking loudly with glee, "Daddy, my daddy!" Then she would grasp his face between her tiny hands, stare into his eyes for a few seconds as if searching for some hidden secret, and smile widely. To say she had him twisted around her little finger was an understatement.

Fishing was unsuccessful. Connor wanted Tara to catch at least one to take back for dinner even though, for her, just being with her dad was all that really mattered. After venturing across the lake in search of a better location, the weather took a turn for the worse. At first the change was only a light drizzle, but Connor saw the dark mass of clouds approaching and decided to make a run back to camp. They never arrived. Motor trouble sent them adrift, then strong winds hit, and waves swamped their small boat, spilling them into the cold water with only light jackets for protection.

For three hours they clung together against the overturned hull. Connor reassured her, as much as himself, help was coming and told stories to keep their minds off the cold. They even laughed some in the beginning, until the shivering became uncontrollable. Connor wrapped his jacket around her as best he could, but the thin fabric was useless. Tara never panicked or even cried, not once. Her trust in her dad was absolute.

When Tara stopped shivering Connor knew hypothermia had reached a critical stage. At first, he begged then cursed God as she slipped into unconsciousness and stopped breathing. A rescue boat found him later in the afternoon, barely alive, still clinging to his daughter, refusing to let go until they pried his arms from her life-less body.

Connor almost died on the way to the hospital, but eventually recovered, except for the nightmares. Months after the funeral he remained withdrawn, blaming himself, wanting to die, unable and afraid to end his own life. Instead, he hid behind a bottle of liquor, pushing away his wife who mourned their daughter's death as much as he.

Within a year his wife divorced him, taking his young son with her. Whether she left because she was unable to find forgiveness or because the thin bond holding them together was broken by his own self-pity, didn't matter to Connor. His family was gone, and in his eyes their departure was well deserved retribution for Tara's death.

Eventually, Connor overcame his grief enough to renew contact with his young son, trying to be a father again. But like so many of his relationships, it also failed. He wanted to blame his wife for taking his son thousands of miles away and giving him a new father who would always be there for him, but in his heart he knew letting him go was best.

Years later, circumstances changed for the better. Once his son reached manhood, the military, ironically, brought them back together. As fellow soldiers they renewed their family bond and learned to appreciate what they had missed for so many years. The blood between them was strong and restored Connor's faith. At least until a roadside bomb in Iraq took his son away for good. Since then, he could barely hang on to the lingering shreds of his own life.

CHAPTER THREE

Sanders watched the flight instruments as the first officer leveled the aircraft, then keyed his transmitter.

Hundreds of miles away, an air traffic controller sitting in front of a large circular screen saw the altitude flash above the radar blip, followed by a routine radio call over his headset.

"Anchorage Center, Northern three-six-zero is level at sixteen thousand."

"Northern three-six-zero, Anchorage Center, roger. Proceed as filed. Advise when passing Drum Intersection."

"Northern three-six-zero, wilco," Sanders replied. He turned his attention outside, captivated by the spectacular scenery. Every so often he looked back at the instruments, verifying the systems were operating correctly.

"Hey Captain, we still going to divert closer to the mountains so the passengers can get some photos before descending into Fairbanks?" Illiamin was hoping they could fly near the peaks and barely hid his enthusiasm.

"Sure. We can divert off the airway after passing Drum Intersection. The winds shouldn't be a problem. I don't want anyone getting sick in the back."

Illiamin thought for a moment. "I know what you mean. The smell is contagious."

"True." Sanders emitted a brief chuckle. "And remember, happy passengers make for return customers. Being jostled around or getting sick could deter future business."

"I guess I'm still used to flying small bush planes," Illiamin said while nodding his head. "We had a captive audience flying into the villages. Repeat customers weren't a problem and rough weather was pretty common."

Sanders smiled as he recalled his own experiences as a young pilot. The flights were almost always long and hectic, lasting from early morning to evening, with multiple stops for passengers, cargo, and fuel. Loading and unloading was done by the pilots, and breaks were often of short duration with only enough time for a cup of coffee or cold sandwich. The schedule was mostly sustained by their youth and eagerness to build flight time, eventually allowing a progression to bigger aircraft and better pay.

"A passenger getting sick is bad enough, but I've got a worse situation for you." A mischievous grin creased the corners of Illiamin's mouth.

"Oh yeah?" Sanders stated suspiciously, familiar with his first officer's penchant for telling stories.

"I was flying a mail run to a village on the Koyukuk River a couple years ago. There was only one passenger, an old sourdough returning from a doctor's visit in Fairbanks. We'd been in the air for about thirty minutes when this awful, disgusting smell hit me. At first I thought maybe one of us had stepped in something before boarding, but the smell kept getting stronger and stronger."

Sanders grimaced. "So what was it?"

Illiamin ignored the question, becoming more animated. "I looked over at my passenger, wondering if he smelled what I smelled.

He was staring out the window, seemingly unaware of the odor even though I was about to gag. The stink was overpowering, and I figured the smell must be from him. I asked if he was all right. He said he was, acting as if nothing was out of the ordinary. Finally, I couldn't stand the stench any longer and slid my window open to get some fresh air. It was the middle of winter and the temperature was thirty below outside."

Sanders smirked, anticipating the rest of the story, but he had to ask. "So what was it? Did the guy crap his pants?"

"Wait a minute, there's more. Not only was the odor getting stronger, the smell reeked something terrible. I mean a noxious, putrid aroma of rotten garbage, mixed with the worst case of diarrhea you can imagine. And of course with the cold temperature outside, the heater was on, making the smell even worse. So I looked at the guy again, and he was still staring out the window but now with an embarrassed look on his face. Well, I didn't want to humiliate the guy by asking if he did what I thought he did, so I kept my mouth shut. I mean I literally kept my mouth shut because I didn't want the stink hitting my taste buds."

"So what did you do?" Sanders asked, laughing aloud.

"I jammed the throttle full open and flew as fast as the damn plane could carry us. All the while I was holding my head close to the open window, trying to keep the smell out of my nostrils, and at the same time trying not to get frostbit from the wind."

"And the old guy still didn't say a thing?" Sanders paused to wipe the moisture from his eyes after laughing so hard. "I'm surprised the guy could sit still."

"Oh yeah, he hardly moved and definitely didn't say a word. Of course, I wondered if the excrement was going to leak through his clothes onto the seat. I mean the smell was so strong there must have been a couple gallons worth. So I flew with my nose out the window, trying not to be obvious about what I was doing. Every few minutes I looked over to check whether he was leaving any residue on the seat, expecting the worse and pretending to look out the opposite window as if watching the weather. I swear if there had been a place to land, I would've been tempted to kick him out. But he was a paying customer, so I kept on flying."

"How long was the flight?"

Illiamin repositioned the mike on his headset. "Another fifteen minutes until we finally landed at the village. I taxied off the runway like a maniac and shut off the engine as quickly as I could. Then I told the old guy to go ahead and exit while I jumped out the other side without helping him. Hell, he stunk so bad I probably would've retched if I got any closer. I deliberately darted toward the tail to get away from him. He headed off to the nearest building, probably in as much of a hurry to get away as I was for him to leave."

"And the smell?" Sanders asked. "Did he take it with him?"

"I opened all the doors and windows to air the plane out, just to make sure. The worst was gone. There was still a lingering odor but nothing else around his seat. After I unloaded the cargo, I sprayed the interior with Lysol and hung an air freshener I grabbed out of the dispatch office. There was probably some residual stink on the way back, but after being hit with the full force on the flight up, I didn't smell a thing."

Sanders shifted in his seat. "So what was the guy's story?"

Illiamin glanced over at Sanders with a serious expression on his face. "I sure wasn't going to track him down and ask. But after I got back to town, I approached one of our experienced pilots and told him what happened. I wanted to know what he would've done. After telling him the story he started laughing his ass off and said, 'you flew Diaper Dan. We only let him fly with the new pilots.' By his expression I knew I'd been set up."

"Diaper Dan?" Sanders asked skeptically.

"Yeah, that was his nickname. Turned out the old prospector had been flying in and out of Fairbanks once or twice a year for decades.

His bowel problems had started a few years before I arrived at the company. Apparently, the guy had read about some weird cure to prevent illness, which involved eating fermented meat and pickled eggs on a daily basis. The less than appetizing recipe became his primary diet. The concoction probably had something to do with the saying, 'if it doesn't kill you, it will only make you stronger.' You can imagine what the ingredients must have been doing inside his digestive system. I bet he had gas something terrible on a normal day. Combined with the pressure changes during flight, his bowels couldn't hold the toxic mixture and unloaded."

Sanders grunted in disgust before commenting. "So obviously the guy started wearing an adult diaper to hold in the goods. Why did the company put up with it?"

A frown etched Illiamin's face as he continued. "The first occurrence was the worst, I was told, since he wasn't wearing a diaper and there were other passengers aboard. After that, the company told him he couldn't fly unless he wore some protection. Even then the smell was terrible. The company was going to stop flying him altogether, but he was a rich old sourdough and offered to pay twice the normal fare. The company agreed as long as the flight wasn't carrying other passengers. Of course, the pilots complained and a few threatened to quit if they had to fly with him."

"But the company said to screw the pilots and kept on allowing the old guy to fly, right?"

"Yes and no," replied Illiamin. "The company had to do something or lose experienced pilots, so they came up with another option. Turns out our director of operations was a practical joker. He decided since the old guy only flew once or twice a year, and since there was always an unsuspecting new pilot around, they would schedule the two together. Unfortunately for me, I was the unsuspecting new guy. This went on for another year while I was there, but I never had to fly him again. A newer pilot always seemed to be available. Poor old 'Diaper Dan' eventually passed away. He probably rotted away from the inside."

Sanders was laughing and shaking his head again. "That's terrible. You're lucky though, new pilots in this company aren't subjected to practical jokes. At least not yet."

"Good to know." Illiamin eye's flashed with humor. "Every new guy should have to go through some kind of initiation. I think we should start right after I'm no longer the new guy."

"I'll keep that in mind. Just remember, no practical jokes on the captain. If I smell a foul odor, I'll know who to blame."

Illiamin nodded innocently and focused back on the instruments, at the same time scrolling through his mental catalog of other interesting anecdotes. He had an engaging personality and could find humor in any situation. He wondered if something might happen today worth remembering.

Sanders looked out the window to the west, noticing the approaching storm in the distance. He spent the next few minutes reviewing an instrument approach chart. When finished, he folded the sheet into a corner of the console below the windshield.

"Three miles until we pass the intersection," Illiamin said, pointing to the digital readout on the instrument panel.

Sanders glanced over to confirm the indication. "Okay, good. We'll break off from the airway in a minute."

Once the distance on the console display decreased to zero, Sanders pressed his transmit button. "Anchorage Center, Northern three-six-zero passing Drum at sixteen thousand, with a request, over."

The response was immediate. "Northern three-six-zero, Anchorage Center, go ahead."

"Northern three-six-zero requests cancellation of our instrument flight plan. We'll continue visually, direct to Fairbanks."

The controller hesitated before answering, making a notation in his tracking log before providing an updated clearance.

"Northern three-six-zero, IFR clearance is canceled. No other traffic in the area. Proceed direct to Fairbanks and contact Approach Control when able on one-two-six-point-five. Good day."

"Northern three-six-zero copies. Good day, sir."

Sanders released the transmit button and placed his hands on the control yoke. "All right, I've got the controls. You have the radios. Let's go sight-seeing."

Illiamin glanced across the cockpit, verifying the captain's hands were on the opposite set of flight controls before releasing his grip.

"You have the controls."

Sanders banked the aircraft in a smooth turn, aiming toward the highest peak in a line of towering mountains.

CHAPTER FOUR

Gil Connor was raised in northern Minnesota, where his father was employed at a local mill. He was content as an only child in the small town with plenty of friends. Luxuries were scarce, but he never lacked for necessities and earned a small allowance for weekend movies at the town theater. His mother kept busy with house-work, church activities and as a member of the local sewing club, which met every Thursday.

On Sundays after service, the family went fishing in one of the nearby lakes or hiked old logging roads that cut through the sur-rounding hills. By the time he was ten, he was included in hunting trips with his father, who taught him to appreciate and respect the outdoors. Life was simple, with plenty of adventurous activities for a kid.

Connor's world changed in his first year of high school. His father had been diagnosed with lung cancer the year before, and his condition worsened until he passed away, bedridden, over the Christmas holi-day. Connor was devastated. He tried to be strong for himself and his mother, secretly wishing for a miracle that never came.

Within a year his mother remarried and the family moved to a small farm near the North Dakota border. Life was hard with full days of work tending livestock and working the fields, but there was still time for hunting, fishing, and other activities.

Connor enjoyed his time alone, even more so as he grew older. His mother became more distant and rarely escaped the presence of his overbearing stepfather. The man rarely spoke to Connor, dealing with him instead through his mother. Sneaking away from the farm became a daily pursuit.

A farmer's life was never a goal for Connor. He was unsure of exactly what he wanted, but a sedate lifestyle was not what he was looking for. College seemed a logical choice in the interim, and following high school he enrolled in the state university. A year later he was still searching for something challenging in his life.

Flying had always appealed to him. Exciting stories of barnstormers and fighter pilots were a conduit into a life of adventure he could only read about in his youth. Finally realizing he was wasting time and money at college, he joined the Army to fly helicopters.

The Army was the only branch in the military accepting applicants for flight school without a college degree. The war in Vietnam was requiring pilots, lots of them. At the time his decision seemed hasty, but it was one he would never regret.

The first time he touched the controls of the small, temperamental helicopter over a small training field in Alabama, he knew he found what he was looking for. The satisfaction and thrill of flying overcame him immediately and would remain with him forever.

Connor was not only good at what he did, he was lucky. After graduating near the top of his class in flight school, he was assigned to a general support company in Vietnam, flying UH-1 Huey helicopters. Connor had the luxury of honing his flying skills in diverse missions and with experienced tutelage from older pilots, who took him under their wings.

By the time he flew his first combat mission, he was already a seasoned pilot and well ahead of his peers. Often flying in situations others avoided, he soon developed a reputation as a fearless pilot with an uncanny ability to survive the worst circumstances. He was known for pushing his aircraft and crew to their limit and always finding a way to accomplish the seemingly impossible.

He sometimes had a feeling someone or something was guiding him, keeping him safe. The presence was faint, barely perceptible. Often the feeling was only a whisper or nudge to his subconscious, but the sensation was real. Whether it was a sixth sense or second thoughts steering his decision, he wasn't sure. He didn't care, but he trusted whatever was there. The voice over his shoulder was never wrong.

Many soldiers owed their lives to his timely rescue or for flying in critical supplies when others couldn't get through. A few jealous pilots considered him a maverick, often accusing him of being out of control and willing to take unnecessary risks. But most pilots, especially those who flew with him, offered a different opinion. To them he was simply the best.

The hardest part for Connor was losing his friends. A few were killed outright during combat missions and some sent home with severe injuries. Each loss made him tougher on the outside, where he appeared determined and self-assured, but inside he was struggling with uncertainty.

Watching Tortello die toward the end of his first tour was particularly hard. Connor and Tortello graduated from flight school together, drank and chased women together, and almost died together. They became close friends. Almost inseparable, they were brothers in arms with the same dreams and ambitions.

He and Tortello were piloting separate helicopters on a joint supply mission to a remote firebase. On the third sortie, they encountered enemy fire over a patch of dense jungle. Tortello's ship was damaged and unable to maintain flight. Connor watched as the ship went down in a small clearing, hitting hard and bouncing before coming to rest on its side.

One of the door gunners, Willie Smith, was thrown clear on impact. Dust was still settling as the pilots staggered out of the wreckage. The copilot, Jack Roberts, barely able to walk, managed to reach Smith and help him sit upright. He was in shock and hardly moved. Tortello pulled the limp body of the other door gunner clear before kneeling weakly beside him.

The small opening in the jungle was impossible to land in without damaging his own helicopter, forcing Connor to circle while radioing for assistance. He knew the enemy was close by and virtually invisible beneath the thick canopy, but he stayed in position, hoping a helicopter with hoist capability could reach their friends in time.

Connor's helicopter began taking small arms fire within minutes after the crash. The rounds peppered the fuselage, causing only superficial damage but forced him to climb higher. His two door gunners blindly sprayed suppressive fire into the thick foliage around the wreckage, with no noticeable effect. Moments later they watched helplessly as over a dozen black-clad soldiers emerged into the clearing, gesturing frantically at the injured survivors with their weapons.

Connor cursed and banked sharply in a high turn overhead, keeping the area in sight. "Cease fire! Cease fire! We don't want to hit our own guys."

"Holding fire," The right door gunner, Private Purelski, spat in disgust. "Just give me the word and I can take the bastards out."

"Keep your finger off the trigger and keep watching. I want to know which way they go when they move out with our guys. I doubt the bastards will stick around for long."

The copilot, Jim Henderson, had been on the radio trying to coordinate a rescue helicopter and close air support. He looked dejected. "Five minutes until the fast movers arrive. At least another ten before an Air Force helo can get here. They're the closest helicopter with hoist capability."

Connor glanced at Henderson with a solemn look. "That will be too late."

Just then, Purelski yelled over the intercom. "They just shot Willie and Mister Roberts. Jesus Christ! Those fucking bastards shot them both."

Connor snapped his head around to see the bodies of Smith and Roberts lying motionless on the ground. The limp body of the other door gunner lay nearby, apparently killed in the crash.

Several of the Viet Cong stood glaring at Tortello, who stayed kneeling with his hands on his head, staring back at them. The others were ransacking the interior of the wreckage, searching for anything useful and completely ignoring the helicopter circling overhead. They knew they wouldn't be fired upon while holding a captive.

"Shit! Those dirty yellow bastards," Henderson exclaimed. "Why? They were unarmed. They weren't even resisting."

"I don't know," Connor answered his copilot even though he knew the reason. Wounded prisoners would slow them down.

"They're tying Mister Tortello's hands," Purelski stated coldly. "Looks like they're getting ready to move."

Connor noticed the activity and watched intently. He was relieved they didn't shoot his friend, but equally worried about his chance of survival as a prisoner of war. The Viet Cong were noted for their brutal treatment of captives, especially airmen.

The soldiers around the helicopter joined the group surrounding Tortello and motioned toward the jungle. Two of them seemed to be arguing. Suddenly, one stepped forward and jammed something in Tortello's mouth. Connor first assumed the object was a gag. But a gag didn't make sense. Why muffle a prisoner deep in their own territory?

Tortello was pushed backward by one of the soldiers, and in that instant Connor realized it wasn't a gag in his mouth. The object was a grenade. He watched in horror as the Viet Cong hurried into the tree line while his friend looked helplessly skyward. In the next second he saw Tortello's upper body disintegrate in an explosion of blood and tissue, collapsing the headless corpse on the ground.

Connor stared wide-eyed at the gruesome scene for only a moment, then pushed the helicopter in a steep dive, yelling at the two door gunners. "Fire! Fire, damn it! Spray inside the tree line. Kill them before they get away!"

Purelski and White were firing before he finished speaking. They let loose a stream of repeated bursts as Connor dove low and fast over the clearing, searching the surrounding jungle for potential targets. They were too late. The enemy was gone. Their friends were dead.

Only feet above the trees, Connor banked tightly for another pass, finally realizing the futility of continuing. "Stop firing. It's over. There's nothing more we can do."

Both gunners continued firing for a few more seconds before obeying. They knew he was right.

No one said anything for a few moments, afraid their emotions would seep through. The four men had been friends. Remaining silent was hard—trying to speak even harder.

"Take us back to base." Connor's voice was quivering as he motioned to his copilot. "You've got the controls."

Henderson noticed the pained expression in Connor's eyes and took control of the helicopter. They were his friends, too, but Connor and Tortello were especially close.

Purelski sat on the metal floor, resting his head in his hands. White sat across from him, staring straight ahead and silently cursing the Viet Cong, the war, and the Army. They all wondered when the killing would end.

CHAPTER FIVE

The six-hundred miles of the Alaska Range curve through the interior like a giant fish hook. Beginning in the Saint Elias Range in Canada, the formidable mountains extend halfway across the state before bending south and joining the Aleutian Range near Bristol Bay. Hundreds of towering, snow-capped peaks and an equal number of massive, seemingly endless glaciers add to the expanse.

Sanders flew the modern commuter plane with an easy confidence. He adjusted the twin throttle levers on the center console as they approached the nearest peak, pulling back slightly on the control yoke. The airspeed slowed as they descended, allowing more time for sightseeing out the windows.

"All right folks, this is your captain speaking. By popular request, we will be passing near a few majestic peaks for some photo opportunities before beginning our descent into Fairbanks. Coming up on the right side is Mount Hayes, which is just under fourteen thousand feet in elevation. A few miles further out, you can see Mount Moffit at thirteen thousand and four other peaks rising above ten thousand.

Closer in on the left side, you will see Mount Balchen at eleven thousand, then Hess Mountain and Mount Deborah at around twelve thousand. Between them is a massive ice field, branching into separate glaciers cutting through the many valleys.

Folks, the view you're seeing up close lies between the Richardson and Parks Highways. Fifty miles across, this small section includes ten peaks above ten thousand feet and seven major glaciers. I'm sure you'll agree the scenery is spectacular, yet the view is only a tiny sampling of all the mountains in Alaska."

The passengers could be heard talking excitedly in the back as a few shifted in their seats, snapping photographs of the scenery. Illiamin was equally impressed and was glad Sanders was flying, allowing him to relax and enjoy the view.

The passenger cabin was designed with only a single seat on each side, extending back for eight rows with a ninth row of three seats across the rear bulkhead. Between the bulkhead and tail section was a large compartment for storing baggage and cargo. A rear exit was located between the last two rows on the left. Two exits were in the middle of the cabin, one over each wing. A forward access door was behind the cockpit, on the left side in front of the first row, and directly across from the entryway were several small storage lockers. Another smaller baggage compartment was located in the nose of the aircraft.

The four girls, their coach, and the retired schoolteacher were sitting in the first three rows. The two out-of-state hunters occupied the fourth row, and the unhappy married couple sat immediately behind. Six of the seven elderly tourists from the cruise ship were spread in the three identical rows further back. The last set of bulkhead seats was filled by the remaining tourist, the old miner, and his nephew.

Susan Douglas smiled as the girls excitedly pointed out the high peaks to each other. Fit and a few inches over five feet tall, at the age of fifty, her curved body still drew admiring looks. Her personality was her best feature, and she was often the center of attention in any social gathering. A cream-colored blouse, boot-cut beige jeans, and fitted waist length jacket highlighted her figure.

One of the girls clicked several images before passing a disposable camera across the aisle for more photos from the opposite window. Their coach, Donna Reagan, seemed less excited about the scenery and more interested in a fashion magazine. Keeping up on the latest trends was one of her obsessions, although she rarely practiced what she read. Only when one of the girls stood up and leaned over her seat, did she divert her attention.

The elderly group of tourists was equally captivated by the towering mountains. The scenery was the main reason they selected Alaska for a vacation. Several had expensive video cameras, which they used liberally from both sides of the aircraft. Voices filled the cabin with talk of Alaska and travels to other exotic destinations.

The two hunters, Dave Kwapich and Hank Bidwell, appeared subdued after a series of long connecting flights over the previous twelve hours. Their seats were separated by the narrow aisle and they seemed content enjoying the view in anticipation of their upcoming hunt.

Kwapich appeared the more relaxed of the two, wearing khaki pants, a plaid shirt, and running shoes on his wiry, five-foot-ten frame. Folded against his seat was a lightweight, fleece jacket. His feet stretched under the seat in front, and he leaned partly sideways against the fuselage. At forty-three years old, he was self-conscious of his retreating hairline and wore a faded, burgundy colored baseball cap.

Bidwell was five inches taller with broad shoulders and thick forearms. Denim jeans and a long-sleeve, heavy cotton shirt rolled above his elbows depicted a typical rancher's outfit. Worn hiking boots covered his large feet, which looked out of proportion in the small opening between the seats. A head of thick, reddish-brown hair and matching goatee speckled with silver gave him a rugged appearance.

In the last row, Danny Simms had given up on trying to see outside from the middle seat. He stretched his youthful legs and immersed himself in music from an iPod, slowly rocking his head to the rhythmic beat in his headphone.

On his left, sixty-three-year-old Otto Hackermann was uninterested in the scenery. He disliked flying and being close to the mountains made him nervous. He usually traveled by vehicle and only made an exception this time because his truck was in for repairs. Aside from personal reservations about flying, he was concerned for his two dogs in the cargo compartment.

The remaining seat in the last row was occupied by an older woman named Doris, who was accompanying two close friends. This was their first visit to Alaska. She spoke excitedly with her companions and encouraged Lenora, directly in front, to take as many pictures as possible.

Sanders maneuvered the aircraft close to the western slope of Mount Hayes until the summit passed off the right wing, then turned left at a sharper angle toward Mount Deborah. At the same time he nosed the aircraft slightly forward, reducing altitude. They began picking up light turbulence as they passed through thirteen thousand feet.

"Flash the seat belt sign for the passengers," Sanders instructed. "I don't want anyone being caught out of their seat."

Illiamin flipped a switch on the overhead console, sending a signal to the passenger cabin. "Seat belt sign is on, Captain."

"Thank you. We'll continue past Mount Deborah, then turn and descend over the Wood River into Fairbanks. The view is awesome up here. I never get tired of it."

"Sure is." Illiamin continued gazing out the window. "This is the first time I've flown over the mountains without being in the clouds."

"I've never been bored flying in Alaska," Sanders stated. "Seeing mountains like this on television doesn't do them justice. I don't think I'll ever get tired of the scenery."

"Yeah, it's pretty amazing. Nature sure has a way of making us feel insignificant."

As Illiamin finished talking, a strong downdraft on the leeward side of the mountain hit the aircraft, forcing Sanders to compensate for a rapid loss of altitude. Stronger bouts of turbulence began shaking the plane.

"We may have to cut this short. Looks like the winds ahead of the weather front arrived earlier than forecast," Sanders explained. "The scenery is a nice bonus, but I don't want the passengers getting jostled around too much."

Illiamin looked out ahead at the highest peak and noticed a trail of blowing snow tapering sharply away from the summit. "Do you see that?" He pointed toward the peak. "The wind wasn't doing that a few minutes ago."

"No, it wasn't. I'm turning toward Fairbanks." Sanders suddenly felt uncomfortable being close to the mountains. He realized he allowed the aircraft to divert too far into the path of the approaching storm.

"Ladies and gentlemen, this is your captain again. I'm afraid we're going to have to cut the scenic tour short. As I'm sure you already noticed, we're picking up increased turbulence. For your comfort and safety, we are continuing on to Fairbanks. I apologize for any inconvenience."

There were a few grumbles of dissatisfaction from the cabin, mostly from the youngsters, but after a few seconds they subsided. The passengers soon realized there was still ample scenery to enjoy during the remainder of the flight.

"Should I give Fairbanks Approach Control a call?" Illiamin watched as Sanders turned on a new heading.

"Not yet. We're still about a hundred miles out. Give them a call at fifty miles."

The turbulence slackened after Sanders turned the aircraft away from the higher peaks. He continued a slow descent, expecting the winds to decrease further. At first they did, and when another sharp downdraft hit the aircraft, he was caught by surprise. The force of violent air took only a few seconds to subside, but in the same time the aircraft dropped three hundred feet.

The next loss of altitude was even worse. The drop wasn't a downdraft, but a loss of power. The aircraft began to roll right, followed by the sound of a high-pitched audio horn and illumination of the number two fire-warning light on the instrument panel. The emergency immediately caught both pilots' attention.

"Fire indication on the number two engine," Sanders declared. He quickly adjusted the power levers to level the aircraft. "Any smoke or fire visible on your side?"

Illiamin quickly turned and leaned against the side window, glancing back toward the starboard wing. His voice increased in pitch. "Roger. We've got smoke trailing from the engine and flames around the cowling."

Illiamin reacted automatically. Without waiting for a command, he reached for the overhead console and placed his hand on the fire suppression handle. "Number two fire handle identified."

Sanders grabbed the starboard engine's fuel and throttle controls, yanking the levers to the off position. He then feathered the propeller, aligning the blades to a zero pitch angle. The procedure stopped their rotation, reducing drag on the aircraft.

Sanders confirmed Illiamin's hand was on the correct fire suppression lever and in a much calmer voice than he expected told him to initiate the emergency procedure. "Pull the fire handle."

Illiamin immediately did as instructed. After waiting a few seconds, he looked back at the engine, relieved to see the fire was extinguished. "The fire's out. No visible flames, and the smoke is subsiding."

Sanders didn't answer. He concentrated on flying the aircraft. With an engine out and a full load of fuel and passengers, the plane was descending rapidly into the mountains. He barely noticed the frantic, terrified voices of the passengers.

CHAPTER SIX

Connor sat in the parking lot, the car's engine off, remembering the events of Tortello's death all too vividly. The memory had been resurfacing more often in the past few months, allowing only fitful sleep.

For a moment he forced his eyes into the glaring sunlight, welcoming the pain. His knuckles turned white as he gripped the steering wheel. He forced the emotion back into a hidden recess, where the memory lingered with the others, waiting to come forward again.

A sharp spasm suddenly shot through Connor's back, reverberating down his left leg. He grimaced and forced himself to lean back against the headrest, closing his eyes. The episodes were becoming more frequent and painful. The throbbing intensified for a moment before slowly fading. He relaxed his breathing, recalling better times when he was healthy and young.

Less than two months after Tortello's death, Connor returned to Alabama as a flight instructor, providing fledgling pilots the benefit of his experience. Away from the war he found a temporary peace. He married and his loving wife bore him a beautiful daughter and son. The time was one of the happiest in his life. He relished each passing day, especially the time with his family. The memories of war, which he hid so well, were left behind, at least for a while.

Once American forces began their systematic withdrawal from Vietnam, Connor thought he would escape being sent over again. His wife didn't want him to go, and for the most part he didn't either. But another part grew anxious with the prospect of returning. Lost friends and personal demons still pulled at his conscious.

Whether he wanted to return or not didn't matter. The Army soon made the decision for him. One day he was in the comfort of his home, surrounded by family, and the next in Vietnam wondering if his new assignment would be his last.

On the second tour Connor always seemed to be in the thick of dangerous situations. Twice, helicopters were shot out from under him in enemy territory, where he barely managed to evade capture. Three other helicopters were so badly damaged they barely made the flight back to base.

Members of his crew, some of them close friends, were killed, each loss making him harder and more determined. Several times he was wounded, although never severely enough to be sent home. He ignored the physical pain, but the mental stress kept building inside. When he finally left Vietnam again, he was near the breaking point. The loss of his daughter on his return finally pushed him over the edge.

By the time Connor pulled himself away from a personal hell of blame and self-pity, reinforced all too frequently by haunting nightmares, his career was in ruin. Two more failed marriages along the way didn't help. Only his love of flying finally turned his life around and eventually his career.

Five years after the loss of his daughter and still in a repetitive routine as an instructor at the Army's flight school in Alabama, Connor asked for reassignment to Germany. There, he flew a more challenging schedule, flying high-ranking officers across Western Europe or supporting tactical operations with specialized troops. The change was rewarding and allowed him to place his personal failures in the past.

His renewed enthusiasm for flying was soon outdone by his next assignment in Alaska. The beauty captured him in a spell of newfound affection and adventure. He was finally able to experience flying in the Last Frontier first hand, outside the pages of the books he consumed as a kid.

Connor was always a step above most pilots and soon became as adept and confident at mountain flying as he had been in combat. He had few equals. His commitment to his career, and more importantly to himself, was restored.

Further assignments followed in Colorado, the Middle East, Louisiana, and Korea. With each new posting came increased responsibility, and as a senior warrant officer he served in multiple administrative positions. His flight hours decreased, but his motivation never changed. He always found time to fly. Flying was his equalizer and a way of reducing the stress of everyday life.

Now at the end of his career, Connor gratefully found himself back in Alaska, ironically assigned to a company of outdated helicopters nearing their own retirement. Unlike the machines, however, he did not intend to fade peacefully away.

Over the years, Connor had seen aviation change for the better and for the worse. As technology improved, so did the capability of the helicopters. Training, tactics, and even the motivation of pilots changed along with them. For some, flying was simply a job, a paycheck and nothing more. As far as he was concerned, they were pilots in name only—unreliable in tight situations.

Following major force cuts after Vietnam and the first Gulf War, flight hours became less available, often only enough to maintain minimum requirements. Pilot proficiency declined, and increased regulation left many disillusioned and bitter. For most, the drawdown was a tough transition, but for others, less enthusiastic about their profession, a lack of flight time was an insignificant diversion. For them, pay and career advancement were far more important than flying, although most never acknowledged the fact outside a close circle of friends.

Those who chose aviation for the love of flying became fewer in number. They alone possessed something special—qualities that set them apart and molded them into the best of the best. The traits were more than physical capabilities or experience, more than even determination and personal drive, which often define success. All were important, even vital, yet there was something else that distinguished the good pilots above the rest.

Some would say the best pilots had a special karma. Their attitude was different, more assured. Not fearless, but an anticipation and unique focus, an uncanny feel for flying most pilots never possessed. The distinction was mostly unspoken, acknowledged with only silent recognition from their peers.

Connor knew there would always be pilots who stayed in aviation for the wrong reasons, but their skill would never equal those he considered real pilots. Wars and other harsh conditions had a way of weaning them out. Even away from the rigors of war, a pilot was often tested. Mountain flying and weather, like combat, were especially cruel discriminators.

Ordinary aviators, of which there were many, often labeled the best pilots as hot-dogs or mavericks, just as Connor had been throughout his career. The critics were partially right, but the best pilots knew and understood their own limitations—how to challenge themselves and master what others considered dangerous.

Even as Connor's well-honed skills became rusty with age and lack of use, he was still better than most. His abilities were fading, but the demons never left. They always were there, reminding him of the past.

Now cancer had joined the fight. The last battle, his last challenge would be to defeat them both, and at the same time, perhaps, destroy himself as well.

CHAPTER SEVEN

Under normal conditions, the twin-engine commuter could maintain level flight with only one operable engine. Unfortunately for the passengers and crew above the mountains, they were not in normal conditions. The aircraft was near maximum gross weight, being forced lower by rough air currents billowing off the peaks, at a rate one engine couldn't compensate for.

At first, the rate of descent kept the aircraft clear of the mountains at a shallow angle toward a distant river basin. Sanders thought they were out of danger. Once the downdrafts began increasing in intensity, he realized he was terribly wrong.

The aircraft quickly began losing altitude at a much steeper angle into the high, rugged terrain. A massive glacier, snaking out of a sharply cut valley several miles away, appeared to be the only hope of a safe landing.

"Get out a Mayday call," Sanders instructed Illiamin. "I can't maintain altitude. Tell them our position is on the north side of Mount Deborah, south of Crosson Glacier, heading northwest. Send our coordinates when you make contact."

Illiamin swallowed hard before transmitting a distress call over the VHF radio. He spoke rapidly, trying to keep his voice from breaking. There was no response. After a few seconds he transmitted again, but the second try also went unanswered.

Sanders could hear the alarmed voices of the passengers through the cockpit door. Realizing they were almost in a panic, he reassured them over the intercom, simultaneously using every bit of skill to maneuver the aircraft for a safe landing.

"Folks, we have a minor emergency. We lost power on one engine and are losing altitude, but the aircraft is still flying. We need to make an emergency landing. Please stay in your seats with your seat belts securely fastened and remain calm. Rescue services have already been notified and we will be safely on the ground before long."

Both pilots wore a look of resignation, fully aware their situation was much more than a minor emergency. Landing safely would require every bit of skill and luck they could muster. A false reassurance might be the only thing preventing the passengers from complete panic.

"Keep sending a distress," Sanders instructed. "Try Unicom and Flight Service frequencies as long as you can. I hope to hell someone hears us."

Illiamin nodded. He transmitted on multiple frequencies without a response. The radios were completely silent, as if they'd entered a zone of dead air. In effect, they had, for the aircraft had descended amid a surrounding wall of peaks, effectively blocking all radio signals.

Sanders pulled back on the yoke, raising the plane's nose, slowing the airspeed as much as he dared to decrease the rate of descent. An ice-covered ridge ahead of the plane was growing at a rapid rate through the windshield. With mountains on each side, there was no room to maneuver and limited altitude to spare.

A hundred yards from the windward side of a jagged ridge, the descent rate suddenly stopped. The flow of air changed direction as it deflected upward against the steep terrain. One second the plane was descending rapidly and the next was being lifted skyward.

Sanders held the same airspeed, capturing as much altitude as possible in the few seconds before the wind changed direction again. He knew what was coming, but there was nothing he could do. Within seconds of clearing the ridge, the aircraft was caught in another, more violent downdraft. Power to the good engine was at maximum, the airspeed was as slow as he dared, and they were again descending rapidly into the mountains. The chance of making the glacier in the distance seemed less and less a possibility.

Susan Douglas had been looking out the window when the engine caught fire. A frightened exclamation from one of the elderly tourists was her first inkling of danger. Within seconds, all the passengers were aware of the situation and becoming increasingly distraught. Everything seemed to move in slow motion, but before anyone could yell to notify the crew, the fire was out and the pilot was talking over the intercom.

Susan sensed the emergency was more serious than the captain stated, and the rest of the passengers soon shared the same feeling. The mountains on each side, the turbulent winds, the changes in their flight path, and variations in engine noise portrayed the ominous truth. She was grateful no one panicked, for it would have triggered her own emotional outbreak.

Three young girls from the swim team were crying softly, traumatized by being alone in their seats with no one beside them. The coach tried reassuring them in a voice teetering on hysteria.

Susan's memory flashed to the death of her husband, killed in the crash of his small plane when the engine failed. She had driven him to the hangar for a brief flight and stood in shock as the engine suddenly ceased on takeoff. Frozen in place and holding her breath in anguish, she stared in horror as her husband made a desperate turn back for the runway.

The tight maneuver was too steep, plunging the aircraft violently earthward. Whether the sharp turn was a panicked attempt to avoid the trees or for some other reason, she never knew. The plane hit nose first in a tangle of bent metal, coming to rest in a grove of high spruce at the end of the runway. There was no sound for a moment. The pause seemed like an eternity before she began screaming for help, hoping someone could reach the wreckage and save her husband.

Susan raced across the tarmac, dismissing the thought he was already dead. Before she was halfway, the wreckage burst into flames, quickly destroying any chance of life. She continued running until her lungs ached, unable to breathe, smelling the acrid smoke blowing across the field. She finally collapsed on her knees, out of breath and sobbing, afraid to go further.

A hand reached from behind the seat in front of Susan, touching her knee and gently jostling her thoughts back to the present. She looked up and saw the face of the young girl sitting in front, her expression was reassuring and surprisingly composed. Her touch was warm, almost tingling, as if carried by a faint electric current. The sensation was comforting. Susan leaned forward to join hands, forcing a smile, suddenly relaxed by the girl's calming influence.

Other passengers were holding hands with mixed emotions, some praying and a few staring outside in disbelief. One of the men was talking forcefully to the plane, unaware he was speaking aloud, coaxing the aircraft to climb and turn as if he was at the controls.

"It's going to be okay," the young girl said easily. "The pilots know what they're doing."

Susan grasped the girl's hand harder in reply before speaking in a shaky voice. "What's your name, sweetie?"

"Lisa," she replied with an almost angelic expression. "Don't be afraid. You're going to be okay."

Susan wanted to ask how she knew but for some reason believed her. She nodded and thought of her husband again. "My husband was a pilot. He practiced this type of emergency all the time." She spoke as much for her own benefit as the other passengers within hearing distance. They needed reassurance, too.

"The pilots will find a place to land." Confidence was evident in Lisa's expression.

"Thank you," Susan replied. Her voice was stronger now. "Thank you for talking with me, Lisa."

"You're welcome. I'll be here with you. Can I still hold your hand?"

Susan was surprised by the question, then realized the gesture was more for her benefit than Lisa's. "Of course. God bless you."

Lisa smiled knowingly, giving Susan's hand a gentle squeeze before facing back forward, her arm still extended behind her.

Illiamin continued sending distress calls. There was no response on any of the frequencies. He knew the terrain was blocking the signal but hoped a high-flying jet might be able to receive the transmission. None did.

Without radio contact, the situation was critical. Even if they landed safely, a quick rescue was unlikely. Basic emergency equipment was carried on the aircraft but no cold weather gear. Weather conditions in Alaska were warm in August near sea level, but the high mountains were more reflective of winter. Freezing temperatures and snowfall were common.

Powerful air currents off the slopes accelerated through narrow channels of terrain, increasing in strength as they pushed the aircraft faster toward the earth. The glacier was no longer visible, hidden behind a saw-toothed ridge extending across their flight path.

Sanders willed the aircraft to stop losing altitude. His silent plea was ignored. If he didn't do something quick, the aircraft would hit below the crest of the ridge.

"Give me thirty-degree flaps," he ordered.

Illiamin glanced at him in surprise and then at the airspeed, a questioning look on his face. With the gusting tail wind, the use of flaps was dangerous. They could tear loose and damage the integrity of the wings.

"Now, damn it! Thirty-degree flaps or we're going to eat the mountain," Sanders exclaimed.

The aircraft buffeted sharply for a brief moment as Illiamin did as instructed. The flaps worked as intended in spite of the fluctuating air currents stressing their design capability. He emitted a slow breath of relief.

The plane steadied as Sanders adjusted the flight controls, keeping the airspeed above stalling, anticipating each gust and trying to gain every foot of altitude he possibly could. The descent slowed momentarily, stopping for a few seconds before continuing again.

"Give me sixty degrees flaps, now." Sanders felt the change before there was an indication on the instruments.

The plane fought for altitude, trying to lift itself higher, struggling with the decreasing distance between earth and sky. The ridge drew closer with each passing second. Sanders knew they needed the wind to help if they were to clear the ridge. An updraft of air was their only hope.

Nearer the windward side of the ridge, the aircraft caught the deflected flow of air, stopping the descent from moments before. Suddenly the plane began ascending. Almost level with the top, the pilots sensed they might clear the ridge after all.

Sanders began talking the plane forward over the sound of the engine. "Come on baby. Come on, you can do it. Keep climbing. Come on baby."

Illiamin listened to Sanders and stared at the ridge, holding his seat as if trying to pull the aircraft higher. He began to repeat the same words, willing the plane upward foot by foot. Slowly, as the edge of the ridge dropped below his line of vision, a smile spread across his face.

His exhilaration was short lived. As they cleared the summit of protruding rock, the strong vertical air current changed to a more horizontal direction. Both pilots were caught off guard. They should have known even if there was nothing they could do.

The updraft disappeared. The wind shifted, varying direction off the steep cliffs angling toward the center of the ridge. At first the change wasn't dramatic but was enough to steal the narrow margin of lift they needed.

Sanders felt the shift in direction and immediately knew they were in trouble. "Full flaps!"

Illiamin reacted quickly, but the action didn't make a difference. Sanders simultaneously adjusted the controls, reducing the airspeed to a dangerous level. An audio horn began sounding a warning and the flight controls began shaking uncontrollably. A stall was imminent.

The mountain ridge was nearly a hundred and fifty yards long, slanting down at a twenty-degree angle from the southwest and curving at a sharper angle to the east. The width was two hundred feet at the widest point, tapering to half that distance between the almost vertical cliffs of the surrounding slopes. Large outcroppings of jagged rock protruded unevenly from the granite surface. Smaller mounds interlaced with patches of colored lichen covered the ground. Snow remained in the deeply shaded areas protected from the sun.

"We're going to hit. Brace yourself!" Sanders exclaimed.

He managed to align the aircraft with the ridge before the aircraft stalled. A split second later he pulled back on the yoke, raising the nose just enough to clear the first seam of rocks. The loss of lift caused the plane to fall violently. Sanders barely had enough time to reach for the throttle and fuel levers, quickly pulling them to the closed position before being knocked unconscious.

CHAPTER EIGHT

Connor's muscles ached as he drove away from the hospital. The intense pain had subsided, providing temporary relief. A bottle of prescription pills was in his pocket, but he was reluctant to use them. He couldn't chance the side effects. He would endure the pain and make do with some less effective over-the-counter medicine.

There was no other traffic on the short drive across base. Soldiers and support personnel were already at work performing a diversity of duties befitting a military base. Over half the assigned soldiers, including the majority of aviation assets, were deployed overseas.

Originally named Ladd Field during construction in World War Two, the airfield and surrounding facilities were renamed Fort Wainwright in the 1960s. Located in the center of Alaska, the base bordered the city of Fairbanks on the west side, and the Richardson Highway on the south. A large airfield stretched across the north end, framed by the Chena River.

Two runways were the biggest features on the airfield, running parallel between an array of hangars and support buildings. Constructed as a staging base for equipment and supplies during World War Two, the airfield served as a transfer facility for thousands of Lend-Lease aircraft bound for the Soviet Union. Following the war, the base was used by a multitude of military units. Many of the original hangars were left in place.

Dozens of scout, medevac, heavy lift, and utility helicopters, normally parked inside the hangars or on the tarmacs, were missing, serving in Afghanistan and Iraq. The airfield appeared abandoned accept for a few remaining helicopters and a small contingent of support personnel.

Connor parked near a large wooden hangar with bleached siding and a pitch-domed roof on the southwest corner of the airfield. He took his time getting out of the car, pausing to straighten the cuffs of his olive-gray flight suit over his boots. He carefully stood erect and donned a camouflage fatigue hat. A silver bar with four black dots, signifying the rank of a senior warrant officer, adorned the front. The flight suit was without insignia, except for a leather nametag above the left chest pocket identifying his name and rank.

Connor glanced at the sky before stepping carefully across the gravel parking lot. He wondered if he would ever fly again or if he should even try. Deep inside, he knew the answer.

Upon reaching a single door on the south side of the building, he entered and removed his hat. The hangar always made him feel welcome. It wasn't much in appearance but had been his place of work for nearly three years—seven if you included his first assignment. Even though the building was old and had seen better days, the memories inside reflected a happier period in his life.

Connor walked through a narrow entryway, past a set of stairs leading to administrative offices on the second floor. The walls were painted light beige, barren except for two safety posters mounted in cheap wooden frames. Vinyl tiles, worn from years of foot traffic and yellowed by over-waxing, covered the floor.

He continued through another door leading into the open bay of the hangar. A familiar smell of oil and grease, the sound of mechanical activity, and the sight of two UH-1H Huey helicopters greeted him.

The hangar bay was a large, spacious area allowing as many as a dozen helicopters inside for maintenance and storage. Telescoping doors, nearly as high and wide as the walls, stretched across each narrow end of the hangar. Thick wooden beams supported the open, elevated ceiling, and the floor was the original concrete, swept clean of dirt and maintained in a polished hue.

Built into the walls on each side were supply and maintenance offices. Directly above on the second floor, other offices were used for classrooms, storage, and administration. All were accessed by identical stairwells on opposite sides of the building. Except for the men and equipment inside, the hangar had experienced only minor change since original construction.

The two UH-1 helicopters were partially dismantled as mechanics worked around the transmission and engine areas, preparing them for shipment to a depot facility outside Alaska. There, the helicopters would either be converted into target drones or auctioned off, more than likely to a foreign country.

The hangar, like the rest on the airfield, was relatively void of the usual activity befitting an aviation unit. Only two of the original six helicopters were left for training and support missions. Their scheduled turn-in was for the following spring. Two others had already been shipped. Six smaller OH-58A scout helicopters had met the same fate the previous year, their pilots and mechanics reassigned to units outside Alaska.

Only the two outdated UH-1 helicopters and a pair of UH-60 Black Hawk helicopters were left at Fort Wainwright—the UH-60s for medical support missions.

Connor strode across the rectangular bay, holding a rigid posture that only added to his discomfort. He acknowledged one of the mechanics working atop the closest helicopter, nodding his head in reply to a brief wave, then continued without stopping. He reached the stairwell and grimaced in pain.

Whispering a profanity, Connor hunched forward and grabbed the railing. The ache in his back seemed to spasm without warning and at the most inopportune times. After a long pause, he straightened and continued gingerly up the stairs.

The worst of the pain subsided upon reaching the top of the landing. He leaned against the wall, took a deep breath, and stretched his back into a fully erect posture. The tension was bearable again.

The hallway was dimly lit. A framed recruiting poster, lithographs of famous military battles and 8 x 10 photographs of the chain-of-command hung in rows on each wall. The paint was clean, applied in a shade of light blue, but did little to alter the drab atmosphere of musty wood and faded ceiling panels. He turned left and approached the open doorway of the company first sergeant.

Voices were emanating from inside the office. Glancing inside, Connor spotted First Sergeant Killian and Sergeant First Class Mayo sitting around a metal desk, discussing a computer printout. Identical mugs of coffee rested within easy reach. The conversation paused as they each took a sip.

Killian wasn't into flashy accommodations even though his position dictated better furnishings. His desk was standard military issue, painted in gunmetal gray and chipped on the corners. A porcelain stein full of pens and pencils rested beside a framed photo on one end. Paperwork piled high in a plastic tray and a desk calendar were positioned in the middle. A thin clipboard and sheets of paper were spread out on the opposite side.

The office was painted in the same shade as the hallway. A worn leather couch and matching chair were positioned along the near wall, and a small wooden bookcase filled with manuals rested below the single window overlooking the tarmac. Three straight-back metal chairs were aligned under a red and white banner along the far wall. A coat rack with two hanging jackets stood in the corner. Another bookcase butted against the desk, filled with more manuals, history books, small mementos, and a pearl-white, push button phone on the top shelf. Above the bookcase was an old lithograph depicting a flight of helicopters over a rice paddy.

The two men looked up as Connor cleared his throat in the doorway. They recognized the senior warrant officer and smiled with curiosity, pleased at being interrupted from the mundane discussion.

Killian was wiry and short in stature, with piercing, dark eyes and a reserved personality. His wrath was legendary, but among friends a relaxed humor was easily visible. He was a career soldier who took a personal interest in each member of the company.

Mayo was the opposite in appearance, tall and powerfully built. His dark complexion revealed his Samoan ancestry. Connor knew him well, having served with him during previous assignments. His intervention following Mayo's drunken brawl at a seedy watering hole saved the young soldier from being booted out of the Army.

"How goes the battle?" Connor asked, leaning against the doorframe. He hid his nagging pain with an easy banter unreflective of his mood.

"Good morning, sir," Killian replied warmly as he looked sharply across the room. "Just trying to keep our heads above the mounting paperwork and putting out the usual fires. How are you today, Mister Connor?"

"Slow and grouchy. Feeling like an old hound dog with nowhere to hunt."

Killian and Mayo both chuckled as Killian set his mug on the side of the desk. "Missing the action in the sandbox, sir?"

Connor forced a smile. "Not so much, really. I was referring more to my age than a desire to battle the faithful followers of Islam. Although dodging bullets might put some motivation in this tired butt. There's nothing like the fear of death to get your adrenaline flowing."

Killian nodded before flashing a look of remorse. "Sitting stateside while our soldiers are getting shot at is eating at you as much as me, I bet."

Connor sighed before answering. "I guess you're right. We're old and slow, but experience trumps youth. At least that's the way it's supposed to be. Can't say I wouldn't trade one for the other though."

"Now you're talking." Killian's eyes brightened at the prospect. "Ten less years of experience for ten less years of age sounds like a hell of a deal."

Connor paused, thinking about the idea. "One for one? Hadn't thought of it that way. At this point I'd gladly give ten for one . . . shit, even twenty for one." He smiled faintly. "But I still get to stay stateside."

"No way!" Killian could see the yearning in Connor's expression and didn't believe the comment. "You'd be the first one in line if you got the chance, sir."

"And I'll be right behind you both, once the MPs drag me on the plane in shackles," Mayo added with a wink.

"Right," Killian stated sarcastically, a hint of a smile creasing his mouth. "Let's see, who recently asked if they could take my place to join the battalion next week in Afghanistan? Something about being stateside behind a desk was like a prison sentence."

Mayo shrugged. "I believe I wasn't in full control of my emotions. The wife had been nagging me more than usual, and at the time the idea seemed like a sure plan of escape."

Connor grinned, forgetting his own problems for the moment, sharing a chuckle with Killian as Mayo smiled and joined in.

"That may be," Killian added. "But I know you'd be on the plane with me if you could, both of you."

Connor's demeanor became serious. "What's the latest from battalion?"

"Nothing new. Flight operations are continuing as normal— mostly reconnaissance and support flights. No losses or injuries for over a month. Occasional damage now and then from small arms fire but no big stuff being sent their way."

"Good. They're fine soldiers. They know what to do if the situation turns ugly."

"Yes, sir. We should be there with them. I know you want back in the fight."

Connor nodded his head. His expression changed as if thinking of something far away. "One last battle? Yeah, I'd go. Until then us old dogs will have to contend with guarding the hen house."

They returned his stare, nodding in agreement. Connor reflected on his many lost friends for a moment, his eyes diverting outside. A flash of sorrow was noticeable before quickly disappearing.

Joking about serious issues was easy for soldiers. Trivial matters bothered them the most. Soldiers were adept at hiding emotional turmoil behind a mask of indifference or humor. Connor was no different and, if anything, was better than most. His change in mood this time was out of character.

Both Mayo and Killian watched Connor as he held a long glance out the window, studying the horizon as if deep in thought. His expression of remorse faded, replaced by a slight smile carrying a hidden secret. That, too, quickly changed.

"Maybe you're right First Sergeant," Connor finally added, focusing his attention back inside. "Always better to go down fighting, right? I'm not ready to be put down just yet."

Connor's comment surprised them both, not for the words themselves but for the hard slate of determination evident on his face.

Mayo and Killian exchanged a quick glance, the relaxed mood somehow broken by the abrupt seriousness. Mayo was the first to break the momentary silence, deflecting the conversation to less important issues.

"Rumor has it the unit might be sent home early. Looks like the towel-heads are ready to give up the fight and embrace the American way. Only problem is, they're asking for ten virgins and twenty goats a piece."

He paused for effect before continuing. "Of course, the president knows that's unrealistic, so he countered with five hookers and ten virgin goats."

Killian chuckled and Connor smirked, barely holding back a wide smile. Mayo always had a way of making him laugh.

Keeping a straight face as if telling a breaking news story, Mayo continued. "Half the hajjis are willing to accept the offer and the other half want double the amount of goats, male or female."

The laughter from Killian was louder. He wiped his eyes before responding. "Where did you hear that, late night with David Letterman?"

Mayo finally cracked an expression of humor. "No, Al Jazeera."

Connor laughed with them, his usual demeanor having returned. He suddenly felt much better. His choice was clear.

"Thanks, Sergeant Mayo. I can rest easier now, knowing the war is almost over. I'll let you two get back to work."

"All right, sir." Killian didn't sound enthusiastic about the prospect. "Feel free to return at your leisure. We can always use an interruption."

"Good to know. Personally, these tired bones could use a nap," Connor quipped in feigned sarcasm. "But I will settle for a cup of fresh coffee. Provided, of course, the pot in the briefing room has been refilled after your generous helpings."

Killian raised his mug in a mock toast and glanced at Mayo. "We have the utmost confidence that should it not be so, you will graciously take the matter into your own hands, sir."

Connor ran a hand through his hair and cracked a well-intentioned smile. "I will, First Sergeant. Thank you for your concern."

Mayo watched Connor push himself carefully away from the door-frame. "How's the back doing, sir? Still giving you problems?"

"Just a little stiff this morning. Nothing serious," Connor lied. "Old age has a way of catching up on all of us."

"You sure you don't want to stay, sir? We can use a break." Killian motioned toward the cushioned chair near his desk. "I'll get you a cup of coffee."

"Don't bother, please." Connor held up his hand and stopped Killian before he could lift himself away from the desk. As much as he enjoyed their company, he didn't want to waste more time. "I have plenty of work to catch up on. Maybe later."

"All right, sir," Killian said. "Let me know if you need anything."

"The same here," Mayo added. "If you get a chance this afternoon, I'd like to talk with you. Nothing important. Reno's doing well, by the way. I think he misses you."

Reno was a German shepherd mix, trained for bomb detection. He was friendly and very protective. Connor acquired him after his handler was killed in Iraq and the military determined he was no longer effective. Mayo and his family occasionally looked after the dog, and before long he was more part of their family than his. He decided to let them keep him. The kids loved Reno, and he was a great companion.

Connor was silent for a second before glancing at his watch. "Good, I'd like that."

"One other thing, sir," Killian added. "Sergeant Jackson has an award recommendation that needs your review. I need the paperwork in by the end of the week if you can take care of it?"

Connor tried not to hurry his exit. He answered while acknowledging them both with a short glance. "I'll make sure the paperwork's completed. Have a good morning, gentlemen."

Killian winked at Mayo as Connor departed. He enjoyed talking with the senior warrant officer. His personality and position as first sergeant didn't normally allow the same openness with subordinates and other officers. Connor and he held a mutual respect for each other, a respect only career soldiers could understand. As such, they occasionally shared a good-natured jab at each other but only in very close company.

Mayo forced a smile. There was something in Connor's mannerism that seemed out of place. He seemed different, as if he was hiding something. There was a determination in his eyes that had been absent for a long time.

CHAPTER NINE

The summer mission schedule was uncommonly slow. Few emergencies had materialized for the 95th Air Medical Company over a typical season of visiting tourists, weekend pilots, and novice adventurers seeking the great outdoors. Only a mother in labor and two lost hikers on an overnight camping trip had broken the spell of inactivity. Boredom and complacency were barely kept at bay by a weekly training flight. Flight time was limited, reserved for the other pilots deployed overseas.

Alaska was a welcome escape from combat duty for the two aircrews, although a temporary one. The few allowed the privilege of remaining behind were mostly recuperating from medical conditions or had family issues requiring attention. They would rotate overseas with another group in a few months.

Two UH-60 Black Hawk helicopters were left behind to support the civilian community in central Alaska. The decision was purely political, based on prior precedence and influenced by the state's senior ranking senator.

By regulation, civilian assistance was secondary to military obligations, but after nearly three decades, the military's support of civilian communities became routine. MAST, short for Military Assistance to Safety and Traffic, became a useful tool. Civilians received vital emergency medical support while aircrews received real-life, hands-on experience required for potential combat missions.

Since most of Alaska was without roads or inaccessible by airplane, military helicopters were often the only means of getting into remote locations. The 95th Air Medical Company provided emergency support by having an assigned aircrew on duty in the hangar, twenty-four hours a day. A helicopter remained ready for departure within twenty minutes, day or night, every day of the year. A second helicopter could be launched within two hours, depending on the status of the previous crew.

The mission schedule was normally accomplished with a full contingent of twelve helicopters and flight crews, rotated on a daily basis for training, support of other military units, and emergency standby duty. Due to the battalion's recent deployment, only two crews remained, each kept on a cycle of one day in the hangar and one day of rest. The day of rest was problematic-dependent on not being called for a second mission.

Even when air medical units were at full strength, medical evacuations, or medevacs, were often more demanding than other aviation missions. Aircrews despised the cycle of repetitive duty sitting on the ground but loved the feeling of accomplishment when involved in an actual mission.

The standby crew in Alaska was composed of two pilots—a pilot-in-command, who was delegated by flight ability and experience, and a copilot. A flight medic and a crew chief made up the rest of the crew. The medic was responsible for patient care and the crew chief for maintenance on the aircraft.

Each morning, a new aircrew replaced the outgoing crew and began a twenty-four-hour duty cycle in the hangar. The helicopter was the first priority. Flight gear, survival equipment, and medical supplies were loaded, if not already aboard. A preflight was conducted and the aircraft taken through a complete engine run-up. Fuel tanks were then topped off, flight gear left on the seats, and the aircraft secured, enabling a quick departure.

Only after the helicopter was deemed mission ready could the crew work on other tasks, but they always remained within ten minutes of the hangar. Flight planning was completed by the pilots, including a weather forecast for the next twenty-four hours. Performance data, based on environmental conditions and the mission configuration of the helicopter, was then computed. A general flight plan was also prepared, based on the same parameters.

Since time was often critical in medical evacuations, preparing in advance reduced time spent on the ground. Each pilot-in-command has a personal routine that included mandatory procedures and their own individual preferences.

At noon, the crew began a mandatory rest period in the duty lounge on the top floor of the hangar. Separated from the rest of the company, they could relax or sleep in a quiet environment, ensuring adequate rest should a mission arise at night or early morning.

On occasion, the standby crew conducted a local training flight, remaining in constant radio contact with Flight Operations and flying no further than a fifty-mile radius from the airfield. This ensured adequate response time should further refueling be necessary.

On a typical day the telephones in any military flight operations office would be ringing continuously. The 95th Air Medical Company was no exception. But following the majority of the unit's deployment, a noticeable reduction occurred in requested missions. When the phone rang, the purpose was generally an innocent inquiry or personal call for one of the soldiers. Not a single medevac mission had been received in the previous month.

Sergeant Donovan barely moved from his chair as the telephone rang for only the third time that morning. He looked up from the training manual he was reading as a soldier sitting at a nearby desk picked up the receiver.

The young private's expression remained placid at first, changing after a few seconds. He sat up straight and locked eyes with his supervisor, asking the person speaking to hold. Cupping his hand over the phone, he spoke quickly to Sergeant Donovan while reaching for the mission book.

"We have a request from the RCC in Anchorage," he said, using the common acronym instead of rescue coordination center. "A satellite picked up an ELT signal ten minutes ago. The signal was confirmed by another satellite several minutes later. I'm getting the full information now."

An ELT signal was an emergency distress transmission sent by an Emergency Locator Transmitter. The device was designed to activate during a crash and was required on all aircraft operating in the United States. When activated, the equipment could broadcast an international distress signal for up to five hours.

Most ELTs were wired into the aircraft electrical system but also contained an internal battery. They could be operated manually or in automatic mode, allowing orbiting satellites and aircraft to monitor the signal.

Donovan nodded at the private's hurried explanation, immediately sliding his chair over to a large handset wired into a loudspeaker system. He flipped the power switch and tapped the microphone, hearing muffled thumps through the speaker.

During the standby crew's mandatory rest period, they would normally be found next door in the duty lounge but at other times were often scattered throughout the hangar performing routine tasks. The potential for delay was obvious. Since a fast and simple method of notification was necessary, a loudspeaker system was installed. With the simple press of a button, each crew member could be quickly and conveniently made aware of the situation.

"Standby crew, standby crew, report to the operations office." Donovan's voice broadcast through the speakers with a slight echo. "This is a mission alert. Standby crew, report to the operations office."

The private hurriedly wrote information on a mission request log as Donovan stood and looked over his shoulder. The form was simple yet efficient, providing essential details such as location, patient information, requesting agency, point of contact, and other pertinent data. Operations personnel could process the request quickly, ensuring an equally effective response from the standby crew.

Regulations dictated mission requests could only be received from five sources—a rescue coordination center, hospital or clinic, the state troopers, a medical dispatch authority, or other military units. The process ensured information was accurate and a military helicopter was necessary. The transportation of non-military patients was specifically prohibited unless there was a life or death situation, and only if a military helicopter was the most expedient travel available.

The requirement assured civilian medical services were not undercut by the military and patients received timely and appropriate care. Mission requests in Alaska were usually not an issue. With most of the state inaccessible, except by helicopter, a military medevac was often the only option.

Search missions were another component of the unit's duty requirement. Locating the source of a distress signal or a missing aircraft often entailed a joint effort between military and civilian agencies. If a helicopter was used and able to verify the signal as a legitimate emergency, evacuating the injured would then become the primary mission.

With thousands of private, commercial, and military aircraft operating in Alaska, inadvertent activation of an ELT was common. An unintentional signal from an airfield could usually be located by airport personnel without the use of additional resources. In remote areas, however, an accidental signal could often only be verified by launching aircraft to investigate. Small bush planes were usually the cause. On rare occasions the signal was authentic, and a real emergency would arise.

Donovan quickly jotted the two sets of coordinates onto a piece of paper. He moved to a large map hanging on a nearby wall and plotted the locations. The area map was pieced together from sectional charts and provided an easy method of geographical reference.

There was a discrepancy of several miles between the coordinates. Satellites had fixed different positions off the signals, both approximately seventy miles southeast of Fort Wainwright and situated in the mountains of the Alaska Range. One location was in the middle of a long, curved glacier and the other further north near the confluence of the glacier and headwaters of a river valley.

Donovan bent forward to read the map, noting the names of various terrain features. The Crosson Glacier, extending from the heart of the mountains and flowing north into the foothills, encompassed both sets of coordinates. He followed the glacier with his finger, tracing the shape into a large ice field spreading in multiple directions between the peaks. The expanse was massive, covering over fifty square miles.

Donovan sighed. The area was extremely dangerous. High mountains and creviced glaciers were unsuitable for most aircraft. If the distress signal was accurate, the medevac crew had a challenging mission ahead. As footsteps echoed down the hallway, he anticipated a long day.

CHAPTER TEN

S usan feared the worst. She sensed the aircraft pitch up and slow, the bile rising in her stomach. The angle was too steep as the plane shuddered from a lack of airspeed. She felt a turn, then a sudden drop almost straight down. Grasping Lisa's hand tightly, she closed her eyes, afraid to watch as the distance above the ground disappeared in an instant.

The aircraft hit tail first, aligned at a thirty-degree angle to the ridge. The rear fuselage buckled from the force of impact, causing a crack to open behind the wings. Screams of terror mixed with the sound of twisting metal as cold air rushed in.

The aircraft careened forward, slamming the nose into the hard earth and crushing the thin aluminum skin. Wing spars bowed and snapped, twisting upward as the propellers curled and locked from the sudden stoppage. Cowlings were torn loose and the engines ripped from their mounts, rupturing fuel, oil, and hydraulic lines. The underbelly grabbed at the rough ground, screeching and bending across the rocks.

The walls inside the fuselage sagged but held around the open fracture, protecting the cabin from collapsing completely. Overhead compartments were jarred open, flinging contents onto the passengers and aisle. Seats were torn loose from their metal rails, the sheared tubing dangerous as sharpened daggers. Other seats collapsed backward or onto the floor, violently jarring anything in the way.

Although the initial collision was violent, enough energy was transferred to the sloping ground for the plane to slide forward and minimize the damage. Or so it seemed at first. The inertia was too great, carrying the aircraft on a course toward the side of the narrow ridge.

Thirty feet into the skid, the right wing collided with a mound of granite, shearing the wing at the fuselage and causing the plane to pivot away from the sharp edge. The momentum slowed, stopping the aircraft with the left wing tip only a few feet from the abyss.

Fuel began leaking from a ruptured line. The ignitable liquid dripped only inches from the hot engine, pooling onto the coarse ground. Ragged wiring hung nearby, luckily void of electrical current because the battery cables were sheared during the crash.

The aircraft's nose was smashed heavily on the right side, pushed inward against the first officer's legs. The curved windshield was webbed and broken in one corner. Sounds of the crash faded against the mountain slopes. A brief silence ensued, broken by a hiss of cooling metal and anguished moans from the surviving passengers.

Inside the cockpit, blood was soaking Illiamin's uniform, and his breathing was labored after hitting hard against the steering column. He was bent forward at an uncomfortable angle against the side window, unmoving.

Sanders blinked his eyes slowly open as he regained consciousness. His lip was split and his hair matted with blood from a deep cut after hitting the instrument panel. He slowly sat upright with his head against the seat rest. One arm rested between his legs and the other hung beside the seat with the sleeve torn open. He emitted a soft groan and tried to focus, only seeing blurred images.

Sounds of pain and shock could be heard in the cabin. The interior was strewn with loose carpeting, torn cushions, and items from the overhead bins. The bodies of several passengers were positioned unnaturally in their seats or on the floor. Those who were able began moving carefully amid the wreckage, holding injured limbs or bleeding wounds. Cries for help and the repeated names of loved ones soon filled the cabin. Some, too traumatized to answer, stared blankly into space.

A few passengers began helping the injured while others, fearing a fire or explosion, exited through the forward cabin. The rear exit was blocked by debris. No one tried using the wing exits after noticing the jagged metal on one side and the position of the other wing close to the edge. Cold air surging in through the open door added a chilling atmosphere to the already gruesome scene.

Two mangled seats still had their occupants belted in, the bodies twisted at odd angles. The frames had been torn from their mounts during the crash and were blocking the aisle. Three rows of seats behind the wings had partially collapsed, throwing the occupants against the walls or other passengers, causing further injury. Except for those who had already exited, no one seemed in a hurry to leave.

Susan felt someone shaking her gently by the shoulder, asking if she was all right. The question seemed like part of a dream, except for a sore shoulder and chilled air blowing across her face.

"Miss, are you all right? Can you hear me?"

She opened her eyes suddenly with a gasp of air. A man was standing beside her with his hand on her arm, looking at her inquisitively. He was well tanned with a day's growth of whiskers and a tired look on his face. She thought he was the passenger who had been sitting behind her.

"Are you all right, any injuries? We hit pretty hard and I guess you were knocked out." He stared at her, waiting for an answer.

Susan blinked a few times, focusing her eyes before the realization of what happened hit her. "Um . . . yes. I'm . . . I'm all right, I think."

"Good. I was worried. You look a little groggy, but I don't see any obvious injuries. Do you think you can stand?"

"What? Yes . . . I think so." Susan placed her weight carefully on each foot while the man held her arm. "I'm okay. Thank you."

"You're welcome. I'm Dave Kwapich. Might be better if you move outside with the others. There's a chance of fire, and we need to get the rest of the passengers out."

Susan looked around the cabin, shocked at what she saw. Injured passengers were sitting in their seats or lying along the aisle behind her, some in great pain with obvious injuries. Several more appeared dead or unconscious. Three of the passengers were trying to help, including the man who had been seated behind her. She noticed all the seats in front were vacant.

"The young girls up front, where are they?" Susan was worried about Lisa, who had been holding her hand.

"They're okay. A little scared, but they're safe with some of the other passengers. One of the girls got them and their coach out right after the crash."

"Thank God. What about the pilots, where are they?"

"I'm going to check on them now," Kwapich replied. "It's only been a few minutes since we hit, and there hasn't been any movement from the cockpit."

"This is all so terrible. So many people are hurt and some are . . ." Susan's voice wavered as she grasped the man's elbow.

"Yes, some are dead. But we have to help the others." Kwapich adjusted the worn cap on his head. "I don't suppose you have any medical training, do you? We could use some help if you're up to it. Some of the passengers are in pretty bad shape."

Susan froze at the pained expressions on some of the faces before regaining her composure. "Of course. I had some first aid training over the years as a schoolteacher before retiring. But it's been a while. I'll do what I can."

"That would be great, miss . . .?"

"Douglas. Susan Douglas. Please call me Susan. Now you go and check the cockpit while I try to find a medical kit."

She couldn't help but notice the cool air blowing through the cabin and looked out through the windows at the high mountains surrounding them, wondering if a rescue was being organized and if they could survive long without one. Off to the side of the plane she saw passengers huddling behind a pile of shoulder high rocks protected from the wind. They were without jackets and looked cold.

Susan touched Kwapich's arm. "With this wind I think we should collect all the bags and any loose clothing as soon as possible. We might need them if we're going to be stuck here for any length of time."

Kwapich looked back at Susan with an appreciative expression. He nodded his head before speaking. "Of course. I'll get one of the other passengers to help as soon as I can. Good idea."

Voices from the back of the aircraft prompted Sanders to try to move out of the captain seat. His face felt sticky, and he tried raising his left hand to wipe his eyes. A sharp jolt of pain immediately shot through his arm, making him grimace in agony.

"Son-of-a-bitch," he cursed, lifting his right hand instead. His fingers wiped away the partially dried fluid until he could focus again. He looked at his hand and wasn't surprised by the sight of blood.

Sanders checked the rest of his face, carefully feeling his cut lip. He moved his tongue around his mouth, tasting blood, but was pleased none of his teeth felt broken. The salty taste made him feel nauseous. He took a deep breath and moved his hand to the wound on his scalp. Blood was still oozing down his brow, causing him to wipe his eyes again.

He looked around his seat until he found his worn pilot's jacket and pulled a linen handkerchief out of the inside pocket. He placed the cloth over the cut, applying pressure while he searched the cockpit with his eyes.

Illiamin sat unmoving and Sanders feared the worst. He checked the warning lights and engine settings, noticing the electrical power was off, but the battery and generator switches were still on. He reached with his good hand and flipped them to the off position, confirming the throttle and fuel handles were also off. Luckily, the fuel had been cut off from the engines just before the crash.

Sanders looked outside, gaining a good perspective of the ridge and surrounding landscape. The view from the ground was as intimidating as the view from the air. Their position appeared inaccessible, somewhere on a narrow finger of rock in a high valley, miles from civilization. Even if they were found, the chance of a quick rescue was doubtful.

The rough terrain and size of the ridge prevented another plane landing anywhere nearby. A mountain rescue team might reach them from the glacier, but the effort would take days. And getting everyone off the ridge without further injury would be impossible. He knew their only realistic hope was by helicopter, but the approaching weather system placed that option in jeopardy. Had anyone even heard their distress call? He prayed a helicopter could reach them in time.

Sanders slowly moved out of his seat and checked Illiamin. His injured arm throbbed with a dull pain, and he was careful not to bump against anything. He could hear shallow, labored breathing. He pulled the first officer's torso carefully against the seat so his head was supported. He was unconscious and appeared to be in bad shape. His face was a mask of half-dried blood covering several deep cuts.

Sanders tried recalling basic first aid from the company's annual training class. He went through the steps, checking the airway, breathing, and circulation. The process allowed him to forget his own pain and concentrate on Illiamin. There was limited room in the cockpit, but he managed to clear his first officer's mouth and throat of accumulated blood and mucus, improving his breathing.

The next step was critical. Moving him could cause further injury. Left alone, he could choke to death or a fire might preclude getting him out of the cockpit. The sound of his labored breathing suggested broken ribs or, even worse, a punctured lung. As long as he remained stable, there was no need to aggravate the injury. Illiamin's unresponsiveness might also indicate a severe head injury. For now he would leave him where he was.

Sanders decided to check the passengers. From the sounds coming from the cabin, there was no doubt in his mind others were in need of attention.

The cockpit door was stuck. He pushed several times before realizing the lock was set. Releasing the latch, he slumped against the doorway as a feeling of light-headedness overcame him.

"Easy now," a deep male voice said from only a few feet away. A firm hand reached out to support Sanders' shoulder. "Let me help."

Sanders nodded and then gasped in pain as the passenger clutched his injured left arm above the elbow. The man let go immediately and apologized. "I'm sorry. Where are you hurt?"

"Not your fault," Sanders said through clenched teeth. "I think my arm is broken. There's some swelling, and it hurts like hell."

The man looked his arm over. "No bulges or bones poking through. Can you manage?"

"I can manage fine as long as no one else grabs my arm." Sanders glared at him, then immediately apologized. "Sorry, that came out worse than I intended. Let me clear my head for a few seconds. How many of the passengers are injured?"

The man sighed. "Most of us, I'm afraid. Several are in bad shape. Some of the seats collapsed and . . . well, we're trying to help them now. There isn't much room to work and some of the wreckage is blocking the aisle. Three are dead. Is there a chance of fire?"

Sanders wiped his eyes with his good hand, regaining his composure while looking over the man's shoulder. "I think we're okay now. Electrical and fuel are shut off. We were lucky." He glanced back at Kwapich. "I need you to help me, okay?"

"Sure, tell me what you need."

"You've been a big help already, mister . . .?"

"My name is Kwapich, Dave Kwapich." He looked at Sanders nametag, then behind him through the cockpit door. "You the captain?"

"Yeah. The first officer is unconscious." Sanders nodded toward the cockpit as he adjusted the handkerchief on his head. "I don't want to try to move him for now. Let's get the less injured passengers outside so we have room to help the others. I'll get the medical kit."

"You look in bad shape," Kwapich said sternly. "Your face took a good wallop. Let's get the head wound bandaged before doing anything else."

"I'll get the cut taken care of as soon as I can. Passengers first, okay?"

"With all due respect, Captain, you've already lost a lot of blood." Kwapich spoke in a firm voice. "Passing out isn't going to help the situation and the rag on your head won't do much, other than put your arm to sleep holding it in place."

Sanders looked hard at Kwapich, who returned the strong gaze without blinking. He knew the passenger was right and relented. "All right. As soon as I get the medical kit, someone can bandage me up."

"One of the passengers is already looking," Kwapich said. He turned and pointed at the attractive, middle-aged woman searching through an overhead compartment near the center of the cabin.

Kwapich was about to call out to her when Sanders stepped sideways and reached toward a waist high storage compartment near the cockpit door. The makeshift bandage fell over his eyes as he removed his hand from the wound. He immediately pushed the cloth back in place and turned to Kwapich, pointing at the compartment door. "In there, in the back. There should be a red canvas medical case. Can you get it?"

"Yeah, of course."

Kwapich twisted and bent forward, dropping to one knee as a dull pain shot through his side. The force of his body being thrown against the seat during the crash had bruised his side. The injury wasn't serious, and he pushed aside the pain. Other passengers had worse injuries to deal with.

"You okay?" Sanders asked.

"I'll be fine. I tweaked my side a little. Nothing serious."

Sanders suspected more than a tweak, but he wasn't going to press the issue. "The case should be in the back, on the upper shelf."

"I see it," Kwapich said. He moved some items around and started pulling everything onto the floor. "This other stuff might come in handy."

A box of thin, navy colored airline blankets, still in cellophane wrappers, was set aside along with a small plastic box containing an emergency flare gun and extra cartridges. The briefcase size medical kit was placed on the floor beside the other items. A yellow flotation device and airline style oxygen mask, used for passenger briefings when a flight attendant was aboard, was left in the cabinet.

"That's everything we can use," said Kwapich.

"Good, you found one." Susan Douglas eyed the medical case as she approached.

When both men turned toward her, she noticed the pilot uniform and the captain's battered face. "Oh my, you're hurt. You better let me take a look at your head wound."

Sanders remembered her from the airport terminal. She had been joking with the ticket agent when he strode by, and her friendly personality brightened the normally boring procedure. Her demeanor was more serious now.

"I'll tell you what, miss . . .?"

"Douglas, Susan Douglas," she replied. "Call me Susan."

"All right, Susan. I'll agree to a bandage from the medical case if you allow Mister Kwapich here to take the remaining contents to the passengers. They need them more than I do." His voice was assertive. "As the captain, I want to make sure they are being taken care of."

"Yes, of course," Susan replied. "I'll have you fixed up in a jiffy. And just so you know, Captain, you appear far worse than you think. I've seen people mauled by bears in better condition."

Sanders would have smiled if not for his split lip. Instead, he relaxed his temperament, returning her gaze and speaking in a softer tone. "I suppose I do. I appreciate your concern. Sorry about snapping at both of you."

"It's okay. We're all on edge right now." She shifted her gaze, unzipping the heavy canvas case so both halves lay open on the floor.

"My name is Scott Sanders. I appreciate you helping out, both of you. I wish we could have met under better circumstances."

Susan glanced back at Sanders for a brief moment. "Of course, we all do. We'll get through this." She retrieved a thick bandage and roll of gauze from the open case, zipping the halves shut.

"If there's a splint in there, he'll need one of those, too," Kwapich interjected. Susan stopped what she was doing, looking at each of the men inquisitively, waiting for an explanation.

"Actually a sling will work," Sanders said softly, embarrassed to admit his physical limitation. "I think my left arm is broken."

Susan reopened the case and withdrew a small packet. A loud cry of pain from the back startled her as she stood to check the pilot's arm. Soft moaning followed. Another loud voice cursed nearby.

Kwapich briefed Sanders in more detail on what he knew of the status of the passengers, while Susan felt gingerly along the swollen forearm. He explained the number of injured passengers and who was outside.

The situation wasn't good but was better than Sanders originally feared. More moans resonated through the cabin.

"I better take the medical kit back there," Kwapich stated. He didn't wait for an answer, instead gathered up the canvas case and hurried away.

"I don't feel any bones out of place," Susan announced. "Nothing obvious, anyway. I'm not a doctor, but consider yourself lucky. The injury could have been worse."

Susan took the nylon sling from the plastic wrapper and tied the ends around Sanders' neck, using the pouch to support his arm at a ninety-degree angle. She then applied a rectangular bandage to his head wound, holding the sides in place with strips of medical tape. Taking a half step back, she looked him over.

"I think you'll live. The bleeding stopped and now you can use your good arm instead of holding a dirty rag on your head. When we have more time, I'll try to clean you up a bit. You have blood on your face and look terrible."

For not being a doctor, she certainly knew what she was doing. Her warm touch added a sense of comfort. He felt better immediately.

"You seem to have experience doing this sort of thing. Thank you."

She smiled weakly. "Raising three boys and a girl as tough as her brothers provided lots of experience. They had their share of cuts and broken bones growing up. I think most mothers learn first aid by necessity."

"I never thought of motherhood that way, but I suppose you're right."

Susan was about to answer when another muffled cry of pain was heard from the back. The person sounded in agony. She looked in the direction of the noise, then back at the pilot.

"Are you ready for this? Some of them will blame you for what happened."

"Blame goes with the job. Right now they need medical attention and reassurance. They can point fingers later."

CHAPTER ELEVEN

Connor continued down the hallway past the vacant commander's office and entered the doorway into the flight planning room. A water cooler and a small table holding a coffee maker rested in the near corner. The pot of recently brewed coffee was a quarter full, barely distinguishable against the stained glass.

The room was divided into two separate areas by a plywood counter—one side for flight planning and the other for operations. On a normal day at least three soldiers would be working the radios or sitting at desks inputting data into computers. Today there was only one.

Connor swirled the brown liquid inside the glass, inhaling the robust aroma, then set the pot back down. He contemplated brewing a fresh pot for a moment and instead filled a paper cup with water from the cooler.

"Sir, I didn't expect you back until this afternoon. Everything okay?"

Connor recognized the booming voice of Sergeant Jackson, his operations sergeant, and turned toward the counter.

"Everything's fine," Connor lied. "My doctor visit was cut short. The lab results weren't ready yet, so I rescheduled for next week."

Lying wasn't easy for Connor, even to a subordinate, but he couldn't tell Jackson the truth. If he did, there would only be more questions and eventually more lies. As the operations officer and Jackson's supervisor, he kept the operations sergeant informed of when he would be out of the office for various appointments. The specifics of his medical condition were kept to himself. Jackson, like everyone else, was unaware of the cancer.

Sergeant Reginald Jackson was a muscular, tough as nails black kid from East St. Louis, who joined the military to get away from the squalor and government dependency prevalent in his neighborhood. In spite of his imposing physical appearance, he possessed a friendly disposition and was the best operations sergeant Connor had worked with. A perfectionist when running operations, Jackson was both demanding and fair with his subordinates, as well as being a mentor. He was at the front of the promotion list for staff sergeant.

"In that case, sir, I have some flight records and weekly closeouts for you to sign. And as you're aware, Specialist Jimenez is leaving us in a couple of weeks to join the rest of the battalion overseas. I'd like your input on recommending her for an award. I was thinking an Army Commendation Medal would be nice. She's done a great job."

A small stack of folders on the counter beside Jackson's beefy right hand caught Connor's attention. "I thought computers were supposed to reduce the amount of paperwork. Doesn't seem to be working, does it?"

"No, sir." Jackson smiled widely. "I can bring these to your office along with the award recommendation if you like?"

"Give me those and bring the rest in a few minutes," Connor said, reaching across the counter. "And I agree with your recommendation. Jimenez deserves the award. Write it up and I'll sign it. Your grammar is better than mine."

"Already done, sir. I hope you don't mind, but I already went ahead and wrote the recommendation, per your approval of course. I'll have the document on your desk shortly if you want to make any changes."

"I'll take a look." Connor doubted there would be any errors. "The first sergeant will be pleased. He mentioned a few minutes ago he wanted the paperwork by the end of the week."

Jackson nodded and stepped away from the counter as Connor turned toward the doorway. Connor trudged down the hallway to his office, being careful to not aggravate his back or show signs of discomfort.

Managing the company's flight operations program was Connor's main responsibility. For the most part, he left the day-to-day requirements in the hands of Sergeant Jackson. His other primary duty was as an instructor pilot, which he enjoyed far more than sitting behind a desk. Unfortunately, with most of the battalion deployed overseas and his medical condition keeping him grounded for the past several weeks, flying hadn't been an option. Today would be different.

The cushioned chair behind his metal desk provided some relief as he sat down. Connor wanted badly to take one of the stronger codeine pills prescribed by the doctor, but the side effects would end any possibility of flying.

Instead, he retrieved a small plastic bottle from his desk drawer and washed down four tablets of ibuprofen with water, hoping they would be strong enough. If not, he was determined to endure the pain as best he could. In a few hours the pain wouldn't matter anyway. All he needed was a helicopter.

Sergeant Jackson entered with another stack of papers while Connor finished reviewing the daily flight schedule.

"Here you go, sir. The award recommendation is on top. After you review the write-up, I'll get the paperwork over to the first sergeant. We should have an approval from battalion and be able to award the medal before Jimenez leaves."

"Not a problem. I'll look it over and add my signature before lunch." Connor glanced briefly back at the flight schedule. "I see both helicopters are scheduled for flights today. Have they taken off yet?"

"Only one, sir. Lieutenant Hovan and Mister Thompson left on a support mission in nine-two-seven a couple hours ago. A training flight with eight-three-zero was postponed until later this afternoon. Captain Hiroldi is busy at battalion, and since you're medically grounded, there wasn't another pilot to fly with Mister Sanchez."

"I see. Well as of this morning I'm back on flight status." Connor lied for the third time that day. "If Mister Sanchez can sneak away from his maintenance duties for a couple of hours, I can take him up on a training flight."

He had no intention of flying Mister Sanchez. Once the aircraft was ready for takeoff, he would simply make an excuse to send the unit's maintenance pilot back in the hangar and depart without him.

"Give me about ten minutes so I can finish signing these records, Sergeant Jackson. Would you mind getting a hold of Mister Sanchez and let him know I would like to depart as soon as possible?"

"Of course, sir. Mister Sanchez should be in the maintenance office. I'll give him a call right away."

"Thank you. And just track the flight internally. We'll be staying local, so there's no need to file an official flight plan."

Sergeant Jackson thought the request odd. Internal tracking sheets hadn't been used for years. There was no regulation prohibiting their use, but why the change?

After Jackson returned to his desk, Connor flipped through the flight records and paperwork requiring a signature. He could hear Jackson on the phone in the next room and began formulating a plan. Getting rid of the other pilot and taking off alone would be easy. What to do then was unclear.

His thoughts drifted to an earlier time. Connor opened the bottom drawer and carefully retrieved a worn photograph in a wooden frame void of glass. He studied the image intently. The scene became sharper in his mind, refreshing the memory of past exploits and a cool mountain breeze he could almost feel against his cheek. For a few minutes the pain in his back was forgotten.

The picture showed a small Army scout helicopter in the foreground, resting on a finger of rock and closely surrounded by high mountains. The small pinnacle jutted from the end of a steep, razorback ridge, nearly a mile above the valley floor. Ice covered peaks reached skyward in the background. Several hundred feet below, a narrow pebble creek opened into a grassy basin. The precarious location appeared tranquil, overshadowed by the panorama of mountains and vibrant colors dotting the lower terrain, hinting at the skill of the pilot who landed there.

Yes, it would suffice, Connor decided. He couldn't think of a better location. The pinnacle was deep in a remote valley of the Alaska Range, at least sixty miles south of the airfield. Seventeen years had passed, but he was certain he could find the site again.

He well remembered past flights in the mountains. Serious mountain flying was done on a much larger scale then, which was surprising considering the older generation helicopters were less powerful and not nearly as capable. Flying those helicopters was always a challenge, especially at high elevations.

Connor didn't appreciate the modern standard of increased regulation. A simple focus on risk assessment and safety had evolved into ridiculous and overbearing requirements, reaching the point where they actually hindered mission accomplishment. Flying wasn't at all like the old days when pilots could push the element of risk, learning the limitations of the machines and their own capabilities. Those days were long over. An era had passed, leaving him behind.

The scene in the photograph had taken place during Connor's first assignment in Alaska. The remote and challenging environment was a welcome change after his second divorce and years of less hazardous assignments following the aftermath of Vietnam. In many ways, the aura of the land mirrored his rigid personality. Mysterious and dangerous, charming and enticing at the same time, Alaska was everything an adventurer dreamed about.

Connor's career was almost a blur, the thirty-plus years having passed all too quickly. He placed the framed photograph back in his desk drawer and thought about the other pictures propped on the bookshelf. One showed his beautiful, dark-haired daughter shortly before her death, sitting happily on his lap with her arms around his neck, their cheeks together, smiling happily at the camera.

Another was of his son, standing proud and tall in full dress uniform before being shipped off to Iraq. The intensity in the steel-blue eyes was identical to his own. But if you looked closely, there was a shade of gentleness, too, a warm sense of kindness that came from his mother.

A third photograph showed a younger Connor during a tour in Vietnam, standing beside a dusty helicopter with his crew, each of them displaying a tired, determined look, much older than their age.

Most were gone now. He still remembered them, but over the years had accepted their passing. Letting go was easier with them. They were men, warriors like himself who shared the same experiences and the same suffering. He missed them, too, but at least understood why they were gone.

Connor stared at the pictures for a moment longer and then turned his face toward the window, acknowledging the individuals silently by name. Soon he would be with them again. His life's journey was longer, but the destination would be the same.

Connor was leaning back in his chair, gazing outside at the empty airfield, when he was caught off guard by a knock on the open door. He heard Sergeant Jackson enter the office but remained unmoving for a few seconds before turning and clearing his throat.

"What have you got Sergeant Jackson?"

There was a strange look of finality on Connor's face, which surprised Jackson, but also a glint of peacefulness that had been lacking for some time. Jackson was pleased and suspicious at the same time.

"Just an update on the training flight, sir. The aircraft won't be available for several hours. I just got off the phone with Mister Sanchez.

After the flight was delayed, he had the crew chief start an engine inspection."

Connor leaned forward on the desk and rubbed his chin, trying to hide his irritation. He didn't want to delay his plan longer than necessary and quickly formulated another option.

"All right. What about the other helicopter, nine-two-seven? Any communication with them?"

"No, sir. The mission was scheduled for four hours, which should have them back before noon, but you know they usually run long."

"Damn, I guess that will have to work." Connor stared at the floor, talking to himself.

"Sir?"

Connor realized his mistake and quickly recovered. "Nothing. I need to speak with young Mister Thompson when he returns, is all. I need to schedule him for his annual evaluation."

"Yes, sir. I'll let you know when I get an update on their mission status."

"Thank you, Sergeant Jackson." Connor returned his attention to the papers on his desk.

Jackson saw Connor's diversion as a dismissal but sensed some urgency in the deliberate lack of conversation.

"Sir, everything okay? You want me to bring you anything?"

Connor wanted him to leave but knew he meant well by asking. He looked up slowly, staring into Jackson's eyes, trying to deflect the sergeant from the truth.

"I'm fine. A little antsy about getting back in the air, is all. Nothing that can't wait until tomorrow."

"Yes, sir." Jackson met the senior warrant officer's stare for several seconds before shifting his gaze toward the empty paper cup and bottle of ibuprofen on the desk.

Probably just a headache, Jackson thought. Maybe that was why Connor was acting strange. No reason to pry on a silly suspicion. He excused himself and returned to his office, unable to shake a nagging feeling that something else was going on.

CHAPTER TWELVE

The fuselage groaned from another strong onslaught of wind. The thin metal offered the only protection as gusts swirled over the mountain ridge. At times the air felt warm, then changed to shivering cold as flurries raced off the icy peaks through the glacier-cut valley, drafting through the narrow entryway. Outside, a few of the passengers huddled around a mound of rocks. The barrier provided enough protection to block the worst of the wind.

Sanders felt a sudden chill. The adrenaline from the crash was wearing off. His company uniform of a white, short-sleeve shirt and dark slacks was only a slight deterrent to the wind.

Susan Douglas was standing beside him, and he noticed she was dressed warmer than he was but not by much. A thin jacket, jeans, and slip-on boots appeared comfortable, but they weren't intended for a high mountain environment. Most of the others were dressed comparatively, having expected a routine flight with temperatures in the seventies upon arrival in Fairbanks. Without additional protection, hypothermia could be a serious problem.

A shiver shook Susan's body. Sanders noted her discomfort. "You're cold. Help me close this entry door. We can at least cut out the draft. I have a leather jacket in the cockpit. You should put it on."

"No, please. It's okay," she answered, shaking her head. "I'm really not very cold. I just need to stay busy. Besides, with only a shirt on you need a jacket more than me. I'll help with the door."

The sound of the wind immediately faded as she helped him pull the access door shut. Unlike some of the others, Susan was still able to function. She ignored the urge to cry, refusing to be distracted by the trauma around her.

Captain Sanders was concerned about the passengers, especially the severely injured. They were all his responsibility, and he had failed them. In spite of his feelings of guilt, he realized there was no time for self-pity. All he could do was save the ones who were left.

"Could you help with the first officer in the cockpit? He's unconscious and has some bad injuries." Sanders' voice sounded less assured than before.

"Yes, of course," Susan replied. She looked past him with a worried look. "When I saw you here I assumed he was outside with the other passengers."

Sanders stepped away from the cockpit door, gently touching her shoulder. "I'm afraid to move him, but I would sure appreciate your checking on him."

Susan nodded before looking inside more closely. The first officer was slumped against the seat. His appearance made her think of her dead husband, whose charred body was found in almost the same position. She gasped, hesitated, and then grabbed Sanders' jacket off the floor. Draping the leather coat over his arm, she returned his gaze. "I'll see what I can do while you check on the others."

A balding, older male passenger was lying in the aisle, clenching his teeth in pain as Sanders approached from the front of the cabin. Someone had placed a thin airline blanket over his chest. A petite, older woman with ebony dyed hair was kneeling at his feet.

The medical kit was open beside her. She was carefully wrapping gauze around a fractured ankle. The other ankle was swollen and bloody and appeared broken.

An obese middle-aged man behind them was leaning on his side against the cabin wall, still in his seat and clutching his lower back in obvious discomfort. Crouching beside him was a well-dressed, auburn-haired woman with bright-red lipstick, speaking softly to him with little effect. He was shaking his head in annoyance and glaring at the ceiling.

On the other side of the aisle, a slim, middle-aged woman with sun-bronzed skin and ivory hair sat slumped in her seat, resting at an uncomfortable angle. Several small airline pillows were tucked around her for support. A bead of sweat rolled down her brow in spite of the cold air. She blinked the moisture from her eye before wiping her forehead with a well-manicured hand.

Immediately behind her, an older woman with a thin, primrose hairdo, rested with her arms tucked under her legs. She appeared to be in shock and stared ahead with a frightened look on her face. Dark streaks of makeup were visible where tears ran down her cheeks. A small abrasion was evident on her forehead, partially covered by a strand of matted hair.

Further back, a tall, male passenger with crew-cut hair was working with Kwapich, attempting to move some seats and a body blocking the exit. They were assisted by a young man with wavy, dark hair pushed behind his ears, standing near the door. He was bleeding slightly from a small wound on his thigh.

Three other passengers were slumped in awkward positions and unmoving. Two were in seats against the rear bulkhead and the other in a broken seat, lying sideways on the floor.

A fourth passenger was pinned in the middle of the aisle. Well attired, he displayed a thin mustache and slick obsidian hair, disheveled from the crash. He was either unconscious or patiently waiting for assistance.

The sound of barking dogs was barely discernible as Sanders approached the first injured passenger. The rear wall was masking their attempts at drawing attention. He listened for a moment, unsure of the sound until realizing the noise was coming from the sled dogs in the cargo compartment. In the turmoil following the crash, he forgot about them. He wondered if they were injured, but for the moment they would have to wait.

Sanders knelt beside the woman tending the man with the broken ankles. "Is there anything I can do?"

The woman dug through the medical kit with a concerned expression. She looked up, then back at the man on the floor before diverting her attention to Sanders. Her petite size was in contrast to her sharp tongue. "Not unless you're a doctor. By your uniform I would say that's not the case unless flying airplanes is a part time job."

Sanders paused. He wondered if she was being sarcastic or trying to lessen the effect of the crash with an attempt at humor. He decided to ignore the statement and asked again.

"Do you have everything you need?"

She looked up again, searching his face before responding. "No, I don't. These people need to get to a hospital, but I imagine it's not an option right now. This medical kit is only for basic first aid and I need equipment for more serious injuries. Splints, backboards, and neck braces would be nice. A warm, clean room to work in, intravenous fluids, antibiotics, some strong pain medication, and a defibrillator would be even better. And that's just to get started."

She paused, catching her breath, glancing at the passengers and then Sanders before continuing in a softer tone. "My husband's ankles are broken and other passengers have serious injuries that need treatment. The man in the busted seat in back has a severe puncture wound. He will probably die if I can't get to him soon. And I can't until the aisle is clear."

Sanders hesitated before responding. She was obviously upset but doing the best she could with what she had. "I see. You have medical training then?"

"Yes, I'm a nurse," she said. "At least I was before retiring five years ago. My husband and I are on vacation—were on vacation, I mean."

"Well I'm glad you're here," Sanders said. "I'm afraid the medical kit will have to do for now, but I think I can make some splints. Would aluminum tubing or wooden boards be okay?"

"Any strong material about a foot long and an inch or two wide would be preferable. We'll need a half dozen or so if you can manage." She blew a tuft of hair out of her eyes, keeping her hands in place around the fracture.

Sanders glanced sympathetically at the man on the floor, then at the rest of the passengers. "What about the others? Is there anything else they need?"

The nurse nodded. "More blankets or jackets—anything warm will help. Fluids, too. Water would be best if you can find some. And get that aisle cleared."

The woman was used to giving orders. She obviously knew what she was doing and Sanders took her instructions without insult. "I'll get right on it."

He stood, realizing he still had the leather jacket on his arm. "Here, take this. Your husband can use it. I'll see what I can do about getting more clothing from the luggage in the cargo compartment."

"Thank you," the nurse said. She smiled for the first time and placed the jacket on her husband's chest.

Sanders caught Kwapich's attention and motioned him forward. The man nodded in reply and maneuvered carefully through the maze of injured passengers and debris.

"Any luck getting through the cabin to the rear exit?"

Kwapich pointed in the direction of his partner and the young man. "Hank and Danny are still working on clearing the aisle. The problem is the injured guy stuck in the middle. We're afraid one of the broken seats is cutting into him. There isn't enough room to free him until we move more debris and the other injured out of the way."

Sanders considered his explanation. "Maybe if we get the rear access door open from the outside, someone can enter and help move the debris through the exit."

Kwapich was about to respond when Sanders continued. "There's also a pallet loaded with mail sacks in the aft cargo compartment. The slats can be broken into splints we need for the injured. Using the wood will be easier than dismantling the aluminum tubing from the seats."

"Okay, I'll take care of it myself." Kwapich shifted his weight, keeping a hand on an overhead bin for support.

"If you can get in there, check on the two dogs," Sanders added. "Be careful. They're in cages, but they might lash out and bite. Most of the luggage is in there, too. Hopefully, everyone packed a jacket and some warm clothing."

Kwapich cleared his throat before motioning toward the rear door. "Danny, the young kid in back, already tried the door. He said it wouldn't open. Something about the frame being bent and wedged in place."

"All right," Sanders sighed. "Let's try pulling from the outside while he pushes from the inside."

"Yeah, it might work. Worth a try, anyway."

Kwapich explained the plan to Hank Bidwell, his tall hunting partner, who followed them to the access door in front. Susan was exiting the cockpit as they approached.

"Anything I can do?"

Sanders paused at the door. "We're going to try to get the rear door open so we can get inside from the back." He noticed the bundle of blankets left beside the cabinet door and nudged them with his foot. "Can you take the blankets and pass them out to the others?"

Susan nodded. Before she could speak Sanders turned to the two men and asked them to go ahead and try the cargo door. They exited quickly, realizing he was no help with his injured arm.

"How is Illiamin, the first officer?" Sanders said, motioning with his head toward the cockpit.

"I don't know what else to do. He's still unconscious and his breathing is labored. He might have a punctured lung, but I can't be sure."

Sanders hung his head. "Maybe the retired nurse can take a look when she gets a chance. Can you ask her while I help outside?"

"There's a nurse onboard?"

"Yeah, she's the one kneeling beside the man with the broken ankles."

Susan's eyes lightened up. "Thank God. What a relief. I was over my head with anything more than a bandage."

"You're doing great," Sanders assured her. "You might be surprised, but even kind words and a caring smile make a big difference in these situations."

"I'm doing the best I can, just like the rest of us," Susan said. She paused and looked back toward the cockpit.

"I wrapped the first officer's head with gauze. The bleeding stopped, but I'm worried. He doesn't look good."

"I know. The nurse might have an idea what to do," Sanders said. He noticed the concern on her face. "He's a tough kid. He'll pull through." Sanders hoped the statement was true.

The words seemed reassuring. Susan smiled weakly as he carefully exited through the open doorway. He stepped down and pushed the door shut behind him.

The wind caught Sanders, cutting through his thin clothing. His hair was blown in disarray and his face stung from the cold blast of air. Turning sideways, he jarred his broken arm in the sling and grunted in agony, fighting to hold a curse under his breath.

Holding his injured arm and shifting his legs slowly over the uneven surface, Sanders turned in a complete circle, gaining a better perspective of the crash site and the dangers they faced. Their predicament looked grim. With the terrain and approaching weather, survival for many of them depended on a quick rescue.

CHAPTER THIRTEEN

Sergeant First Class Mayo sat rigidly in his chair in the maintenance office. A sour expression reflected his attitude toward
paperwork. His office was located on the lower floor of the
hangar and as usual was cluttered with boxes of old parts and equipment. His desk was in similar disarray, littered with notes and scattered papers in a semblance of order only he understood. Although the
appearance was disorganized, he knew the precise contents of every
box and the exact figures on each scrap of paper.

Mayo had decided to catch up on some daily maintenance forms
after leaving the first sergeant's office. Beginning with the aircraft repair
logs, he confirmed the timetable for each helicopter was on track for
turn-in to depot. Once they were completed, he scheduled a weekly
training class around the daily maintenance requirements. Even though
maintenance was a priority, his job also entailed juggling numerous
administrative issues for his platoon, ranging from leave requests and
medical appointments to physical training and classroom instruction.

Sergeant Mayo considered life behind a desk almost as displeasing
as the wound he received during his first combat tour. The injured

shoulder still bothered him, especially during the winter. At the time, he was a private in an infantry platoon, supporting an armor unit during the first Gulf War.

Like his father before him, Mayo was drawn to the military at a young age. His father served in Vietnam as an infantry officer, receiving a silver star for valor and a career ending disability. Mayo was a reckless kid growing up and being a soldier appealed to him, especially the challenge of being a grunt on the front lines. Four years of slogging through mud, rain, and scorching heat changed his perspective.

After finishing his enlistment in the infantry and a year pursuing an unproductive civilian career, he re-enlisted as a UH-1 Huey helicopter mechanic. His first assignment in Germany was almost his last. A bad breakup with his stateside fiancé left him depressed and angry. Drinking and fighting soon resulted in disciplinary action by his company commander, requiring extra duty and a one-month reduction in pay. The penalty did nothing to ease his hostility. He was arrested for assault and battery a short time later.

At the time, Connor was in the same unit, tasked as the post duty officer the night Mayo was taken into custody. He received the late night call from the military police station and recognized Mayo's name. The telephone call was annotated in the duty log, and he was supposed to notify the chain-of-command. Nothing else was required. Depending on the charges, a soldier would either be signed over to his unit or held in custody to face arraignment for court-martial proceedings. Mayo was facing the latter category with a strong possibility of a prison sentence. His short career would be over.

Connor held off notifying the chain of command, deciding instead to visit the military police station where the desk sergeant was a former grunt he pulled off a hot LZ in Vietnam. They had a short conversation, ending with the NCO agreeing to let Connor try to talk some sense into Mayo before filing any paperwork.

Mayo was sitting on his bunk, still mad at the world, when Connor entered the cell. The last thing he wanted was a lecture. He told

Connor to go screw himself, expecting the warrant officer to be furious and add more charges to his growing rap sheet. Digging a deeper hole was becoming a pattern he couldn't seem to avoid.

Instead, Connor nodded his head as if expecting the response, for he understood more than anyone what Mayo was going through.

"You get it out of your system yet?"

Mayo stared at Connor and smirked sarcastically, testing how far he could push his act of defiance. "What? The taste of your wife's puss . . ."

Before Mayo could finish, he was hit so hard his head slammed against the wall. He shook it off and came back fighting, but Connor hit him with two quick blows to his throat and stomach, collapsing Mayo's big Samoan body onto the floor. He lay there gasping for breath, eyeing the warrant officer with disdain.

"Now you're going to listen." Connor sat on the cot and spoke in a firm, yet forgiving voice. "You think you've got it bad, Mayo? You think your life stinks and everyone is out to get you? Bullshit! I've been in your shoes more times than I can count. I know what you're feeling. Life isn't fair. No one ever said it was supposed to be. The booze, the fighting, the anger, they only make what you're feeling worse. Whatever you're going through, get over it and move on."

Mayo coughed, hacking in air, keeping his eyes trained on Connor. His voice was almost a whisper as he spoke, but the sarcasm had disappeared. "And why should I listen to you?"

"Because this is your last chance. You can swallow your pride and walk out of here with a fresh start or hold the hate inside and keep traveling down the same road. The destination is far worse than you think. I've been there."

There was a measured change in Mayo's expression, a hint of self-doubt followed by a flash of suspicion in his dark eyes.

"You're a good crew chief," Connor continued. "The pride shows, whether you intend it or not. I could see you enjoyed what you were doing when we flew together. Let the good things in life guide you, kid.

101

Don't let the bad things be a distraction. They'll eat at you until you're nothing but a wasted shell."

Mayo struggled to his feet, leaned against the wall, and massaged his bruised throat. "You've got a powerful punch for an old man."

Connor met his stare without showing any antagonism. "I had my share of fights, usually when drunk and hating the world. Hate is a constant battle you'll never win."

There was a long moment of reflection from Mayo. He suddenly realized Connor was sincere and respected him for the advice, and his left jab. Unlike anyone else in recent memory, Connor had knocked some sense into his thick skull.

"I'm in deep shit, sir." He hung his head and looked at the floor.

"Yeah, you are. Now here's the deal." Connor pointed at the door. "I'm going to talk with the desk sergeant out there. He'll be back to see you in a few minutes. If he gives you the option of walking out of here tonight, I suggest you take it. The decision is yours. I'll be waiting outside."

The desk sergeant was a head shorter than Mayo but fifteen years his senior and far tougher. He opened the cell door and waved him out.

"You don't know how lucky you are, soldier. That warrant officer went out on a limb for you. I owed him a favor—a big one—and he just collected."

"You mean I'm free to go?" Mayo stood outside the door, surprised in spite of what Connor told him. "What about the charges?"

"The charges have been dropped. The other three punks changed their mind when I told them they could be cited for being drunk and stupid. The MP you took a swing at will be pissed, but I'll convince him my decision is in everyone's best interest. The pub owner said he'll withdraw his complaint as long as the damage is paid for."

There was an expression of relief on Mayo's face he didn't try to hide. He wiped some dried blood from the corner of his mouth. "Why? I mean why did Mister Connor go out on a limb for me?"

"Damned if I know." The sergeant's eyes narrowed as he looked Mayo over. "I'll tell you this though. You screw up again and he'll be dragging you back himself. Now tuck in your shirt and get on your way. I see you in here again and you'll be answering to me."

Mayo didn't screw up again. He turned his life around and his career, becoming a well-respected maintenance NCO. A wife and several kids helped him along the way.

Years later Mayo found himself in Alaska serving as the maintenance platoon sergeant. He was coordinating the transfer of the unit's remaining UH-1 helicopters while the rest of the battalion was overseas.

Mayo looked up as Connor entered the office, pleased he stopped by. They remained in contact after their tour in Germany. Connor often kept a watchful, if distant, eye on him, at times offering advice but never again intervening in his career. Mayo considered him both a mentor and a friend.

"Pull up a seat. You look a little tired." Mayo motioned to a nearby chair. "How's the morning going?"

Connor decided being downstairs was a better location for carrying out his plan. After finishing the paperwork in his office, Sergeant Jackson informed him the mission helicopter would be returning within the hour. He was still contemplating how to take the Huey without arousing suspicion when he found Mayo.

"The usual. How's the family?"

"They're great," replied Mayo. "Stop by sometime. Maria and the kids would enjoy seeing you. The old dog misses you, too. The kids are wearing him out."

Connor smiled. He missed Reno's company but knew the dog was in better hands with Mayo's family. "How have you been? Other than this morning, I haven't seen you in a while."

"Maintenance is keeping me busy." Mayo stretched back against the chair. "We're still short-handed but staying on schedule. Once the last helicopter is turned in, I'll be joining the battalion or be reassigned to another aviation unit."

Connor nodded. "You have any orders yet?"

"Nope. I'm pretty sure the Army won't move me for a while. Even if I'm deployed, the family can stay here until my oldest kid graduates from high school next year. What about you? You've been here for three years already, right?"

"Almost," Connor sighed. "I'm not sure what the Army has planned for me. Not that it matters. I don't plan on leaving Alaska."

"You mean you're actually going to retire? I don't believe it." Mayo laughed good-naturedly.

Connor held back a grimace and turned away before speaking. "I've thought about retiring, but at my age and in my condition there aren't many jobs out there. Sitting around doing nothing could get boring real quick."

"The last time we discussed retirement, you said you couldn't survive without getting another job. Maybe you should find a rich widow instead." Mayo was referencing a prior conversation concerning Connor's ex-wives and stiff alimony payments.

Since Connor could only collect half his retirement upon leaving the military, the rest going to the ex-wives, there would be little left to live on. Two of the three exes never remarried, remaining eligible for portions of his retirement.

"Nothing's changed." Connor ignored Mayo's attempt at humor. His ex-wives weren't a happy subject. "Not unless the two collecting alimony find different sugar daddies, which is unlikely with the monthly allotment they're getting. I'm sure a large chunk of my retirement would be icing on the cake."

"I suppose." Mayo became serious. He could tell something was bothering Connor. "I'd think with your experience, a civilian helicopter company would pay good money to hire you. You'll do fine."

Connor started to speak and then hesitated, almost giving his secret away. "Maybe. A civilian life isn't what I have in mind though."

Mayo was unsure of what Connor meant. He was about to inquire further when another figure entered the office.

Anthony Sanchez was an athletic, mid-career warrant officer who had a penchant for racquetball and poker. A disregard of fraternization rules had already delayed one promotion after he received a medio-cre officer evaluation. Several enlisted soldiers took offense and com-plained when they lost big in an all-night card game. Aside from his personal indiscretions, he was a good maintenance officer, taking great pride in the condition of his aircraft.

"Good morning," Sanchez said, noticing Connor. "Sorry about the helicopter. I didn't know you were available to fly until after we started the inspection."

"Not a problem." Connor kept a neutral expression. "The idea was just a spur of the moment thing when I heard there was an aircraft available."

"Well, at least you're back on flight status. Both helicopters should be flyable for tomorrow. Hell, you can even have my slot this afternoon and fly the commander if he doesn't postpone again."

Connor shook his head. "It's okay. I've got other things planned. You go ahead. Enjoy flying the old Hueys while you can. They'll be gone for good before long."

Sanchez nodded and turned his attention to Mayo. "I'd like to pull one of the mechanics off two-six-nine for an inspection on nine-three-four. It needs to be finished by this afternoon."

"I would prefer not to." Mayo sighed. "But if you really need another mechanic, go ahead. I need him back on two-six-nine as soon as possible though. We only have another week to get the engine up to specs for turn-in. Besides, once Lieutenant Hovan and Mister Thomp-son return, their aircraft is done for the day. The crew chief is new and could use some help on the daily inspection."

Connor shifted in his chair, realizing the mission helicopter wouldn't be available as planned. His options were quickly disappearing. He'd hoped to fly under the guise of a training flight without revealing his true intentions, at least until well after takeoff. Now he had little choice in the matter.

"I understand Sergeant Mayo," Sanchez said. "If the turn-in is delayed, and it won't be, I'll be the one taking the heat."

Mayo wasn't trying to be impertinent and only stated the obvious. He was irritated at Sanchez's attitude and considered reminding him, had he stuck to the previous schedule, there wouldn't be a need to shuffle mechanics now. Not to mention, should the scheduled turn-in be delayed, they would both be equally responsible.

Instead, Mayo held his comment. "Yes, sir. Thank you for the heads up."

Sanchez marched out the door. Mayo shook his head in response, displaying a look of fatherly resignation.

Connor noticed Mayo's frustration and waited until Sanchez was gone. "Give him a break. He's a good maintenance officer even if he's a little overzealous at times. We've both been in his shoes."

"Yeah, you're right," Mayo stated. "Sometimes dealing with officers is worse than raising kids. Neither listens very well. Present company excluded of course."

Connor almost smiled, in spite of his plan falling apart. He contemplated being honest with Mayo about his medical condition and desire for a last flight. Mayo would probably help but could end up being reprimanded or even court-martialed. Altering the schedule to allow another flight, especially once Connor's medical condition and real intentions were exposed, would have serious consequences.

Connor couldn't allow someone else to take the blame. Instead, he decided to lie and, if necessary, just steal the damn thing before anyone could stop him.

Mayo leaned forward in his chair, cupping his hands together. "And when did you get back on flight status? The way you were moping around here the last few weeks, I thought your flying days were over."

The truth of the statement, although spoken in jest, caught Connor by surprise. A pained look crossed his face before being masked with a look of indifference. "The flight surgeon cleared me this morning. I was hoping to get back up today on a refresher flight."

Mayo had no reason to doubt him. "Well, I'm glad you're back flying, but there won't be any time left when the helicopter returns from the mission. The pilots were told to log no more than three hours, otherwise they would be in deep shit with Captain Hiroldi."

"Why, what's the problem?"

"I forgot you missed the last staff briefing. The commander limited our flights to ten hours a week. Otherwise, we exceed the allotted budget. You know things are tight with the battalion deployed overseas. Those guys are the priority, as they should be."

"I remember now," Connor answered. "Sergeant Jackson briefed me last week after the meeting. He's been doing the flight schedule while I've been bouncing between medical appointments. The change slipped my mind."

Mayo understood his desire to fly. "Too bad we don't have more flight hours and the maintenance wasn't keeping me so busy. I'd go up with you if I could. Flying with your crazy ass again would be a nice distraction. Just like the old days."

Mayo waited for a response, noticing a sparkle return to Connor's eyes. Out of all the pilots Mayo had flown with, Connor was the best. They had flown together many times after their encounter at the MP Station in Germany, through a diversity of demanding missions. He was young and fearless then, and Connor was at the peak of his flying ability.

He wasn't fearless anymore. Time had a way of changing an individual's perspective. The sense of invincibility when you're young always ends. Experience ultimately reveals a person's vulnerability, and having family and friends alters selfish priorities.

Over the years, Mayo noticed the change in his own attitude. He became more responsible as his vitality was slowed by age and wisdom. The change in others was even more apparent, especially his elders. Flying was a perfect example.

Young pilots reflected strength and energy but were unrefined, possessing limited experience. Eventually, as knowledge and skill increased, physical and mental aptitude combined to make a better pilot. Later on, as physical attributes began to decline, wisdom and judgment maintained an effective balance, at least for a while. Over time, there was a change in direction. Experience no longer remained the deciding factor. The continued deterioration of mind and body became the predominate influence, making a pilot less and less effective.

Mayo realized the same changes were occurring in Connor. He didn't like what he saw. The transformation reminded him of his own mortality.

"We had some great times flying together." A flash of sorrow crossed Mayo's face. "Seems like only yesterday. Hard to believe, but a lot has changed over the years. We're both growing old. Soon our memories will be all we have left."

There were more than memories to look forward to, of course. But Mayo didn't tell Connor what he was thinking. Mayo had a wife, children, and future grandchildren to share his life. Connor was alone. There was plenty of female companionship and a few friends but no family. At least none he spoke about. For whatever reason, Connor's life had taken a solitary turn years ago.

"I always enjoyed flying with you," Mayo said. "Looks like you'll have to wait awhile to get back in the air, unless you reconsider Sanchez's offer."

"No, I don't think so. I've got other issues to take care of."

"Sure, I understand. So what did the doctor say about the aches and pains you've been having lately? Just old age or what?"

"Pretty much," Connor answered, prepared for the question. "Arthritis mostly, but some disc problems in my back. And just tired bones, I guess. He also said I have a mild ulcer. Apparently nothing a few pills and a bottle of Maalox can't help. Truthfully though, I think it's my overactive sex life."

Mayo laughed and flexed his hands together. "Good to hear. I guess we don't have to commit you just yet."

"Yeah, at least not for a while." Connor became more serious, deciding to test Mayo's reaction. "To tell you the truth, I was worried about my back problems being something far more serious."

"You mean cancer?"

"Damn right. Both my parents had cancer. My dad died when I was a teenager and my mom when she was about my age. Both were smokers. I remember when tobacco and caffeine were staples during long days in Vietnam. They helped keep us alert on long missions. Smoking didn't seem like much of a threat when we were dodging bullets every day. Part of the indifference of our youth, I guess. Good thing I quit a long time ago."

Mayo nodded, leaning back with his hands behind his head. "You should have told me, Gil. Not that I could do anything, but I can listen, especially over a few beers."

"I appreciate it," Connor said. "You know, if I was diagnosed with cancer, I wasn't sure how I was going to react. Lying in a hospital with tubes and wires barely keeping me alive is not the way I want to die. A nice quick death would be much better, don't you think?"

Mayo had thought about his own mortality. Death was something everyone considered at one time or another, especially in their line of work. "Some say dying in your sleep would be best or while making love to a beautiful woman. I sure can't think of a better way to go."

"That might be a little traumatic for your wife," Connor stated.

Mayo chuckled agreeably. "I suppose, especially if she wasn't the one I was making love with at the time."

Connor smirked. "I'm sure Maria will make up for your passing with plenty of male companionship."

There was a pause in the conversation. Connor looked at Mayo before continuing, studying his reaction. "If passing away in your sleep wasn't an option, dying suddenly in an accident would be preferable. Flying would be my choice."

The laughter faded from Mayo's face as he noticed the seriousness in Connor's expression. Just then, the phone on his desk rang, diverting his attention. He picked up the receiver on the second ring and spoke loudly into the handset.

"Charlie Company Maintenance Office, Sergeant First Class Mayo speaking."

Mayo listened for a few seconds and raised his eyebrows in puzzlement. "As a matter of fact he's right here. Hang on."

The phone was handed over and Connor wasn't surprised to hear Sergeant Jackson's voice on the other end. "Sir, a doctor Akers called here a couple minutes ago looking for you. He wanted you to call him right away."

"Really?" Connor answered as if unaware of the reason for the call. He assumed doctor Akers was checking on his absence from a cancer counseling session he was scheduled for. He was supposed to be there now but had no intention of showing up.

"Did he say what the call was about?"

"No, sir."

"All right, thank you, Sergeant Jackson. I'll get a hold of him."

"Yes, sir."

Connor handed the phone back to Mayo, who placed the receiver on the cradle.

"You get yourself in trouble again?"

"No, just forgot to pick up some paperwork this morning. Nothing important." Connor realized his chance of commandeering a helicopter was rapidly decreasing.

He also realized another call would eventually be placed to his acting commander, describing in detail the terminal cancer and his reaction to the news. Once that happened, the possibility of taking a last flight would be virtually eliminated.

"At least your medical problem isn't anything serious," Mayo added. Something was bothering Connor, but he wasn't sure what, exactly. "Looks like your grumpy ass will be with us for a while."

Connor glanced at a portrait of Mayo's family proudly positioned on his desk, reminding him of his own family many years before. He was about to comment when the sound of a helicopter began reverberating off the hangar walls.

The helicopter's early return gave Connor another idea. His plan had just changed back in his favor.

CHAPTER FOURTEEN

The baritone voice of Warrant Officer Joe Shultz resonated off the walls as he entered the 95th Air Medical Company's flight operations room. "What have you got?"

His office was on the same floor at the end of the hallway, allowing him to respond quickly to any mission alert. He was one of only two pilots-in-command left in the unit.

Shultz was short and stout with hair in need of a trim around a thin spot on the crown of his head. A baggy flight suit gave him even more of a rotund appearance. Most people mistook him for an out-of-shape clerk or salesman when he wasn't in uniform. His appearance was deceiving. He was, in fact, well fit and could easily outrun most of the officers in the battalion. He was also an experienced and respected instructor pilot.

Stopping at the counter, Shultz eyed the mission request log on the private's desk. In his right hand he held a small nylon trifold enclosing a flight computer and writing pad he used for jotting down information. The black case was opened and set aside as he waited for an answer.

"Satellites picked up an ELT signal." Donovan pointed at the coordinates on the large wall map. "The RCC in Anchorage sent in the mission request, sir. So far, the signal is unconfirmed."

Shultz moved closer to inspect the map. He took the piece of paper showing the coordinates from Donovan and quickly verified the locations. "Could be the real deal this time. No landing sites I'm aware of in the area."

"The RCC didn't give us much information to go on," the soft-spoken private stated after hanging up the telephone. "He was more interested in how he could get a ride on a helicopter."

"Let me take a look," Shultz said, holding out his hand for the mission sheet.

"Yes, sir." The private handed over the sheet and went back to his desk for the file book.

Quickly scanning the paper, Shultz noted most of the spaces were left blank. The times of the satellite tracks caught his attention, and he glanced at his watch.

"The last satellite fix was less than ten minutes ago," he announced to no one in particular. "A couple more satellite passes and we should be able to narrow the search area considerably."

Donovan was about to ask if he intended to delay the takeoff until more information was available when Warrant Officer Damien Ferguson, the copilot, entered the room.

Ferguson had barely heard the mission alert over the loudspeaker. He was in the supply office with the door closed on the opposite side of the hangar. His attention was on typing a memorandum, and only the piercing squelch of static halfway through the announcement alerted him to the mission. After saving the document on the computer and locking the door, he hurried his lean, six-foot frame down the stairs and across the hangar floor.

With only a couple of medevac missions under his belt, Ferguson was anxious. He'd been taught to have a sense of urgency without being in a hurry and hid his excitement. When you were in a hurry, you made mistakes. Mistakes made you unsafe and being unsafe caused accidents. Still, a rush of adrenaline was only human nature. He forced himself to remain focused.

The crew medic, Sergeant Steiner, a tough, blond-haired, ex-golden glove boxer, followed Ferguson across the hangar floor. Alaska was Steiner's third assignment as a flight medic and one he especially enjoyed after serving a tour in Afghanistan.

Specialist Brilnesko, a slim, slick-haired crew chief, nicknamed "Bril," caught up to Steiner as they reached the stairway. He was new to the medevac mission but previously crewed UH-60s in an air assault company.

They entered the operations office only a few steps behind Ferguson as Bril finished telling a joke.

His voice had a slow, rhythmic quality of someone accustomed to telling stories. The difference between fact and fiction was often well shaded. "So the blonde told the bartender she wanted a fifteen."

Steiner looked over at him suspiciously as they entered the office. "A fifteen? What exactly is a fifteen, Bril?"

The smile on Bril's face widened, but he glanced around the office before answering, confirming there were no females present who might be offended. "That's exactly what the bartender said. So the blonde rolled her eyes at the bartender and spoke slowly. 'Fiiif-teeen! A seven and seven, duuuh!' As if he was a complete moron."

He looked at each of them and laughed good-naturedly, his eyes sparkling with humor.

Steiner groaned and rolled his eyes in disbelief. "You owe me two minutes of my life back for listening to your bullshit story. I should have known any account of you and a blonde in a bar had to have a punch-line."

Shultz tried suppressing a smile and handed the mission sheet over to Steiner. "Here's all we know so far." He motioned Ferguson over to the area wall map and pointed to where the coordinates corresponded to locations on the glacier.

"This is where we're going. We'll only be on a search mission to confirm the signal. We have no information other than the satellite coordinates. Could be a real emergency or a false alarm. Questions?"

Ferguson shook his head no.

Steiner was the first to respond. "Looks pretty routine, sir. Probably some bush plane made a hard landing and activated his ELT. Even if the plane was damaged, there won't be more than a couple guys to pick up."

"Probably, but maybe an aircraft really did smack into the glacier." Shultz made eye contact with each of his crew while continuing to speak. "Wouldn't be the first time. What do you say we go find out?"

A relaxed smile creased Steiner's mouth. He loved the exhilaration of a real mission, especially the potential for a medical emergency. He was often the first responder, providing critical care for a patient and their only hope of staying alive. Bad weather, harsh terrain, and sometimes enemy fire only added to the risk. The hazards somehow made the lives he saved more meaningful, as if death had thrown everything possible at him and failed. Being a medic was what he lived for.

During a mission the pilot-in-command was responsible for the crew and aircraft, while the flight medic was responsible for patient care. The medic's assessment for treatment and priority of transport played an integral part in the overall decision-making process.

On missions where no patients were involved, the medic still served as an important member of the crew and as another set of eyes during search operations. Aside from medical training, their flight experience was a valuable asset.

"How soon before we launch, sir?" Steiner raised his wristwatch to note the time. "I need to grab something before we go."

He caught the questioning looks of his fellow crew members and offered an explanation. "I left my jacket in the medic office. If we're heading in the mountains, it might come in handy."

"Okay. We'll launch as soon as everyone's onboard." Shultz shifted his gaze to Ferguson, thinking it would be quicker to have the copilot start the APU, the helicopter's auxiliary power unit, while waiting on the rest of the crew. "You and Bril head down and go up on the APU. Get everything running, short of starting the engines. I'll be there as soon as I call for a weather update. We can file a flight plan over the radio."

"Should we top off the external tanks?" Ferguson thought additional fuel might be a good idea with the potential for a long flight.

Shultz had already figured the fuel required for the mission but went over the mental calculations again as he looked back at the map. A normal mission configuration was flown with the internal fuel tanks filled to capacity and the two external long-range tanks only partially filled with a hundred gallons each. This provided roughly three and half hours of flight time, depending on environmental conditions and gross weight.

Shultz figured twenty-five minutes to reach the glacier flying a direct course between Fort Wainwright and the mountains. Factoring in time for the return flight left two hours and forty minutes on station, more than enough time to find the source of the signal and rescue possible survivors. Provided, of course, there were no unforeseen problems.

"Let's go with the fuel we have. I'm thinking worst-case scenario. If we have to conduct a rescue at high altitude, the additional fuel will increase our gross weight and limit our hovering capability. Once the RCC sends updated information, we can reduce the size of the search area and won't need as much fuel. Operations can pass any new information while we're en route. The off-duty crew can be called in to launch if we start running low on fuel."

Steiner and Bril stepped into the hallway as Ferguson nodded in reply and followed. They looked at each other without speaking, each thinking of the mission ahead.

Shultz moved toward a telephone on a nearby flight-planning table. He hesitated before lifting the receiver. Something was nagging at him. An intuition he developed over the years, telling him this would be anything but a routine mission. He ignored the warning and dialed the weather office.

The operations and planning area were located in the same room, separated by a long wooden counter. The design was similar to other operation offices on the airfield. Flight publications and aircraft manuals were stored in a long metal bookshelf near the window. A large wooden desk was situated in the center of the floor for plotting routes and filling out flight plans and weather briefing sheets. Maps of the local training areas and charts of Interior Alaska hung from the walls for easy reference, clearly marked with updated hazards.

An updated briefing from the Air Force Weather office only took a minute. The forecaster was happy to break the monotony of boredom. Medevac missions had priority anyway. En route conditions were basically the same as forecast earlier, except for an approaching frontal system over the southern mountain range. The storm was moving faster than originally predicted, with moderate to severe turbulence developing over rough terrain. Rain was forecast with possible snow at higher elevations. Icing in clouds was expected above six thousand feet.

Shultz took the information in stride. The forecasters were usually on the money with their analysis. Flight conditions were deteriorating and could get downright nasty, but he wasn't overly concerned. The helicopter was capable of flying in almost any weather, and if necessary they could turn back should the situation worsen. Flying in the mountains was a dangerous business, a business in which he was well experienced. In the mountains, the winds could be a pilot's worst enemy, unpredictable and deadly.

Sergeant Donovan was looking out the window at the mission helicopter on the tarmac when Shultz got off the phone. He turned to see Shultz staring at the large wall map again.

"Weather good, sir?"

Shultz didn't respond for a few seconds before glancing back at the Donovan. "Good enough for a couple of hours. Then conditions will get a lot worse. We should be able to identify the ELT signal by then."

"New satellite fixes should be coming through soon." Donovan crossed his arms over his chest as he spoke. "I already informed the RCC you're launching."

"Roger," Shultz said. "Right now the search area is well over three square miles, assuming the coordinates are accurate. The transmission was probably bouncing off the surrounding mountains and distorting the signal. The source could be outside the three-mile area, but I guess we'll find out soon enough."

"Yes, sir. Would you like me to notify the off-duty crew, just in case?"

Shultz scratched his chin and looked at his watch. "No. Don't bother until we have more information. The mission could be a false alarm. I don't want them coming in for nothing. If the RCC doesn't send an update by the time we reach the search area, I'll reconsider."

"Yes, sir. I'll notify battalion, so they're aware of the mission." Donovan began dialing one of the phone numbers stenciled on a sheet of paper under the Plexiglas cover on his desk.

Shultz waved in reply and headed out the door.

As the phone on the other end began ringing, Donovan yelled in his direction. "Good luck, sir."

CHAPTER FIFTEEN

S anders confirmed his earlier assessment of the crash site. The ridge was far too uneven and strewn with large obstacles for even a small bush plane to land. He didn't know much about helicopters but guessed even the most capable would have problems with the high, surrounding slopes and swirling winds. Hoisting the survivors off the ground seemed the only possibility. He saw the procedure performed at an air show once, but it was on a fair weather day at a much lower altitude. With the current weather and terrain, the possibility of a quick rescue was slim at best. He decided to plan for the worst.

Sanders watched as Kwapich and Bidwell pulled hard on the rear access door. Immediately behind them the tail section had bowed upward and sideways at an abnormal angle. The wing was also heavily damaged. Large sections of aluminum skin were deeply dented and the engine cowling was broken, twisted away on one side. The propeller blades were curved sharply backward from the tips contacting the ground.

Sanders let out a slow breath and shook his head. His company's multi-million dollar aircraft was now a pile of twisted junk.

The noise of the wind was interrupted by a dull groan of metal as the rear access door slowly opened. One problem solved, Sanders thought. The two men had the situation under control, and he moved toward the wing for a closer inspection.

There was no sign of leaking fuel. The self-sealing bladder had remained intact. He ran his hand over the wing affectionately. Fire was still a possibility, although remote, and he made a mental note to remind everyone about not using lighters or open flame.

Tufts of hair blew across his face as he turned away from the biting wind. Off the front of the aircraft, he could see a woman and four girls clustered behind a pile of rock. They were all wearing similar sweat jackets. Sitting shoulder to shoulder, they seemed protected from the worst effects of the wind.

There was little he could do for them at this point. Even so, he wanted to check their condition and assure them the situation wasn't as terrible as they might assume. Actually, the situation probably was, maybe even worse, but he wasn't about to scare them further with the truth. At least not until he knew for sure a rescue wasn't imminent. Until then, there was always hope.

The woman and all but one of the girls stared at Sanders meekly as he approached. One of them, who appeared to be the youngest and yet most composed of the group, rose to meet him when he was a few feet away. Her eyes were bright and unafraid as if a crash on a high mountain in the middle of nowhere was a typical day at school.

He extended his good arm in an attempted hug, forcing a smile and introducing himself, trying to appear fatherly as if everything would be all right. The young girl seemed surprised by the gesture and instead of falling into his arms, took his hand and looked at him reassuringly.

"I'm Lisa," she explained, stepping beside him to face the others. "That's Sheryl, Becka, Mary Beth, and our coach, Miss Regan." She pointed to each of them by name.

The three girls appeared more scared than in shock, awaiting guidance Sanders supposed since they were outside the wreckage with only the wind and each other for company. Their coach concerned him the most. She had a look of hysteria on her face as her eyes darted back and forth between him, the girls, and the surrounding mountains.

"Miss Regan?" Sanders asked. "I need you and the girls to do something for me."

Her expression didn't change at first until he repeated her name more forcefully. She tilted her head and recognition slowly returned. Her lips quivered as she spoke, and the sound of her own voice seemed to focus her attention.

"Yes? . . . what? . . . okay." Donna's mind seemed to prioritize her thoughts before she returned to a positive state of awareness. Self-preservation was her main concern. The girls were secondary.

"But the plane . . . shouldn't we stay here? We were told to stay here."

Sanders was about to answer when Lisa squeezed his hand and began speaking. "Mrs. Douglas, the nice lady sitting behind me on the plane, told us to wait here until it was safe. I wanted to help, but she insisted. Can't we do something? It's hard not knowing what's going on."

The other girls nodded their heads in agreement. They were content to accept Lisa as their spokesperson. The excitement of doing something was suddenly more important than staying out of the wind, although Sander's noticed one of the girls appeared less excited than the others.

"We should stay here," Donna stated weakly. "For the girls' sake I mean. This is the safest place, right? These girls are my responsibility. I'm their coach."

Having the girls remain where they were was Sanders intention all along. The trauma inside the wreckage wasn't something they should be exposed to more than they already had been. But Lisa's offer had merit. She was persuasive. Her maturity was far more reflective of an adult than a child.

"This is the safest place for the moment," Sanders acknowledged. "I could still use some assistance though if you'll allow it, Miss Regan?"

She was shaking her head as Sanders ignored the gesture and continued. "Perhaps a couple of the girls could help with the baggage? Sort through them for warm clothing, jackets, sweaters, and such. There might be some food as well. The items might make our situation more comfortable until help arrives."

Donna's expression changed as the thought of warmer clothing and food appealed to her. She pretended to think about the offer for a few seconds. "Oh, I guess it would be okay. Just a couple of the girls?"

"Two or three should be enough. The rest can stay here with you, where they'll be more comfortable." Sanders felt Lisa squeeze his hand again.

"I'll help." Lisa was the first to offer, then Sheryl and Becka. Mary Lou hesitated and Sanders could tell she was reluctant to offer.

"You three will be enough. There aren't many pieces of luggage. Mary Lou and Miss Regan can stay here so the rest of the passengers will know where to meet."

There was a visible show of relief on Mary Lou's face as she looked at the ground. Donna smiled slightly as if getting the best of Sander's without him knowing.

"Okay, girls, this is what I need you to do." Sanders turned and, out of reflex, attempted to raise his broken arm. The pain made him grimace and stop. He released Lisa's hand, motioned toward the rear of the wreckage with his good arm, and gingerly repositioned the sling.

"Most of the luggage is in the compartment behind the wing, further back from the exit door. Open the bags and take out the things I mentioned. Keep the loose items in the cargo compartment so the wind doesn't blow them away. When you're done, reclose the bags and set them on the ground under the tail. If they're too heavy, leave them. Someone can move them later. Any questions?"

Sheryl and Becka shook their heads, each answering in the negative. Only Lisa had a question. "Can I let the dogs out? They might be injured."

Sanders realized he forgot about the dogs again. Their occasional barking was heard over the wind, yet he had been ignoring the sound since exiting the wreckage.

"Leave them alone for now, Lisa. The dogs will be frightened, maybe aggressive. They could bite or attack you. One of the other passengers will check on them."

Lisa noticed the sling when Sanders' first approached and saw his grimace of pain. She gently grasped his wrist and placed the fingers of her other hand lightly under the injured arm. Her words carried a gentle strength.

"The dogs won't hurt me."

She held his arm for a few moments longer. He didn't answer, but he believed her. There was a reassuring smile on her face, as if she knew what he was thinking. He'd never met such an insightful young girl. Before he could reason a response, she was talking with the other girls as they drifted away.

He watched them go for a moment, then nodded at Donna and headed toward the nose of the plane. Already focused on something else, he didn't notice the pain in his arm was almost gone.

Without the landing gear extended, the top of the windshield was no higher than Sanders' head. He could see the cockpit through the broken, spider-webbed glass and Illiamin in his seat, still unconscious. His chest was moving, discernible by the fabric of his shirt flexing with each labored breath. The narrow cockpit door was half open. Someone was standing, facing away on the other side, but he couldn't tell who the person was.

His eyes moved over the fuselage. The starboard side of the cockpit sustained the heaviest damage, pushed inward by the impact. Directly below the windshield the nose was misshapen from scraping over the rough ground. Less than five feet away, a sedan size boulder lay partially embedded in the ground. If the plane hadn't stopped where it did, the collision would have crushed the cockpit, killing both pilots.

Sanders studied the damage, thankful he survived. He said a silent prayer for the injured. He remembered reading a story where someone said there were no atheists in foxholes. Considering what had transpired, he doubted there were any atheists after an airliner crash either.

He moved around the nose to check the starboard wing—or what was left of it. Only a few feet of broken metal remained attached to the fuselage. The rest of the wing remained twisted around a rock formation behind the tail. Its aluminum skin was bent and torn open, leaving a broken spar pointing upward at an odd angle. The engine was still attached, dangling by a single mount with the propeller hub stuck in the ground. The cowling was missing, torn loose sometime during the crash.

Sanders could smell fuel as he neared the jagged section attached to the fuselage. The combustible liquid was dripping from a ruptured line and seeping into the ground. Using his good hand, he bent the end of the tubing, pinching it tight to stop the leak. He finished by wrapping the line with a strip of torn handkerchief. The fix seemed to work. For the moment at least, he was satisfied.

Hydraulic fluid and oil were another potential hazard. He checked the broken lines, but other than a few drops, there was no obvious accumulation. He plugged the lines anyway.

The small nose compartment was the last thing Sanders examined. The surface was heavily damaged, but the door opened with a sharp tug. A separate access panel was built into the wall. Mounted inside on a rail was a bright red, brick-size ELT with an antenna attached. He retrieved the metal box and checked the three-position toggle switch, verifying the position was ON and the power light illuminated.

Knowing the device was operating correctly was a relief. The ELT activated automatically when the plane crashed. An orbiting satellite would eventually pick up the transmission, forwarding the signal location to a rescue coordination center where the information would be passed to search and rescue facilities. Unless someone heard their earlier radio calls, the emergency locator was the only hope they had of a timely rescue.

Sanders placed the ELT back on the rail, leaving the small access door open. He repositioned his head and arm so he could retrieve the few lightweight bags stored inside. They might be useful.

A scuffle of boots across the rough surface was indiscernible above the sound of the wind. Sanders' head was still in the compartment when he recognized Kwapich's voice.

"There you are. We managed to get the rear cabin door open. Hank is helping Danny free the passenger entangled in his seat. The aisle should be free of debris soon."

Sanders pulled his head clear, holding the last bag. "Good. Nice job. Some of the passengers might require help getting outside if they find the urge. And there's the dead to consider. We should move them as soon as possible. Did you check the cargo compartment?"

"The pallet is there. The dogs, too, and they seem uninjured. I left them in their kennels, but one of the girls going through the luggage insisted it was all right to let them out. She's very persuasive."

"Yes, she is." Sanders was grateful for the help he was getting from many of the passengers.

"Figured I'd let you know what was going on before breaking apart the pallet. The girls are busy getting the suitcases open. They've already found some jackets and sweaters. Moving the bags outside when they're finished shouldn't be a problem. I'll go back and give them a hand in a minute after I check on the injured. Maybe we can move the bodies into the cargo compartment."

"I was thinking the same thing," Sanders replied.

Kwapich stared through the side window at Illiamin's body. "The retired nurse and Susan Douglas are patching up the injured, but some of them are in pretty bad shape. A few might not make it."

Sanders let out a sigh. "I know. The thought has been on my mind since the crash. I guess I've been avoiding the injured by trying to stay busy. I'm the one at fault." He hesitated before continuing. "I'll check on everyone in a minute."

There was no blame on Kwapich's face, only a sad expression of understanding. "What are you doing here?"

"I thought we might need these bags. I also wanted to check our emergency locator to ensure it was sending out a distress signal."

"Is it?"

"Yeah," Sanders said. "The battery's strong. Someone should be looking for us before long."

Kwapich raised his eyebrows. "What do you mean? You said earlier search and rescue had already been notified."

Sanders hesitated but looked directly at him. "Yes, I did. I didn't want to alarm the passengers any more than necessary. Giving them hope of a quick rescue seemed the right thing to do at the time."

"I see," Kwapich said, shifting uncomfortably. "Then we might be here awhile?"

A thick layer of clouds was clearly visible among the distant mountains, obscuring the high, rugged peaks as the dark mass slowly advanced toward the crash site.

Sanders watched and gauged the storm's approaching speed, estimating they only had a couple hours at the most before the weather was upon them. He turned back to Kwapich and noticed his questioning expression. Sanders couldn't lie about their predicament. They would all find out soon enough.

"Let's hope not," he said. "If no one finds us by the time the storm arrives, we could be here for days."

CHAPTER SIXTEEN

A blast of hot air swirled outward in a surrounding wave of dust as the helicopter approached the hangar. The UH-1 flared, slowing to a stationary hover over a faded yellow line on the parking ramp. As it turned to face the hangar, the tail caught the wind, causing the fuselage to wobble and dip before regaining position. The helicopter slowly settled, touching down with a gentle bump.

Two pilots sat in the cockpit, an expression of cocky enthusiasm partially hidden by the dark visors of their helmets.

A third helmeted figure jumped out of the rear cargo door as the engine spooled to idle. The deafening roar of the turbine engine changed to a low rumble as the harmonic beat of the rotor blades softened in the fresh morning air.

The crew chief stood close to the fuselage, attached to the intercom system by a long cord for communication. He looked on both sides of the helicopter, ensuring the area was clear and no one approached the tail rotor. A small door in the cowling of the engine compartment was then pushed open as he checked for fluid leaks. He could hear the pilots talking through the intercom, one reading from a checklist as the other confirmed each step.

The UH-1 Huey had been in military service for over fifty years. An iconic symbol of the Vietnam War, the UH-1 earned a well-deserved reputation for an ability to perform any mission, setting a high standard for several decades. Even after being replaced by the more advanced UH-60 Black Hawk in the 1980s, the Huey remained in service with various military units for another twenty years. The Army in Alaska was one of the last active commands still using them.

Medical evacuations, or medevacs, had always been one of the most important missions. During the Vietnam War, the Huey, in particular, was regarded as an angel of mercy. Thousands of wounded soldiers were rescued from death's door—a legacy that continued throughout its lengthy service.

All Army pilots were aware of the UH-1's storied history. Many of the older pilots had flown them during their career, but Connor was one of the few still on active duty who had flown in Vietnam.

None of those facts mattered to Connor as he listened to the helicopter approach the hangar. He waited until the engine decreased to idle, then exited the hangar through a small side door. Standing outside the spinning rotors in front of the cockpit, he waited until the pilot in the left seat made eye contact and motioned him forward.

The primary pilot, or pilot-in-command, normally sat in the right cockpit seat of a helicopter, opposite the arrangement in an airplane. When two pilots were flying together, however, they often switched seats to maintain competency from both positions. Many pilots actually preferred flying from the left, or copilot's seat, which provided a better view of the tail rotor and possible obstructions. Pilots Thompson and Hovan were similarly positioned as Connor approached.

Warrant Officer Al Thompson, twenty-two years old with a swimmer's physique and chestnut hair, held a questioning look on his face as the senior warrant officer hastened beneath the spinning rotor blades. He opened his left cockpit door to greet him but was surprised when Connor continued past and opened the side cargo door.

Connor retrieved a headset draped over one of the folding seats along the bulkhead and plugged into the intercom. Thompson turned to face him with a questioning expression.

"Al, can you hear me?"

"Yeah, loud and clear. What's up Mister Connor?"

Even though Thompson considered Connor a mentor and friend, he rarely addressed him by his first name. Out of respect for his rank, he usually used the formal warrant officer title of Mister unless they were flying together.

Thompson was a warrant officer one, with less than two years of service, while Connor was a senior warrant officer four, with over thirty. Military protocol wasn't as prevalent among warrant officers as other officers, but there still existed a strong bond of respect. Addressing Connor by his first name didn't seem appropriate to Thompson in front of Lieutenant Hovan.

Connor sat down on the folding seat nearest the door before answering. "Don't shut down. You guys have another mission. Some visiting dignitary requested a last minute flight. I'm not sure of the details, but your helicopter is the only one available. Captain Hiroldi wants to brief you both right away. He said the mission is urgent and to give him a call."

"Both of us?" Lieutenant Hovan asked, interrupting before Thompson could answer. He was a stocky, West Point graduate fresh out of flight school. "Where's the Captain now?"

Connor's voice was calm and direct. "He's in his office at battalion. Give him a call from the operations office. All I know is he wants to brief you both."

Hovan glanced at Thompson in the opposite seat and frowned with uncertainty. As the copilot he was still under Thompson's authority where the helicopter was concerned. The difference in rank wasn't usually an issue, and like most aircrews they considered each other part of an integral team.

"All right, we're almost ready to shut down." Thompson's voice had a hint of eagerness.

"Don't shut down," Connor said forcefully. He paused, hoping they hadn't sensed the deceit in his voice. "Captain Hiroldi wants you back in the air as soon as possible. I'll keep the engine running while you're getting briefed."

Thompson's eyebrows raised in brief surprise. He was baffled by the subterfuge surrounding the mission but figured any chance at acquiring more flight time was good enough reason for him. He had been out of flight school for only a year, but aside from spending time with his wife and newborn son, he preferred flying over anything else.

He was a good pilot and had only obtained his pilot-in-command status a few months earlier. Unfortunately for him, available flight hours were substantially reduced after the battalion's deployment. The disappointment of limited flying was offset by being with his wife when she gave birth to his son and an opportunity to acquire more of Connor's tutelage before heading off to a combat zone.

The few times Thompson had flown with Connor had been particularly enlightening. The senior warrant officer's approach and techniques for flying were invaluable, something that couldn't be found in a manual. What impressed him most was the relaxed, almost effortless way Connor flew. His personality was different on the ground. In the air, he seemed at ease and in complete control of his surroundings.

"I'll stay on the flight controls, Lieutenant, if you want to climb out first," Thompson said.

Hovan glanced over at Thompson before relenting. "All right, you have the controls. I'll meet you inside."

Lieutenant Hovan was a former linebacker on the West Point football team. Weighing close to two hundred and forty pounds, he spent a good part of his off-duty time lifting weights and running. Rumors were circulating he was being groomed for a high position of command. His uncle was a United States Senator and chairman of the powerful Armed Service Committee.

Connor climbed out the opposite cargo door, still wearing the headset, and waited as Hovan unbuckled his shoulder harness and seat belt. He held the door open as the brawny lieutenant unplugged from the intercom system and backed out of the pilot's seat, smoothly stepping onto the ground. They nodded politely. Hovan hurried away toward the hangar and Connor took his place, gingerly stepping on the toe of the skid before pulling himself in the seat.

The simple movement of climbing into the cockpit was painful. Connor tried not to show discomfort. His time was running out, but he willed his strength to overcome the stabbing pain emanating from his lower back. Acting as if he was unaffected, he forced a weak smile, nodding to Thompson.

Thompson waited until Connor plugged in his headset before speaking. "This must be an important mission if the commander is briefing us."

Connor swallowed, guilt sticking in his throat. He hated lying, but the ruse was necessary if he intended to continue with the plan. Thompson's trust mirrored his innocence. In many ways, the young warrant officer reminded Connor of himself, early in his career.

"I doubt it," Connor replied. "More than likely the flight is a sight-seeing tour around the local area so some ranking official can feel important. I'm sure Hiroldi is only doing what the post commander asked him."

"Too bad." Thompson smiled mischievously. "I guess flying the Swedish Bikini Team would be too much to hope for."

Connor couldn't suppress a grin. "Not today, anyway. I'll check and see what we have on the mission schedule later. Maybe some Playboy bunnies can fill in on short notice."

"Now you're talking. Try to include the latest Miss August in the request. By her warm expression in this month's issue, I'm sure she'll want to give me a good send off before I head overseas."

"You bet. I'm sure your wife will appreciate the patriotic gesture. Now get going. Don't keep the commander waiting."

Thompson relinquished the flight controls. Before climbing down from the cockpit, he paused and looked back at Connor with a more serious expression. "So when do I get to see the autographed picture you promised to show me over a month ago?"

Connor shook his head good-naturedly, in spite of the delay. He couldn't help but like the energetic warrant officer. "Get out of here and quit wasting time."

The picture was of a Playboy centerfold Connor had flown while supporting a USO troupe in Korea years ago. The voluptuous kiss from the model was nothing more than a friendly gesture on her part, but soldiers got a kick out of the story when he mentioned spending three days with her on a series of flights to different bases.

"Uh, sir?" Private Epstein asked from outside the helicopter, still hooked into the intercom system. He had been silent since Connor emerged from the hangar.

"Yeah, what's on your mind?"

"Sir, I've got to piss something fierce. Do you mind if I go and use the bathroom real quick?"

Until Epstein interrupted his train of thought, Connor had been unsure of how to get him away from the helicopter. "Sure thing. Take your time. Before you go inside though, make sure the cargo doors are secure."

Epstein was only going to be gone a few minutes but did as requested after unplugging from the intercom and setting the cord near his helmet bag. He waved, indicating all was secure before moving hurriedly toward the hangar.

Connor watched every step, urging him faster as he approached the hangar. He finally sighed with relief as the crew chief disappeared inside. *Hovan should be upstairs by now, with Thompson right behind.*

No one was around the parking ramp as Connor rolled the throttle to the full open position, applying left pedal to counter the torque from the rotor blades. Quickly, with the precision of flying thousands of hours in the air, he checked the engine gauges and verified the fuel status. The tanks had been topped off before the aircraft was flown back to the hangar, providing another two hours of usable fuel. More than enough for what he intended.

Sergeant First Class Mayo was sitting in his office. He could hear the helicopter running when Private Epstein shuffled by the open door. "Private, where are you going in such a hurry?"

The crew chief halted and stuck his head in the doorway. "To the bathroom, Sergeant. I need to go before we take off again."

"Take off again? What are talking about? Your aircraft isn't scheduled for any more flights."

"I know. I mean it wasn't," said Epstein as he shuffled his weight nervously from one leg to the other. "We have another mission. Lieutenant Hovan and Mister Thompson are getting briefed right now."

Mayo frowned in irritation, doubting if Epstein knew what he was talking about. "Then why the hell is the aircraft still running?"

"Mister Connor is at the controls. He told the pilots he'd keep it running. Said the commander wanted to brief them over the phone about another mission."

A look of concern flashed across Mayo's face and his eyes widened in disbelief. The earlier conversation with Connor seemed innocent enough at the time, but he'd sensed there was something else going on. The suspicion was nothing he could put his finger on, but Connor had been acting strange. The turn of events now was disturbing. He had to figure out why.

"You stay here, Private. I'm going to find out what's going on."

Epstein moved aside as Mayo hurried through the door. *What was the big deal? If the commander wanted them to fly another mission, what did the sergeant have to be concerned about?* All he wanted to do was use the damn bathroom.

Before Mayo reached the hangar door, he could hear the helicopter's engine increasing to full power. The hot wind from the rotor wash hit his face as he stepped outside.

Connor was looking right at him but started pulling in collective to bring the helicopter off the ground. Mayo ignored the attempt to lift off. He shielded his eyes against the swirling dust and ducked beneath the spinning rotor blades above his head. Connor stopped, clenching his teeth in anger.

"What the hell are you doing?" Mayo yelled over the sound of the engine as he flung open the cockpit door.

"I'm taking the damn helicopter," Connor answered sharply.

"Why? What's going on? You don't have authorization to fly. Where the hell are you going?"

Connor knew he had no choice but to tell his friend the truth. His voice strained against the loud noise.

"I need to do this. Remember what we were talking about earlier? The situation I described? Well, it's real. I have terminal cancer. They won't let me fly anymore. I want one last flight on my own terms, just me and the helicopter. I'll be back later and face the consequences."

Mayo suspected Connor was sicker than he admitted earlier but never thought cancer was the culprit or that he would resort to such an extreme measure. Now knowing the truth, his suspicions made sense.

"So this is what you're going to do? Take the damn helicopter without permission? Throw your reputation and career away? You're better than that."

"Not anymore," Connor said with a choking voice. "My career is over. My personal life was over a long time ago. I'm not taking the chance I'll never fly again."

Mayo hesitated before responding. He could see the determination etched in his friend's face. The set jaw and rigid stare defined Connor's resolve.

"That's your excuse? Bullshit! Shut the helicopter down and let's talk this over. There's plenty of time to speak with the commander and get his approval. He'll understand."

Connor shook his head solemnly. There was no way he was changing his mind. Unwilling to explain his true intentions, he offered a
partial explanation.

"No way. I'm off flight status, permanently grounded. My pilot
days are over. The commander will never let me fly by myself or even
be at the controls with another pilot. I appreciate what you're trying to
do, but you won't change my mind. Taking the helicopter is the best
option. I'm doing this on my terms." Connor pulled the door closed
and nodded a final farewell.

Mayo stepped back. There was nothing he could do, short of trying to drag his friend out of the helicopter by force. He reluctantly
moved away, convincing himself to trust Connor and hope he came
back safely. In his gut, he knew differently.

As the helicopter lifted, Mayo turned. He shielded his eyes
from the rotor wash, watching as the helicopter floated in a smooth
motion over the tarmac, disappearing around the hangar. He stood
there for some time, even after the sound of the engine faded across
the airfield.

Connor was irritated at Mayo even though he was trying to help.
Why couldn't he have stayed in the hangar? The confrontation only made
the situation worse. He hovered at a moderate pace toward the takeoff
pad, putting his emotions aside. In the air he didn't need any distractions. His plan would be carried through to the end.

"Wainwright ground, Army . . .," Connor paused while checking
the placard with the aircraft number on the instrument panel. "Nine-
two-seven, east side of hangar three for south departure."

Almost immediately, a voice with a slight southern twang responded.
"Roger, nine-two-seven. Taxi into position on pad three and hold for a
zero-six-zero departure. Winds are one-two-five at five knots, altimeter
three-zero-one-two. Contact tower when ready for departure, over."

Connor did as instructed, anticipating the change in wind direction as he hovered over the pad and aligned the helicopter in the direction of takeoff.

"Tower, nine-two-seven is in position on pad three, right crosswind departure to the south."

A different, lower voice responded this time. "Roger, nine-two-seven. Right crosswind departure is approved. Call exiting the surface area."

Connor adjusted the flight controls for a steep climb away from the helipad. After passing through a hundred feet, he banked right on a southerly heading, maintaining a steady climb. At twelve hundred feet he pushed the nose forward to gain airspeed and reduced power, smoothly leveling the helicopter at the desired altitude. Directly ahead and approximately fifty miles away, the high mountains of the Alaska Range were visible as a wall of chiseled peaks stretching across the horizon.

Connor crossed the Tanana River south of Fort Wainwright, surprised no one had attempted to call him on the radio with instructions to return to the airfield. His surprise was short lived, however, for no sooner had the thought occurred, then the FM radio barked through his headset.

"Nine-two-seven, Operations, over?" There was a slight pause before the voice continued, becoming more excited each time. "Nine-two-seven, Operations, over? Nine-two-seven, this is Operations, please respond, over?"

Connor recognized Sergeant Jackson's voice but chose to ignore him. Answering would only lead to more questions he was in no mood to answer. Captain Hiroldi or Lieutenant Hovan probably directed Jackson to attempt contact, which was confirmed a moment later when Lieutenant Hovan's voice chimed in.

"Nine-two-seven, this is Lieutenant Hovan. You are instructed to return to the hangar immediately. Do you copy, over? Nine-two-seven, do you copy, over? Mister Connor, bring the helicopter back to the hangar, now. That's an order! Mister Connor, this is . . ."

The lieutenant wasn't used to someone ignoring his instructions. His voice increased a few decibels in frustration after each sentence.

Connor selected another frequency on the FM radio, cutting off Hovan as he spoke.

There was no benefit in responding or listening any further to the radio. Explaining himself would only inflame the situation. Not answering the calls might buy more time. He was about to change the frequencies on the other radios when the control tower operator broke in over the UHF. Apparently, the tower personnel had become aware of the unauthorized flight.

"Nine-two-seven, Wainwright Tower, over? Nine-two-seven, Wainwright Tower, you are requested to return to the airfield immediately. Nine-two-seven, Wainwright Tower, do you copy, over?"

Instead of turning the dial, Connor tried a different tactic. "Wainwright Tower, this is nine-two-seven, you're coming in broken and unreadable. I'm clear to the south. Have a nice day." He selected a civilian frequency the military had no control over, hopeful the radio would remain silent.

There was no turning back. Connor had no intention of changing his plan. He was pleased with the decision, although the subterfuge stayed fresh in his mind. The lying had bothered him at first. Now he found the deceit easier to push aside. His desperate course of action would be carried through to the end.

CHAPTER SEVENTEEN

Ferguson put on his flight helmet and survival vest before strapping himself into the left cockpit seat. Bril stood outside the door, slightly to the front and side with his helmet visor down, and plugged into the intercom system by an external cord. He held a small fire extinguisher at the ready. Less than three minutes had passed since leaving the operations office.

"Clear!" Ferguson yelled. He waited for confirmation from Bril before switching on the APU.

A sound of rushing air briefly filtered through the cockpit, followed by a high-pitched whine as the small engine came to life, powering the helicopter's electrical and hydraulic systems. The four-bladed rotor system remained motionless, requiring power from the main engines before being engaged.

Army regulations required two pilots in the cockpit for all engine starts and flight operations. Because of a separate power control for each engine, the UH-60 was considered an advanced aircraft. One pilot was easily capable of starting both, but in case of an emergency, safety dictated two pilots be in the cockpit to handle independent switches and controls.

Ferguson went through the checklist just short of starting the engines. He then turned on the radios and informed operations he was standing by.

Bril remained outside, waiting for the other members of the crew. Sergeant Steiner soon approached with his jacket tucked tightly under his arm. He reached the sliding cargo door and grabbed a second fire extinguisher, positioning himself on the side opposite Bril where he could watch the starboard engine. Shultz exited the hangar a moment later carrying a sheet of paper in his hand. He hurried at a fast walk, moving around the nose to the side of the cockpit.

Medevac helicopters were configured differently than other UH-60 Black Hawks. Because of the specialized mission, each helicopter was only fitted with two seats in the passenger/cargo area behind the cockpit, one for the medic and the other for the crew chief. Both seats faced the rear, aligned with the gunner windows. The bulk of the rear area contained a large, rotating carousel, capable of holding up to six litter patients, three on each side.

In flight, the carousel was turned sideways between the sliding doors, allowing more space for the medic to monitor the patients. On the ground, the carousel could be rotated forty-five degrees, allowing easier loading and unloading through the cargo doors.

Although the UH-60 had a larger capacity and roomier interior than the older UH-1 helicopter, space was still tight. With the carousel installed, there was barely enough room for mounting a rescue hoist inside the right cargo door. The remaining space was filled with medical equipment and survival gear.

"Evac one-one-four, Flight Operations, over?" Sergeant Donovan's voice crackled over the radio.

Ferguson immediately keyed the transmit switch on his cyclic control. "Go ahead, Ops."

"I have the RCC on the phone with additional information if you're ready to copy?"

Grabbing a pencil out of the shoulder pocket of his flight suit, Ferguson opened the trifold flaps of his kneeboard to a blank note page. "Ready, go ahead."

Shuffling papers could be heard in the background as Donovan continued. "A satellite picked up another set of coordinates further south than the previous two. The location is still on the glacier feeding into the East Fork of the Little Delta River. A triangulated position using the three coordinates is as follows . . ."

Opening the cockpit door, Shultz grabbed his helmet and gloves from the seat and slipped them on before donning his nylon mesh survival vest hanging on the armor plating. He noticed Ferguson writing on his kneeboard and plugged into the intercom, remaining silent while positioning himself in the seat.

Sergeant Donovan's voice could be heard passing a series of latitude and longitude numbers over the radio. The message ended as Shultz finished strapping himself in.

"We have a better location on the ELT signal," Ferguson explained after confirming Shultz was plugged in. "The RCC triangulated a fix further south. I entered the coordinates in the GPS. The engines are set for start if you're ready?"

"I'm ready," Shultz replied, verifying the medic and crew chief were in position with fire extinguishers on opposite sides of the helicopter. "I have the controls, you start the engines."

"Roger, number one clear?"

"One is clear!" Bril yelled back, signaling with a raised arm.

Ferguson pushed the start button for the left engine on the overhead console, keeping his hand close to the power control lever. He monitored the clock and system gauges on the instrument panel as the start sequence was initiated.

"Blades are turning," announced Shultz.

Repeating the same start procedure on the number two engine, Ferguson carefully watched the engine gauges for a malfunction, only diverting his eyes when both engines indicated a normal start.

Bril and Steiner moved along opposite sides of the fuselage, check-ing inside the engine cowlings for fire or leaks before repositioning inside.

Ferguson pushed the engine power control levers forward until they were at full RPM. The noise from the powerful engines increased dramatically, shaking the airframe and hangar windows as the sound reverberated off the tarmac.

"Everyone secure?" Shultz asked, directing the question at no one in particular but expecting a response from each of them. When each verified they were safely buckled in, he called the control tower for takeoff clearance.

"Wainwright Tower, Evac one-one-four is on the north side of hangar six. Request present position, two-four-zero departure over the taxiway. Left crosswind to the south."

Shultz didn't wait for a reply and handed the controls off to Fer-guson, motioning for him to bring the helicopter to a hover. Aircraft with Evac call signs had priority as long as the departure didn't conflict with traffic. The controllers were accustomed to medevac helicopters departing without a flight plan, so not having one on file wasn't a concern.

The tower responded indifferently. "Evac one-one-four, cleared as requested. You have a slight tailwind. Winds are out of the southeast at five knots. Altimeter is three-zero-one-two. No other traffic reported in the area. You're cleared to change frequencies at your convenience. Have a safe flight."

Shultz thanked the controller while cocking his head to look at the instrument panel. All engine and system indications were normal. Fer-guson held the helicopter at a stabilized hover, waiting for confirmation.

"Takeoff check is good. Let's rock and roll."

"Clear on the right—clear on the left," the voices of Steiner and Bril announced in sequence over the intercom.

"On the go." Ferguson pulled the collective higher, increasing power in a steep climb, simultaneously applying forward cyclic to lower the nose and increase speed over the taxiway. He smiled, glad to be flying again.

Fourteen minutes after receiving the first call from the RCC in Anchorage, Evac 114 passed the Tanana River on a course for the Alaska Range. The crew settled in as the helicopter cruised comfortably at 130 knots, holding a level altitude two thousand feet above the ground.

Shultz called in a flight plan to the local Flight Service Station before briefing the crew on the latest weather and ELT coordinates.

"All right guys, this is what we know, which isn't much. The RCC plotted three fixes off an ELT signal deep in the Alaska Range. The terrain is probably distorting the signal, so the location could be off by a few miles. Once we get closer, we should be able to pick up the signal on our radio and hone in on the source. If not, we'll have to conduct a visual search.

"At this point, we don't know if a real emergency exists. Could be a signal triggered by accident or plane crash. We have a twenty-five-minute flight each way, leaving a good two and a half hours of blade time on station. By then, the weather conditions might force us out of the area anyway. If need be, the backup crew can be called in to relieve us."

"Sir?" asked Bril. "Has there been a confirmed ELT signal in the area from other aircraft?"

Shultz answered. "Nothing yet. A plane would have to be at a high altitude or within a few miles of the source. Otherwise, the terrain masks the transmission. And some bush planes don't have the right type of radio to monitor the emergency frequency."

Steiner wasn't thinking about a search mission as much as he was about possible survivors. His training as an emergency medical technician allowed him to handle almost any emergency. During his five years as a flight medic, he had treated a multitude of injuries, from vehicle accidents, plane crashes, gun shots, bomb detonations, drug overdoses and even a shark attack. The injuries covered a full spectrum from abrasions and broken bones to heart attacks and severed limbs.

He never lost a patient and wasn't sure if their survival was from luck, skill, or acts of God.

The GPS mounted above the instrument panel showed a steady course toward the mountains. Ferguson kept a firm, yet gentle grasp on the controls, adding only subtle corrections every few minutes. He maintained a straight track over the ground, keeping a fixed reference point in the distance and periodically glancing inside at the GPS and directional indicator. Both engines were operating smoothly, carrying the helicopter easily through the autumn air.

Shultz verified the external tanks were transferring fuel and the burn rate was normal. A VFR sectional chart was open on his lap as he plotted the coordinates, confirming the previous triangulation. Although he trusted his own and Sergeant Donovan's ability to read a map, human error was always a possibility, and he wanted to double check the locations for accuracy.

He studied the chart in more detail. The mountains surrounding the glacier were at a minimum of five thousand feet in elevation, with some of the peaks rising above seven thousand.

Tracking the distress signal direct to the location was the easiest method but not always an option in the mountains. If the source couldn't be verified from the coordinates, a systematic search would be required. Flying a grid pattern required an altitude high enough above the ground to maximize coverage, but low enough to spot wreckage or visual signals from survivors. The rugged terrain dictated constant variations in the helicopter's flight path, making the process even more difficult and time consuming.

The silhouette of an aircraft was the most obvious indicator of the crash location. Smoke or a reflection from a signaling mirror was the next noticeable sign. Otherwise, a glint of metal, strange shape, disturbed area on the ground or unusual contrast of colors was the only means of finding potential wreckage.

Shultz was pleased with his decision on not adding extra fuel. Even though the UH-60 was an advanced helicopter, the engines still had limitations. Landing at high elevations required additional power, and hovering required even more. The increased power demand limited the maximum gross weight and altitude the helicopter could operate. The careful balance between available fuel and usable weight was always a calculated risk.

The Black Hawk helicopter had audio alarms and a visual display of segment lights for alerting the crew of a malfunction. Rows of gauges provided indications for the engines and transmission, and other instruments showed navigation and flight information, all organized on the instrument panel and center console for easy viewing. Shultz and Ferguson scanned the systems periodically as a matter of routine, ensuring everything was operating correctly.

Something caught Shultz's eye. The temperature gauge for the number two engine was higher than the other engine. The vertical display bar was within normal range, but the disparity between the two seemed higher than before. He watched the temperature for a few minutes, finally convincing himself there was no noticeable change.

Shultz adjusted his radio selector to call operations as the helicopter approached the foothills of the Alaska Range. Communication would be limited in the mountains, and he wanted an update on any new information while they could still make contact. Once inside the towering terrain, they would be isolated and alone.

CHAPTER EIGHTEEN

A gust of wind cut through the baggage compartment door, rustling Kwapich's clothes and almost knocking the faded hat from his head. He pulled the sides snug around his thinning hair and struggled with the remaining luggage inside the small enclosure. The girls had left the larger bags they were unable to move. He positioned them near the door and then stacked the two empty kennels atop each other in the corner, freeing space around the pallet loaded with four canvas mail sacks.

There was a sound of barking outside, a child's voice, some muffled conversation from inside the passenger cabin, and a shuffling of padded feet when he felt a bump against his leg. He turned to see one of the malamutes had joined him, content for the moment on watching the activity with an inquisitive expression. The dog's pink tongue flicked over his sharp canines with its head tilted to the side, studying him with suspicion.

"Well, hello there," Kwapich said pleasantly. "You forget something or just want some adult company?"

The ears cocked forward before the female dog turned to look out the door, then back inside as if accepting the offer and lying on the floor near his feet.

Kwapich reached down and let the malamute sniff his hand. Kneeling, he rubbed behind her ears with his other hand, stroking the thick fur around her neck. She raised her gray muzzle, letting his fingers caress under her chin so both hands were busy providing the desired attention.

Just then, a second bundle of fur jumped through the door in a flash of energy, startling the older malamute and Kwapich. The younger of the two nudged the other playfully—curious as to why she wasn't outside keeping him company.

"So, you miss your playmate?" Kwapich asked. He could tell the male was younger by the spirited movement and constant tail wagging. He was also smaller, but the same breed and color.

The younger dog responded by licking his hand and bowing for a friendly pat. Kwapich obliged, using a hand for each of them.

"They ran away," a russet haired girl explained apologetically from the doorway. "They don't listen very well. That's Muck. He's the youngest. And that's Copper, his mother." She pointed at each of the dogs.

"Oh," Kwapich replied. "Well, they're friendly enough. I don't think they'll be any trouble if you want to leave them here."

Before she could answer, another girl called from further away. Kwapich recognized Lisa's voice as the young male dog immediately scampered out the door. The female was more reluctant but followed a moment later with a slight limp.

Kwapich watched them go and saw the girl at the door sigh in frustration. "At least they listen to somebody."

He was as surprised as she was. "I guess so. Problem solved."

Kwapich refocused his attention on the pallet of mail. Each sack weighed over forty pounds, and he positioned them in a neat pile beside the kennels. The wooden slats on the pallet were nailed in place, but by using a small fire extinguisher, he managed to break them apart and split the boards down the middle. When he finished, there was an assortment of usable splints.

He then retrieved some cotton shirts from one of the suitcases and ripped them into long strips, hoping whoever they belonged to wouldn't be upset. He tucked the bundle of splints under one arm and returned to the passenger compartment with the ribbons of cloth in his hand.

The young man, Danny Sims, was clearing the last of the debris from the aisle when he entered. Bidwell was busy dismantling a broken seat partially impaling one of the passengers while the retired nurse held the aluminum leg in place against the man's torso. They worked slowly, careful not to push the severed shaft in deeper, finally succeeding in detaching the end from the frame without causing further injury.

Kwapich set the items he was carrying on the floor. He helped the others reposition the injured man so the nurse could bandage the wound, leaving the metal rod protruding from his side.

He was an older man of slight build and dark hair. His appearance suggested he was barely conscious. There was only a fluttering of eyelids and a soft murmur of pain.

Mildred cleaned and wrapped the man's injury, carefully taping the obstruction in place, while the others finished clearing the aisle. What remained of the loose debris was tossed outside and stacked under the left wing. The three passengers who died in the crash were moved into the cargo compartment out of sight of the others. They were covered with a canvas tarp used for protecting the luggage.

No one noticed Susan leave amid all the activity. She tried staying busy so she wouldn't focus on the trauma. Distributing blankets, assisting the injured, and speaking words of comfort kept her occupied. Between errands she shared bottles of water found in a storage bin and checked on the comatose first officer. She was near exhaustion and her fatigue showed. Her hair was disheveled, her clothes smudged with dirt and her makeup ruined, but she somehow maintained a reassuring poise.

"You should take a break." Sanders noticed Susan standing beside the damaged tail section and approached her with concern.

She turned to the sound of his voice, the wind blowing wisps of hair across her face. She brushed a strand aside. "I am. I just needed a few minutes alone."

"No, I mean take a long break and relax. We have the injured passengers and cabin organized now. You can sit with the others by the rocks. At least you'll be out of the wind."

Susan contemplated the suggestion for a few seconds and then shook her head no. "That would be nice, but I would rather stay busy."

Sanders saw she was determined. "At least take a few minutes. You've certainly earned it."

"I will. Thank you."

"Is there anything I can get you?"

"No, really, I'm fine," Susan reiterated. "The injured man in the back of the plane reminded me of my husband. I just wanted a moment alone."

"Of course," replied Sanders. He waited a few seconds, embarrassed by his own callousness. "I shouldn't have bothered you. I'm sorry."

"It's okay. I guess I wasn't expecting the poor man to look the way he did. His injuries brought back memories of my husband's accident. Frank was killed in a plane crash. I saw it happen."

Susan sighed, staring into space, recalling the tragic event. His death was hard on her and the kids. Over the years she learned to focus on the good memories and push the bad ones away. Separating the emotions gave her an inner strength, somehow, helping heal the family when they needed closure the most.

Sanders didn't know what to say. At first he thought she might break down and cry but instead was impressed by her ability to control her emotions. She possessed a strong demeanor—a trait that reminded him of his grandmother. "I don't think the man's injuries are as bad as they appear. He'll be all right." The statement was truthful, except for Sander's omitting the part about a recovery being dependent on getting the man to a proper medical facility as soon as possible.

"That's good to hear," Susan stated. She pushed a windblown curl of hair away from her eyes. "I was worried. The other injured passengers . . . some are even worse, aren't they? Mildred wouldn't say for sure."

"I don't know. I'll talk to her again in a few minutes."

"Okay. What about you?" she pointed at his arm.

"If I said it doesn't hurt, I'd be lying. The pain comes and goes but is bearable as long as I don't bump into anything. Then it can be rather intense but I imagine insignificant compared to what some of the others are enduring. I'll survive."

"Hey!" The girl's coach, Donna Regan, announced in a frightened voice. She moved with a nervous demeanor, almost stumbling across the ground and seemed not to notice as Sanders reached out with his good arm to catch her. Before he could even ask what the problem was, she began talking rapidly.

"Is there any chance we can move inside the plane? The girls are getting chilled from the wind. They could use something to eat, too. And drink if there is more water. We aren't going to be here much longer, are we? It's been almost an hour. Shouldn't someone have been here already?"

Sanders waited until she paused to take a breath before answering. "I don't know how much longer a rescue might be. I wish I did, but without radio contact we'll just have to wait and hope for the best."

"But the . . ." the coach tried interrupting before Sanders raised his hand to silence her. Her eyes widened in protest.

"There are still seriously injured passengers in the plane. Until their injuries are taken care of and we can make them comfortable, the others need to remain outside. I'm sorry, but there isn't enough room inside right now. Give us another ten or fifteen minutes, okay?"

Susan gently grasped Donna's arm, speaking softly. "We need to give the injured a few more minutes, honey, and get the plane organized so we can all fit in comfortably. You don't want your girls seeing all the blood and the injured still traumatized in their seats, do you?"

The coach glanced from Susan to Sanders, then back again, finally shaking her head. "Well, no. I guess not, but . . ."

"That's good, honey. It's for the best. Let's do as the captain asks and give the others a chance to get situated. Can I walk you back over to the rocks? Maybe I can fill the others in on what's happening?"

Susan caught Sanders' nod of thanks and smiled in reply. The coach seemed unsure of what to say with both of them coaxing her away but relented after realizing she couldn't win the argument. She appeared frustrated, then concerned as another gust of wind caught her. She altered her balance with a pained expression.

"What if a rescue doesn't arrive soon? What are we going to do then?"

"We'll do the best we can. Someone will come," Sanders replied.

The statement sounded convincing. If only the words were really true. They were all in for a long, cold, and miserable experience. Even though the temperature was moderate, somewhere in the low fifties he guessed without the wind chill, the approaching storm would change conditions dramatically.

Sanders didn't want the panicked coach to know the extent of their situation and withdraw into a shell again. Better she maintains a positive outlook. Even though he was responsible for ensuring the safety of the survivors, without a timely rescue their safety was in serious doubt. A fact he could do little to avoid.

"There is something you can do," Sanders said suddenly, wanting to provide the swimming coach with a positive goal to focus on. "Keep a sharp ear for the sound of an aircraft. If you hear anything, come and get me right away. We have a flare gun inside and it can be used to signal our position when one arrives in the area."

Her eyes lit up, and she looked toward the lower valley as if expecting an aircraft at any moment. "Yes, that's a good idea. I'll tell the girls."

Sanders scrutinized the surrounding terrain. He sighed and pondered what was in store for all of them. More than anything he wanted to lie down and rest but couldn't afford the luxury. His arm and head throbbed with enough pain he doubted he could relax, and from the queasy feeling in his stomach, he was afraid he might vomit at any moment.

Sanders wanted to improve the passengers' situation but was unsure of what else needed to be done. Almost everyone was busy. Once the injured were cared for and the cabin cleared of debris, he could gather everyone together and discuss their options.

The wreckage would provide shelter from the wind and weather. Conserving water was the immediate concern. If necessary, they could find another source nearby. Food wouldn't be essential for the first few days, and in any case, there was nothing they could do except hoard the few candy bars and crackers the passengers brought with them. Staying warm was another matter. If the temperature dropped significantly, as it was sure to do with the coming storm, the passengers' clothing and a few thin blankets would be the only protection from the cold.

Inside the aircraft the retired nurse was getting frustrated. She managed to move the obese man into a more comfortable position against some seat cushions on the floor. He was the last of the injured to be taken care of and made everyone within hearing distance know he was not happy about the lack of attention. He was in obvious agony from a back injury and when not groaning in pain, blamed the airline, the pilots, and other passengers for his predicament. His wife stayed by his side, trying to calm him with limited success.

Mildred wanted to slap him but was content for the moment in telling him to shut his mouth. She had remained silent long enough and was tired of his tirade. He only relented for a few seconds before accusing her of medical misconduct, threatening a lawsuit. If a strong sedative had been available, she wouldn't have hesitated in giving him one.

Sanders entered the access door at the rear of the plane. He could hear the obnoxious passenger berating Mildred. She and the man's wife stood over him with looks of disgust, unsure of what to do. For the moment Sanders ignored them and glanced around the interior.

Four of the undamaged seats were left in place over the wings. The rest had been dismantled and carried outside after the cushions were removed. Four of the injured were sitting against the walls or lying on cushions near the front, including the first officer and the man with two broken legs. Three others were in similar positions in the back.

Two fresh stains were noticeable on the floor where blood had soaked through the carpet—one in front and the other in back. Another area on the wall was smeared where a stain had been wiped with a rag. Otherwise, the interior was much cleaner than he hoped. Sanders made a mental note to have the blood spots covered before the youngsters were allowed back inside.

Kwapich was taking a break in one of the over-wing seats. His attempts to silence the overbearing passenger had fared no better than Mildred or the other occupants. Short of knocking him unconscious, which was becoming more of a possibility, there was little he could do. For the moment he was content staying in his seat.

Sanders noticed Bidwell and Sims weren't inside and assumed they were with the others by the rocks, staying out of the wind. They had been a welcome presence following the crash. Without them the situation would still be in turmoil. He would thank them later.

Mildred noticed Sanders near the door and approached him, a strong look of resignation on her face. She gestured outside where they could talk without being overheard.

Their precarious location on the high ridge and the extensive damage to the aircraft surprised her. She looked around the surrounding area with wide eyes. This was her first time outside since the crash. She was amazed at how isolated they were among the towering mountains.

Mildred was sweating from the activity of tending the injured. The outside air, chilled by the wind off the icy peaks, cut through her summer weight pantsuit like a knife. She zipped the thin jacket closed and began speaking over the wind in a low enough voice so only Sanders could hear.

"The bandages are used up and there's only a half bottle of aspirin left. There isn't much else I can do except keep an eye on the injured."

"Thank you, Mildred," Sanders answered. "I don't know what we would have done without you. There's probably more clothing we can use for bandages in the luggage."

"White cotton would be helpful." She glanced toward the cargo compartment where the bodies were stored. "We were lucky no one else was killed, weren't we?"

"Yeah, we were. Very lucky. I only hope we don't lose anyone else. How bad are the injured?"

Mildred shook her head sadly. "Two are in critical condition. As you know, the first officer is unconscious from a head injury. There could be neck or spinal damage, so we were careful moving him. He has a punctured lung from a broken rib, which is causing the shallow breathing and a buildup of pressure in the lung. The pressure needs to be equalized, but I don't have the right tools."

Sanders rubbed his forehead. "Are there any options?"

She gave him a stern look. "Very few. Other than a pair of scissors from the first aid kit and a pocketknife from one of the passengers, there's nothing else available. I don't want to risk trying anything unless we absolutely have to. Bottom line, he needs to be transported to a hospital as quick as possible."

Sanders could only nod his head as Mildred continued.

"The man who was impaled on the seat has been in and out of consciousness, but nothing vital was hit as far as I can tell. There's some bleeding, but I've left the rod in place and bandaged the wound the best I can. Until he gets to a medical facility, I don't want the object removed. The rod helps plug the wound and suppress the bleeding. I'm more concerned about his head injury. He took a terrible beating when his chair broke loose during the crash."

"I see," said Sanders. He wanted to reassure her they would be fine but knew she would see right through him.

"My husband is a strong man. He hasn't complained in spite of his fractured legs and they have to be hurting terribly. He has a compound fracture of his left tibia. The lower right is also broken but not near as serious. I've immobilized them with wooden splints and wrapped them in cloth, but they'll need to be reset. I'm afraid he'll need surgery."

She paused and took a deep breath, holding back her emotion. "Gangrene is another concern."

Sanders shifted his gaze for a moment, thinking about what she said before refocusing on her stern expression. "And the rest of the injured, how are they?"

Mildred searched his eyes, noticing a compassion she hadn't expected. She wrapped her arms together against the wind.

"Better than I anticipated, except for the one named Connover. He's the obese man with the bad attitude. He has a spinal injury, probably a herniated disc or pinched nerve causing a lot of pain. We had a hard time moving him on the floor, and I don't want to chance moving him again without a spine board. At least he's not paralyzed. He has full motion in his legs. If we can just get him to shut up and relax, it would be much better for all of us."

"I'll talk to him. Maybe my presence and some of your aspirin can calm him down."

Mildred smiled for the first time since the accident. "I think we would all appreciate that."

She paused, looking back at the wrecked fuselage before continuing. "One of the women, Mrs. Delucci, has a dislocated hip. I stabilized the injury for now. She's in terrible pain though. Her husband is the man with the severe puncture wound. He was sitting directly across from her."

"I see," Sanders said with sad eyes. He was concerned, but there was little he could do.

"Another woman from the back is pretty traumatized. From what I can get out of her, she was traveling with two friends. They were both killed in the crash. She's in shock and doesn't seem to comprehend their deaths. I got her name as Rosa before she started weeping again. She's outside now."

Sanders took a deep breath. "Is she okay with the others?"

"Yes, I think so. Susan and the girls are keeping an eye on her, providing comfort as best they can. As for the rest, there are a few minor sprains and abrasions but nothing too serious. Most are handling it well. A few have been asking about a rescue."

She was hoping for a positive response but instead saw a resigned look on his face. "Is there something you're not telling me?"

Sanders didn't respond immediately. Instead, he took a few seconds and carefully scanned the dark clouds moving lower over the western sky.

"We might be here for more than a few hours, maybe even a few days."

"What do you mean?" Mildred gasped in reply. "Rescuers are coming, aren't they?"

"Yes, but I don't know when," Sanders said solemnly. He pointed to the approaching storm so she could see what he was concerned about.

"Our aircraft has an emergency transmitter that has been sending out an electronic distress signal repeatedly since we crashed. Rescue services are sure to have been notified, but it could be several hours before our position is pinpointed and anyone arrives. Unfortunately, that nasty storm might arrive before then. Any chance of a rescue will be delayed until the storm passes, and it could take days."

"Oh my God! Are you sure? What will we do?"

"For now let's get everyone inside. It's time I told the others."

CHAPTER NINETEEN

"We should be over the foothills in a few minutes," announced Shultz, studying the horizon. "If Operations doesn't call by then, I'll try to make contact. Another fix from the satellite would be nice before we begin a search."

"Roger that," Ferguson answered. He watched the heavier clouds filter across the line of rugged mountains and sensed more than felt a change in the wind velocity. A quick glance at ground speed on the GPS verified the winds were intensifying.

"Looks like we picked up a stronger headwind."

Shultz had been expecting the increase. "We're in for a bumpy ride. The winds pushing those clouds don't look very friendly. I've got a feeling we're going to earn our pay today."

"Just another day, flying the Army way," Bril added. He always seemed ready with a quick comment.

Steiner looked over at Bril and shook his head before responding. "Just another day in paradise, right?"

"You got that right. I'm not complaining. Three more months until sun and guns in the land of the righteous."

"Don't you mean unrighteous?" Steiner could tell Bril was baiting him. He couldn't resist. "You turning raghead on us?"

Bril held a somber expression. "Muslims have done great things in history. Granted, most were over a thousand years ago, but in recent history the radical sect we know as the Taliban actually invented condoms by using the lower intestines of goats."

Steiner was skeptical. He let Bril continue without comment, expecting a punch line.

"Of course, Western society improved on the invention by removing the intestines from the goats first."

The crew had a good laugh. Even Bril broke a wide smile at his own joke. Steiner wiped his eyes and started chuckling again.

Shultz listened to the exchange and recalled his two previous deployments. His thoughts became serious again. The first was during the Gulf War and the second a decade later in central Iraq. He wasn't looking forward to a third tour in the Sand Box but knew another deployment was inevitable.

Both Steiner and Ferguson had experienced war but not Bril. His casual attitude reflected his inexperience.

Shultz knew Bril was only being his usual self, but he wanted to keep everyone focused on the mission. When he spoke, his voice sounded harsher than intended. "Stay sharp guys. We might not be taking enemy fire, but this won't be a cakewalk either."

Ferguson momentarily shifted his eyes toward Shultz. What he said was true. They were all experienced enough not to be offended by the comment.

Steiner hesitated then keyed his mike switch. He knew Shultz was confident in their ability, as they were in his. "We're ready, sir. We aren't taking anything for granted."

"That's right, sir," added Bril. He looked serious but winked mischievously at Steiner, who was looking at him from the other rear-facing seat. "If the mission was easy they'd send a contingent from the United Nations."

"Or the French," piped in Ferguson after a brief chuckle.

A smile etched the corners of Shultz's mouth. He was about to respond but turned and glanced in back where Bril was seated, not surprised to see him staring blankly out the window.

The first jolts of turbulence began hitting the helicopter a mile from the foothills. Light in intensity and gaining in frequency, they gave a clear indication of what was ahead. The path of the helicopter changed a few degrees each time but quickly recovered with almost imperceptible inputs from Ferguson. Simultaneously, he adjusted for a higher altitude above the rising terrain, maintaining a slow climb through three thousand, then four thousand feet.

Looking up from the sectional chart spread on his lap, Shultz pointed through the windshield in the direction they were heading. "Level at forty-five hundred and follow the larger drainage opening up ahead to the southeast. In about another twenty miles, it'll hook southwest into the deeper mountains. Once we get around the corner, we should be able to see the face of the glacier."

Ferguson couldn't help but notice the wide drainage of intersecting creeks flowing into the larger fork of the river. Across his field of view, lesser streams branched from the soaring mountains like cracks in a pane of glass. He was captivated by the chiseled beauty—the hidden dangers as yet unfamiliar to him.

"Man, what an awesome sight. I always imagined flying in Alaska would be like this."

Shultz was equally impressed with the scenery. Even though he had flown missions and training flights in the mountains, the view never grew old. He shifted his vision across the instruments panel, then outside again for the tenth time in as many minutes.

"We certainly have the best seats. I've flown in the Rocky Mountains and the European Alps, and both pale in comparison. Flying doesn't get any better than this."

Ferguson nodded in reply as Steiner and Bril remained silent in back, content while enjoying the view. Passing the first set of foothills, he noted the time on the digital clock, satisfied with their progress. He wondered if Shultz was going to make the radio call to Operations as intended. He thought about asking and instead decided to wait a few more minutes.

On cue, as if reading Ferguson's mind, Shultz reached for the radio switch on the center console.

"Flight Ops, Evac one-one-four, over?"

There was a lengthy pause before a slightly garbled voice answered. "Evac one-one-four, this is Flight Operations. Go ahead, over."

Shultz motioned for Ferguson to climb higher with a quick hand gesture. "Standby, Operations."

The helicopter immediately began increasing altitude as Ferguson adjusted the controls. Shultz waited as they gained several hundred feet before trying again.

"Operations, Evac one-one-four. Any further information on the ELT signal?"

"Evac one-one-four, that's affirmative. We received an update a few minutes ago. A fourth fix was plotted by the RCC about a mile from the others. The location places the signal further south on the east side of the glacier. I have the coordinates and additional information when you're ready to copy, over."

Shultz held a pencil over the pad of paper on his kneeboard. "Ready to copy. Go ahead Ops."

"Roger, Evac one-one-four. Coordinates are as follows. . ."

The tone of the transmission grew clearer as Shultz copied the new figures. Ferguson leveled the helicopter at fifty-five hundred, following the drainage south.

After writing the coordinates, Shultz repeated them back for clarification. Satisfied they were correct, he continued.

"Go ahead with additional information."

"Evac one-one-four, it looks like you might have a real rescue on your hands. We received a report from the RCC and another from Fairbanks Flight Service moments before you called. A Northern Mountain

Air commuter plane with twenty-one people aboard is missing on a flight from Gulkana. Their last position report was almost an hour ago. At the time, the flight was diverting off the airway south of Big Delta. The pilot canceled their instrument flight clearance, apparently for sightseeing over the Alaska Range before continuing into Fairbanks. Air Traffic Control has been unable to establish contact. The plane's route would have placed it in the vicinity of the ELT signal, over."

Shultz exchanged a serious look with Ferguson before keying the intercom. "Sergeant Steiner, Bril, you monitor?"

"Yes, sir." Their voices were crisp and alert.

"Good. We've got about ten minutes until we get in the area. I hope to hell we find them."

He didn't wait for a response from the crew. "I copy, Operations. Our position is approximately twenty-two miles north of the last set of coordinates. Should be in position to initiate a search in the next ten minutes. Do you have a description of the aircraft or further information, over?"

"Evac one-one-four, roger. The plane is a twin-engine turboprop. It has a low wing configuration with a T-tail and is painted white with a red accent stripe below the windows. The company name should be visible on both sides of the rear fuselage. Two pilots and nineteen passengers are aboard. Some cargo, but we don't have specific details, over."

"Ops, have you notified the standby crew yet?"

"Affirmative, one-one-four. They're being called as we speak. You're probably looking at around two hours before they arrive in your area. The Civilian Air Patrol at Eielson has been notified. The RCC was coordinating and advised no aircrews are available until this afternoon. The Air Guard's C-130s in Anchorage were also notified, but their aircraft are committed on another mission."

Shultz expressed a look of irritation. Success would depend on them alone. With the approaching weather, time was critical, and as the only rescue aircraft available, there was no room for mistakes. He knew his crew was prepared but didn't want any doubts distracting them. His voice was confident and reassuring, hiding a troubled feeling they were getting into a situation more dangerous than any of them could imagine.

"We copy, Ops. Sounds like we'll be on our own awhile. Any weather updates? It looks like the bad stuff is moving in rapidly. The way the storm's developing, we might have a narrow window to rescue survivors, over."

"Standby, one-one-four." A lengthy pause ensued before Sergeant Donovan answered.

"Evac one-one-four, no new updates on the weather. Flight Service did request a confirmation on the missing commuter plane if you can locate it. There's still a possibility the ELT signal might be from another source, over."

"Roger, will do. We're entering the higher mountains now. We'll attempt contact again in another hour or after confirming the source of the signal."

"Evac one-one-four, good copy. We're standing by. Good luck. Operations out."

"Damn! Twenty-one people," Steiner stated. "This is going to be a long day."

"Probably so," Shultz responded. "Provided the ELT signal is from the missing plane. If we find survivors, we'll have to haul them out in shifts. Plus, the weather is going to be a limiting factor. We might only have an hour or two before the weather closes in, so there isn't enough time to run back and forth to Fairbanks with each load. You're the boss when it comes to the patients, Sergeant Steiner. Any suggestions?"

"Yeah, I've been running the numbers in my head. Depends on how fast we can get them inside the helicopter. The critically injured need to go first. I'll make a medical assessment on the ground. If Bril and either you or Mister Ferguson can help me, it will speed things up. We'll be able to load them quicker."

"Not a problem as long as we can find a place to land. Otherwise, we'll have to use the hoist."

Steiner turned sideways in his seat. "Then I'll go down first and do what I can."

"What about setting up a relay point somewhere close?" Ferguson asked. "We can move the survivors to a safe area close by and still be in position to transport them out of the mountains. The narrow time constraint won't be as critical."

Shultz thought for a moment. "It could work. Good idea. But only as a last resort. Once we pick them up, we're responsible for them. I don't want to drop off passengers in the middle of nowhere without shelter and provisions unless we have to. If we can't get back to them, they might be in a worse situation than before."

"I agree. But a nearby landing site might make a difference," Steiner stated. "If nothing else, moving them can buy time until our other helicopter arrives. Sure wish I had grabbed more gear before we left. Extra blankets and rations might come in handy."

"What we have onboard will have to do," Shultz stated. "I'll have Ops tell the backup crew to load extra kits from the supply locker."

Bril had been surprisingly silent, busy with his own thoughts. He was the first to hear a faint beeping through the background static of the VHF radio, and at first didn't associate the noise with a distress signal. His hearing was better than the others, due more to having spent less time around helicopters, than because of his youth. Several seconds passed before he realized what the sound actually was.

CHAPTER TWENTY

"I'm picking up a signal over the radio," Bril announced excitedly. "Sounds like an ELT, but the static is making the tone hard to distinguish."

Silence ensued as the others listened intently. Shultz turned up the volume on the VHF radio.

"I hear it now. Good ears Bril." Shultz fiddled with the volume again. "The signal should intensify as we near the glacier."

"You still want me to follow the drainage or cut the corner over the ridge?" Ferguson asked.

Shultz looked over at his copilot. "Go as direct as possible. We'll hit more turbulence, but the shortcut will save a couple minutes. This altitude should be good."

"Roger."

Shultz attempted contact with the missing aircraft on several frequencies, including the emergency guard channel. There was no response. If the commuter plane crashed, the radios were likely inoperable.

The medevac helicopter cleared the rounded spur of a lower mountain, encountering less turbulence than expected, and entered the ice-carved valley. The glacier ahead was ominous and majestic in appearance. Pools of ice-blue water and mounds of deposited moraine stretched across the basin. From the two-mile wide face, the creviced and dirt-stained ice extended into the heart of the mountains, changing course over several miles in a gradual, climbing curve. At the end was an immense ice field, thick and blinding white, spreading in multiple directions like outstretched fingers.

The expanse of ice and layers of heavy snow increased five hundred feet in thickness for every mile of distance until the glacier was nearly as deep as it was wide. Deep chasms were cut in the surface and the sides discolored from the force of ice crushing and eating away at the mountain.

"Another five miles to the GPS coordinates," Ferguson said. "The signal is getting stronger every minute."

Shultz nodded in agreement. "Hold a thousand feet above the ground as we pass over the front of the glacier and slow to sixty knots. Fly up the center on the first pass. Maybe we'll get lucky."

Steiner turned and faced the cockpit, leaning between the seats for a view out the windshield. "It's a big area. If the missing plane isn't intact, the wreckage will be hard to spot."

"We'll find the plane," Shultz added confidently. "It might take us a few orbits, but we'll find the wreckage. Everyone stay sharp and use your visual cues like you've been trained."

He knew his crew was dependable. Search techniques were part of their training and repeatedly practiced until they became routine.

The visual area was divided into separate, overlapping sectors. The pilots scanned out from the windshield and to the side, covering an arc of approximately sixty degrees, while the crew in back searched a similar pattern, scanning in an overlapping arc from the sides to the front. The technique maximized the coverage, allowing multiple sets of eyes to search the same area.

By maintaining a thousand feet above the terrain and flying a moderate airspeed of sixty knots, a wider area could be searched more effectively. Even if one set of eyes missed something, another crew member would hopefully spot what the other had overlooked.

The first leg took four minutes to fly. The helicopter passed the last set of coordinates and continued another mile before reversing course. The signal was strong in all directions, bouncing off the high mountain and making an accurate fix impossible to identify.

The eyes of the crew slowly moved back and forth across the glacier, searching for the outline of a plane, tracks in the snow, misshapen objects, or discoloration—anything that might indicate a presence other than ice or snow. There was nothing.

"We have to be close," Shultz announced. "If we don't spot anything on this pass we'll fly another pattern on the opposite side."

He attempted contact with the missing plane again, not surprised by the lack of response. Shultz imagined a worst-case scenario where the plane might have slid into one of the large crevasses after crash landing on the glacier. If so, the chance of spotting wreckage and finding survivors was drastically reduced.

Upon completion of the third leg, the crew doubted the accuracy of the ELT signal. The decreasing fuel left them with few options. They could repeat a search pattern at a lower altitude, ignore the coordinates and try searching a different area, or fly higher where the signal might be less distorted by the terrain.

Shultz opted for the latter, hoping at least one high pass over the glacier might confirm a definitive location. If not, they would try a lower altitude and hope they could spot something they might have missed earlier.

"Initiate a climb and let's see if we can get a more localized signal from the ELT. We need to pinpoint the source to a smaller area."

Ferguson increased power. "You think a higher altitude will work? The closest mountains have to be over eight thousand feet and the cloud base is already obscuring the peaks."

"I don't know. Staying at the same altitude isn't working. See if we can reach seven thousand without going into the clouds."

The winds were stronger and more turbulent as the helicopter ascended. Funneled by the mountains, the winds increased in intensity as they raced through the valley, deflecting off the protruding ridges, and causing sudden, vertical changes in the flow of air. The light turbulence changed to moderate, shaking the helicopter with stronger and more frequent bursts of wind. The helicopter was pushed violently up and down and sideways through the air, causing rapid changes in altitude and airspeed. Seat belts and shoulder harnesses were pulled tighter. Hands held the seat frame or braced against the wall. There was little talk. The crew was unwavering, maintaining their search without complaint.

A knowledgeable pilot would say the turbulence was one level from severe and two levels from extreme, neither of which were desirable. Severe turbulence would render an aircraft momentarily uncontrollable while extreme would cause a complete loss of control and possible structural failure.

Shultz had flown in severe turbulence twice during his career and the encounters were something he never wished to duplicate. Both times were only for a short duration, but the experience left a lasting impression. He would continue the search as long as the safety of the helicopter and crew wasn't in jeopardy. They took priority over anything else.

The helicopter leveled at seven thousand, a few hundred feet below the thick clouds settling over the valley. Ferguson adjusted the flight controls, fighting the turbulence to begin another pattern. He listened silently with the rest of the crew to the rhythmic tone of the ELT signal.

The signal strength increased momentarily, almost imperceptibly in tone, then just as suddenly returned to the previous volume. The change was subtle, but enough to get the attention of the crew. Ferguson quickly turned and slowed, trying to isolate the stronger tone. Ninety degrees through the maneuver, the signal increased again. He corrected the turn, leveling the helicopter as they headed for an almost vertical peak less than a mile away. Each of the crew was searching intently along the lower glacier and nearby slopes. Nothing caught their eyes.

"Damn! Where the hell is the signal coming from," Shultz said in frustration. "We have to be right over the source."

"Sir! I've got something," Bril stated excitedly. "A few hundred feet lower at two o'clock. About a half mile ahead on the ridge."

Shultz was on the same side of the helicopter as Bril and immediately shifted his focus higher up the terrain. He scanned back and forth across the area. "I don't see anything."

"At three o'clock now. Turn right."

The helicopter banked thirty degrees until a spur of rock jutting from a steep slope was directly ahead, only a few hundred feet below their flight path. Bril shifted around in his seat so he could keep the area in sight through the windshield.

"There!" Bril pointed. "You see it?"

Ferguson and Shultz both recognized the broken profile of the commuter plane at the same time, at first confusing the white fuselage for snow. Only as the distance narrowed did the outline of the fuselage with red lettering become clear.

They concentrated on the wreckage, searching for survivors and wondering how the plane managed to end up in such a perilous location without sliding off the edge. The position was the result of one of the best landings they could imagine. Or one of the worst.

Silence ensued as the extent of the damage became obvious. This would be the first time any of them was involved in the crash of a large plane or under such hazardous conditions. Without speaking, each of them knew there would be injured and dead waiting. How many, if any survived, was a question yet to be answered. Whatever the outcome, they realized a rescue would be anything but easy.

The question of survivors was answered a moment later as movement was detected near a mass of boulders in front of the wreckage. The plane's survivors became aware of the approaching helicopter at about the same time, for a bright orange flare shot out from the ridge into the overcast sky.

CHAPTER TWENTY-ONE

A clear turquoise sky above the Tanana River basin was indicative of fair weather, not an approaching storm, yet signs were obvious further south of Fairbanks. High clouds, stretching into wisps of vapor by the powerful winds ahead of the frontal system, were visible over the distant mountains. Below and further west, a dense layer of dark stratus moved in a solid line, smothering the peaks in a slow progression across the horizon. Heavy with moisture and turbulent air, the rippled overcast billowed around the summits and into the lower valleys, angling toward a lone helicopter flying low over the ground.

The Tanana Valley stretched hundreds of miles through the belly of Alaska, cutting a swath from the Canadian border westward across the state. Nearly fifty miles across at the widest point, the valley was situated between lesser mountains to the north and towering mountains of the Alaska Range to the south.

A major river bearing the same name flowed in a broad channel along the length of the valley, stained with mud and silt from the surrounding mountains. Joined by hundreds of lesser rivers, creeks, and tributaries, the current grew in strength and size, eventually meeting the mighty Yukon River before emptying into the sea.

Encompassed within the valley were huge tracts of scrub timber and marshland, intermixed with lakes and scattered growths of willow, alder, birch, and spruce. A few pockets of rounded hills, formed by the deposits of ancient glaciers, lay scattered across the lowlands, jutting from the surface in contrast to the mountains rising in the distance.

Connor maintained a steady course, intent on his destination. With each passing mile, the aged helicopter brought him closer to the mountains. The fall landscape was ripe with vibrant patterns of texture and color. Red, orange, and golden hues filled the trees and bushes, their leaves bright with a last gleam of life before winter.

He was enjoying the flight. The feel of the controls, the way the aircraft moved through the air, the acute sense of touch, speed, and harnessed power gave him a momentary aura of invincibility. The helicopter glided gracefully in his hands above the terrain. The distinction between flesh and metal disappeared as he flew with a smooth, instinctive touch. Man and machine became a perfect combination of thought and motion, testing the complexity of flight with effortless simplicity.

Flying had always been easy for Connor. He had a talent for flying that few could equal. He was at his best in the air. Even his personality seemed to change away from the confines of earth. Life was more enjoyable, although death and sadness found him there, too. In the air, the burdens of sadness and guilt were eased, if only for a while.

Connor headed toward a series of rounded buttes jutting from the flat muskeg of the valley. From there, he followed a clear, narrow stream, staying low over the bordering trees as the exposed banks twisted southward. By springtime, the creek would be overflowing with melting ice and snow.

The area was abundant with wildlife. Connor's son had accompanied him on a moose hunt the previous year before departing for Iraq. They were successful, but spending time together and talking for hours around a campfire were the most memorable. The days passed all too quickly. Before he could find the words to tell his son how proud he was of him, he was gone.

Expressing his feelings had never been easy for Connor. He was brought up in an era and a household where emotion, seen as a weakness, was frowned upon. Toughness was expected from men, and he was as tough as they came. Tears did not come easy, nor did he want them to.

He had loved his son and daughter without reservation. Showing love to his daughter was always easier. At least he had more time with his son. They were drawn to each other by their bond of blood and war. His biggest regret was not being closer when he was a child, never being there to guide him and help him learn about life or watch as he matured from a boy into a man. He knew his son had forgiven him. Forgiving himself was not as easy.

A minor spasm of pain stabbed at Connor's lower back, forcing him to shift uncomfortably in the seat. He grimaced and concentrated on what lay ahead. His plan wouldn't have to wait much longer.

A tranquil lake passed underneath the helicopter, reflecting the welcoming mountains. There was a slight ripple across the surface from a pair of loons. He smiled with renewed exuberance.

His mood was short lived. He pulled in power, gaining altitude nearer the mountains. A buffeting and slight yaw of the helicopter told him the winds were increasing. Off to the southwest he could see wisps of moisture curling off the peaks. The tapered line of lenticular clouds was a sign of bad weather, something he should have noticed earlier. Even so, the weather wouldn't deter him. There was no turning back.

The strong winds were accelerating over the ridges and snow cornices hanging off the peaks. Currents of air pushed the building clouds into elongated fingers pointing menacingly along the horizon. The winds were deceptive, calmer near the lower foothills but increasing in intensity and unpredictable at higher elevations. Danger lurked in the air, hidden and elusive in a subterfuge of sky and wind.

Flying in the mountains was not an endeavor to be taken lightly. Safe flight required more than just a weather briefing. Being able to accurately assess weather conditions, react to changes, and know your limitations were far more important. Knowing when or when not to fly was as important as knowing how to fly.

Over the years Connor had benefitted from that wisdom many times. Pilots who ignored the same vigilance paid a heavy price. The mountains of Alaska were littered with the wreckage of their mistakes.

Connor pulled back slightly on the control stick to increase altitude, flying the helicopter effortlessly above the rising terrain. A narrow canyon cut through the slopes in the center of the foothills, holding a small creek of fast flowing water. A mile further on, the gap opened onto a low basin, widening into a large drainage leading toward the mountains.

Connor followed the contours of the terrain, making almost imperceptible movements with the controls—more reflex than conscious thought. The old pilot and obsolete helicopter flew with a vigor and purpose missing for far too long.

Vegetation grew sparse in the heart of the mountains. Spruce and thick brush along the lower creek beds were replaced by low grass and tundra moss, mixed with patches of colorful willow. The slopes were covered with lichen and alpine flowers, thinning with the rising terrain toward the steeper rock walls framing the valley. At the far end, the drainage changed into barren moraine and stained blue ice from a small glacier, packed tight against the base of the mountain.

Carved canyons and narrow draws joined the valley from each side, adding to the glacial waters flowing north. One particular canyon was almost hidden from view, noticeable only by a shaded expanse of rock where the opening entered a turn in the valley.

Connor remembered the location and began climbing on an intercept course. The helicopter angled eastward toward a high pass, staying a thousand feet above the ground. The fast moving silhouette disappeared against the darker slope, only to appear again a half-mile further, climbing rapidly over an alpine meadow near the summit.

The last thousand feet were the steepest. Connor slowed and circled in a wide spiral. Strong gusts swirled above the canyon as they deflected off the peaks and spread across the terrain. He anticipated the changing currents, maintaining a steady climb.

The wind was strong and building in intensity ahead of the storm. At the crest of the canyon the pass narrowed, funneling air through the gap with increased velocity. The helicopter ascended through the jolts of turbulence, rising in an updraft of air over the slope. On the opposite side of the pass, the wind changed, shooting downward with equal speed.

Understanding the wind and using the proper technique was a matter of routine for Connor. After climbing several hundred feet, he reduced power and pushed the nose forward, dropping into the adjacent river valley. He kept the helicopter on the right side of the pass, allowing enough room to reverse course if the weather deteriorated.

Experience had taught him the wind could be different from one valley to the next, sometimes blowing in opposite directions or with greater force. Good pilots anticipated change, allowing for the unexpected and leaving themselves another option.

The valley was similar in appearance to the last but ran in a northeast direction instead of north. Connor nosed the helicopter into a dive away from the pass and strong winds, banking back and forth in a series of tight turns until the helicopter was only a few hundred feet above the dry creek. For a moment he was young again, flying without pain and only the thrill of flight to guide him.

Near a shallow, grassy slope on the opposite side of the valley, a band of Dall sheep heard the approaching helicopter and grew agitated by the noise. They were cautious animals, accustomed to running at the first signs of danger. The oldest ram began moving toward a distant ridge, quickly followed by the others. Safety was in the high, rugged terrain. They continued their escape until the sound of the helicopter faded in the distance.

Connor saw the sheep and ignored them. In the past he might have desired a closer look but not today. Today he was intent only on flying.

This day he would savor his time in the air. Every thought, every input of motion, told him he controlled his own destiny. Today was his last day, and he would go out on his own terms.

For another two miles the helicopter soared above the valley floor. When the mountain valley widened at a sharp turn in the graveled creek, he began increasing altitude. Ahead and higher up on the west side of the basin, a small pinnacle jutted from a jagged spur. The pile of rock was the same as the photograph in Connor's office. Without the constraints of a glass cover and frame, it appeared far more formidable.

The pinnacle was obtrusive and uninviting, a simple obstruction of boulders protruding menacingly from the steeply angled ridge. Landing there was something most pilots would never consider. Connor wasn't one of them. He had seen the value and used the site to train new pilots. The cornice of rock became an excellent tool for sharpening a pilot's technique and building trust in the helicopter's capability. The last time was years ago before regulations and limited flight hours prevented its use.

Connor recognized the turn in the valley and pulled into a steep climb, trading airspeed for altitude. The vertical speed indicator increased dramatically, reading over two thousand feet per minute.

The helicopter's nose pointed toward the sky as if launched into the heavens. Connor smiled in satisfaction, relishing the sensation as the weight of his body seemed to leave the gravity of earth. For a brief moment, the pain was completely gone.

As the helicopter slowed to forty knots, Connor eased the nose forward, maintaining a sustainable climb. Near the closest slope of the drainage, he banked slowly left in a continuing ascent, completing a full circle. The maneuver increased altitude over a short distance and soon had the helicopter reaching six thousand feet. Connor adjusted the controls, placing the helicopter on a level course slightly higher and a quarter mile away from the pinnacle.

The rock ledge was directly ahead as Connor rolled out of the turn. The outcropping seemed out of place, extending unnaturally from the mountain in a protrusion of misshapen granite. At a distance the site appeared unsuitable for landing. On this day the suitability didn't matter, for he had no intention of landing.

A faint beeping filtered over the radio. The sound began when Connor ascended above the valley floor, growing stronger with increasing altitude. By the time he leveled at six thousand, the beeping was louder and distinctive. The tone was easily recognizable as an emergency locator beacon.

Hearing the signal surprised Connor. The strength indicated the transmission originated from somewhere nearby. At first he ignored the sound, assuming a small bush plane must have inadvertently activated its ELT. A worse scenario crossed his mind, but he dismissed the thought and concentrated on flying. Now was not the time for distraction. He turned down the volume on the radio, determined to end the flight as intended.

Connor could feel the effect of the wind on the helicopter and noticed the movement of air over the slopes. Turbulence was becoming stronger and more frequent and the clouds seemed to be building faster over the peaks. Every control input became a move and countermove, anticipating and fighting the different forces trying to take control of the helicopter.

To Connor the effect of the wind didn't matter. He thought of the weather as nothing more than a contest and knew he would win.

As he neared the pinnacle, Connor stayed above and off to the side, continuing past for several seconds before reversing course in a tight teardrop pattern. He maintained a hundred feet above the rocky outcropping and circled in a slow arc, unwilling to commit.

Connor was both ashamed and grateful for what he was about to do. He thought back over his life and career, as he had done many times in the last few days, and saw no other option. He hated giving up and not fighting like a warrior, but whether he died now or waited six months for the disease to kill him, the outcome would be the same. Better to end it all on his terms.

He saw no reason to continue the struggle. The years of guilt were overpowering, the haunting memories becoming more and more of a burden. There was no will left to fight. He could see his daughter clearly, smiling with a bright gleam in her eyes and expression of love, beckoning him home. *Yes, now was the time.*

Connor turned and reversed course again in a tight pattern, this time accelerating so the helicopter descended at a steep angle. The airspeed continued to increase. The crest of the pinnacle grew larger in the windshield with each passing second.

He wanted to instinctively pull back on the cyclic or turn away but forced himself to continue. He held a firm grip, focusing on a fixed point, willing his hands to remain steady. At a hundred feet he clenched his teeth in an act of final determination. At fifty feet he closed his eyes, leaned back and waited for the inevitable.

CHAPTER TWENTY-TWO

Trailing a thin line of smoke, the burning flare arced high into the overcast sky above the valley. The bright phosphorous disappeared momentarily into the clouds before re-emerging in a slow descent toward the glacier. Carried by the wind, the flare drifted harmlessly away from the crash site. The crew of the helicopter and the survivors on the mountain ignored the signal, already concentrating on each other's position as the distance narrowed between them.

"I count six survivors. Make that seven, near a rock formation forward of the left wing of the plane." Shultz spoke in a steady voice without shifting his gaze away from the wreckage. "Anyone see other survivors?"

Bril was the first to answer as Steiner slid sideways for a better view. "No one else that I can see, sir."

There was silence for several seconds before Bril spoke excitedly again. "There's movement near the plane. I see two more coming out of the fuselage. Wait! Make it four more. Eleven total on the ground. Damn, they sure look glad to see us."

Steiner shook Bril optimistically by the shoulder. They watched the four survivors waving enthusiastically near the wreckage, joining the others near the rocks. The display of emotion was as much elation as relief.

The sound of the engines was barely distinguishable above the wind when the helicopter first arrived over the glacier. Only the shifting air currents carried a distant echo from the lower valley, providing a sudden spark of interest from the survivors. Some stood and turned their heads, trying to identify the source, but the noise was elusive and distant.

They became convinced the faint echo must be a trick of nature. Several times the sound disappeared and their eyes squinted against the wind, searching the sky. Firing a flare was considered and then dismissed. They waited for positive proof the noise was something more than their imagination.

Minutes passed before Mary Lou and Lisa noticed a movement over the glacier. Kwapich looked over the edge and confirmed the helicopter's presence before the others become convinced. Only then was a flare used. The first was fired in haste and carried behind the path of the helicopter by the wind. A second flare duplicated the same error.

The pistol was being loaded for another attempt when the helicopter turned and climbed higher. The survivors were certain someone must have spotted them, but instead of flying toward their position, the machine stayed over the center of the glacier, following a course away from the ridge. Groans of frustration carried over the wind. They argued whether to fire another flare immediately or wait. Only three remained.

Another minute passed, then two, and the helicopter turned on a parallel course taking it further away than before. Their chance of rescue appeared to be lost.

There were cries of protest. The gunner raised the pistol and was about to pull the trigger in an act of defiance when the helicopter suddenly veered in their direction. They all watched, fixated, as the silhouette altered course a few degrees before heading straight toward them. They were found. The loaded flare was fired anyway, just to be sure, and arced perfectly in front of the aircraft.

The survivors grew more animated the closer the helicopter approached. Several of the young girls and their coach hugged each other, jumping and waving their arms. Others were more subdued, waving an arm or pumping a fist in the air, but wide smiles expressed their true emotion.

Ferguson began a slow turn into the wind, gradually losing altitude while lining up for an approach. Only a narrow space between the broken tail of the wrecked plane and the edge of the ridge appeared suitable for landing. He wasn't sure if the helicopter could fit, but they needed to get lower for a better look.

"What do you think?" Ferguson asked, glancing over at Shultz. The flight was his first real mission into the mountains, and he was nervous about landing with the winds and high elevation.

"You're doing fine. Stay on this heading and make a low pass so we can get a better view of the ridge. Watch your airspeed and power and don't get below sixty knots."

Shultz was an experienced pilot who understood the dangerous conditions they were flying in. Although he was comfortable with the situation, he sensed Ferguson was apprehensive. For the time being, he decided to let his copilot continue flying.

A pilot's personal limitations and those of the aircraft were always a concern, but Ferguson needed to trust his own judgment. At the same time Shultz didn't want to push him too far. He was ready to take the controls if necessary.

The high, narrow ridge and the scattered wreckage grew larger in the windshield as they approached. Shultz studied the ground for a possible landing site. The two strong turbine engines provided enough power for landing at the high elevation, but if they couldn't find a large enough area to set down, they would have to use the hoist. The power demand required to maintain a high hover above the ground would be near maximum. Multiple lifts would be even harder as each hoist added a survivor and more weight to the aircraft.

The small opening on the ridge was almost big enough for the helicopter, but almost wasn't good enough. The helicopter's elongated fuselage and tail required an area of relatively flat ground, a minimum of sixty feet in length. Even then, the distance only allowed five feet of clearance behind the tail. Additional clearance was needed to the front and sides for the four rotor blades. Landing in a tight location with gusting winds only increased the risk, leaving a limited margin of error.

Shultz and the rest of the crew realized the site was unsuitable for landing. Fitting the helicopter between the surrounding obstacles and high boulders would be impossible under the best of circumstances. Their options were limited to only one. If they were going to rescue the survivors before the weather closed in, they would have to use the hoist.

"We won't be able to land," Ferguson said reluctantly.

Shultz was satisfied Ferguson made the right decision. Real situations were the best means of determining a pilot's judgment. Although he had flown with Ferguson before, Shultz hadn't flown enough with him to fully trust his ability. Any situation was an opportunity to teach and learn, regardless of the experience level. Since this was Ferguson's first flight in the mountains, the mission was an opportunity to evaluate his competency. Even, perhaps, to reaffirm his own.

Shultz felt slightly uneasy, not so much about the copilot but about the mission in general. He had already concluded the rescue would be a test for both of them.

"I agree. Good job." Shultz acknowledged the decision not to land. "Steiner, looks like you're going down on the hoist. You ready?"

"Yes, sir. A bundle of blankets and my medical kit are already in the basket. I'm taking a case of rations along, too."

"Everything is set, sir," added Bril. "Let me know when to lower the hoist."

"We're coming around for another approach," Ferguson added, already banking the helicopter in a left turn away from the ridge.

"Climb higher on the turn," coaxed Shultz. "But stay below the clouds. I'll see if I can contact Operations and pass along an update. They need confirmation on the missing plane and an exact location."

The wind was more turbulent as they turned downwind, yawing the helicopter sideways as Ferguson compensated with quick pedal control. The airspeed quickly dropped from sixty to forty knots during the change in direction, catching him off guard. He immediately added power to compensate.

"I know, watch the airspeed," he said without waiting for Shultz's instruction. "It won't happen again."

There was no comment from Shultz. Instead, he switched the fuel indicator between the external and main tanks to check the status, then attempted radio contact with Flight Operations.

"Operations, Evac one-one-four, over?" Continuous static was the only answer. "Medevac Operations, Evac one-one-four. Do you copy, over?" There was no reply.

Without waiting Shultz switched to the VHF radio and tried contacting Fairbanks Flight Service on a different frequency. "Fairbanks Radio, Evac one-one-four on one-twenty-two point two, over?"

Only silence reverberated over the radio. "Fairbanks Radio, Evac one-one-four on one-twenty-two point two?"

Shultz was not surprised at the lack of response. They hadn't heard traffic on the frequencies since entering the mountains. The higher terrain was blocking all radio reception. "I was afraid of that."

Ferguson glanced over at Shultz before offering a suggestion. "We can turn back north until we're out of the valley and try radioing again?"

The idea was dismissed by Shultz. "Not yet. Let's get Steiner hoisted down first. He can do a medical assessment and assist the survivors while we fly north and contact operations. We can still communicate with Steiner through his survival radio and be in position to relay the medical information until the survivors are ready for pick up."

Each member of the crew wore a lightweight, nylon survival vest, equipped with basic survival gear, including a hand-size emergency radio. The portable radio was capable of voice communication or of transmitting a continuous electronic distress signal, much like an ELT.

"Sounds good, sir. I'll check in on the radio as soon as I'm clear of the helicopter." Steiner seemed eager to go. He leaned forward between the seats watching their progress through the windshield.

The helicopter maneuvered over the wide glacier in a careful turn back toward the ridge. The rotors pulled at the rough air below the clouds, biting the drafts of strong wind to maintain course as the fuselage bucked and slipped in reaction to the turbulence.

"I'm coming around on final. These winds are going to be a bitch at a hover," Ferguson stated. He fought the sharp movements with rapid inputs on the flight controls.

The thin air and strong gusts were challenging, but he felt more comfortable with each passing minute. He stayed focused, anticipating the effects on the helicopter and reacting almost simultaneously with each movement. He began perspiring and felt the first bead of sweat forming under his hair. He ignored the sensation and turned at a slight angle toward the ridge, deliberately staying away from the higher slope where the winds were more unpredictable.

"You're looking good. Maintain this approach angle until you're in position for a stabilized hover," Shultz directed.

Shultz watched the torque gauge with sideward glances and kept his hands within easy reach of the controls, pleased with Ferguson's smooth inputs. Applying power too quickly at the bottom of the approach could over-torque the engines. "I'll monitor the instruments and call off altitude and power. Focus on your outside references."

"Roger. I'm aiming for the middle of the open area off the plane's left wing." Ferguson's voice sounded calmer than he felt.

Turbulence buffeted the helicopter as they neared the crash site. The winds hitting the lower edge of the ridge swirled over the rough terrain in multiple directions and mixed with more vertical gusts deflecting off the slopes, requiring quick reactions from the pilot. Ferguson applied constant input on the controls, his feet and hands moving in a choreographed rhythm, testing his ability.

"One hundred feet," Shultz announced. "Fifty knots . . . fort-five, forty. Seventy-five feet, thirty knots. Seventy feet. Sixty feet. Going through effective translational lift." The helicopter shuddered and shimmied slightly from the changing airflow through the rotor system. The amount of lift in the rotor blades decreased, requiring a higher power demand.

"Fifty-five feet. Now at fifty feet. Hold your altitude. Power's good."

Bril slid back the right cargo door and stuck his head into the wind. "Right side is clear. Tail is well above the rocks and there's plenty of clearance behind us."

Steiner duplicated the same procedure out the opposite door. "Left is clear. Position looks good."

Shultz acknowledged. He was impressed with the approach. "Nicely done. Stay oriented outside and keep us in a fixed position. Bril, you've got control of the hoist."

"Roger that, sir. Door's sliding full open." The sound of rushing air through the microphone could be heard over the intercom.

The helicopter rocked and yawed as Ferguson fought to remain in the same position, keeping the nose aligned with the wind. Shultz observed the airspeed needle fluctuating around twenty knots, jumping with each hard gust to nearly thirty. As the wind speed changed, the lift through the rotor system also changed, requiring variations in power through the flight controls.

Anticipating the abrupt movements was impossible, demanding quick and precise response from the pilot. The technique was more reactive than deliberate thought. Some pilots never mastered the delicate precision.

Shultz felt the wind's erratic effect and watched Ferguson out of the corner of his eye. He could see the stress building, exemplified by the expression and color on his face.

"Stay on the controls for this hoist and I'll do the next one." Shultz's calm voice was reassuring.

"This is harder than a workout at the gym," answered Ferguson, never taking his eyes from the reference points on the ground. "These winds are squirrelly as hell."

Several of the survivors stood out in front of the helicopter with their faces into the wind, watching with anticipation. Ignoring the stinging gusts, they offered silent encouragement. Others remained crouched near a mass of boulders, holding the collars of two dogs agitated by the noise of the engines.

"I'm hooking up the basket," Bril announced.

Keeping one hand on the cable and the other on the pistol-grip control, he used his thumb to work the three electrical switches controlling the boom, cable speed, and voice communication. A temperature light was also configured into the control box to provide a warning if the electric motor began overheating. A switch for cutting the cable in case of malfunction was controlled by the pilot.

The hoist assembly was attached to the helicopter by heavy bolts in the floor and roof of the cabin, just inside the cargo door. The lower assembly contained the gear motor and winch and the upper assembly a moveable boom for controlling the cable. When hoist operations were required, the boom was swung outside, allowing unobstructed movement as the cable was unspooled or retracted. On missions where a hoist wasn't necessary, the apparatus was stored out of the way inside the door.

The end of the cable was attached to a hook assembly, which could be connected to one of several devices. A rescue basket was the most convenient. The basket allowed a person to sit inside unaided or for an injured person to be strapped onto a separate device, called a Stokes litter, which fit inside the basket. The litter was constructed of tubular aluminum and looked like a larger version of a plastic food basket found at any local diner.

The helicopter carried two or four litters, depending on the mission configuration. With the carousel in place, four were carried, each with its own backboard.

Steiner seated himself on the litter with a case of blankets, two medical kits and a box of military ready-to-eat meals between his legs. Prior to climbing in, he put on his jacket and kept his helmet in place with the visor down for protection against the rotor wash. His survival vest was worn over his jacket.

"Basket is going out," Bril announced.

He lifted the basket a few inches off the cabin floor and carefully swung the boom until Steiner was positioned between the door and external fuel tank attached to the side pylon.

Steiner gave a thumbs-up signal as Bril guided the wire with his hand, ensuring the cable wouldn't swing back into the helicopter. He gradually lowered the basket below the belly before increasing speed. He stood in the doorway, watching the load descend, giving instructions over the intercom so Ferguson could position the helicopter directly over the intended touchdown point.

"Basket is five feet below the helicopter. Basket is halfway down."

The wind and downward flow of air from the rotor wash spun the load in a slow circle. In a short time the basket was on the ground.

"Basket is on the ground. Hold your position." Bril let out more cable until there was enough slack the basket wouldn't drag with changes in the helicopter's position.

Steiner threw out the gear and exited before removing the detachable litter. He moved several feet off to the side and signaled Bril he was clear. Only a few seconds had passed.

"Steiner's out. The basket's clear." Bril continued watching the ground. His finger depressed the intercom button. "You're drifting forward . . . slide back a foot. Hold it! That's good, sir. I'm bringing the cable up."

Shultz diverted his attention back and forth from the engine instruments to the ground. Their hover position remained steady. He couldn't see the basket on the way down, trusting Bril to keep them oriented over the correct point. Instead, he watched for any excessive movement of the helicopter that could cause the hoist to become entangled or to swing out of control.

Both engines were operating efficiently with power to spare. All gauges were normal, except for the number two engine's oil temperature. Shultz noticed he was correct in thinking the display bar had increased earlier in the flight. Now the indicator was at the upper edge of the range, near redline. The green bar had been moving incrementally higher since they started hovering over the crash site.

At first Shultz thought the sensor might be faulty, but now he wasn't sure. He kept a constant eye on the display bar, deciding to continue with the mission as long as they could. He didn't tell Ferguson. He didn't want him distracted from holding a steady hover.

Unaware of what was transpiring in the cockpit, Bril began motoring the cable upward. He watched the basket slide sideways slightly over the ground as the tension increased. Clear of the ground the basket began spinning again. He let the motion continue until the load was only a couple feet below the helicopter.

Stopping the hoist with a push of the button, he twisted the cable with his hand, aligning the basket parallel with the fuselage. He then continued bringing in the cable until the basket was beside the cargo door. Using the other finger button on the control, he swung the boom back inside and lowered the basket to the floor.

Once the hoist was complete, Bril felt a sense of relief. "Basket is in. Hoist's secure. Closing the door."

"Roger. We're on the go." Shultz motioned out the windshield in front of Ferguson. "Keep the same power and push the nose forward to accelerate. Straight ahead until we're clear of the ridge. Nice job, both of you."

Ferguson smiled. "Thanks." Passing sixty knots he turned and began heading north through the valley. The cloud base was lower now, allowing a climb of only a few hundred feet before leveling off.

CHAPTER TWENTY-THREE

The helicopter circled and came to a high hover over the ridge, the Red Cross symbol clearly visible on the nose. The survivors watched in awe, transfixed by the machine and the helmeted figures inside. For most, this was their first time seeing a helicopter up close. They stared with wind stung faces and blowing hair, cold and shivering, afraid to move for fear of changing whatever fate had in store for them. One of the girls said it looked beautiful. Another commented the silhouette resembled a salamander. No one argued with either assessment.

An eternity seemed to pass before they saw the hoist being lowered. A broad shouldered crewman wearing a flight suit and jacket sat in the attached basket. Boxes and several bags of gear were positioned between his legs. When he reached the ground, he quickly unloaded the cargo and detached a long board from inside. He waved at the survivors, grabbed as many bags as he could carry, and approached the wreckage.

Their exhilaration disappeared a moment later when the helicopter retrieved the hoist and flew away. Only after the medic removed his helmet and explained the crew would be back in a few minutes, did their enthusiasm return. Smiles and handshakes quickly followed. Two of the men hurried to retrieve the rest of the gear. They knew the worst was over.

Captain Sanders was the first to introduce himself to Steiner. He provided an explanation of the crash and the situation leading up to the helicopter's arrival. Other brief introductions were made as they proceeded inside the wreckage.

Steiner looked around the interior and began triaging the injured, prioritizing them for treatment and transport. The retired nurse assisted him. She had done a nice job caring for the injured, considering the lack of medical supplies. The large first aid kit and rescue/trauma packs he brought with him were immediately put to use.

Steiner was able to send a situation report to the helicopter and begin prepping the injured for transport within a few minutes. Each would be loaded by their level of priority. The seriously injured would go first, along with the nurse, who could assist on the helicopter while Steiner prepped the remaining injured at the crash site. Reluctant at first, she agreed when he explained the hoist procedure required him being on the ground.

Next would be the four girls. The remaining adults would be transported on the second helicopter, provided the other medevac arrived in time. If not, and the weather was still good enough, they would go on a second lift with his helicopter.

The unconscious first officer was the closest when Steiner entered the wreckage. He was positioned near the cockpit and covered with a pair of thin airline blankets. A seat cushion had been placed under his neck for support. Gauze bandages were taped over his forehead and around a wound in his calf, the last partially hidden beneath a tear in his dark slacks. His white shirt was stained with dried blood from the head wound.

Steiner left the bandages in place and removed the blankets, then pulled back the already unbuttoned shirt. Mildred briefed him while he performed an examination.

The raspy breaths, shallow breathing, and broken rib, told him Mildred's assessment was correct. A punctured lung was causing the labored breathing.

Equalizing the pressure in the lungs was the first priority. Steiner cut away the undershirt and then used a large gauge intravenous needle, or IV, to pierce the rib muscle and tough chest membrane. He was aptly familiar with the procedure after treating a number of similar combat injuries.

The needle was pushed through the latex finger of a surgical glove and inserted between the ribs. A slight popping sound signified the passage through the chest wall and surrounding membrane, followed by a hiss of escaping air as the needle entered the lung, equalizing the pressure. A piece of surgical tubing was attached to the end of the needle with the glove hanging over the end, acting as a flutter valve. This allowed the lung to expand and contract properly as the patient breathed.

The first officer's improvement was immediate. Steiner finished by taping the tube securely in place and then covered his torso with a heavy wool blanket he brought with him from the helicopter.

While Mildred inserted an IV and started a solution drip, Steiner continued prepping him for transport. Since there was head trauma and a possible spinal injury, Steiner attached a rigid cervical collar, or C-collar, around the first officer's neck. A backboard and litter would also be necessary before moving him, but for the moment he was satisfied. The first officer's condition was critical. He would go out on the first load.

Steiner moved to the next injured survivor and knelt beside him with his trauma bag. The balding man's injuries were obvious. Wooden splints placed on the fractures were crude but effective. One of the pant legs was torn and bloody, the protruding bone wrapped loosely with a folded shirt. His name was Ralph, and he was Mildred's husband.

They made eye contact and Steiner introduced himself. In spite of his stoic demeanor, the man's eyes couldn't hide the pain. Aside from the fractures, there were no other injuries.

"Glad you could join the party, soldier. I'd get up to shake your hand, but that's not an option right now." He forced a smile and raised his arm part way in greeting.

Steiner wasn't entirely surprised by the patient's response. He had witnessed the best and worst of emotions while treating a variety of injuries during his career. The human spirit was amazing in both strength and weakness. Trauma never affected everyone the same way. Some tolerated the worst of pain with humor and grace, while others couldn't handle a minor injury without an emotional display of suffering.

"Yes, sir. I never miss a good rescue. You relax now. We'll get you fixed right up."

The man winked at Mildred, his wife. His eyes were moist from the pain, but he grinned as if broken bones were nothing more than an annoyance. She patted his arm lovingly.

Steiner gave him a dose of morphine, and in seconds the pained expression was replaced by one of euphoria.

The injured legs needed better protection before transport. Steiner withdrew two air splints from his trauma kit and set them on the floor. They were more effective than fixed or wooden splints, designed to stabilize arm and leg fractures by inflating a protective membrane around the injured limb. Steiner carried several in each kit. They were important components of any medic's gear, and he had them in place within a few minutes. Ralph's condition was serious. He, too, would go on the first helicopter.

A muffled curse of anger welcomed Steiner as he knelt by the obese man dressed in expensive slacks and a silk shirt. An Armani leather jacket was draped over his chest for warmth. On his left wrist was a Rolex Submariner watch and around his neck a roped gold chain. He was well tanned and smelled of expensive cologne.

"I think my back's broken. You need to get me out of here. I'm going to sue this damn airline if it's the last thing I do."

"I'm Sergeant Steiner, sir. I'm an Army medic and I need to check your injuries and ask some questions, then we'll see about getting you out of here."

Mildred explained his back injury before he could lapse into another tirade. This one would be a real struggle to move, Steiner realized. The man had to be close to four hundred pounds. Carrying him to the hoist site would be extremely difficult with only four men. For the moment, he needed to stabilize him. He'd worry about moving him later.

Steiner felt along the man's neck and spine and had him move his head and limbs to check their range of motion. There was no pain other than in his lower back. The man cursed under his breath and then thankfully remained silent.

Only one C-collar remained from Steiner's medical gear. Normally he would use one for a back injury, but the location of the man's pain and range of motion indicated a minor risk of paralysis. He decided to save the collar until the other injured survivors could be assessed.

Steiner asked a few more questions before retrieving the morphine bottle from his medical bag. Because of the man's size, he used a larger dose.

The man relaxed almost immediately. His eyes dilated, and he lapsed into a quiet demeanor. Mildred's eyebrows raised, and she smiled with a look of satisfaction, disappointed the medication hadn't been available earlier to shut him up.

"Is Harold going to be all right?" A nicely dressed woman with stylish hair and meticulous makeup slid closer beside the obese man.

"I'm his wife, Marla Connover." She had remained silent until now and appeared worn out from the trauma of the crash and the ordeal of tending to her husband.

Steiner looked at her with a reassuring expression. "Yes, ma'am. I think so. They'll make sure once he gets to a hospital. Until then, he needs to be as stationary as possible. He's stable and there's no immediate concern. Is he in good health, otherwise?"

She looked surprised. "What? I thought with him being overweight and having . . . well, you know, his injury might be serious."

"I don't believe so. Probably just a pinched nerve, but we'll be careful and stabilize him before he's moved. Does he have any other medical concerns, heart disease, hyperten . . ."

"No," She stated deliberately, interrupting Steiner's question. "At least none he's told me about, and he's always very specific. I'm sure everything he told you is accurate."

In reality, her husband was a chronic diabetic, but she kept the fact to herself. She wasn't surprised her husband omitted telling the medic about his disease, one he most certainly construed as making him less of a man. Power, money, and self-esteem were his primary concerns.

Further back in the cabin, an older woman with short ivory-colored hair was lying on her side, barely enduring fits of sharp pain. Her shoulder and hip were throbbing from being thrown against the side of the fuselage. She managed a weak smile as Steiner approached.

"Check on my husband first. I'm okay for the moment." She was insistent and Steiner did as asked, nodding to her in reply.

Her husband had lost a large amount of blood from a deep puncture wound in his side, below the ribcage and had been slipping in and out of consciousness since the crash. He had thinning hair and wore a bright polo shirt with beige khakis. The shirt was stained crimson around the torn fabric. A metal rod protruded from the opening. Gauze was packed around the base of the rod and taped in place.

Steiner checked his vitals and had a plasma bag supplying fluid in his arm within minutes. He removed the old gauze and treated the puncture wound with a strong antiseptic. A clean dressing was placed around the rod and secured. Some foam padding from one of the torn seats and medical tape was used to protect his side. The last C-collar was used to immobilize his neck.

Steiner sat back with his knees on the floor and checked the man's vitals again. The dark hair and thin mustache reminded him of a character in an old black and white movie. Steiner wrapped him in a wool blanket and nodded to Mildred. His condition was critical, but for the moment he was stable.

He, too, would need a backboard and litter for transport.

"Okay, miss. Your turn." Steiner spoke warmly as he repositioned beside the injured, woman. "I understand you have a sore shoulder and hip."

"Sore might be an understatement." She grimaced in pain. "How's Bill. Is he okay?"

"Yes, ma'am. He's injured, but we'll get him to a hospital as soon as we can."

"Please take good care of him." She became more concerned the more she talked, causing more pain.

Steiner tried diverting her attention. "Only the best, ma'am. We'll take good care of him. Mildred tells me you once worked in a publishing house. What was that like?"

She told her story while Steiner checked her shoulder and hip, trying to be gentle. The shoulder was heavily bruised, but he didn't think the bone was broken. Her hip was either fractured or dislocated, but without an x-ray he couldn't be sure. Immobilization and pain medication were the best options until she arrived at a hospital.

Steiner padded and taped the hip securely. A small dose of morphine seemed to ease the pain and worries about her husband. Her condition was serious but not critical.

Steiner motioned Mildred closer so they could talk in lowered voices. He pointed at the unconscious man with the puncture wound. "This man's the worst, but I don't want him to be loaded first. If he stops breathing, one of us needs to be there with him."

"Okay," whispered Mildred. "How do you want to prioritize them?"

"Your husband's first. I don't want anyone stepping on his legs and causing further injury. Once he's out of the way we can move the others." Steiner looked her in the eyes reassuringly. "I'd like to send you next if you're up to it?"

Mildred glanced toward the front of the cabin. She was reluctant and felt uneasy. "What about the first officer and the man with the foul mouth?"

"Mildred, you'll be okay," Steiner spoke softly, touching her hand. "You can do this. The first officer isn't stable. I need you in the helicopter before I send him up. The crew chief—the guy running the hoist—will help if you need assistance."

She frowned and reluctantly agreed. "If you insist. I've never liked helicopters, you know. Don't think I like airplanes much anymore, either."

Steiner suppressed a smile. He squeezed her hand in thanks. "After you go, I'll send the first officer. This gentleman will follow."

She glanced at the man's wife, Mrs. Delucci, who seemed content for the moment with the dose of morphine.

Steiner knew what Mildred was thinking. "She'll go after her husband. The big, mouthy guy can wait. He's in no danger, and I'll need several strong bodies to move him. I'll need another spine board from the helicopter before I can move him, anyway."

"You know I'm supposed to be retired," Mildred stated half in jest.

Steiner shrugged innocently. "Medics and nurses never retire. Taking care of others is in our blood."

CHAPTER TWENTY-FOUR

"How you feeling?" Shultz asked Ferguson. "You want a break?" Ferguson thought for a second. He was still sweating from holding the helicopter in position but otherwise felt good. "No, I'm good. I'll fly awhile longer. You can take the controls when we head back to the crash site."

"Sure, but keep an eye on the number two engine temp." He pointed a finger at the gauge. "The temperature started running hot while we were hovering above the ridge but has dropped some since. Bril, you do any maintenance on the number two engine lately? The oil level looked fine during preflight, but something isn't right."

"No, sir. After the last training flight, I added half a quart to the tank. The level was a little low but nothing out of the ordinary. Everything looked good on the daily inspection."

"All right, we'll keep watching. I don't like the high indication though. If the engine shits itself while we're in the middle of a hoist, we're screwed."

They flew only a few miles before Steiner's voice, barely recognizable, was heard over the UHF radio. Static and wind noise in the background were distorting the usually clear tone. "Evac One, Medic One, commo check, over?"

"Receiving you slightly broken but readable, Medic One," Shultz responded. He kept his hand near the radio selector switch while he waited for an answer.

A pause ensued as Steiner knelt out of the wind behind a boulder. "I have you loud and clear on my end. Making contact with the survivors now. Expect an update in a few minutes. Medic One out."

"Roger, Medic One. Standing by." Shultz switched back to the FM radio. He glanced at the engine temperature again and noticed a slight decrease. The indication was still higher than normal, but diverting from the mission wasn't an option. The weather was worsening every minute. He estimated less than an hour to get the survivors off the mountain.

"Operations, Evac one-one-four, over?" Shultz wasn't surprised at the lack of response. A good distance remained before clearing the higher peaks. He waited until they climbed another five hundred feet before trying the VHF radio. "Fairbanks Radio, Evac one-one-four on one-twenty-two point two, over?"

There was no answer. He switched to the emergency guard frequency, hoping another aircraft might pick up the transmission. "Any aircraft on one-twenty-one point five, Evac one-one-four, over." He hesitated a few seconds. "Any aircraft monitoring emergency guard on one-twenty-one point five, this is Army Evac one-one-four. Please respond, over."

Shultz shook his head in disgust. Time was critical, and they were wasting what little they had trying to make radio contact. He needed to send an update so additional aircraft could be notified of the crash location. If they didn't reach the survivors in the next hour, the opportunity of a quick rescue would be gone. The only hope was the other Evac helicopter had already launched.

"If we can't reach anyone in the next five minutes, head back to the crash site. We'll hoist as many as we can before the weather closes in. If we're lucky, our other medevac helicopter will be here by then and can pick up the remaining survivors."

Ferguson held their altitude just below the cloud base. He noted their fuel but was unsure how many passengers they could carry at the elevation of the crash site. He turned to Shultz. "How many survivors can we take without unloading? We've already burned off a third of our fuel."

Shultz thought for a second, running the calculations through his head. "Eight or nine I think if we pack them in tight. Maybe more as the fuel weight decreases. With the carousel we'll be limited on space. We'll watch our power and keep bringing them aboard until we max out. As long the number two engine doesn't crap out first."

Ferguson gave him a questioning look. Glancing at the temperature again for the umpteenth time, he wished the display bar would drop lower on the scale. At least the oil pressure appeared normal. If the oil system were leaking, the temperature would have increased with a corresponding decrease in pressure, which hadn't occurred.

They had almost forgotten about Steiner when his voice interrupted the radio silence. "Evac One, Medic One with a sitrep, over?"

"Yeah, go ahead," Shultz answered after moving the radio selector to the correct position.

"Eighteen survivors on site. Three fatalities. Two in critical condition and three others serious. The rest are stable and mobile. I'll have the first ready for transport by the time you return. There is minimal survival gear on site. Request you have the second Evac bring more blankets, water, and rations."

"I copy that, Medic One. We'll advise once we make contact with Operations."

Over the next several minutes, Shultz attempted contact on different radios. Static filled silence was the only answer. Not even a broken syllable interrupted the void. He tried again as they passed the face of the glacier and again a minute later. There was still no answer.

Shultz glanced at his watch. Five minutes had already passed. "Let's head back to the crash site. We've wasted enough time. The clouds won't allow more altitude for communication. Looks like we're on our own."

Ferguson banked the helicopter hard left without speaking. He agreed with the decision. Flight Operations wasn't aware of their position or even if they found the missing aircraft, but they knew the general area of the search. The second duty crew was en route and should arrive within the hour. He only hoped all the survivors could be rescued before the weather set in.

They headed back over the glacier as Shultz tried a last radio call. There was no immediate answer. He was about to reach for the flight controls and relieve Ferguson when a clear, loud voice answered.

"Evac one-one-four, this is Army nine-two-seven on one-twenty-one point five. Can I be of assistance, over?"

By the strength of the transmission, Shultz knew the other Army helicopter was close. He recognized the voice, but the realization didn't make sense. The person talking was supposedly grounded for medical reasons back at Fort Wainwright.

Could the voice really be from his old mentor? He gave the issue only a brief thought before answering, grateful someone finally heard their radio call.

CHAPTER TWENTY-FIVE

A sharp pain pierced the nerves in Connor's back, causing the muscles to tighten instantly in reaction. The involuntary reflex was enough for his body to recoil sharply, jerking his arm and the hand grasping the cyclic sideways. The helicopter pitched upward and hard left, missing the narrow pinnacle only a moment before impact.

His eyes shot open automatically as the burning spasm along his spine shattered his concentration. His ability to manipulate the flight controls was lost for a few seconds, but those few seconds were long enough to give him a second chance at life, whether he wanted one or not. In frustration, he cursed his reflexes and the helicopter and then laughed away the agony and his own personal outrage with morbid contempt.

"What's the matter old girl?" Connor spoke to the helicopter as if the machine had veered off course on its own. "You afraid to die?" At the same time, he wondered if the sudden jolt of pain, at the last moment before impact, was coincidence or a message from his subconscious to reconsider his desperate action. He quickly dismissed the thought.

"To hell with that," Connor stated emphatically to himself. "I'm coming around again."

The pain remained, although on a lesser scale as he pulled the cyclic back and to the side in a steep climbing turn.

The weather had noticeably worsened since first entering the valley. Connor felt the difference by the way the helicopter reacted. The winds were stronger, pushing harder with the changing airflow as the fuselage fishtailed during the turn. Constant pedal inputs were necessary to keep the nose streamlined. The altered heading caused the airspeed to decrease noticeably, requiring more power to accelerate and maintain the climb. He reacted quickly, ignoring the pain that only moments before had caused him such anguish.

Connor watched the clouds moving faster over the mountains. The movement was clearly visible as the moisture laden mass shifted around the uneven terrain, surrounding and smothering every inch of higher ground in a methodical dance. Narrow fingers of mist hung below the overcast in scattered pockets, following the clouds like strands of a jellyfish. At times they seemed to move with a purpose all their own, separating into smaller wisps of vapor or changing shape and size before forming similar patterns all over again. Others formed from converging currents of warm and cold air, moving with the drafts of wind into the valleys or mixing into the dense layer blanketing the mountain range.

The helicopter continued climbing on a downwind turn above the pinnacle. A composed voice broke through the silence on the radio, surprising Connor by the clarity of the transmission. He realized the call must be associated with the ELT signal he monitored earlier. The electronic beeping was no longer audible over the VHF radio, replaced instead by the Evac helicopter's request for assistance.

Connor debated whether to ignore the call or respond, frustrated at the turn of events. The realization of someone in distress was hard to push aside. He slowed the helicopter, keeping the pinnacle in sight off the nose, trying to justify his selfish reasons for placing himself in this predicament. Something else inside told him the unfolding situation was deadly serious and lives were in jeopardy.

He circled once more but already knew the answer. The decision was easier than he imagined.

Connor's old instincts kicked in. So many people from his past were never saved, just like he would not allow himself to be saved now. But there was a chance someone might be if he could silence his personal demons. *Maybe this is what I really need, another chance at redemption. Yes, there was still time.*

His original plan would simply be placed on hold. Determined to see both choices through to the end, Connor found new resolve and ignored the pain. He turned away from the pinnacle and changed the radio selector to the emergency frequency.

Most military and a few civilian radios were designed to receive transmissions on the emergency guard frequency, regardless of the frequency the aircraft's receiver was set on. For an aircraft to transmit, however, the specific frequency needed to be selected.

Connor pulled in more power, climbing higher in another circling turn above the valley. Leery of getting too near the cloud base for fear of being pushed in by a strong updraft, he leveled the helicopter several hundred feet below the overcast and headed on a northwest course toward the head of the drainage.

The terrain gradually began tapering from rugged mountains to rounded hills a few miles in the distance. He continued until he was sure the other aircraft could hear him before answering their call.

"Evac one-one-four, this is Army nine-two-seven on one-twenty-one point five. Can I be of assistance, over?"

There was no immediate response and Connor was about to try again when a loud, positive voice answered. "Roger, nine-two-seven. We're on a rescue mission in the Alaska Range, near the northeast side of the Crosson Glacier. We need to pass coordinates of a crash site to Medevac Operations or to Fairbanks Flight Service. Can you relay over?"

"That's a roger, Evac. I'm currently about ten miles west of you, heading north out of the West Fork drainage." Connor knew the approximate location without having to check the map. "I should be able to establish contact once I'm clear of the higher mountains."

The inflection was more familiar the second time. Shultz was certain the voice was from his old mentor, Gil Connor. "Is that you, Gil? This is Joe. Let me know when you're ready to copy the information."

He sounded different over the radio, but Connor recognized his voice through the static. His former student always spoke in a relaxed tone, unreflective of a particular dialect. Connor couldn't remember where he was from.

They had never been close friends but always found time to reminisce when running into each other at the officer's club or around the airfield. They first met when Connor was the chief instructor in Contact Phase at the Army's helicopter flight school in Fort Rucker, Alabama, fifteen years prior. Shultz was a student pilot at the time and having problems. His assigned instructor had failed him on an important check ride, after which Connor was asked to perform a follow-up evaluation. The ride went badly at first, but once Connor demonstrated better techniques, Shultz quickly mastered the maneuvers. Eventually, he went on to become a fine pilot.

Over the years, they had been assigned to the same aviation unit on two occasions. Shultz was one of many former students and Connor remembered them all in some way or another. Something about each of them stayed with him, whether it was their name, a particular mannerism or how they flew. The ones he helped the most—those who used his experience and knowledge to the greatest benefit, learning from his techniques and refining their own flying style to become good pilots—they were the ones he remembered above the others. Shultz was one of them.

"Roger, Joe. I thought I recognized your voice. Glad I can help out."

Without waiting for an answer, Connor pulled a pen out of the shoulder pocket of his flight suit and looked around the cockpit for something to write on. A pocket-size Alaska Flight Supplement was sticking out of a black canvas bag on the side of the console and caught his eye. He quickly pulled the book out and laid it open on his knee.

"Lucky for us you were in the area. The terrain has been hampering our radio calls. We need to send an update on our situation ASAP." Shultz waited for an answer.

"I'm ready to copy. Send your message." Connor had questions about the ongoing rescue mission but held off for the moment. Reluctant to be on the sideline passing information, he wanted to be directly involved, yet knew Shultz and his crew in their more powerful helicopter was a better option.

"Information as follows . . . missing Northern Mountain Air flight found east side of Crosson Glacier at sixty-nine hundred feet. Coordinates are sixty-three, zero-six point two-nine North; one-forty-seven, zero-four point sixty-one West. Eighteen total survivors . . . three fatal, two critical and three others serious. Crash site is on a narrow ridge requiring hoist capability. Weather is closing in rapidly. Need a second Evac helicopter ASAP. Request they bring extra provisions and blankets. How copy, over?"

Connor wrote quickly, only diverting his attention outside every few seconds to confirm the helicopter's course and altitude.

"Got it, Joe," he answered before reading back the message for confirmation. "I figure another couple minutes before I'm in position to relay. Anything else?"

"Negative. We're about the same time out from the crash site."

"I'll advise when I make contact." Connor thought for a second before adding a suggestion. "Let's use the FM radio for communication. I'll need the VHF to contact the civilian agencies."

"Roger. Use the medevac frequency. We're already monitoring the channel," Shultz advised.

After changing the FM radio setting and moving the selector to the number one position on the communication panel, Connor was ready.

He verified the new frequency. "Evac one-one-four, you copy on Fox Mike?"

"Loud and clear, Gil." There was a long silence before Shultz continued. "Good thing you were in the area. What brought you out here?"

Connor was ready for the question. "One last flight. I thought I'd revisit some old stomping grounds. Didn't figure I'd be involved in a high mountain rescue though."

The answer was honest, but deceptive at the same time. Shultz thought Connor was referencing the helicopter's last flight and not Connor's own intention. He hoped his mentor could remain in the area as long as they needed him.

"How's your fuel situation?"

Connor answered without hesitation. "About an hour and a half." He had already checked the fuel several times in the past few minutes.

"We're good for two hours. Should be enough to get most of the survivors off, provided the weather holds."

Connor mentally calculated the amount of passengers Shultz's helicopter could transport. The carrying capacity of the Black Hawk was limited by the high altitude and the internal carousel configuration. Even though the capability was greater than his own helicopter, it was not enough to get everyone off the ridge in one load. Unless the second medevac helicopter arrived, some would have to be left on their own. He was already thinking of a second option.

"Joe? Is any area at the crash site big enough for my helicopter to land?"

There was a lengthy pause. Shultz thought back to his time flying the older helicopters, years earlier. "Maybe, but I don't think so. A landing would be awfully tight. The ground isn't level and with the winds, I wouldn't advise trying. Even on a good day an attempt would be risky."

Connor had hoped for a more positive answer. "Okay, Joe. A couple more minutes till I'm in position to make contact."

"Roger, standing by."

"Evac One, Medic One, over?" Steiner's voice broadcast over the radio. His words were being muffled by the wind in the background.

"Go ahead Medic One. What's your status?"

"One ready for hoist. Another prepped and waiting." Steiner's voice reflected his confidence.

Shultz took the controls from Ferguson. The crash site was clearly visible through the windshield as he maneuvered the helicopter into the wind for the approach.

Northwest of the valley, Connor reached a position clear of the higher mountains. "Medevac Flight Operations, Army nine-two-seven, over?"

A barely decipherable voice responded. "Callin . . . tation . . . unreadab . . . say . . . gain . . . ver."

Connor realized he was too low and turned on a sharper angle toward the foothills before trying again. "Medevac Operations, nine-two-seven. How do you hear, over?"

"Understan . . . broke . . . unreadab . . . ver."

Unable to climb higher and not wanting to waste more time, Connor dialed in the Fairbanks Flight Service Station on the VHF radio. An unexpected and much clearer voice responded on the medevac frequency before he could press the transmit button.

"Nine-two-seven, this is eight-three-zero on Fox Mike. Do you copy?"

Connor hadn't expected another helicopter in the area and was caught off guard by Al Thompson's concerned voice on the radio. He realized they must have been sent to find him and coerce him back to base. Hoping to avoid an argument over the radio, he kept the conversation focused on the rescue mission.

"I read you loud and clear eight-three-zero. I've got an emergency message from Evac one-one-four for their flight operations. Can you relay, over?"

"Roger, nine-two-seven. We were instructed by Wainwright Tower to monitor this frequency in case the Evac flight attempted contact. Medevac Operations was getting concerned. Go ahead with the message."

Information on the crash and the survivors was passed quickly by Connor. He listened as the same details were passed by Thompson to someone else. A garbled, unrecognizable response followed, taking much longer than anticipated. He turned east toward the confluence of river drainages north of the glacier, putting the helicopter on a more direct line with the crash site. In position, he slowed to preserve fuel.

"Nine-two-seven, Medevac Ops is requesting you pass information back to Evac one-one-four. Are you still in contact with them?"

"Affirmative."

"Inform one-one-four the second medevac helicopter is delayed with a mechanical problem. They estimate another hour before they're able to launch. Other rescue services have been notified, but none will arrive in the area for some time. The State Trooper helicopter is currently on a mission in Nenana and doesn't have hoist capability. The Air Guard rescue unit in Anchorage will be launching in the next few minutes. They were waiting for confirmation of the crash. That's all the available helicopters. Operations requested updates as the situation changes, over."

The news was discouraging. Connor realized the weather would be a deterrent before other helicopters could arrive. Shultz was on his own.

"Roger, eight-three-zero. I copy." Connor began a slow circle below the clouds.

"Break! Evac one-one-four, this is nine-two-seven. Information on the rescue has been passed. I have a message when you're ready, over."

"Thank you, nine-two-seven. Ready to copy." A different voice than before answered. Ferguson was now handling the radios while Shultz flew the helicopter. They had heard Connor talking with the second aircraft but couldn't monitor the other end of the conversation.

Connor delivered the bad news, pausing until he was sure Shultz's copilot had time to comprehend the message, then passed Medevac Operations' request for an update.

"We'll keep you advised," Ferguson replied.

The hoist was already out the door and on the way down for the first patient.

CHAPTER TWENTY-SIX

Lisa was the first to see the helicopter return. She stood, ignoring the wind, staring into the distance for signs of movement. The young dog leaned against her leg, sensing her anticipation.

She stroked his neck, then yelled and pointed over the glacier. "They're coming back! I see the helicopter. Over there. They're coming back!"

The sound of the helicopter was muffled by the wind. The sleek fuselage moved quickly through the cold air, passing over the center of the valley on a course toward the crash site. Only when the powerful machine flared on short final could the high-pitched whine of the engines be heard.

Survivors outside the wreckage pointed and shouted over the wind as the helicopter came into view. Their eyes eagerly followed the approach with each passing second. They were huddled together from the cold, each wrapped in a heavy wool blanket the Army medic had brought with him. One of the girls hurried inside to tell the others.

For some, the wait for the helicopter was even harder the second time. Even though rescue was close at hand, they realized the injured would go first. They wondered if there would be enough room for all of them or if another helicopter was on the way.

Only a few thought of the consequences of the worsening weather. No one noticed the clouds had dropped several hundred feet in the short time the helicopter was gone.

Steiner received a call when the helicopter was a minute out. Shultz emphasized the need to hurry.

"Time to go. You ready?" Steiner gently squeezed the shoulder of the injured man with the broken legs. He didn't expect an answer and was surprised when he nodded his head in acknowledgment.

Steiner motioned to the passenger grasping the front of the litter. They lifted in unison and carefully moved toward the plane's doorway.

Sanders stood to the side, letting Bidwell and the medic carry the load. Both were strong and easily moved with the injured man. Once outside, Simms grabbed a corner of the litter beside Bidwell, helping steady the weight. Kwapich took the other corner position beside Steiner as they moved cautiously over the rough terrain. In a short time, they had the litter at the pickup point.

The basket arrived a moment before they did. The bottom scraped across the ground before coming to a complete stop. Slack was added and Bril waved from the hovering helicopter to proceed.

Steiner gave brief instructions before they set the litter inside the rescue basket and strapped the board in place. He had to yell over the sound of the engines. He knelt beside the aluminum frame and wrapped one end of the blanket already tucked in the litter around the patient's head for additional protection. The rotor wash immediately pulled at the fabric, trying to pull it free.

The men with Steiner moved away from the swirling winds biting at their exposed skin and thin clothing. He remained and donned his flight helmet left next to the basket. Flipping down the visor, he glanced up and saw Bril leaning out the open door, waiting for the signal to begin the hoist.

Sanders watched the helicopter hover over the pickup point. He stood in the doorway of the wrecked plane, grateful the medic was taking charge. He was weak from his own injuries and the mental strain of keeping everyone focused but wasn't about to let his fatigue show. Once everyone was safe, he could rest. Until then, the survivors were still his responsibility.

Someone brushed against Sander's shoulder. Susan peeked out the doorway while trying to shelter her face from the wind, squeezing his good arm in a reassuring gesture.

"Rescue is only a matter of time now." She spoke loud enough to be heard over the sound of the helicopter. "I had my doubts for a while."

Sanders nodded then motioned toward the injured passengers. "Once they're aboard, the rest of us can leave. We couldn't have done this without you."

Susan shook her head in denial. "Everyone did what needed to be done."

"Maybe, but you did your part with a smile and charm. You helped us relax and stay focused."

She lowered her eyes without speaking and patted his arm in thanks. Directing her attention back outside, she noticed the rescue basket leaving the ground on a rapid ascent toward the helicopter. The load began spinning beneath the fuselage. The medic moved to the side and watched for a moment, then turned and stepped toward the wreckage, pulling a hand-held radio from his jacket.

Steiner took a deep breath. The sense of relief was only temporary. There was still much to do. He hadn't been sure what to expect when he first arrived. The number of injured was a surprise after observing the extent of damage from the air. He anticipated far more fatalities.

The amount of survivors was the only positive outcome of the crash. Getting them off the mountain wouldn't be easy. The passenger's combined weight and limited space on the helicopter would only allow half of them in one load. Shultz's ability to make another trip or the chance of a second helicopter arriving was still in doubt.

****

Holding the helicopter at a fixed point over the ridge wasn't easy for Shultz. His hands and legs remained tight on the controls from constant corrections, reacting with less finesse in a battle against the swirling wind. Subtle inputs were not an option against the strong air currents hammering the helicopter. The t-shirt under his flight suit was already damp with sweat.

Bril leaned out the open cargo door, watching the ground while guiding the cable with his free hand. The basket came down within a foot of where Steiner and the others were waiting. Bril was quick to pass corrections to the pilot as they drifted. His position directly above the basket provided the best view for judging movement.

Steiner and the men moved quickly to unfasten two empty litters from the hoist. Bidwell carried them away while Steiner and Kwapich helped position the injured man in the basket. He was wrapped in a heavy blanket with air splints around his legs. Bril watched patiently, waiting for the signal to start the hoist.

The speed of each lift was determined by how quickly the load could be attached and the pilot's ability to maintain a fixed position over the ground. The lift was also at the mercy of the winch, which could only operate at a certain speed.

Bril and Steiner were a good team. Steiner was more experienced, having multiple rescue hoists under his belt. He was an expert at getting the basket loaded and hooked correctly to the cable in a minimal amount of time. Bril was equally adept at operating the hoist. His sharp vision and ability to judge speed and distance made up for his lack of experience.

Steiner used one hand to hold the metal ring attached to the harness of the basket and the other to guide the cable's hook assembly into the ring, ensuring they locked together.

He confirmed the equipment was secure by jerking sharply downward. The hook and ring remained locked. He signaled Bril and stepped away, letting the hoist lift the basket free of the ground.

"One patient coming up. The man's wife is next." His voice was distorted by the wind as he spoke through his hand-held radio. "She's a retired nurse. I want her aboard so she can assist with the two critical patients."

Ferguson could see Steiner standing near the wreckage with his back to the wind. An older woman stood beside him, looking up at the helicopter with apparent apprehension.

"Roger," Ferguson answered. He turned and watched Bril as the basket was pulled inside.

The temperature display for the number two engine was climbing. Ferguson kept a sharp eye on the gauge after Shultz took the controls, his uneasiness growing with each incremental increase.

"Number two engine is running hot again. The indicator bar is near the top of the green. Pressure's unchanged."

Shultz was already aware of the change. He stole an occasional glance at the gauge in spite of his attention being focused outside. "We might have to call this off. Let's get as many aboard as we can before the temperature hits redline. Bril, how we doing?"

"Another ten feet, sir." Limited by the speed of the hoist, he was forced to slow the cable as the load neared the underside of the fuselage. From there, the basket was carefully maneuvered between the door and external fuel tank. Once abeam the door, he swung the boom holding the basket and patient inside.

Bril moved as quickly as he could without needlessly jarring the patient, unhooking the metal ring of the basket and unfastening the straps holding the litter. Removing the litter from the basket was the hardest part.

He slid a corner onto the lowest rack of the carousel, repeating the maneuver with the opposite end while pushing the device all the way in on the rack. Straps were then attached to the side to hold the device in place. The last empty litter in the helicopter and three backboards were placed inside the basket before being reattached to the hook. The procedure took less than two minutes.

"Patient's secure. Basket is loaded with remaining equipment and going back out."

"Okay Bril. Keep them moving." Ferguson stated. "Let's hope this engine doesn't crap out first."

Glancing at the temperature, he noticed the indicator was at the top of the normal range. Only minutes remained before the limit was exceeded. The emergency procedure was clear, and he quickly went over the steps in his head.

Shultz offered an opinion that did little to ease their uncomfortable feeling. "I sure as hell hope the temperature sensor is sending faulty information. Otherwise, things will get ugly real quick."

"You want to break off now?"

"No. Not until we absolutely have to." Shultz's voice was firm with determination. "It's my ass in the sling. I might lose my pilot position, but if we rescue the critical survivors before the weather sets in, the reward will be worth the risk. Sure hope I don't have to pay for the repairs."

Ferguson knew he was being honest. Damaging a multi-million dollar helicopter was never trivial, especially when the pilot knowingly violated regulations. The safety of the aircraft and crew were always the priority. The loss of a helicopter, especially because of bad judgment, would have serious repercussions.

Ferguson didn't worry about the consequences. His only thought was about the survivors trapped on the ridge, with no chance of rescue except the lone helicopter and a wish for delay in the deteriorating weather. "I'm with you. I'll back you up."

Shultz glanced over at his copilot. He nodded his head in thanks. After a long pause he spoke. "Get Connor on the radio. Give him an update to send to Flight Operations. Then see if he'll reposition to our location."

"You think he can land on the ridge?" Ferguson stated in surprise.

"I don't know, maybe. No harm in him taking a look. He's a damn good pilot. He might see something we missed."

Ferguson frowned. "You can't land a helicopter where it won't fit, without breaking something."

"There's another option. If our engine craps out, I think maybe we can rig our hoist inside his helicopter. We'll have to find somewhere we can land together. What do you think, Bril?"

Bril had remained busy with the hoist but monitored the conversation. "Don't know, sir. I don't have any experience with UH-1s. Don't know if our hoist mount is compatible. The attaching points and wiring might be different. The install could take some time."

"From what I remember the attaching points are the same." Shultz paused, picturing the hoist assembly. "Both helicopters use identical mounts. You might be right about the wiring though. Worth a try if our engine fails."

The statement didn't elicit a response. None was necessary. They each knew the option was there if needed and concentrated on the task at hand.

As Bril watched from above, the second person was positioned in the basket. The woman didn't require a litter and sat at one end with her legs extended. The basket jerked as the bottom lifted off the ground, causing her to flinch and hold on tighter. She seemed frightened at being hoisted fifty feet in the air by a thin metal cable and kept her eyes closed through the ascent. Her arms were wrapped tightly around the support straps, and her legs were pulled up to her chest for protection.

Ferguson pressed the transmit button. "Nine-two-seven, Evac one-one-four. You still with us?"

The answer was almost instantaneous. "Roger, go ahead."

"Request you pass another update to Flight Operations. One patient is aboard, another hoist in progress. Engine problems require a possible abort of the mission. Other injured still on the ground. We need the standby crew on station as soon as possible, over."

CHAPTER TWENTY-SEVEN

Connor processed the information. An engine problem during a hoist could be catastrophic, especially over a high pinnacle in the mountains void of a level landing area. He thought of asking for clarification and then decided to wait. Forwarding the message was the priority.

"I copy. I'll relay through eight-three-zero. Standby."

Ferguson could only hear Connor transmitting to dead air. Monitoring the other helicopter was impossible with the high terrain masking the signal. He waited, allowing enough time for the message to be confirmed and then sent a second transmission. "Nine-two-seven, one-one-four again. Can you relocate to our location?"

There was no hesitation. "Affirmative. What's the status of your engine?"

"Number two is running hot. Don't know how much longer we can maintain our hover, over."

Connor didn't like the copilot's response. His voice had a hint of anxiety, reflecting more than concern over a hot engine. At their altitude, with only one operable engine, the helicopter had insufficient power to maintain flight. They would have to find an emergency land-ing area or limp back to base on the remaining engine, provided it could handle the increased load. Neither option was acceptable for the survivors stuck on the mountain. He figured Shultz must have an idea and wanted to check the crash site for himself, anyway.

"I'm on the way. Should be there in a few minutes. I'm at the north end of the valley, just off the face of the glacier. I repositioned closer to your location since eight-three-zero is nearing the foothills."

Shultz exchanged a look of approval with Ferguson. "He always seems to be in the right place at the right time."

"Basket's coming in," Bril announced. He pulled the frame inside until the weight rested firmly on the floor, not surprised to see the nurse breathe a sigh of relief.

On the way up she forced herself to open her eyes. She squinted, stealing a peek at the ground. A moment later her eyes shot wide open when the hoist slowed below the fuselage. Once inside, she glanced around the cabin, then at Bril, waiting for instructions.

"You're okay now, Miss." He yelled over the sound of the engines. Extending his hand, he helped her out of the basket and into the crew seat.

She immediately bent forward to check her husband, grasping his hand out of concern and relief at being free of the basket. He smiled through glazed eyes. After a few seconds she patted his hand and slid back into the crew seat.

Bril handed her a headset, which she placed over her ears. "You hear me okay?" He looked into her wide eyes for confirmation.

She tried answering but couldn't hear herself speak and nodded her head instead.

"We're glad to have you with us. I'm Specialist Brilnesko. Call me Bril. Place the microphone so the front touches your bottom lip and press the black button on the cord to talk." He pointed to each item. "Okay?"

"Yes, I understand, young man. Call me Mildred. What would you like me to do?"

"Basket is going down." Bril lifted the basket and swung the boom out as he continued talking. "Mildred, I'm going to let the copilot, Mister Ferguson, brief you while I'm busy with the hoist."

Ferguson turned in his seat, facing Mildred as he reached back to get her attention. "Hi, Mildred. Monitor the patients as they come aboard. Take care of them, just like you did on the ground. You're our onboard medic, okay?"

She nodded in reply, looking back at Ferguson, then around the cabin again as if searching for something in particular. "Where is your medical equipment?"

"There's a small first aid kit and a trauma bag in the red cases below the platform in front of you. A stethoscope and other medical instruments are inside the larger of the two. There's a defibrillator in the bright orange case below your seat. If you need to use it, Bril can help, but the instructions are written inside. Let me know if you need anything. Otherwise, stay seated. Okay?"

Mildred seemed more at ease once her familiarity with the medical equipment kicked in. She reached for the cases before he finished talking. "I know how to use them, young man. You just keep this machine in the air."

"Ahh . . . yes, ma'am." Ferguson replied in a broken voice, unsure of what to say. He noticed Bril smirking before turning forward in the cockpit.

In the short time Ferguson diverted his attention, the engine temperature increased above the normal range. A segment light on the caution panel illuminated, notifying the pilots of the fault.

The caution panel contained small, rectangular segment lights, which when illuminated, identified a specific problem in the aircraft systems. A separate master caution light was activated in conjunction with the segment lights, designed to attract immediate attention from the pilots, who would then check the caution panel for the specific problem.

Shultz was aware of the light before Ferguson but waited until he focused back in the cockpit and saw the fault for himself.

"Reset the indicator."

Ferguson immediately reached over and pressed the reset button to extinguish the master caution light. This allowed the light to illuminate again should another system fault occur and didn't interfere with the operation of the first segment light. He glanced at Shultz, waiting for a response.

Instead, Shultz addressed Bril. The tension in his voice was noticeable. "How much longer on the next hoist?"

"Almost on the ground, sir. Steiner is moving another patient into position. Three minutes, maybe more."

Out the bottom corner of the windshield, Shultz could see Steiner and the men carrying a second litter patient from the wreckage. He debated his options for the tenth time in as many minutes.

Emergency procedures stipulated an immediate reduction in power to get the engine temperature back to normal or shutting down the engine before serious damage occurred. Either option meant aborting the mission and abandoning the survivors.

He didn't care about the repercussions of violating regulations. Keeping his crew and the survivors safe was the only consideration. If the engine was fine and sending information through a faulty gauge, the risk was no greater than before. If the temperature was accurate, the risk could be fatal. He knew what he should do, but the choice wasn't what he wanted to do.

"Be ready on the cable shear switch," Shultz instructed. He glanced sideways to ensure Ferguson moved his hand near the covered switch on the center console. A second switch on the hoist control box could be used by Bril if the primary failed.

"The temperature is still climbing," announced Ferguson. He watched the gauge intently.

Shultz seemed to ignore the comment. "Is the patient in the basket yet?"

"Almost, sir. Another minute."

Judgment finally got the better of Shultz. *This is insane. What the hell am I thinking?* "Bring the basket up, Bril. Right now."

Bril could see Steiner and the others only a few feet from the cable. There was a moment's hesitation before he responded. The hoist began winching in the slack just as Steiner kneeled and lowered his end of the litter on the basket. Bril immediately stopped the hoist.

"The litter's on the basket. I can't bring the cable up until the patient's secure."

Shultz was about to have Ferguson advise Steiner they needed to abort when Connor's voice broadcast over the FM radio.

"Evac one-one-four, nine-two-seven has you in sight. I'll do a slow pass overhead. I want a good look at the area."

"Acknowledge him and tell Steiner to abort," Shultz Instructed. "Bril, bring in the basket when they're clear."

"Roger, nine-two-seven," Ferguson stated. He attempted contacting Steiner, without success. The emergency radio was inside his vest pocket and couldn't be heard below the roar of the helicopter's engines.

On the ground, Steiner moved quickly and had the patient secured in the basket in under a minute. He failed to notice Bril's attempts at getting his attention.

"The patient is secure. I'm bringing the basket up."

Christ! Thought Shultz. They were committed now. "As quickly as you can Bril."

"The weight's off the ground. Five feet . . ."

A bearing in the number two engine finally failed under the heavy demands of the mission. The bearing should have been replaced during a previous engine inspection, but evidence of excessive abrasion was missed by an inexperienced, overworked mechanic and a supervisor distracted by an ongoing divorce.

The Teflon coating around the bearing, already worn down during a hundred previous flight hours, was too thin to be effective. The exposed metal became hot, increasing the temperature of the lubricating oil, causing the caution light to illuminate. Eventually, the bearing became hot enough, the core split into multiple pieces. Metal ground against metal, squealing in protest. The engine lost power, the turbine stopped turning, and the helicopter was left with only half its capability.

Steiner and the others were almost back to the wreckage when a change occurred in the sound of the helicopter engines. The men accompanying him didn't notice or couldn't comprehend the significance. Steiner did. He turned around in alarm.

A variation in engine noise was barely recognizable in the cockpit. An immediate change in the engine instruments was. The number two engine's power, or torque, decreased rapidly. The other engine automatically compensated. In a split second the functioning engine reached maximum power, attempting to maintain the high demand of continued flight. The attempt was unsuccessful. A warning horn blared over the intercom and warning lights flashed on the instrument panel.

There was minimal time to react. Shultz quickly focused on the instruments, confirming the loss of power as he sensed the helicopter descending. The predicament was exactly what he hoped would never occur.

The patient was twenty feet above the ground when the helicopter's engine failed. Bril felt the change and immediately reversed the hoist. In an instant, he realized the load was falling with the helicopter and moving too fast. He tried bringing the basket up again.

"Where's the load?" Ferguson demanded. His thumb flipped up the protective cover on the cable shear switch. He didn't want to cut loose until the patient was on the ground.

Bril answered immediately. His quick reaction and the helicopter's own descent had set the basket back on the ridge with only minimal force.

"Cable's on the ground. Hit the shear switch!" He moved his finger on the control box at the same time, ready to duplicate the action if the cockpit switch failed.

A pressure cartridge in the hoist assembly activated instantly, shearing the cable cleanly as soon as Ferguson toggled the switch. He moved the knob three times in rapid succession, but once was enough.

"Cables free! Go! Go!" Bril yelled. He watched the ground getting closer by the second. Thirty feet of altitude was already gone.

The length of cable was still falling when he was thrown sideways. Only his safety harness and his arm instinctively grabbing the doorway kept him from being tossed outside.

Steiner stared, transfixed by the movement of the helicopter. He watched as the loss of power caused the heavy machine to spasm, then catch itself and hang in midair before falling. The basket remained suspended below, at the mercy of the thin metal cable as the assembly lurched and began swinging, falling with equal speed.

Incredibly, the basket slowed just before impact and slid onto the hard ground with barely a bump. Steiner was dumbfounded, certain the patient would be killed by the fall. A second later the cable sheared and snaked wildly in the wind as the frayed end fell earthward. The hook, still attached to the harness on the basket, bounced off the side of the frame and landed sideways. The rest of the cable landed nearby, barely missing the patient.

The event seemed to occur in slow motion even though the entire incident took only seconds. The rescue basket lay safely upright on the ground as the helicopter disappeared over the side of the ridge. Steiner hesitated and then ran toward the immobile patient still strapped safely inside.

Mildred had been leaning over her husband, checking his air splints when the engine lost power. Startled by the loud warning signal and abrupt movement, she fell back in her seat. The hurried commands from the crew and sudden yaw of the helicopter terrified her. All she could do was stare and hold on tight.

Shultz pushed in right cyclic as soon as the cable sheared, simultaneously kicking in more right pedal to swing away from the ridge. The helicopter slid over the outer edge of the mountain and turned sharply, dropping nose down and accelerating into the expanse above the glacier. The tail boom missed the rocks by only a few feet.

CHAPTER TWENTY-EIGHT

"On my command, shutdown the number two engine!" Shultz's voice was forceful, edged with only a hint of anxiety and sounding more assured than he felt.

Ferguson grabbed the engine power control lever on the overhead console. His voice became more excited. "Number two engine identified."

A quick glance by Shultz confirmed the position. "Pull the power control lever and shut off the fuel."

Ferguson did as instructed. The procedure was routine after reacting to dozens of similar emergencies in flight simulators. But the tension he felt certainly was not. His adrenaline increased faster as they descended toward the crevice-scarred glacier below.

Shultz maintained the helicopter's airspeed at forty knots to maximize lift. Keeping the torque at the top of the normal range, he used the slow airspeed and available altitude for a controlled descent to the valley floor.

With one operational engine, the helicopter only had sufficient power to maneuver and land at a lower altitude. The thought of flying back to the airfield was dismissed. He was uncertain of the extent of damage and the distance was too great a risk. Getting the helicopter on the ground was the immediate priority.

Shultz adjusted the helicopter's attitude for a more gradual descent. The rate was hopefully enough to distance themselves from the jagged glacial ice field and rough mounds of deposited moraine. The maneuver also provided the crew with more time to evaluate their predicament and to coordinate a rescue attempt with the other helicopter.

After his initial flash of panic at the thought of being thrown clear of the helicopter, Bril managed to swing the boom inside and close the sliding door. He breathed in deeply before taking his seat, nodding to Mildred, who was as wide-eyed as an owl. He motioned for her to fasten her seat belt and forced a smile in an act of reassurance. From her expression, she would most likely be driving a car from now on.

"We're okay back here. Thought I was a goner for a second." Bril was going to comment on needing a clean pair of underwear when he realized the pilots were busy enough without listening to his inane comment. Instead, he began thinking of the survivors left on the ridge.

Shultz began looking for a level place to land. Even though the immediate danger had passed, he remained tense. His legs were cramped from the strain of hovering over the ridge and sweat had soaked through his undergarments into his flight suit.

He couldn't help but second-guess his decision to stay over the ridge. His stubbornness had almost cost them their lives. Hindsight aside, self-evaluation could often be the harshest critic. Shultz knew the loss of the engine and near fatal crash were because of his own poor judgment. He also knew chastising himself was only going to make the situation worse. With their Black Hawk out of commission, Connor and the old, outdated Huey were the only option remaining.

Almost on cue, the radio barked an acknowledgment. "Evac one-one-four? Joe, how you doing? Everything all right?"

Connor was less than a quarter mile away when he saw the medevac helicopter dive away from the ridge. From the abrupt maneuver and sight of the rescue basket and cable lying on the ground, he realized they must have lost power. There was nothing he could do but watch. Only when he was certain they were out of danger did he break radio silence.

"I've got the radio," Shultz told Ferguson. He wanted to talk to Connor himself.

"We're doing okay, Gil. The number two engine crapped out. No power at all. We had to cut the hoist and break off. We still have single engine power, but the output isn't enough to keep us flying safely much longer. We're coming down slow. Still plenty of altitude to find a landing spot. You get a look at the crash site?"

There was a delay before he answered. "Yeah, I did. I think I might be able to get in there. I need some help though. A couple more sets of eyes would be useful."

"I hope you're right. I didn't see a suitable place on the ridge I'd want to try, especially in this weather. But you've got a smaller helicopter."

Connor ignored the comment. "I'm staying up high to talk to eight-three-zero. There's a small airstrip on the east side of the river, about five miles ahead of you. The dirt runway is just inside the tree line, about a hundred yards south of where the larger drainage joins the next valley. The ground is nice and level and small bush planes sometimes use the site during hunting season. Can you make it?"

Shultz stared ahead at the location Connor described. "I think so. What have you got in mind?"

"Eight-three-zero and I will meet you on the ground. I'll brief you there."

Ferguson looked at Shultz with obvious skepticism. "You think he can really land on the ridge?"

Shultz didn't answer at first. His face reflected a blank expression before frowning with concern. "Maybe. There was a time I wouldn't have doubted him."

"And now?" Ferguson asked.

Shultz thought for a moment, keeping his eyes focused outside. "I don't know. He's older now, not exactly at the top of his game. Only he knows if he's still as good as he used to be."

In a moment of reflection, Shultz recalled past stories other pilots told of Connor's exploits in Vietnam. Following the war, his reputation grew even more. Somehow Connor managed to build an impressive legacy, even with his personal life in shambles. Most of his career was ancient history now, forgotten or overlooked by a new generation of pilots. To most of them he was a relic of another era, an old horse past his usefulness who should've been put to pasture years ago.

In the past, Shultz would never have questioned Connor's ability. Now, he wasn't sure. He still had doubts, but he kept them to himself. He wondered if the combination of man and machine, in this case Connor and an equally outdated helicopter, were good enough to accomplish what needed to be done.

The soon to be retired UH-1 Huey helicopters were underpowered, under-equipped, and over-extended for the demands of modern aviation. At the high altitude necessary for a successful rescue, Connor's Huey would be at the limit of its capability. Factoring in the dangerous wind conditions, the idea of trying seemed unrealistic. The unknown was the ability of the pilot at the controls. Was Connor's skill in the air still sharp, or diminished by age? Much like the machine he was flying, no one could argue he was well past his prime. Any attempt at rescue could be a recipe for disaster.

Shultz couldn't stop Connor from trying. Allowing members of his crew and the survivors to participate in the same risky attempt was a different story. If the risk was too extreme or the chance of success too small, he could insist they wait and not place their lives in greater jeopardy. Silence or unwillingness to object to Connor's attempt could reflect directly back on Shultz.

Shultz pondered his options, finally deciding the chance was worth taking. He would support Connor as much as he could, for now. He didn't dwell on the consequences of failure but instead on the hope of achievement. Some of the survivors would surely die if they were left at the crash site. An attempt at getting them off the ridge seemed just as risky as leaving them there on their own.

"You've got control of the radios. Advise Steiner what's going on." Shultz relinquished the communications back to Ferguson. "I'm sure he's wondering what happened. Tell him Connor will attempt a landing on the ridge and to have the survivors ready."

Ferguson did as instructed. He reached Steiner on the second attempt, explaining the situation as simply as possible. Steiner took the news in stride, as he always did, equally prepared to remain for days, if need be, or leave on a moment's notice. His priority was the safety of the survivors, nothing more, nothing less. Ferguson was amazed at his calm demeanor.

The ridge first appeared unsuitable for landing when Connor flew over. The rough ground was too uneven, full of obstructions and far too small. On his second pass over the site, however, he saw a possible location.

An opening in the rocks near the forward side of the wreckage, several yards ahead of the port wing, appeared large enough. The space was just wide enough to position the skids on the ground without the rotor blades hitting the surrounding obstructions.

The uneven surface was another concern. The intended landing area sloped back and to the side, allowing little margin for error. Only the main fuselage of the helicopter would fit. The entire tail boom, half the length of the helicopter, would have to hang over the ridge with the wind quartering at a sharp angle. The positioning was risky, maybe too risky, but Connor was willing to try.

With the weather worsening every minute, Connor contemplated landing on the ridge by himself. The recurring pain told him to reconsider. His physical discomfort and the need for another set of eyes to help align the helicopter between the rocks was enough for a temporary delay.

The turbulence continued pounding the helicopter, hammering the already strained muscles along Connor's spine as he flew north.

The pain was intense. Age and disease were collecting their debt. The distractions were requiring all his willpower to maintain control.

Masking the tortured beating he was enduring became harder and harder when talking on the radio. Limited time remained before his body collapsed from the repeated stress. He needed a break from flying, and fast.

CHAPTER TWENTY-NINE

Lower in the valley, away from the higher slopes, there was less turbulence pounding the helicopter. The winds were more predictable, maintaining a consistent direction and velocity. The funneled air currents and vertical bursts of wind lost intensity as they spread over the flatter terrain of the valley, allowing a smoother descent into the river basin where Shultz intended to land.

"I think I see the landing area ahead at one o'clock, about a half mile." Ferguson pointed at a spot in the distance. "Looks like plenty of gravel bars in the area we can land on, too."

Shultz looked where he pointed. The dirt airstrip was visible as a narrow cut in the sparse timber on the east side of the drainage. At either end the runway widened into low growth spruce and willow bushes. "I see the opening. We still have plenty of altitude. No need to rush the approach."

A quick glance at the radar altimeter confirmed they were still fifteen hundred feet above the valley floor. As they continued their descent, both pilots realized Connor's recommendation was probably the correct one. The dry riverbed they initially intended to land on was unsuitable. Gravel washouts, uprooted trees, and windblown mounds of sand had transformed the terrain into an uneven landscape. Some areas were still adequate for landing a helicopter under normal power, but they didn't have that option. The one operational engine provided insufficient power for a standard approach. A long, relatively level surface was needed, allowing a faster touchdown speed.

Bril remained silent during most of the descent, content to let the pilots handle the emergency. He kept switching his gaze from the lights on the instrument panel to the rising ground. Only after they were safely away from the glacier did he glance at Mildred. Visibly upset after the helicopter lost power, she seemed less distraught with each passing minute.

Bril unbuckled his seat belt so he could talk to Mildred directly without interrupting the pilots over the intercom. He leaned forward and pulled the headset away from her ear. Speaking loudly over the drone of the engine, he explained the emergency and their intention of landing to assist another helicopter with the rescue. She seemed confused, then irritated as she motioned toward her injured husband. He assured her the situation was under control. She frowned and shook her head, wondering what else could go wrong.

Shultz banked the helicopter on a downwind course for landing, bleeding off altitude and allowing more time to observe the area. The clearing was narrow and rutted with old tire tracks, only used by single-engine bush planes a few times a year. The width was barely big enough for the fifty-four-foot diameter rotor blades, but it would suffice as long as the helicopter didn't slide more than a few feet to either side. Near the far end, the strip opened into a large turnout, twice as wide and big enough for the other two helicopters to land.

"We'll be okay. It'll be tight though." Shultz glanced over at Ferguson, who had his head turned, looking out the side window. "Any of the gravel bars look like a better option?"

Ferguson turned back to face the cockpit. "Too many obstructions. Looks like the landing strip will have to do."

"Then the strip it is. I'll extend the downwind leg to set up a better approach angle. Watch the torque on final."

Ferguson acknowledged with a hand signal as he pressed the intercom button. "Bril? How is everyone doing back there? Everything secure?"

"Roger, sir. Passengers and gear are secure." He sat on the edge of the crew seat with his seat belt unfastened but remained attached by the safety harness so he could slide the cargo door open on approach.

"Coming around on final," announced Shultz.

The helicopter lost speed in the turn as the wind shifted from the tail to the nose. Shultz anticipated the change. Even though the helicopter was moving slower across the ground, the headwind provided more lift, allowing less power for the approach. He adjusted the controls perfectly, feeling the wind, raising the nose so the helicopter rode the same wave of speed and angle all the way to the ground.

At fifty feet, Bril stood and pulled open the cargo door. A rush of air hit him in the face as he leaned outside. The tail easily missed the trees by a several feet.

"Tail is clear." He pushed himself back into the seat and buckled in.

Mildred stared in fright and frustration as the helicopter approached the ground, certain she was going to crash all over again. She grasped her husband's hand and said a silent prayer. Her husband smiled back with a content, medicated expression.

Shultz applied power to cushion the tail wheel as it touched the ground. The tire bounced slightly over the rough surface. He raised the nose, reducing power and slowing the helicopter's momentum. As the speed decreased, the nose gradually fell forward, placing the main wheels firmly on the ground.

The helicopter continued rolling until clear of the surrounding trees. Shultz applied light brake pressure until they came to a stop at the end of the airstrip. The area was filled with clumps of low brush, broken by the weight of other aircraft. Skid marks and ruts were clearly visible where airplanes had parked and turned around to unload cargo.

Shultz grinned at his copilot. "Set the brakes."

Ferguson had watched the power during touchdown, but exceeding the torque limit was never in doubt. Shultz made the approach look easy. He pulled the brake handle and returned the grin. "Brakes are locked. Damn nice job."

"Ditto, sir." Bril was back to his usual form as he climbed out the cargo door. "Piece of cake, right?"

"Better to be lucky than good," Shultz stated. "Would have been a lot worse if we landed on the riverbed."

Nothing else was said. They all knew luck had nothing to do with it.

Outside the helicopter, Bril positioned himself near the front with the fire extinguisher. He stretched his legs and stood staring at the mountains as they went through the shutdown procedure.

Mildred turned and faced forward. She leaned in toward the pilots. After being hoisted off the ground, falsely assured of her safety then subjected to another in-flight emergency, she didn't appear happy to be stuck in the middle of nowhere.

"I knew I was right to be concerned about this helicopter business. Two crashes in one day would have been a little much, don't you think? Do all your rescues go this badly?"

Ferguson's dark eyebrows arched slightly from the criticism. His hands turned up in a sign of surrender. He held a blank stare, reluctant to address her question. This one he left for the pilot-in-command.

Shultz grimaced. He wasn't sure if she was serious or not. Usually the crew chief and medic handled interactions with the passengers. "No, ma'am. Not usually. I apologize for the inconvenience. I'm sure . . ."

"The inconvenience?" she interrupted. Her tone immediately provided any doubt Shultz had about her comment. "Not having the option of coffee or soda is an inconvenience, young man. Being on the edge of a nervous breakdown, twice in the same day, because the aircraft I'm flying in suddenly decide they don't like being in the air, now that's something else entirely."

All Shultz could do was apologize and try to reassure her help was on the way. Dealing with civilians, especially an irate woman was something he was unfamiliar with. All of a sudden, an ass chewing from his chain of command didn't seem too bad. Even though he was a senior warrant officer and an experienced pilot, his status meant nothing to the traumatized woman in the back and probably her patient-husband as well.

"I'm sorry about the situation. I really am." He turned so he could look directly at her. "Right now, there are other helicopters on the way. One is going to try to get the rest of the survivors off the mountain. Another can transport you and your husband to the hospital. You've both been through a lot and we appreciate your cooperation. Are you both all right?"

Mildred stared back into his eyes for a moment. They projected a surprising calmness that eased her anxiety. Her desire to verbally lash out at someone subsided. She nodded okay.

"You can unbuckle your seat belt now and move around if you like, Mildred. Is your husband conscious? Would you like anything?"

She kneeled beside the litter and ran her hand lightly over her husband's brow. His eyes opened slightly in response. "Yes, he's conscious. He's not in any pain. The medication your medic gave him is still working."

She leaned forward and kissed her husband on the cheek. Their hands were locked together. He managed a weak smile.

Once the rotors stopped turning, Shultz kept the helicopter running on auxiliary power so they could use the radios and keep the heater on. Ferguson remained in the cockpit while he exited to look at the damaged engine.

Bril was on the engine deck with the upper cowling open as he approached. The young crew chief shook his head in doubt. They both removed their helmets to talk.

"Can you tell what happened?" There was no apparent damage Shultz could see.

"No, sir. Everything looks fine on the outside. All the lines and control fittings are tight. No oil or fuel on the deck." Bril bent over the engine, running his fingers and eyes over each section.

He jerked his hand away in pain. "Son of a bitch, that's hot!" He should have known better. The engine had malfunctioned for a reason even if the damage wasn't obvious.

"The forward section is hotter than normal." Bril blew on his fingers. "My guess is one of the components failed. A bearing or a pinion gear probably overheated, which caused the oil temperature to rise. Once the part failed, the turbine ate itself and lost power. No way to tell for sure until the engine is taken apart."

"Sounds reasonable." Shultz rested his arm on the open cowling. "We'll be here awhile then. Maintenance won't be happy about needing to replace the engine."

"I guess they can get in line behind everyone else. Shit. I'll be as busy as any of them, sir."

"We all will. Close the cowlings. Right now we need to focus on getting the rest of the survivors off the mountain."

A mile away and fifteen hundred feet higher, Connor watched as the Black Hawk turned into the small landing strip. He lost sight of the silhouette below the trees but could see dust billowing skyward from the rotor wash. Once the cloud dissipated, he saw the helicopter coasting to a stop. One figure was outside almost immediately.

Connor diverted his attention to the other helicopter. "Eight-three-zero, this is nine-two-seven. How far out are you?"

The voice of the copilot, Lieutenant Hovan, sounded concerned. "We just passed the foothills near Dinosaur Ridge. We're over the East Fork now at four thousand. Do not have you in sight."

Lieutenant Hovan was under orders to bring Connor back and suspected the senior warrant officer taking the helicopter involved more than he was told. Captain Hiroldi was evasive about Connor's intent, only stating he wanted Connor and the helicopter back without delay. Consenting to a rescue attempt was not something he wanted to be involved with.

"You should be about three miles away." Connor searched for a dark speck of movement against the sky. "I'm also at four thousand and directly over the river."

His back felt better once he was clear of the constant pounding from the turbulent winds. The muscles still ached, but the spasms had eased, relieving the sharper pain. He was able to stretch by extending his legs on top of the control pedals.

Thompson's voice broke over the radio. "I've got you in sight. We're at your ten o'clock position."

Connor placed his feet back on the pedals. He scanned the horizon. "I don't have a visual on you."

His eyes couldn't distinguish objects at a distance as well as they once could. On the second scan of the horizon, his eyes caught a speck of movement. "I have you now. Follow me down. Evac one-one-four is already on the ground."

Connor waited for an answer before calling Shultz. "Evac one-one-four, you still on the radio?"

"Go ahead, nine-two-seven." Ferguson motioned out the window at Shultz there was a call on the radio.

"Is your medic monitoring the emergency frequency? I want to talk to him before we land."

"Affirmative, nine-two-seven. He's using his survival radio." Ferguson watched Shultz climb into the pilot's seat while he continued talking.

"What's his name?"

"Sergeant Steiner. He's using Medic One as his call sign."

Connor switched to his other radio's emergency frequency. "Medic One, Army nine-two-seven."

Background static muffled the response. "This is Medic One. Go ahead, nine-two-seven."

"Medic One, I can hardly read you. Do you need any additional equipment from your helicopter? I should be there in the next thirty minutes, over."

"Standby, nine-two-seven." There was a break in the transmission before he continued. "Negative on the equipment. But I could use some extra help moving the survivors. One of the injured is a very large man. Two of the other injured are critical, but stable for now. Bring Bril, the crew chief, if you can. We'll be ready."

"I copy, Medic One. Any change in the weather?" Connor could tell the conditions were worsening by the minute but asked anyway.

"Ceiling is still dropping, nine-two-seven. Suggest you don't delay, over." No sarcasm was intended. The statement was an honest assessment.

If there was any anxiety on the part of the medic, Connor didn't hear any in his voice. Either the medic was one cool operator or he wasn't aware of the danger the weather posed for all of them. Connor hoped the former was true. "Roger, Medic One."

He relayed the medic's request while turning on final approach. He flared and touched down off their right side a few seconds later. By the time he rolled the throttle to idle after the two-minute cool down, Thompson was landing nearby.

A flurry of dust and leaves spread out from the helicopter's rotor wash and quickly subsided. Thompson was flying and Lieutenant Hovan sat with a stern expression, visible below the visor of his helmet.

CHAPTER THIRTY

Connor checked the fuel quantity on the instrument panel. The amount was insufficient to rescue the survivors and make the flight back to base. His helicopter could carry more passengers with the reduced weight, but they would need to be transferred at some point to a second helicopter. The time involved and the chance of the weather limiting a return made a second option necessary. Since Thompson's helicopter carried more fuel, he decided they would use his.

When he looked up from the cockpit, Lieutenant Hovan was hurrying toward him. He was all of Connor's height with wide shoulders and thick muscles. His Nomex flight suit bounced from the weight of items in his pockets as he ran. His square jaw was clenched, and he didn't appear to be in a good mood.

Connor wasn't sure what the lieutenant wanted. He assumed Hovan would try to take charge of the situation. Connor had neither the time nor patience to put up with his arrogance.

Al Thompson had done most of the talking over the radio while Hovan listened in annoyance. As a lieutenant who outranked the young warrant officer, he wanted to be more involved in the decision process, whether he was a copilot or not. He was already under orders to find Connor and bring him and the helicopter home. How, exactly, he wasn't sure. The ongoing rescue mission only made his dilemma worse. Now he was having second thoughts about whether he should even go along with the rescue at all.

Connor's company commander had been informed of his terminal cancer by the flight surgeon, shortly after the helicopter was stolen. Hovan and Thompson were told a short time later. The commander was obviously worried about Connor's true intention but held off on sharing his concern Connor might be looking for a more dramatic end to his illness.

Even though Hovan lacked experience in a command position, he was smart enough to realize the rescue trumped his previous order. He wanted to clarify the situation with his commander, but now they were out of radio range and unable to notify anyone of their intention. Delaying the rescue or stopping Connor's involvement might be the best course of action, yet he was hesitant about what to do.

His expression said enough as he climbed into the copilot seat of Connor's helicopter and plugged into the intercom. He was unhappy with the predicament he found himself in. The outcome of the rescue could well depend on his decision.

"Mister Connor, I hope you know what you're doing because I'm having serious doubts. What were you thinking taking the helicopter without authorization? You've put my ass in a real jam here. Now you want me to go along with a dangerous rescue plan?"

Connor didn't turn from Hovan's intense stare. He wasn't sure if the words were an attempt at intimidation or an expression of frustration. The lieutenant's demeanor was easily overcome by Connor's confidence.

"I'm sure you know about my cancer by now. The reality of impending death has a way of making a man do things in a hurry. I took the helicopter so I could have a last flight on my own terms, nothing more.

If I went through proper channels, the request would be denied or permitted with so many conditions I would be lucky to sit in the back seat on a trip around the traffic pattern."

He paused to see if Hovan accepted the explanation. Although the details were accurate, his intent was not.

"As for the rescue, we're their only hope. I can get the survivors off the mountain, but I need help."

The lieutenant blinked and looked away toward the shrouded peaks. "You're sure you can do this?"

"As sure as I can be. Nothing is ever a sure thing."

Hovan studied Connor's expression before exhaling noticeably. "All right, I guess there's nothing I can do to stop you. Even if I order you to fly back to base, you would probably ignore me. Either way I'm probably getting my butt chewed."

Connor realized he had underestimated the lieutenant. Some officers, especially West Point graduates, often demonstrated an air of superiority around subordinates. The process of junior officers becoming good leaders usually required a series of mistakes and delicate manipulation of their egos before they learned to trust more experienced soldiers in their charge. Hovan was already ahead of many of his peers by accepting that fact.

Connor automatically reverted to the role of mentor without being aware of the change. "Being in a position of command is never easy, Lieutenant. We all have to make choices; they're just harder when someone else's life is at stake. For whatever reason, this rescue was placed in our laps. Don't worry about an ass chewing. You're making the right decision."

Hovan nodded. He shifted in the seat and glanced at his watch. "Does the medevac crew know about your theft of the helicopter?"

"No, sir. I didn't mention it. They probably suspect something, but I'm not offering up any information."

"Good, keep quiet for now. You can answer to Captain Hiroldi later."

Connor finished the shutdown as the blades coasted to a stop. Hovan stepped from the cockpit and was already on the way back to the other helicopter. Bril headed in the same direction, joining him halfway there.

Shultz stood and leaned against his own helicopter, watching Connor intently. He waited until the pilot's door swung open before approaching.

Connor left his headset on the seat. He managed to mask the pain as he exited, but his slow movements and bent torso gave away his obvious discomfort. He leaned against the fuselage and forced himself into an upright position. The constricted muscles resisted, protesting in annoyance. The nerves flared for a few seconds before the pain ebbed, the movement helping stretch and loosen the tension.

"Hello, Gil." Shultz approached Connor with a stern expression. "Sorry to get you involved in this . . ." He paused when he saw Connor grimace. "You okay?"

He reached to help support him, but Connor waved his hand away. "I'm all right. I tweaked my back getting out of the helicopter." He grimaced again but managed to stand upright. "Good to see you, Joe."

Shultz was concerned about Connor's condition. He looked weak and in pain. He'd never seen him this way before. "Good to see you, too. You sure you're up for this?"

The intense gleam in Connor's eyes was all the answer he needed. "Yeah, I am. I'm taking Thompson with me. He can spell me on the controls if I need a break."

Shultz studied his face for a sign of uncertainty. There wasn't any. "Bril, my crew chief, is already onboard. You ready?"

Connor nodded and slowly pushed himself away from the helicopter. "Your crew chief okay with flying with me?"

They started walking. "Specialist Bril doesn't have a problem. He's always looking for an adventure. He did ask me what kind of pilot you are though and if you knew what you were doing."

"And what did you tell him?"

"The truth." Shultz suppressed a grin. "I told him you're a hard-headed bastard and a below average pilot with minimal experience. And even less skill."

Connor shook his head. He would have laughed if not for the dull ache piercing his body with each forced step. "Careful, you're going to inflate my ego."

The expression on Shultz's face became serious. "I told him I trusted you with my life. And he could do the same."

There was a moment's silence. They exchanged a look of respect before Shultz changed the subject. "Watch the winds up there. I'll stay on the radio with you and keep an eye on the weather. If the clouds start closing in between here and the ridge, I'll let you know."

Connor nodded. "I figure ten minutes en route and another ten or fifteen on the ridge, depending on how long we take to load the survivors. Some will have to be left at the crash site. I can't take them all in one trip. There won't be time for a second."

"I know. Let Sergeant Steiner decide who goes and who stays. The survivors have blankets and food we dropped off earlier, and the wreckage should provide enough shelter. I know you don't want to leave anyone. Either do I, but there isn't another choice with the weather closing in."

He was about to tell Connor to be careful and not take unnecessary risks, then caught himself. What the hell. If anyone was aware of the risks, Connor was. The last thing he was going to do was lecture him on what being a good pilot was all about. Connor had given him the lecture years ago.

"I've got two survivors in my helicopter. One is in serious condition with two fractured legs. If the other medevac doesn't reach us in time, I'd like to get them out of here. Is the lieutenant signed off as a pilot-in-command in the Huey?"

Connor hadn't thought about Shultz's passengers. "No, not yet. He's capable though. I'll talk to him. He can fly nine-two-seven back. I'm guessing you're not current in UH-1s?"

"Not even close. The last time I flew one was years ago. I can go along as a copilot and keep him out of trouble."

They reached the idling helicopter where Thompson sat at the controls. Hovan met them outside the arc of the spinning blades. He spoke in a loud voice so Connor could hear him over the sound of the engine. "You're all set. The crew chief is aboard. You sure you don't want me to go along."

"We'll be fine, Lieutenant. Thompson and the crew chief can help load the injured. Your extra weight would only be a hindrance. That's why I'm taking Thompson instead of you. He's a good forty pounds lighter."

What he didn't mention was his preference for Thompson because of his better flying skills. Hovan was okay but less experienced. Thompson had more flight hours and a better feel for the aircraft. Connor had flown with him enough to trust his ability and knew he was capable of handling a tight situation. In many ways, Thompson reminded him of himself early in his career.

Hovan seemed satisfied with the answer. "Okay, makes sense." He stared at Connor's parked helicopter where the skids rested between clumps of willow bushes, the blades left untied. "What about nine-two-seven?"

"There's enough fuel for a return to Fort Wainwright. I know you're not signed off yet, but you can fly back. I'm designating you a pilot-in-command. The paperwork can be done later. Joe is your witness if anyone questions the flight. He'll go along if the other medevac doesn't arrive to take his passengers."

Lieutenant Hovan seemed skeptical. "I don't know. The commander might not buy the explanation."

There was no time to argue the point. "The decision is yours, Lieutenant. I've got to go. The weather isn't going to wait." Connor displayed an air of confidence. Silently he wondered if any of this was a good idea.

Before Connor could step away, Shultz grabbed his arm. He hurriedly removed the flight jacket he was wearing. "Take this. It's too small to wear, but roll the material and use it behind your back for support."

There was no argument. Connor was grateful and nodded in thanks. He turned and approached the waiting helicopter as fast as his aching body would allow.

Climbing into the left seat was just as difficult as the other side. He placed one foot on the toe of the skid and stepped into the cockpit with the opposite leg, pulling himself in by grasping the doorframe and seat. The simple movement taxed his tender muscles. Once in position, he bent forward, placing Shultz's folded jacket against his lower back. The pressure eased some of the pain.

Being in the copilot's seat was routine for Connor. He was comfortable flying from either seat. Instructor pilots usually flew on the left side and often preferred the position, although some instrumentation wasn't as visible.

Thompson increased the throttle to a hundred percent and waited while Connor fastened his shoulder harness. There was no headset, and he was forced to wear the flight helmet left by Lieutenant Hovan. The size was almost a perfect fit, and he pulled the straps tight.

"You ready?" Thompson was apprehensive but trusted Connor.

"I'm ready." Connor's voice sounded strained as the projection of pain become more obvious. He checked the engine instruments as they lifted off.

"Head for the center of the valley and follow the drainage south into the mountains," Connor added. "I'll mark coordinates on the GPS as we go. I want a good track to fly out of there if the weather goes to shit."

They shifted their eyes to the weather closing in on the mountains. Stronger winds were already buffeting the helicopter. Thompson glanced at Connor, hoping he knew what the hell he was doing.

"Pull in max power and climb to seven thousand," Connor directed. "The crash site is about fifteen miles ahead."

Thompson did as instructed, increasing power against the strength of the head wind blowing through the valley. He noted the time. They spent eight minutes on the ground. Not a lot, but enough to make a difference. The clouds already appeared lower on the slopes, masking the top third of the higher peaks. Another layer was forming below, covering the valleys with a patchwork of broken stratus. The weather was spreading faster than he realized.

Connor began glancing around the interior of the cockpit, verifying radio settings. All were on the correct frequencies. He made a quick radio check with Shultz's helicopter and let the medic know they were on the way.

Looking behind into the cargo area, he noticed the seats were still in place, arranged in a standard load configuration. Five were mounted across the rear bulkhead, facing forward. Two more were in each corner, facing the doors, and two additional seats were situated directly behind the cockpit, facing rearward.

Although suitable for carrying a load of soldiers, the configuration limited the space for carrying multiple litter patients.

"Specialist Bril, is it?" Connor eyed the back of the crew chief's helmet.

"Yes, sir." He turned to face the cockpit.

"I'm Mister Connor, Bril. You up for this?"

His voice was emphatic in reply. "Yes, sir. I'm glad I can help."

"We're glad to have you. You have any experience in UH-1s?"

"No, sir, I don't. From what I can tell, the interior is pretty much laid out like the Black Hawk's, only smaller. The doors and exits are about the same. Mister Thompson gave me a briefing when I first hopped in."

Connor pointed to the folding seats. "I need you to fold the back row of five seats against the bulkhead so we have more room for the injured passengers. Pull up on the circular brackets on the bottom of the legs. They'll come loose and you can fold the whole assembly up and out of the way."

The task only took a minute for Bril to accomplish. The seats were identical to those on the UH-60. "Done, sir."

Connor waited until he strapped himself back into the seat. "When we come in for landing, I need your head outside watching the tail rotor. Do the same thing you do in the Black Hawk, except you'll be looking out the left side instead of the right. Watch for any obstructions. The landing area is real tight. I'll be positioning the tail between several outcroppings of rock. You need to give me directions so the tail remains clear."

"I understand, sir."

"You want the controls, Gil?" The question was asked out of courtesy. Thompson preferred to fly as much as he could. In this case though, he was more than happy to relinquish them to Connor.

"Not yet." Connor fully extended his legs over the control pedals instead, allowing the tension in his muscles a brief respite. Now that they were airborne, he was not as concerned about showing his discomfort.

Thompson noticed Connor's uneasiness. He was aware of the cancer and the demand the disease must be placing on his body. *Surely he would call off the rescue mission if he felt incapable of handling the aircraft. Even though his body might be weakened, his judgment wouldn't be impaired. Or would it? Could he really trust Connor's decisions?*

A moment of uncertainty flashed through Thompson. He quickly dismissed the feeling when Connor's calm voice interrupted his thoughts. "The crash site is on the east side of the glacier, on a narrow ridge butting out from the mountain. Seven thousand feet will give us enough altitude for the approach as long as the weather holds. I'll take the controls about a mile out."

When they were in position over the center of the valley, Connor pressed the waypoint button on the GPS to lock in the position. The green box rested on top of the instrument console so either pilot could access the information. He usually didn't like using the device. He was old school and still preferred using a map, plotting the time and distance manually. In his opinion, the GPS caused basic navigational skills to lapse.

When the GPS technology was first implemented in Army helicopters, Connor noticed younger pilots became overly reliant on the device and couldn't follow a regular map across the airfield, much less on a cross-country mission. They were completely dependent on the GPS system for basic navigation. As far as he was concerned, any mechanical device could and probably would eventually fail, usually in a critical situation. A pilot needed a backup plan, especially in combat or adverse weather. He ensured every pilot he flew with knew how to use the GPS and a map equally well.

As they continued south, Connor noted the course they were tracking and the ground speed. The wind was blowing almost directly off the nose, so by correlating the ground speed on the GPS with the airspeed indication, he could determine the wind velocity and time back to the waypoint. The GPS computed the time automatically, but he was not going to rely on the device alone. He wrote his own calculations on a piece of paper taken from Thompson's kneeboard. The procedure would be repeated where the valley changed course with the glacier.

There was no comment from the young warrant officer. He was well trained and knew exactly what Connor was doing. The procedure had been instilled in his flight planning from the first time they flew together. *Always give yourself another option. Think ahead and plan for the worst.*

The turn in the valley was still ahead. Connor set the paper aside and retrieved the operator's manual from a metal box mounted on the rear of the center console. Opening the book with familiarity, he carefully studied a performance chart, confirming some mental calculations. Satisfied, he closed the pages and placed the manual back in the metal tray.

The pain in his back intensified. He adjusted the folded jacket against his spine, shifting into a straighter posture. He felt better as he briefed Thompson and Bril on what he knew of the crash site.

"Our power will be limited. Even with reduced fuel we can't carry all the survivors. There are sixteen civilians and four of us, including Steiner. I figure eight or nine passengers is all we can carry, depending on their weight. We'll load as many as we can until we're maxed out on power. Any questions?"

Bril was the first to answer. "Maybe we'll get lucky and the weather will hold for another trip."

"Yeah, maybe," Thompson added. From the cockpit he could tell the clouds above the glacier were not going to cooperate. "It's a shame we can't carry them all."

As the helicopter flew further into the sharply cut mountains, the overcast could be seen angling lower over the glacier. The clouds encompassed the valley in a solid blanket, leaving no way out except the same way they came in.

Increased turbulence buffeted the helicopter, shaking the airframe and jostling their stomachs with intense and unpredictable rhythm. Shoulder harnesses and seat belts were pulled tighter in response.

Connor set another waypoint in the GPS as they turned, taking a second to write down their course track as he had done before. The gusts were increasing over the glacier, fluctuating the airspeed as much as thirty knots. Nearer the slopes the vertical drafts would be even stronger and more violent.

A light drizzle began speckling the windshield. A quick glance at the outside temperature showed they were in a range where icing could occur. Both pilots understood the implication, but just as quickly the rain stopped. If the precipitation returned, icing could be a serious problem.

The Huey only had limited de-icing capability, a simple device for directing hot air onto the engine inlets. Unlike the more advanced Black Hawk, no de-icing was available on the main rotor and tail rotor blades. The potential for icing was a serious concern. Ice could add weight and cause a loss of lift-disastrous for any aircraft.

Two miles from the ridge the cloud vapor touched the top of the spinning rotor blades. The weather was closing in with each passing minute. There was less than a hundred feet of clearance between the base of the clouds and the crash site, providing less time than Connor hoped for. Ten minutes at the most, then the weather would be on them.

Connor moved his aching torso, placing his hands and feet in position on the flight controls.

"I've got the controls. Time to earn our pay, gentlemen."

CHAPTER THIRTY-ONE

The rhythmic beat of the rotors resonated through the mountain air as the helicopter disappeared from sight toward the glacier. The sound became fainter and fainter until the noise was only a whisper, finally changing to a soft, intermittent echo before fading completely.

Shultz and Hovan watched the helicopter lift and turn southward, following the departure silently with their eyes. They waited until the silhouette was a tiny speck, cocking their heads to follow the last perceptible din with their ears. When it, too, was gone, all that remained was the rustle of wind through the trees and the drone of the Black Hawk's APU in the background.

There was nothing left to do but wait. Shultz looked at the lieutenant, who he had met only once before, and wondered what was going through his mind. *Did his thoughts really matter?* The events were already in motion and there was little either of them could do.

"Well, Lieutenant Hovan, what say we get into the helicopter out of the wind? We can monitor the radios until the other rescue helicopter arrives."

"What about your passengers? The weather could close in before they get here."

Shultz studied the sky. "I think we'll be fine for a while, judging by the base of the clouds. The passengers can wait a bit. We still have the Huey if the weather deteriorates faster than expected."

"I thought you were worried about the passenger with the broken legs?"

Shultz pushed at a clump of dirt with his foot before looking at Hovan. "I am, but Connor could use our help. I'd like to stay here and keep in radio contact until we know he's back off the ridge."

Hovan seemed relieved. "I guess so. I'll tie down the blades on nine-two-seven. Like you said, we can use the helicopter to fly out of here if we need to."

They strolled together, keeping an easy pace over the rutted ground. "How well do you know Mister Connor?"

Shultz looked hard at the lieutenant. He wasn't sure how to respond. The question was simple enough. He just wasn't entirely sure of the answer. Even though he had known Connor for at least fifteen years, he considered him more a teacher than a close friend. The experiences he gained flying with him were invaluable. Stories about him from other pilots, long since retired, were legendary. In that regard he knew him very well. Connor's personal life was different. In that aspect Shultz didn't know much at all.

They stopped at the left cargo door. Hovan grabbed the tie-down strap from under the seat before Shultz responded. "I've known him since I was in flight school. We've flown and worked together several times over the years. Most of what I learned about being a good pilot came from him. He's the best pilot I've ever flown with, if that's what you're asking."

Hovan pondered the answer. "I haven't flown with him myself, but I heard similar things from Thompson. I guess I was just looking for confirmation."

Maybe, thought Shultz. He suspected there was more to the question. Did the lieutenant doubt Connor's intentions? But why would he, unless Hovan knew something important he wasn't sharing? Then again, Connor did seem different somehow. Exactly how, he wasn't sure.

"Is there something you're not telling me, Lieutenant? I'm sensing something more than a concern about the weather and those survivors stuck on a mountain."

Hovan ignored the question. He tossed the end of the tie-down over the forward rotor blade, attached the hook, and swung the blade over the tail boom, wrapping the line around the metal stinger. The rotor blades were secured. He took a deep breath and exhaled noticeably.

"Mister Connor has terminal cancer. Did he mention that?"

The expression on Shultz's face turned sour. He looked at Hovan as if he were crazy. "You're sure? How do you know?"

"The flight surgeon called our commander. Connor received confirmation of the cancer this morning. He was obviously upset, refused treatment and counseling, and then left the hospital." Hovan glanced down at his boots. "The doc told him he only had a few months, more if he chose the chemotherapy option."

"Damn!" Shultz's voice dropped. "Life can really suck sometimes. No wonder he looks in bad shape. What type of cancer does he have?"

"I didn't get the full story, but apparently he has tumors in his lungs and spine. And they're spreading. The doctor was concerned and thought the commander should know. He assumed Connor could be persuaded to take chemotherapy treatments, which might give him more time."

"I can't say I blame Connor for refusing. He doesn't have any family to speak of, so what's the point?" Shultz crossed his arms and contemplated what he would do in the same situation.

Hovan ran his hand along the fuselage. "Connor also took this helicopter without authorization. I bet he didn't mention that either? Thompson and I were sent to bring him back. The rescue mission threw a wrench into the plan."

"What?" Shultz looked toward the mountains and then smiled. "It explains why he was flying alone. He said he was on a last flight.

I assumed he meant for the aircraft, not him. I guess he deserves that much."

"Yeah, well there's something else. The commander wanted us to bring him back, but he didn't tell us everything. He was concerned about something else. I think he thought Connor might be suicidal."

"No way, I don't believe it." Shultz's smile had disappeared. He stared hard at Hovan. "You don't either, otherwise you wouldn't have let him take off again."

"I could be wrong. But even if he intended suicide, I don't believe he'd take anyone with him. Why even get involved in the rescue at all?"

Shultz sighed. "From my experience and from what I've heard about him over the years, he always has a tendency to be in the right place at the right time. Maybe fate brought him here, instead."

Hovan nodded, reassured of his decision. "I'll have a lot of explaining to do when I get back."

"Both of us will. I just hope to hell we're right. Otherwise, two members of my crew and those survivors are going to pay the price."

Shultz was already moving away without waiting for an answer. Hovan finished a quick inspection of the helicopter and followed, walking heavily over the rutted ground.

The disabled Black Hawk rested among a patch of knee-high willows with the cargo doors closed against the wind. Ferguson had a navigation chart spread out in front of him against the instrument panel, hiding all but the top of his head. He was comparing what he was seeing on the chart to the terrain visible from the cockpit.

Shultz stepped behind a thick bush behind the helicopter to relieve himself. He finished as a gust of wind rustled the nearby trees. A chill shook his body. He looked skyward at the fast moving clouds and felt a small raindrop pelt his forehead.

Shultz walked around the tail and met Hovan at the cargo door. He pulled hard on the handle, sliding it open, motioning to Bril's empty crew seat. "Might as well get comfortable, sir. Grab a headset and listen in. We can monitor the radios while we wait."

Hovan pulled himself in and nodded to Mildred, who leaned in over her husband, checking his pulse. She gave him a cursory nod in reply before shifting her gaze toward Shultz.

"How is he Mildred? Any change?" Shultz showed concern for the patient even though there was little he could do.

She finished counting silently before taking her hand away from his wrist. Her husband's eyes fluttered but remained closed. "He's comfortable. The medication is still working. Any news on the other helicopter?"

"No, ma'am." He glanced down at his watch. "The other rescue helicopter should be here before long. An hour, maybe less."

Mildred didn't appear pleased by the answer. Before she could comment, Shultz deflected the conversation. "This is Lieutenant Hovan. He was on the last helicopter. He gave up his seat to a more experienced pilot for the rescue attempt. They should be nearing the crash site any minute."

She attempted a weak smile, which Hovan returned. "Nice to meet you, ma'am. I'm sorry about your husband's injury."

"Thank you." She focused her attention on the other helicopter parked on the airstrip, wondering why the machine wasn't being used to transport her husband. "Is that one broken, too?"

Shultz knew why she was asking. Even though the Huey was flyable, trying to explain the lieutenant was a reluctant pilot-in-command, and he and Ferguson weren't current in the UH-1 helicopter would take too long. Besides, the explanation wouldn't make sense to her anyway. The real reason was he intended to remain in the area as long as possible. Connor might need weather updates to get the survivors safely off the mountain.

Instead, Shultz decided to keep the answer simple and lie. "Yes, ma'am." In the back of his mind, he kept the other option open. If the second Black Hawk didn't arrive before the weather closed in or if a life and death situation arose, they would use the Huey.

Hovan glanced at Shultz with raised eyebrows but didn't say anything. Instead, he pulled out two chocolate bars from a leg pocket of his flight suit. "Anyone want something to eat? I grabbed these before I left."

Mildred seemed satisfied with Shultz's answer and suddenly realized how hungry she felt. A light breakfast and the ordeal of dealing with the trauma of the crash had left her famished.

"Yes. That sounds good. I could use something to eat."

Shultz shook his head, as did Ferguson. Mildred took one and peeled the wrapper away slowly, grateful for the treat. When she had the wrapper half open, she broke off a piece and placed the morsel gently against her husband's lips.

He responded, flicked his eyes open in brief attentiveness as the chocolate melted on his tongue. They exchanged a few warm words the others couldn't hear. He closed his eyes again after a few small bites, letting his wife finish what was left.

Shultz closed the cargo door before climbing into the pilot's seat. He stretched his helmet lightly over his ears to listen to the radio, leaving the chin strap unfastened.

"Anything?"

"Just a radio check after they took off," Ferguson answered. He reached for the radio selector. "You want me to call them?"

"No, it's okay." Shultz leaned back in the seat and crossed his arms. "No need to distract them. They'll let us know when they arrive."

Ferguson finished studying the chart and folded the sheet neatly to the original size. "I hope Steiner and the survivors are doing all right up there. The pilot of the plane sure picked a hell of a place to crash, didn't he?"

"I'd say he did a damn good job without causing more injuries. Crashes in the high mountains are usually fatal."

Ferguson tilted his head back, massaging the sides of his neck. He stopped after watching the movement of clouds through the overhead Plexiglas. "You think Connor can get all the survivors off before the weather closes in?"

"Not all of them." Shultz's voice changed to a softer tone. "Some will have to be left behind until the weather breaks. At least overnight, maybe a couple days. Steiner will decide who stays."

Ferguson noticed Shultz staring outside. He could see a look of regret in his expression and sensed Shultz was as disappointed in their inability to help as much as he was.

"There's nothing else we could have done, Joe."

"I know. We pushed too hard as it was." Shultz turned his attention to the cockpit and blinked his eyes into focus. "Good thing Connor and the other helicopter showed up when they did. Kind of ironic though when you think about it."

"What do you mean?"

"Well, here we are, the new breed of pilots with a technologically advanced, more capable helicopter, sitting broken on the ground while the old aviator in the aged helicopter flies off to save the day."

Ferguson laughed. "Sort of like the cavalry arriving at the last minute. Except they're riding old mules while the horses are laid up at the fort."

"Yeah, exactly. But don't sell the Huey short. In capable hands the old workhorse is still a damn good helicopter." Shultz raised his voice slightly for emphasis. "Even with terrain and weather, I'll put my faith in Connor."

There was no response from Ferguson. He stared out the window again at the far mountains. The break allowed Hovan to ask a question.

"Mister Shultz? You said you've known Connor since you were in flight school. Was he your instructor?"

Shultz thought for a moment. The simple answer was yes, but there was much more to the explanation. Years had passed since he last told the story. He was certain Hovan and Ferguson were unaware of the circumstances. Now was a good time as any to tell them.

"No, not at first." Shultz paused as if choosing the words carefully. "He was the senior instructor for my class when we started flying in Contact Phase. His role was more of an administrative position, supervising the class instructors and managing the curriculum. He gave morning briefings and handled the organizational duties, letting the junior instructors handle the students. Most of the time he was stuck behind a desk. He never looked happy and many of the students were intimidated by him, including me."

"Sounds like he hasn't changed much." Ferguson smiled at the attempt of humor.

Shultz grinned. "There was a rumor floating around he kicked half the previous class out of flight school for poor performance. The story was false, but we believed it. One day a student in my class made a stupid remark while Connor was giving the morning briefing. The room went completely silent and I swear Connor's stare melted the guy in his seat. His stern look was enough. Later the same day the student talked to a bunch of us and swore Connor's eyes burned like a blue heat."

The corners of Shultz's mouth curled in a smile as he took a deep breath. "Of course, the rumors persisted even more after that, for a while anyway."

A mutual look, part skepticism and part belief, passed between Hovan and Ferguson. They let Shultz go on without interruption.

"Toward the end of the Contact Phase, the class had only lost three students, and two of them were for medical reasons. By then Connor had flown with a couple of my classmates, filling in for their assigned instructors when they were absent. The students he flew with all came away with positive comments. Still, most of us remained intimidated by him."

Ferguson cleared his throat. "When did you fly with him?"

"I'm getting to that." Shultz tried recalling some finer aspects of the story. There was a pause of several seconds as he rubbed his chin in thought.

"Our perspective of Connor changed after a holiday break from training. Several of the older students had visited a local watering hole and saw Connor drinking heavily. They were telling the story in the hallway during a break in class, making a joke of how he must be an alcoholic. We all laughed. Connor never showed up for work either, and we drew the obvious conclusion.

One of our instructors overheard the conversation. He could have reprimanded every one of us for insubordination but didn't. Instead, after we returned to class he got up in front of the room and said he wanted to talk about what being a real aviator means. We didn't know why he brought the subject up or who he was talking about, until the end. The premise of the speech was you can't always judge a pilot by their actions on the ground. The true test of an aviator is how they perform in the air."

Hovan turned sideways to face the cockpit. "So he was talking about Connor?"

A smile curled the edges of Shultz's mouth. He could tell the lieutenant and Ferguson were becoming captivated by the story.

"The instructor talked about courage and sacrifice and what they mean being a pilot. He was a Vietnam veteran and took what he said very seriously. They were just words to us students. Important? Sure. But they lacked perspective until he began reading an old newspaper article from Stars and Stripes. The story was published during the Vietnam War.

The article described how a young warrant officer continued risking his life to save a company of soldiers stranded in a hot LZ. Two medevac helicopters were shot down trying to extract the wounded and no other pilots were willing to try until the warrant officer in the story did. He made a dozen trips and pulled every soldier out before they could be overrun by a battalion of North Vietnamese.

The article went on about how the young warrant officer switched aircraft three times due to extensive damage from enemy fire, barely making the flight back on each occasion. His bravery motivated others to go with him. Two of his gunners were killed and another gunner and a copilot were seriously wounded. He was wounded twice himself. For his actions the warrant officer was awarded the Distinguished Flying Cross."

Shultz paused for effect. "The instructor then put away the article and looked over the class. He explained the warrant officer in the story was later reprimanded for showing up late to receive his award. At the time, he was attending a different ceremony with the men he rescued, honoring their fallen comrades. The soldiers he saved meant more to the warrant officer than a medal.

As the instructor continued, he surprised us all by stating he was one of the soldiers who had been rescued that day and was with the warrant officer toasting their fallen comrades. The young warrant officer was the reason he decided to become a pilot. The instructor let the significance sink in, then finished by telling us the man who rescued them was our senior instructor, Mister Connor."

Ferguson let out a slow breath as Shultz finished talking. "No shit! I never knew that."

"I didn't either." Hovan seemed embarrassed. "I knew he was in Vietnam, two tours I think, but this is the first time I've heard any details."

Shultz continued. "There are other incidents just as amazing. He confided in me once when we were assigned together in Germany. We both had more than a few drinks before he opened up. It was the only time he ever talked about his combat experience. I was humbled, to say the least."

Ferguson leaned forward with his hands open. "So you going to tell us what he said or what?"

"No. They're his private memories. I think he would rather tell them himself. Besides, I thought you wanted to hear about the first time we flew together."

Hovan glanced at Mildred in the seat beside him. She was not wearing a headset and seemed content looking out the side window at the trees bending in the wind. Maybe it was a good thing she wasn't listening to the conversation.

CHAPTER THIRTY-TWO

A strong gust bent the tops of the tall spruce on the edge of the clearing and raced across the waist high willows, swirling across the narrow dirt runway. Leaves and dirt pelted the Black Hawk's windshield, quickly passed and then subsided to a light breeze. The heavy rotor blades flexed and bounced from the onslaught before returning to a rigid position.

"Perhaps a sign of things to come?" Shultz's somber remark elicited silent acknowledgement.

"Okay, tell us the rest of the story," Ferguson prodded after a moment. He wanted to hear about Shultz's first flight with Connor.

Glancing at his watch, Shultz estimated Connor was nearing the crash site. He decided to continue with the story until they received a call.

"After the class instructor read the article, the perspective of many of the students changed. For me, he no longer reflected a hard-assed figure of authority, but a real American hero. If anything, the truth was even more intimidating.

About a week later, I flew with him for the first time. I busted my end-of-phase check ride the day before and was feeling pretty down on myself. He was the instructor giving me a recheck."

"You busted a check ride? Your exalted status just dropped a notch," Ferguson chided.

Hovan laughed and Shultz ignored them. "My busted check ride started off poorly with the first maneuver. I bounced the helicopter heavily during a simple touchdown. After that I was even more nervous and overcompensated, trying to finesse everything, which made me erratic. Each maneuver got progressively worse. My evaluator wrote notes like crazy and all I could think about was being kicked out of flight school. He ended up taking the controls during an autorotation and I knew then I busted for sure. He flew us back to the airfield without saying much."

"Man, and I thought my check rides were bad." Ferguson laughed with Hovan at Shultz's misfortune.

Shultz answered with chuckle of his own. "When we got back to base the evaluator actually went pretty easy on me. I think he knew I could do better. He said the flight wasn't bad, but I needed to be reevaluated on a couple maneuvers. After reading previous write-ups in my training folder, he said a different perspective from another instructor might help. I felt better, but then he hit me with a bombshell. I would be flying with Connor the next day."

"Out of the frying pan and into the fire?"

The comment from Ferguson made him grimace. "Exactly what I thought. I was apprehensive as hell when I showed up the next day. His attitude was nothing like I expected though. From the moment I sat down, I actually felt comfortable. The experience is hard to explain, but the flight was like an epiphany. All of a sudden everything I'd been taught about flying made sense.

I still remember what he told me at the table. He said, 'I know you know how to fly. Anyone can fly. You've made it this far, so relax. Before long you'll learn to trust your instincts. Think ahead and fly like you're an extension of the helicopter. When you can do that you'll be a good pilot.' His words put me at ease."

Ferguson nodded in understanding. "And how did the flight go?"

"The flight was one of the smoothest check rides I ever had. Nothing seemed to fluster him, and he explained everything in such a calm manner, everything just fell into place. He wasn't satisfied with just evaluating my performance, he wanted to make me a better pilot. I made a couple of mistakes, but he either smiled or laughed them off and showed me a different technique. By the end of the flight I not only felt comfortable flying with him, I felt comfortable with myself. I think that was the important thing. I never imagined a check-ride would actually be enjoyable."

Hovan thought about his own performance during past evaluations. Every pilot seemed to have at least one bad experience. They were easy to laugh off after the fact, once the embarrassment faded. Since pilots were known for their big egos, the process could often be a lengthy one. "Was that the only flight you had with Connor?"

"The first of many." The two younger pilots fixated on Shultz, waiting for more information while he adjusted his helmet.

"He was my assigned instructor later during Tactics Phase. It was there he really taught me about flying. His experience in Vietnam was a real benefit. Being able to draw from his knowledge was a huge advantage over flying with less experienced instructors."

The gleam in his eyes expressed the warm memories of flying with Connor. Shultz enjoyed telling the story as much as they enjoyed hearing the details.

"Half way through my first assignment at Fort Carson, Connor showed up as the new standardization instructor. We flew together several times, mostly on training flights but on a couple of support missions, too. He kept busy flying with all the battalion pilots, especially the more inexperienced ones like myself. His flying skills were phenomenal. He made everything look easy. I learned more about flying from him than I ever imagined."

Shultz watched Ferguson scratch his nose in thought. The lieutenant sat unmoving with a wide-eyed look on his face. Shultz wasn't sure if they believed him, but the stories were all true. He checked his watch again before continuing.

"Later on in my career, we were assigned to the same aviation brigade in Germany. He wasn't doing much flying then, at least not until our deployment to Saudi for the first Gulf War. His emphasis on realistic training helped most of us survive without a mishap. He wasn't afraid to speak his mind, either, and always stuck up for the men.

I remember one incident after the ground phase began. He got in trouble for arguing with our commander about an improperly planned assault mission into Iraq. He ended up being relieved for insubordination. Turns out he was right though. We lost two helicopters on the mission, including six men. They gave our commander an award for the fiasco. Connor ended up reassigned to a training unit at Fort Polk.

After his reassignment, I didn't see him for several years. The next time was here in Alaska."

"He's had a colorful career," Hovan interjected. "Getting himself into trouble with his commander seems to be a pattern." The remark sounded harsher than intended. He only made an observation, but by the reaction of the two warrant officers, he could tell the comment was not well received.

Like most warrant officers, Ferguson and Shultz didn't appreciate negative comments about one of their own even if they were true. Shultz appeared irritated the most, but he was smart enough to let the remark slide. Ferguson followed his lead.

Hovan knew by their expressions that he had said the wrong thing. "I didn't mean to imply anything derogatory. I'm sure he thought he was right."

"And you don't think he was?" Shultz could let one comment go by but not two. He kept his tone respectful.

Ferguson looked down at the console, all of a sudden wishing he were outside where he could avoid being drawn into the conversation.

He knew the usually mild mannered Shultz could clamp onto an issue as hard as a pit bull, if he wanted to get a point across.

"Well, that depends." Hovan hadn't expected to be questioned. "I mean, look, there are ways to express your opinion without having to fall on your sword."

Shultz thought for a moment. He slid sideways and cocked his neck so he could face Hovan as directly as possible. He wanted the lieutenant to think about what he said without being adversarial. "I would agree, most of the time, sir. But I also think there are situations when a different course of action is necessary. Sometimes you have to be willing to sacrifice more than an opinion to elicit the right response."

Hovan leaned forward for emphasis. "We do have a chain of command for a reason. A good commander makes a decision based on many factors. Advice from subordinates is only one of them. Just because a subordinate doesn't like a decision, doesn't give the right to become disrespectful or disobey an order. All Connor did was get another black mark on his record. For what?"

Shultz swallowed hard. "Saying he was wrong after the fact is easy. Maybe he did get out of line for nothing. I'm not justifying his action, but at the time maybe he thought his persistence would make a difference. And you're right about the black mark. His career wasn't exactly on the fast track anyway."

"So how can you equate his action with the need for anyone to make a similar mistake?" Hovan sensed a weakness in Shultz's argument.

"Because I believe a good soldier will sacrifice his career and even his life to save others from being killed by a misguided decision."

Hovan shook his head. "I disagree. Any soldier, especially an officer, has to go along with a commander's decision. Otherwise, what's the point of having a rank structure? We can't tell the future. We don't know what is the right or wrong decision until after the fact."

Shultz pressed the issue. "Sure, in principle. All I'm saying is there might be a situation where falling on one's sword, as you say, would be beneficial."

A frown crossed Hovan's face. He thought Shultz might be pulling his chain for the sake of argument or was unwilling to concede without some agreement to his line of reasoning. Even though the logic might be valid, he wasn't about to tell him so. "Maybe you're right. But I can't think of one. Can you?"

Ferguson glanced back and forth between them, beginning to enjoy the debate. He agreed with Shultz but couldn't think of a specific situation to substantiate his side of the argument.

"Absolutely, sir." An innocent expression hid Shultz's real emotion. "How about what we're doing right now, with the mission to rescue the crash survivors?"

"It's not the same thing. We have no specific instructions concerning the survivors. Having the authority to make decisions on our own is part of our training."

Hovan knew the consequences but didn't say anything. He was walking a fine line by agreeing to the rescue, and he could be severely reprimanded if the attempt went wrong.

Shultz considered his own consequences even though he wasn't aware of what Hovan thought. His actions caused them to be stranded in a broken helicopter. Someone inevitably would second-guess the decision. Still, Hovan was right in one respect. Their present situation was a far cry from the issue they were talking about.

"Okay, you're right."

Hovan smiled in perceived victory.

Shultz shifted the conversation. "When I mentioned the instructor reading the article in front of my class, I didn't tell the whole story."

There was pause as Shultz waited for a reaction. Ferguson was the first to bite. His eyes were wide with curiosity. "What else happened you didn't tell us?"

There wasn't much time left until Connor arrived at the crash site. Shultz hurried his explanation.

"I found this out later, but something else took place during the rescue in Vietnam. At the time, Connor was flying the unit's brigade commander so he could observe the troop insertion. The colonel was content on directing the mission from a safe distance, especially after the attack turned into a disaster. Troops on the ground were taking serious casualties. They were close to being overrun.

"Connor refused to stand-by and watch our troops getting slaughtered. The commander ordered Connor to stay away from direct involvement, apparently concerned with only keeping his own ass out of danger. Needless to say, Connor went in anyway. The commander was furious and repeatedly threatened Connor with a court-martial.

"I don't know if this part is true, but a rumor circulated after the battle the commander was told by Connor to shut up or get out of the helicopter and fight with his men."

"Wow!" Ferguson added. "I'm sure that was received well."

Hovan was skeptical but remained silent. Shultz's expression remained serious.

"They returned with the first load of wounded and the helicopter heavily damaged. The commander stormed off without saying another word. Connor flew more flights, risking his life on each one. By the time the division commander learned of Connor disobeying a direct order, he was already being lauded as a hero. At that point the situation was beyond the general's control.

"Connor was initially submitted for the Medal of Honor. His actions were verified by other aircrews and every member of the infantry unit he rescued. In the end, because of the objections from the irate brigade commander, the award was down-rated to a Distinguished Flying Cross. I guess he was lucky he didn't get court-martialed, but I doubt if he really cared. What was important to him was saving those soldiers."

Lieutenant Hovan didn't speak. A humbled expression was his only reply as he nodded his head in agreement. Shultz was right. But like all situations, the results of an individual's actions often dictated the consequences. If Connor had failed, the outcome would have been far different.

"No, shit." Ferguson spoke softly as he contemplated what Shultz said. He couldn't help but be impressed. He was in awe and could only wonder if he would have done the same thing. The events then and those transpiring now would be a story to tell his kids.

Shultz settled back in his seat. He was checking his watch when a voice broke over the radio. The words were slightly distorted by static but still easily understood. He listened intently, focusing his attention on Connor's transmission.

CHAPTER THIRTY-THREE

A sharp jolt of turbulence pushed the helicopter sideways, followed by a strong vertical burst of air, rattling Connor's teeth. He fought the gusts with quick corrections, trying to keep the helicopter from being tossed out of control. "Hang on guys, this is going to get bumpy."

Thompson clutched the sides of his seat, trying to appear unconcerned as if the flight was perfectly normal. Bril sat in the back with hands on his hips and legs spread for balance. He treated the turbulence as a challenge and tried anticipating each movement, making his body react to the motion.

Connor made a pass over the ridge with only fifty feet to spare. He judged the wind's movement off the higher slopes and could feel the altered airflow near the ridge. The burbling currents were causing strong downdrafts on the leeward side, making a straight-in approach at their low altitude almost impossible. He decided to come in at an angle, over a wider extension of the ridge where the winds were less vertical. Once over the landing site he would swing the helicopter into position. There wasn't much room for error. If the helicopter didn't have enough power at the bottom of the approach to stop the descent, they would have to dive away from the ridge.

Connor pointed out the intended location to Thompson before explaining the plan. There were no questions. Any apprehension they felt remained unspoken.

Thompson relayed to Steiner they were beginning their downwind turn. As the helicopter altered course over the glacier, the direction of the wind changed in relation to the aircraft. The wind was no longer off the nose, where it provided the most lift, but off the tail, where the effect was the most dangerous. The airspeed dropped noticeably, the fuselage fishtailed, and the altitude decreased. His muscles were slow to react.

Connor clenched his jaw in determination. He needed to get his head in the game. Another episode of inattention and they would be an accident statistic. He had to stay sharp or relinquish the controls. Slow reactions in these conditions would get them all killed.

The strong tail wind pushed them past the ridge in only a few seconds. Once abeam the intended landing area, Connor turned back into the wind for the approach. He was quicker on the controls this time and easily kept the tail streamlined behind the fuselage. The wind tried pushing them into the clouds, but he reduced power in the turn, keeping the helicopter at the same altitude.

Constant control inputs were critical. The helicopter bucked like a wild horse with a burr under the saddle, rolling and pitching with every change of turbulent air. Connor stayed focused, his mind shutting out the physical pain, concentrating only on flying the helicopter. His arms and legs moved in unison, countering the effects of the wind in a struggle of power and control. His muscles ached but he refused to quit.

"Watch the torque for me, Al. These damn downdrafts are making me pull every inch of power we have. They should decrease once we're over the ridge."

"Roger. You're at forty pounds." A strong burst slammed into the helicopter. Thompson felt his stomach skip. He saw the torque jump to forty-eight then go back down. "Fluctuating between forty and forty-five now."

Connor seemed impervious. "All right guys. Stay sharp. If we lose power, I'll break right over the glacier. The wind should help us nearer the ground. We'll be out of the downdrafts closer to the surface. When we're below fifty feet, I need you both looking outside, giving directions. Keep us away from the rocks."

Bril had remained seated for much of the ride. He watched silently as the helicopter approached the granite carved ridge, shifting his gaze from the almost vertical cliff out the left to the narrow pinnacle of rock out the front. With fifty feet remaining, he unfastened his seat belt and moved toward the door. "Door's coming open, sir."

Checking first to secure his safety harness, he slid the door open, grabbing the doorframe for support as he leaned into the slipstream. Angling his torso slightly so the wind deflected off his back, he leaned out further until he could see the entire length of the tail boom. The edge of the ridge was passing behind them.

"Looking good, sir. Keep coming."

Just as Connor anticipated, the wind was less violent over the flatter terrain of the ridge, blowing in a more horizontal direction away from the slopes. Sharp gusts still hammered the helicopter but from a more consistent direction.

"Thirty-seven on power . . . thirty-five." Thompson kept his eyes moving from the instrument panel to the terrain, shifting a split second at a time between the narrowing distance and indications of torque and airspeed. "Airspeed is forty. Thirty-five now."

Connor pulled more power to reduce the descent, maintaining a constant approach angle. "Power's at thirty-six. Thirty-seven . . . thirty-nine. Holding at forty. Airspeed is at thirty knots."

Bril's instructions during the approach were equally important. By watching the side and rear of the helicopter, he could judge the terrain and hazards that would otherwise be invisible to the pilots in the cockpit. With twenty feet of tail boom behind the engine and its tail rotor supplying directional control for the helicopter, remaining clear of any obstruction was imperative.

The same was true for the main rotor blades. They provided lift and needed an equal amount of clearance out the sides and front. If any component hit a rock or other obstacle, the consequences would be disastrous.

"Thirty feet above the ground, sir. Now at twenty feet. High boulders on the left. Keep moving straight ahead. Don't turn the tail yet." Bril's voice was steady. He seemed unaffected by the danger they were placing themselves in. "Ten feet. Hold your altitude. Swing the tail right five feet. Another three feet . . . that's good. You're clear to come down, sir."

As Connor slowed to a low hover near the spur of the ridge, he could see the intended landing area was barely big enough. The rocks were only a few feet below the rotor blades and the ground sloped at a sharp angle, but he was confident in continuing.

The airspeed fluctuated between twenty-five and forty knots, indicating the velocity of the gusting wind. The power demand decreased closer to the ground, aided by increased lift from the strong current of air.

Slowly, with directions from Bril and Thompson, Connor maneuvered the helicopter so the tail remained positioned between the obstacles. As he turned, the wind hit at a forward angle off the right side, demanding increased pedal inputs and more power. He compensated perfectly, but the constant movement began taking a toll on his thighs and back. Already strained by over-exertion, they were nearing a point of exhaustion.

"How we doing on power, Al?"

"Staying steady at thirty-eight. My side is clear to descend. You've got four feet of room if you need to slide my way."

Connor's gaze remained focused on the rocks and uneven ground. He shifted his eyes constantly, using his outside references to maintain a fixed position. "Coming straight down."

"The skids are five feet above the ground, sir. The tail is looking good." Bril kept his head moving, shifting from one point to the next, ready with quick instructions should the helicopter drift one way or the other.

A strong gust suddenly raced across the pinnacle and rocked the helicopter. The nose yawed right as the tail began swinging left into the boulders. Connor fought to maintain position. The airframe shimmied noticeably from the force of the wind but corrected itself in time.

Control inputs were constant and less subtle now. His muscles were working at peak intensity, increasing and decreasing pressure on the controls—just enough to hold the helicopter steady. Not enough pressure and the wind would swing the tail into the rocks. Too much, and he could overcompensate, fighting his own corrections as much as the wind until he lost control. The outcome would be the same.

"Power is thirty-seven, Gil. You're still good on my side. Ten feet of clearance below the blades."

Connor didn't answer. Thompson glanced sideways at him. He felt more than noticed the change in demeanor. His mentor's jaw was rigid and the eyes determined, but there was an aura of doubt he had never sensed in him before. He knew the increased stress of flying in these conditions must be taking a heavy toll and kept his hands and feet within easy reach of the controls, just in case.

The landing area was almost triangular, surrounded by obstacles of varying heights as much as six feet tall. Large boulders and smaller granite deposits formed a barrier on each side. A large gap opened to the rear before falling into the void below the ridge. A narrower cut was visible to the front, barely wide enough for a person to walk through.

Connor could judge the skid height above the ground as easily as Bril or Thompson, but he needed their help in avoiding the obstructions to the sides and rear. Without their directions, he knew landing in so tight an area would be impossible with the wind. Inch by inch, he lowered the helicopter to the ground. In spite of his pain, he never allowed the tail to shift position more than a foot. Each time he caught the movement before Bril could announce a correction.

"Three feet now. Two feet . . . one foot. Toes are on the ground, sir. You've still got a foot and a half below the back of the skids. The tail looks good."

The ground sloped downward toward the rear, causing the helicopter to touch on the toes of the skids. Connor slowly decreased power, feeling for a solid footing as the nose pitched higher.

They began sliding backward. The angle was too great. The helicopter couldn't maintain a safe attitude, and he was forced to increase power to hold position.

With only the toes of the skids resting on the slope, the position acted as a pivot point, making the helicopter more susceptible to the effect of the wind. Balancing the weight and shifting center of gravity was a struggle. Powerful gusts made the corrections even harder. Constant control changes were necessary, requiring Connor's full attention.

"What's our clearance on the sides?"

"Rotor blades are four feet above the rocks on the right." Thompson had his torso turned toward the window so he could see farther back toward the tail.

"About the same on this side, sir." Bril pulled himself back into the doorway so only his head was outside. "You've got about six feet of clearance on either side of the tail boom."

"I'll have to have to hold the front of the skids on the slope until the helicopter's loaded. There's too much of a slope to set completely down." Connor's voice sounded strained for the first time.

"Let me take the controls for a while, Gil. I can hold us in position while you take a break."

Connor's legs were aching even more than his back from the repeated pedal inputs. He worried his legs would start cramping or, worse, the back would spasm again, but he knew what he had to do. Judging by the level of the clouds, they only had a short time before being engulfed in the dark mass.

"As much as I'd like that, we don't have time. Steiner needs you both to help carry the injured. Get going before this damn ceiling drops any lower. And step lightly getting in and out. I don't want any unexpected movement."

There was no argument from Thompson. He knew Connor was right. Bril was already outside the helicopter and moving toward the break in the rock formation. "I'm unplugging. I'll turn my survival radio on so we can talk."

A head nod was Connor's only reply. He watched Thompson step down and glance up at the spinning rotor blades above him. He turned and made eye contact before hurrying after Bril. In a second he was gone, out of sight behind the maze of rocks surrounding the helicopter.

"Medic One, we're on the ground. Bril and the copilot are heading your way."

Steiner's strong voice answered immediately. "Roger eight-three-zero. I see them. We'll bring out the litter patients first. The youngsters and women next, over."

Connor didn't care who was first as long as the loading was done quickly. "Your call, Medic One. I figure about ten minutes before the clouds obscure the ridge."

"Roger that, sir. Standby."

Shultz monitored the conversation between Steiner and Connor. He pressed his transmit button when there was a pause on the radio, wanting to verify they could still receive him from the ridge. Ferguson and Lieutenant Hovan were staring at the console, listening intently.

"Eight-three-zero? This is one-one-four. I copied your transmission with Medic One. How do you hear, Gil?"

"You're weak but readable. The weather isn't getting any better. We picked up some light drizzle on the way in. The ceiling is only a hundred feet above us now. How does the weather look from your position?"

"Not good, Gil. The broken layer over the valley has turned into a solid overcast. There are also some lower clouds building further south.

They're broken, but getting thicker every minute. I figured you were busy enough with the landing or I would have notified you earlier."

A series of blows rattled the helicopter as repeated gusts swirled over the ridge in rapid succession. Connor fought the movement with a series of corrections, letting the wind subside to a constant velocity before he dared respond to the radio. The fuselage was almost pushed backward, forcing him to pull in full power with the collective. He could feel sweat building under his armpits and the first drops of moisture starting to slide down his brow.

Shultz tried again when Connor didn't answer. "You copy, Gil?"

"I read you, Joe. I was a little busy for a second. I'm light on the skids with only the toes on the ground. Too much slope for the helicopter to set down completely."

Shultz exchanged looks with his copilot and Hovan, noticing their mixed expressions of skepticism and wonder. He was more worried about Connor's physical stamina than any concern over his flying ability. "How you holding up?"

"So far, so good." Connor's voice didn't mirror the optimistic answer. "I guess I still have some energy left in these old muscles. Even the doctors would be impressed."

Shultz could hear the strain in his voice and knew the situation was anything but good. He could only listen and provide encouragement. "Never a doubt from this end. We're standing by."

Lieutenant Hovan was amazed Connor still maintained a sense of humor. The doctors might indeed be impressed but more likely would be furious he was flying at all, much less rescuing survivors off a mountain. Connor's condition could deteriorate at any second and put everyone at risk. Hovan was past second-guessing the flight. Now all he could do was hope the rescue succeeded.

"I'm stepping out for a minute," Shultz announced to no one in particular. "I want to see how the foothills look behind us."

He kept his helmet plugged in as he stepped down and scanned the northern horizon. The clouds overhead stretched for several miles in the distance, well into the lower Tanana Valley. They seemed to be holding their height above the terrain, but patches of lower mist were developing around the hills in the river basin. The worsening weather was another problem they didn't need.

CHAPTER THIRTY-FOUR

Bril was the first to make contact with the survivors. The plane's injured captain met him near the helicopter, obviously relieved to see them. Talking over the wind and the noise of the helicopter's loud turbine engine was impossible without shouting. They nodded at each other and continued to the wreckage. Thompson joined them a moment later.

As they approached the broken fuselage, four young girls, a dog, and two adults could be seen huddling near a pile of rock, watching them intently. They seemed uncomfortable in the cold weather with only blankets and light coats for warmth but managed weak smiles.

A pile of twisted seats and luggage was visible near the rear cargo door. The forward entrance was open and two more survivors stood in the doorway. One, an attractive middle-aged woman and the other a lean, middle-aged man wearing a worn cap, greeted them. Both looked tired from their ordeal.

Thompson and Bril raised the visors of their helmets and unhooked the chin straps so they could hear better before entering. They were shocked by the conditions. Even though the exterior damage was obvious, they innocently expected a more serene setting inside. Most of the seats had been removed and the floor space was occupied by the rest of the survivors. Two of the injured lay on litters in the rear of the cabin and another two on litters in front. The few seats were occupied and the rest of the individuals were standing or sitting where they could. The smell of dried blood and sweat hung in the air.

The two adults from outside followed them to the wreckage. They remained near the door so they could hear what was going on. A look of concern etched on their faces as if they thought they might be left behind.

Steiner and an auburn-haired woman were kneeling over one of the litters in back. Bril and Thompson made eye contact, signaling Steiner to join them. He hurriedly maneuvered between the survivors, taking a deep breath before explaining the plan.

The unconscious first officer and a woman with a dislocated hip would be carried first to free more room near the door. The man with the puncture wound would go next. The four young girls and the dazed older woman would follow. The overweight man would go ahead of the remaining survivors, who would in turn be added one at a time, depending on the weight the helicopter could still carry.

"Time is critical," Thompson explained. "The weather is closing fast."

"We're ready." Steiner pointed to where the first officer lay. "Bril? You take the front and Bidwell will take the rear. Once the litter is clear of the doorway, Mister Thompson and Captain Sanders can grab a corner. Myself, Kwapich, and Simms will follow you to the helicopter with the second litter."

Each of them nodded in understanding.

"We need to be careful," Steiner added. "Watch your step and don't let go of the litter. If you need to stop and rest, say so immediately. These people have severe injuries. More trauma could be fatal."

Steiner let his explanation sink in before continuing. "Any questions? Good, let's go."

The space was tight, but with only one man on each end, they quickly got the front of the litter through the hatch. Bril stepped out first, tripping backward slightly before regaining his footing.

"Easy now! Slow and easy until you get turned around." Steiner's stern voice cut the cold air, making Bril slow his movements.

Thompson quickly positioned himself in front, joining Bril so they faced the direction of travel. Several careful steps later, Bidwell was clear of the fuselage with his end. They stopped so Sanders could help carry a corner and then proceeded toward the helicopter at a moderate pace over the rough ground.

Steiner and Simms lifted the second patient once the first was through the door. Kwapich waited outside and helped ease the weight past the opening before changing position.

The litter bumped against the doorframe as Steiner stepped and twisted sideways. The weight wasn't a factor as much as the awkward position. He easily supported the load and quickly regained his balance.

A low moan escaped from the woman. Even with the strong medication, she felt a stab of pain in her hip. Clenching her teeth, she breathed in sharply from the shock, exhaling slowly.

"Sorry about the nudge. You're clear of the plane now." A quick apology was all Steiner could offer. He didn't want to tell her the helicopter ride would be worse.

"We'll be back in a minute," Steiner yelled over the wind at the group nearby. Their expression immediately changed to anticipation.

Donna Regan shivered with concern. On the verge of hysteria following the crash, she had managed to calm down after reassurances from Susan. Once the second helicopter arrived, her fears returned. *What if there wasn't enough room for them all?* She didn't think she could handle a night on the mountain under these terrible conditions.

On the positive side, the four young girls seemed calm. Two of them were in tears during the emergency and the others held hands across the aisle, but all quickly recovered their emotions following the crash. Only Lisa seemed unfazed by the event.

Since then, they had been sticking close together and helping with whatever was asked. Watching over the two dogs was a good distraction. As long as they held their emotions and didn't panic, Donna thought she could do the same.

Connor began wondering what was taking so long when he saw movement through the opening in the rocks. He needed desperately to get out of the helicopter and relax his aching muscles but knew he had to hang on for a few more minutes.

A tight, burning sensation was building from the exertion on his legs and his back felt as if the muscles had been pummeled with a baseball bat. He could only grit his teeth in response.

Thompson and the others squinted against the swirling downwash as they approached. They carried the litter to the right side, where there was more room between the cargo door and rock wall. Stopping short, Bril used one hand to pull the door open before setting the litter on the metal floor. He carefully repositioned inside and helped the others slide the patient further through the doorway.

A quick assessment of the interior made him realize the litter would occupy a large portion of the floor. The patients would have to be positioned on the side, parallel to the doors. The uninjured passengers could then be seated in the middle against the rear bulkhead.

Connor felt a shift in weight but couldn't risk turning to look. He could hear a voice without being able to distinguish the words. There was movement behind his right shoulder and a slight change in the attitude of the helicopter.

He compensated with cyclic control to adjust for the weight. Each increase caused a change in the center of gravity, altering the stability of the helicopter. He anticipated the movements to minimize the corrections, taxing his overburdened muscles. Keeping the helicopter balanced without losing control was becoming more and more of a challenge.

"Push the litter all the way across the floor," Bril yelled over the engine. Thompson hurried around the front of the helicopter to the opposite door, helping align the patient in the corner.

Connor watched a second litter emerge through the gap in front of the helicopter. They stopped, waiting on the others, then moved in position on the same side. As the first group left, Thompson looked back at Connor and pointed to his ear, indicating he intended to call on the radio. A moment later he turned and disappeared.

Bril remained by the helicopter to assist the second group. He removed both rear facing crew seats, allowing more space toward the front where they could slide the patient in a perpendicular position across the floor.

"I figure a third litter can be placed beside this one." Bril had to shout near Steiner's ear. "We'll place the last one inside the right door."

Steiner nodded in agreement. The space was tight, but the configuration was the only way there would be enough room for the other passengers. The two litters in the middle would have to be pushed forward against the console.

"Help me move this one in position. Be careful, she has an injured hip. Turn the litter so her head is facing the right side. I don't want anyone bumping into her while getting into the helicopter."

They worked quickly. The petite woman didn't utter a sound except to take in a sharp breath. Her eyes were partially shut as if expecting a flash of pain any moment. Once the litter was in place, she managed a weak reply. Her voice was too slurred with medication to be understood, but her gratitude was evident.

Kwapich and Simms were impressed with the crew's professionalism. They were careful to keep their feet away from the skids. "Nice job," Kwapich shouted. "We're ready for a second load."

"Eight-three-zero? Gil, can you hear me?" Thompson's voice squawked through the emergency frequency.

"Go ahead." *Are you kidding me? I'm only fifty feet away. Of course I can hear you.* He caught himself before making a sarcastic reply. The stress was getting to him.

"I'll spell you on the controls once we get the next two loaded," Thompson continued. "We need six men to move the heavy guy. How you holding up?"

Barely, he wanted to say but instead lied. "I can manage." The strain in his voice told a different story.

Thompson didn't like the weak response. *Connor must be struggling.* He thought about going back to the helicopter before deciding to continue. The others needed help with the overweight man. Without assistance they would take more time. Time they didn't have.

"We're going as fast as we can, Gil. A few more minutes. How much more weight can you carry?"

"Standby."

He had watched the torque gauge increase during the loading but waited until Steiner and his group were clear before making a determination. By the indication on the gauge, he estimated they could carry another six or seven survivors, depending on the weight. Probably six with the heavy man included. Plus there was Thompson, Bril, Steiner, and himself. Almost half their fuel was gone. They would have just enough to make the trip home.

"Twelve hundred pounds, I think. Probably six or seven additional passengers. After the next litter give me an estimated weight on who's left."

"Roger, will do."

"No extra baggage. Everything stays except what's absolutely necessary."

"Understand, Gil. The next one is on the way."

CHAPTER THIRTY-FIVE

Thompson placed the hand-held radio back in his vest while Sanders and Bidwell tried moving the obese man closer to the plane's rear cargo door. He was lying on a thin but sturdy backboard, barely able to fit on the litter.

Positioning him on the board was a struggle in the narrow aisle. They labored to roll his body so the board could be slid underneath. Lifting the man's large mass onto the litter was even harder. All the while he mumbled insults and threatened legal action in slurred, broken sentences. Somehow, in spite of the morphine, he could still focus his anger.

Reassurances fell on deaf ears. The man's personality needed something to complain about. Sanders finally had enough. Listening to the man insult the other survivors and now the men trying to help him was the last straw.

"Shut your mouth and listen. I know you're upset. Cussing at us isn't making this any easier. You can remain quiet and allow us to move you, or you'll be staying here until another helicopter arrives. That means you won't be leaving and will remain on this mountain for another day or two. You can moan all you want, but the next time you bad-mouth one of us, I'm putting you at the bottom of the list. You got that?"

The man stared back in wide-eyed disbelief, but he nodded his head in understanding. He wasn't accustomed to being lectured to and was unsure how to respond. One thing was clear, he would do whatever was necessary to see the pilot fired and the company penalized. He was an important man. No one got away with treating him like this.

Marla, his pampered and submissive wife, had remained near his side following the crash. She now displayed an open-mouthed expression of disbelief. A slight smile of gratitude briefly framed the corners of her mouth before being suppressed by a look of feigned concern. *Someone finally had the nerve to tell him what an ass he is.* With him or without him, she wanted on the helicopter.

Moving the heavy man was easier with Thompson helping. They managed to slide the litter across the aisle a few inches at a time.

Marla moved outside, out of the way. Her husband grunted and moaned loudly several times, more out of spite toward the captain than feelings of pain. His silence was a welcome change.

Susan could only watch the spectacle. There was no room in the confined space for another body. As it was, the men could hardly move without bumping into the severely injured man with the puncture wound. He rested in a semi-conscious state against the rear bulkhead. An intravenous bag hung from the ceiling, the tubing attached to his arm left dangling in the open. The obnoxious man almost snagged the line with his foot before Bidwell moved it out of the way.

Susan had no misgivings about remaining at the crash site, fully aware some of the passengers couldn't leave on the first load. If necessary, she could endure a night or two on the mountain. The weather was a minor issue. She was a lifelong Alaskan and knew how to make do in difficult situations.

With Bidwell pushing and Thompson and Sanders pulling, they eventually managed to maneuver the obese man out of the way. They could now move the other injured man without tripping over each other.

Steiner arrived a moment later with Kwapich and Simms. They entered the fuselage while Steiner stopped and pulled out his survival radio. He turned his back to the wind, ready to transmit when Thompson yelled at him from the doorway.

"I just talked with Connor. He figures seven more passengers. And we need to be careful loading them, especially the big guy, so we can keep the helicopter in balance. Too much weight on one side, and he could lose control."

"Okay." Steiner looked back at the survivors standing around the wreckage. "Only seven more?"

Thompson shared his concern. "That's what he figured. Depends on how much they weigh."

"We better get moving then. The guy with the puncture wound goes next. I'll talk to Connor after we get him loaded. The girls and the older lady will follow, then the fourth and last litter with the heavy man. He has to be set directly inside the door."

Steiner moved inside out of the wind with Thompson when Sanders pulled them aside. "There might be a problem with a couple of the women." The expression on his face showed he was serious.

"What do you mean?"

"Marla, the large man's wife, and the girls' coach are pretty adamant about leaving on the helicopter. The coach, in particular, looks a little panicky."

"Christ!" Steiner thought for a second. "You have to talk to them. Explain there isn't enough room."

"And if they get into the helicopter, there'll be too much weight. It could crash," Thompson emphasized.

Sanders understood. He turned his eyes to Steiner. "Just be prepared with a sedative if you have to."

The group inside the fuselage waited for instructions. They understood the urgency as Thompson briefed them on the intended loading procedure. Bril left, intent on briefing the others already outside.

Steiner designated the litter teams. Thompson, Bidwell, Kwapich, and himself would carry the severely injured man. Once he was loaded, they would hurry back and help with the heavier patient.

Sanders tried to appear optimistic. He gathered the girls and women behind the rocks, out of the wind, including Susan and Marla. Each of them was disheveled and held a blanket around their shoulders for warmth. A few hours ago they would have been upset at their appearance. No one gave a second thought now.

Bril hurried over from the wreckage and joined them. His easy demeanor had faded as the weather worsened. He wasn't concerned about himself as much as the survivors, knowing time was against them. The worried look on the young girls' faces made him more determined. Even the dog looked distraught, resting between one of the girl's legs.

Bril tried appearing optimistic while explaining the situation. "This is what we're going to do. As soon as the next litter is loaded, I'll take five to the helicopter."

Steiner pointed at the girls and older woman, omitting Donna, Susan, and Marla, who would remain behind. They appeared receptive, except for Donna and the traumatized, older woman who held a blank stare. She was still lethargic and in shock from her close friend's death.

Donna became emotional when he explained the limited seating. She started arguing on her necessity to remain with the girls. One of the girls, who seemed unflustered by the situation, volunteered to stay behind. The other three became visibly upset.

Bril was taken off guard. Unsure of what to do, he let Susan and Sanders talk with them. After some reassurances, they calmed down and relented. Donna remained reluctant, but she didn't have a choice. She sat and stared at the ground, shaking and holding back tears.

Marla, on the other hand, was surprisingly rational. She accepted the decision without comment. Perhaps she decided time away from her husband might be a nice change, even in these conditions.

Susan was different from the other women. She didn't need convincing. In fact, she reiterated her willingness to stay behind. He admired her spunk.

"All right, it's settled." Bril nodded a thank you to Susan and Sanders.

The girls were uncertain of their own weight and the older woman was in no condition to speak, so Bril made an educated guess. He'd pass the information to Connor.

"A couple of other things," Brill added. "We'll be approaching the helicopter from the front, walking under the rotor blades. Don't be afraid, they're well above your head, but the downwash can tear the blankets from your shoulders. Before we go, I need each of you to fold your blanket tight against your chest. Once you're inside the helicopter and the doors are closed, you can open them back up. Okay?"

He looked at each of the girls as they nodded in reply. Someone would have to help the traumatized woman. She was unresponsive.

"The helicopter's engine will be very loud. Try to ignore the noise. You'll get used to it. Keep holding your blankets and don't try covering your ears."

They waited until the men carrying the litter were almost to the helicopter. Sanders took the older woman by the hand while the girls trailed behind Bril. Their coach became teary-eyed right away and started sniffling. Whether her emotion was out of concern for the girls or herself, no one was sure. They took a last look at the wreckage before hurrying away.

Marla and Susan waited until the girls were out of sight before escorting Donna inside the wreckage. They guided her into one of the seats, talking as if everything was normal so she wouldn't focus on the helicopter.

The dog that had stayed close to the girls joined them, seemingly content to remain with the women for the time being. The high-pitched sound of the turbine engine scared him. Lisa's command to stay and the loud noise from the direction she departed was all the coaxing he needed. The older malamute lay in the cargo compartment, guarding her owner's body.

Marla excused herself for a moment, retrieved an item from an overhead bin, and then knelt by her husband. With her back turned, blocking their view, no one noticed her prick his finger with a small lancet. He flinched, muttered something incoherent, and lapsed back into glaring at the ceiling. She spoke to him softly so the other couldn't hear.

Connor's pain was becoming intense. His thighs were cramping from over exertion, causing his back muscles to tighten in response. A small spasm flared in the already bruised tissue, sending a grimace of agony through his gut. Sweat beaded on his forehead, trickling down into his eyes and nose. More perspiration pooled underneath his arms and along his back. His clothing was soaked, but the irritation helped take his mind off the pain, at least temporarily.

The distraction only lasted until the next gust of wind. Moving the controls in quick response became more difficult. He thought his muscles would give out any second. They felt like iron blocks moving under water. His reflexes were sluggish, making him over-compensate and nearly lose control.

Where the hell are they? Please, let me hang on another minute. Connor grimaced in pain and couldn't even laugh at the irony, for less than an hour ago, he tried to kill himself.

The throbbing was becoming unbearable when he noticed movement in front of the helicopter. Steiner was holding a litter from the front. Kwapich and Bidwell were positioned on the sides and Thompson at the back. They moved quickly, concentrating on the uneven ground.

Thompson stole a glance through the Plexiglas window. He was stunned by Connor's appearance. His face was red and clammy from exertion, yet he somehow maintained a look of pained determination.

Sweat beaded above his eyes and drops were streaking along his nose and temples. Exhaustion was only a matter of time. Thompson realized there wasn't much time before he was completely spent.

Positioning the patient inside the helicopter was a careful process. Steiner set his end on the metal floor and crouched in the door. He moved slowly. The others pushed as he guided the litter behind the cockpit, next to the woman with the injured hip. Barely enough room remained in the back for the uninjured survivors and a narrow space for the heavy man beside the door.

An IV bag between the man's legs was hung from the ceiling. The man had been in and out of consciousness since the crash, but his eyes fluttered for a moment before closing again. A neck brace supported his head, and a blanket covered his torso with the sides tucked tightly underneath.

Steiner leaned over and spoke into his ear, unsure if he comprehended what he said or could even hear above the sound of the engine. "You're safe. We'll be at the hospital before long." He then slid across the floor and checked the other two patients. There was no change.

When Steiner stepped down from the helicopter, Thompson motioned him closer. Concern was obvious on his face. "I need to relieve Connor. He's in bad shape. I don't think he can hang on for the next load. Can you carry the last litter without me?"

Quickly glancing at the cockpit and then back at Thompson, Steiner relented. "Yeah, I think so. We'll hurry as fast as we can."

Steiner and the other two men hurried away from the helicopter. A moment later, Thompson met the girls and older woman escorted by Sanders and Bril. He helped them climb inside one at a time, having them sit on the floor where they wouldn't bump the three litter patients. He slid the cargo door closed. When he turned, Bril and Sanders were gone, hurrying after the others.

Lisa stared at Connor in the cockpit as if she needed something, but the space between them was blocked. For the first time, she seemed unsure of the situation. She sat on the floor, barely able to move, thinking of what to do. The other girls ignored her, overwhelmed and shocked at the injured lying close by.

The wind blew with enough force Thompson strained to pull the cockpit door open. The door slammed harder than intended as he positioned himself in the pilot's seat. In the few seconds required to fasten the shoulder harness, he noticed Connor grimace in pain. Sweat dripped noticeably from his brow, yet he never lost focus, intent on holding the helicopter's delicate balance.

He keyed the microphone so Connor could hear him through the intercom. His feet and hands were already in place. "I've got the controls."

There was no hesitation in Connor's voice, but his muscles were slow to respond. He forced himself to let go. "You've got the controls."

Free of the physical exertion, Connor's body sagged noticeably in the seat. His legs shook from fatigue and the taut muscles in his back left him slightly hunched forward. Using his arms against the frame of the seat, he pushed his torso tight into the mesh backing, stretching his spine an inch at a time until the pain gradually subsided.

With slow movements, he massaged his locked knees and extended each leg carefully over the pedals. Finished, he let his head rest back against the seat and closed his eyes for a moment. He was in no condition to continue. Thompson would have to fly the helicopter on his own.

CHAPTER THIRTY-SIX

An overwhelming feeling of exhaustion and agony engulfed Connor. He couldn't remember a time when the pain was ever this intense. Only once, when he was much younger, was the similarity even close. During his two tours in Vietnam, his body in prime condition, physical injuries and pain weren't an issue. Minor wounds were easily suppressed by the heightened anxiety of battle.

As his thoughts drifted to a different era, he barely noticed the helicopter's subtle motion. Thompson was doing a better job of compensating for the wind than he had done.

A few moments of rest was all Connor wanted, and then he could give up his seat to someone else. In his present state, the way he felt, there was no way he would be much use in the cockpit. Remaining on the mountain would provide more time for carrying out his plan.

He stared straight ahead without seeing, letting his mind drift to another time, many years before. The memory took away the physical agony for a moment, substituting a different pain he was all too familiar with.

The day began like many others in Vietnam. He rose early after a fitful sleep and forced a few bites of food with several cups of coffee. The other members of his crew were late risers, so he preflighted the helicopter on his own. He then checked the latest intelligence report, the mission board for changes, and finally the weather forecast. Nothing significant was projected. The flight was a routine supply mission, except routine was rarely the norm in combat.

The air was heavy with the smell of dense vegetation. The crew was alert as they headed out over the jungle. By mid-morning, the heat and humidity were already causing them to perspire. They didn't say much. Their thoughts were on staying alive.

Nine months into his first tour, Connor was already considered an experienced veteran. He was on the controls and working the radios, occasionally pointing out landmarks to a new copilot who tried processing the influx of rapid information. The fresh-eyed kid, only a year younger than himself, monitored the instruments and attempted to follow their course on a rumpled map unfolded in his lap.

Water cans, cases of C-rations, ammunition and boxes of fresh oranges sat stacked in the rear, secured by a cargo net to the floor. The crew chief and gunner sat by the open doors behind their machine guns, watching the terrain. Small arms fire was always a possibility, but no threat was anticipated.

The mission progressed easily enough. They flew high above the jungle and encountered no surprises on the first leg. Once the supplies were unloaded, they continued with an orientation of other firebases in the area, avoiding locations of known enemy activity. Connor let the new pilot fly on the return.

A flash of light reflecting off a piece of metal on a nearby hill was the first indication of trouble. Connor immediately took the controls and banked the helicopter, trying to pinpoint the position. The enemy could be moving troops into the area for an assault. If so, he could radio artillery for a quick fire mission. As he passed overhead, several figures were seen along the edge of the tree line.

High-caliber tracer rounds were the second indication of trouble. They rose skyward from a partially concealed anti-aircraft gun, flickering red through the air like sparks from a bonfire. Connor had flown into a trap. A series of rounds hit the fuselage, tearing through the thin aluminum skin and engine housing.

A sudden and instinctive dive away from the hill saved them, initially. The maneuver cleared the helicopter from the line of fire, but the damage was done. The engine compressor disintegrated, flinging shards of metal and severing the drive shaft. They were going down without power.

"Mayday, mayday, mayday!" Connor's voice was higher than normal. "UH-1 helicopter five-five-two, 129th Assault Battalion, taking enemy fire. Going down ten miles southwest of Firebase Zebra. Four on board."

The copilot sat riveted in his seat, the engine alarm blaring, waiting for instructions. Connor's voice prompted him out of his trance. "Shut off fuel and electrical power, now!"

"Roger," the copilot muttered. His hand reached across the console.

The words were barely out of his mouth before Connor flared the helicopter, slowing their forward momentum above the jungle canopy. They hung for a moment over the trees, and he pulled in an armful of power, trying to cushion the fall.

The thick foliage was too high. The helicopter hit, bouncing and jerking from side to side as the rotor blades sliced through the branches, splintering against the thicker limbs. The tail boom tore loose from the fuselage and the helicopter fell back and sideways, sliding between two mangrove trees before hitting the ground. The broad trunks and dense underbrush helped slow the momentum but only slightly.

The copilot had shut off the fuel and electrical switches a split second before they hit. There was no immediate fire, but with one of the fuel tanks ruptured, the threat was imminent. More dangerous was the possibility of being captured. The enemy was nearby and would soon be hunting them.

Connor's shoulder throbbed from slamming hard against the door and his thighs ached where the control stick had been wrenched back and forth during the fall. His adrenaline eased some of the pain, encouraging him to look after his crew.

"Anyone hurt? If not, grab what you can and get the hell out of here!"

The left door gunner was dead. His neck was broken. The copilot, a kid named Gillant, had a twisted knee and could barely walk. Both of them were on the side where the helicopter took the brunt of impact. Hicks was the least injured and first out of the wreckage.

Connor and Hicks pulled Gillant through the broken windshield. The path was faster and easier than trying to lift him through the door. Once he was safely clear, they assessed their situation.

In their mesh survival vests, they each carried a thirty-eight caliber pistol and emergency handheld radio. Additional pockets held flares, a signaling mirror, flashlight, extra ammo, bags of hard candy, and a laminated map.

The crew chief also had an M1 carbine and bandoleer of extra magazines he kept tucked behind his seat. He always flew with the weapon for just such an emergency.

"What about Chauncey, sir?" Hicks didn't want to leave his dead friend.

Connor understood his concern, but they were out of options. "We can't take him. He's gone. We have to get away from here as fast as we can. The VC are already looking for us."

"They'll mutilate his body, sir. You know they will."

"No, they won't. I'm burning the helicopter. Maybe we'll get lucky and the bastards will think we all died in the crash."

Hicks appeared stunned for a moment and then nodded his head in agreement. A cremation was the best they could do.

A flight helmet was quickly filled with fuel and splashed inside the wreckage. Connor's Zippo did the rest. In seconds, the interior was ablaze and spreading throughout the wreckage. The remaining fuel and magnesium parts ensured there would be nothing left in a matter of minutes.

Leaving no obvious signs of their presence, they moved deeper into the jungle. Connor and Hicks supported Gillant from the sides while he placed his arms around their shoulders, allowing him to use his good leg.

They headed toward the opposite side of the valley, away from the enemy. Their route worked well for a half mile until the terrain slowed them down. They knew they needed to get in position for a rescue as quickly as possible. The chance of capture increased dramatically after the first day. A realistic hope of survival depended on increasing the distance between themselves and the enemy. Being captured was not a consideration. The Viet Cong were notorious for their treatment of prisoners.

When they stopped to catch their breath, Connor activated his survival radio. He spoke softly so his voice wouldn't carry.

A returning flight of F-105 fighter-bombers picked up the first mayday call and diverted in their direction. They easily spotted the smoke from the burning helicopter, and they were flying cover over the valley when Connor's second call came through. Rescuing downed airmen was a priority in Vietnam. Connor and his crew were no exception.

Within fifteen minutes, other Air Force jets were on station, keeping the enemy occupied with repeated strafing runs. A rescue helicopter had been notified and was on the way. Connor knew they needed to get to higher ground. He informed the fighters of their intention so they could cover the route, talking on the radio every few minutes.

Working through the thick jungle was a struggle with the injured copilot. They traveled as fast as they could, stopping only enough to catch their breath and listen for the sound of pursuers. From what they could determine, the enemy was busy hiding from the circling aircraft.

Connor kept the fighters aware of their position and direction of travel. A small clearing located by one of the planes became their intended pickup point. The site was over a mile away but the closest large enough for extraction. Hopefully, the enemy soldiers were some-where else. Getting there wasn't going to be easy.

After two hours of hard walking and climbing through the under-growth, they were within a hundred yards of the landing zone. The last rays of sunlight were just settling below the horizon as they neared the top of a curved knoll. Only when they heard the beat of the helicopter in the distance, did they think they were home free. A group of enemy soldiers had a different idea.

A squad of soldiers was camped below the ridge when Connor and his crew stumbled into them. The surprise was obvious on both sides, but the enemy was slower to respond. They were relaxing under the shaded canopy, safely hidden from the fighter jets, when Connor and his crew unexpectedly appeared. The VC's weapons were lying on the ground or leaning against trees. Having their weapons out of reach was a disadvantage, one they paid for with their lives.

Hicks reacted first. Releasing his hold on the copilot and bringing his carbine to his shoulder in a burst of fire, he cut down half of them. Con-nor raised his revolver and got off a couple shots before grabbing Gillant in a hasty retreat. Half carrying the copilot with Hicks close behind, each of them began firing on the run as the remaining enemy followed.

The confusion allowed only a brief head start. The firing had alerted other enemy soldiers dispersed around the ridge. Troops hurried over the hill in a hasty attempt to surround the airmen's escape route, while others followed their trail and were shooting blindly through the underbrush. Several times an enemy soldier materialized ahead, only to be gunned down by Hicks or Connor. More than once, the return fire missed them by inches.

One of the enemy soldiers froze in disbelief when they almost ran him over. Connor fired point blank into his face, only slowing down long enough to grab the soldier's Russian-made assault rifle. He tossed his empty revolver aside.

Still running and talking on the hand-held radio, Connor informed air support of the worsening situation. The enemy was dangerously close and most likely had the landing zone surrounded. They needed immediate suppressive fire.

Recently arrived gunships began blasting the tree line, adjusting their fire a hundred feet ahead of the airmen and along the perimeter of the clearing. Connor and Hicks ran into the open with Gillant between them.

The rescue helicopter was already flaring and touched down hard in front of them. Enemy fire immediately opened up from the edge of the jungle. A flight of ground-attack jets rolled in on a strafing run, but before they could release their ordnance, Gillant was hit and went down.

Connor hesitated, looking at the helicopter then back at the tree line. He lifted the copilot over his shoulder and continued running, yelling at Hicks who was kneeling and firing at the enemy.

With the gunners in the helicopter spraying fire over their heads, Connor tossed Gillant on the floor. Hicks, who had been at his side a moment before, was missing. Connor turned and saw him twenty feet away, crawling toward them.

Increasing fire blazed from the edge of the jungle. The helicopter crew screamed at him to get in. Connor ignored them and ran back to his crew chief. Both of Hicks' legs were hit, and he was bleeding profusely.

Connor pulled him up and over his shoulder as bullets began peppering the ground. Within seconds they were inside the helicopter and lifting above the dark jungle, the door gunners firing in rapid bursts as more fighter jets rolled in on the ridge.

The battle was over. Gillant was dead. A bullet ended his life only feet from the helicopter. He had been in the country less than a week. A medic worked on Hicks' mangled limbs in a spreading pool of blood. He was hemorrhaging profusely, seemingly unaware of the damage and pain. There was a look of resignation on his face. Connor turned away and closed his eyes. He didn't want to see him die, too.

The sound of the engine lulled his eyes closed. He was exhausted, physically and mentally. The warm jungle air made him sleepy. After awhile he opened his eyes and stared out the open door, watching the sun disappear below the horizon.

A week after the death of Hicks and Gillant, Connor was flying again. The scrapes and bruises from the crash and escape through the jungle had mostly healed. His only other injury was a flesh wound from an enemy bullet creasing his ribs. At the time he never even knew he was hit.

CHAPTER THIRTY-SEVEN

Thompson's voice jarred Connor back to the present.

"The four girls and the woman are loaded. Bril estimates their combined weight at four hundred and fifty pounds. The man on the last litter is three-forty, according to his wife. She isn't positive, but it's the weight he told her a month ago. Steiner doubts the accuracy though. He estimates the weight around four hundred with the litter and backboard. Steiner's weight is two-ten and Bril weighs one-seventy. You think we can carry them all?"

Connor diverted his attention to the torque gauge. The needle fluctuated with control inputs as the helicopter jostled with the varying air currents. The weight would be close, maybe too close. Under different circumstances he might have tried carrying them all but not here. Not now.

During Vietnam he faced a similar challenge. The engine was at maximum power with a full load of troops. The helicopter could only get light on the skids and was unable to hover. With a much larger enemy force approaching, the soldiers couldn't wait. Connor forced the engine past maximum, sliding the helicopter over the rain slick grass until building enough airspeed to lift off. Luckily, the surface was flat and long without obstructions.

The present situation was different. There were no other options. The altitude was too high and the terrain too uneven. If the helicopter didn't have enough power for a stabilized hover, they would be forced to lighten the load.

"No. We can't carry him. Even at three-forty we'll be overloaded. Two hundred pounds more is all we can take. The engine can't handle any more weight."

"What if Bril remains behind? He said he'd volunteer if we need the weight." Thompson didn't relish leaving him behind, but the option was there.

Connor knew time was of the essence. "Okay. Get on the radio and tell them to bring the last litter. The man's wife better be accurate. If he's over her estimate, we're still screwed."

Thompson trusted Connor's judgment. Still, he worried about excessive weight causing a loss of power as much as the clouds closing in around them. He radioed Steiner to hurry.

The expanse over the glacier was already obscured, masking the creviced ice field and canyon walls. Low clouds were already hugging the ridge behind the wreckage, limiting visibility to less than a hundred yards. There was only twenty feet of clearance above the spinning rotors, which worked against them by pulling the cloud vapor closer. They barely had visual references for takeoff.

Connor saw the visibility decreasing and sensed Thompson's concern. The anxiety was no different than his. He wanted to take the controls himself but knew his physical condition would make the situation worse. His legs were still shaking and the muscles in his lower back pulsated with burning pain.

A flash of agony tore at his side as he tried pulling his legs back against the seat. The spasm made him grunt against the door. He bent forward, unable to push himself upright without aggravating the muscles further.

"Christ, you okay, Gil?" Thompson saw his body lurch forward in obvious discomfort.

Placing his hands behind him and pushing forcefully against the tension in his back, he managed to ease the pain. His voice tried hiding a feeling of helplessness.

"Are you comfortable flying us off of here? I can't manipulate the controls. My back and legs are failing me."

There was a moment of hesitation before Thompson responded. His voice sounded confident, in spite of his concerns. "Yeah. I think so. I'll get us home."

The answer made Connor's decision easier. "Watch the power on takeoff. Lift straight up until you're clear of the boulders. If you need to, pull an extra inch of torque above redline. The helicopter will handle the load. Keep your nose in the wind and slide sideways until you can accelerate off the pinnacle."

"Roger, I understand." Thompson didn't comprehend he would be flying alone.

Connor's expression didn't waver. "After you clear the ridge, fly direct toward our last waypoint. From there, track the GPS route we programmed on the way in. You'll be in the clouds over the glacier. Stay on instruments and don't descend until you're clear of the mountains."

"Okay, Gil. Everything is set. I'm ready."

There was no doubt in Connor's mind he was. The torch had been passed months ago, but Connor hadn't realized the fact until now. The same confidence and passion that once framed his own personality was now a part of Thompson's.

In the doorway of the plane wreckage, the last litter was being maneuvered into position. The men grunted as they struggled with the weight. Three of them lifted from outside while the other three lifted and stepped one at a time through the opening. Bidwell was in front and Steiner was at the back. Kwapich and Simms were on one side, Bril and Sanders, using his good arm, were on the other. They moved at a slow pace, laboring with the heavy load over the rough ground.

The wind seemed colder and stronger than before. A chill bit at their exposed necks, sending shivers through their light clothing. The skin on their hands and faces grew numb, but they ignored the sensation and pushed on.

Seconds later, a strong gust hit them with enough force Sanders almost lost his balance. He estimated the wind was near forty knots. He checked the sky and could tell the clouds were lower than before. The ceiling was dropping rapidly. There was barely enough room for the helicopter to depart.

Trying to maneuver the cumbersome litter through the narrow opening of boulders was difficult. The men on the sides were pinched between the stretcher and rocks, forcing them to move in unison only a step at a time. The weight strained their endurance, but they were soon through and beside the helicopter.

"Okay, stop here," Bril shouted a step away from the helicopter door. "No one move until I tell you."

Already briefed on how they would load the patient before leaving the wreckage, Bril explained the plan again, yelling over the engine noise so there would be no misunderstanding.

"Mister Bidwell will take Sergeant Steiner's spot on the other end. Once he's in position, Captain Sanders will let go of the litter and move with Steiner to the opposite side of the helicopter. On my signal they'll step on the skid to balance the weight while we slide the litter in. No one on my side can step on the skid. Is that clear?"

They all nodded and moved as directed. As soon as Steiner and Sanders let go, the remaining men strained with the increased load. Each held over a hundred pounds. They waited anxiously with aching arms, silently hoping their strength didn't fail.

The obese man remained silent. The medication kept him sedated enough for a temporary silence. Still, he appeared upset after being jostled and almost dropped on the trip to the helicopter. His eyes widened in fear under the swirling wind of the rotor blades. His perceived mistreatment was forgotten as the loud whine of the engine pierced his eardrums.

Sanders and Steiner were in position in a matter of seconds. Bril motioned for the end of the litter to be set on the floor. As the weight transferred to the helicopter, Sanders stepped on the left skid, equalizing the center of gravity. Steiner waited until the litter could be pushed further inside before doing the same.

Before the four men could begin sliding the weight across the floor, a shout from the cockpit stopped them. "Stop! The litter's too heavy. We can't carry the patient. Pull him back out."

Connor watched the torque gauge jump to a needle's width below redline. He knew immediately the litter was too heavy. Even without Sanders standing on the skid, the weight limit would be exceeded once the patient was fully inside. Steiner was right. The man had to be over four hundred pounds. Valuable minutes had been wasted carrying him to the helicopter.

As soon as Connor yelled, the four men lifted the litter off the floor. They stood on the side, straining with the load, unsure if they should wait, set the patient down, or take him away, when Connor opened his door and began speaking with Steiner.

The heavy patient didn't comprehend what Connor yelled to the others. He could hardly move but shouted to be put back into the helicopter. His strained voice, garbled by the medication and wind, was ignored.

Another figure appeared by the opening in the rocks. Donna couldn't stand the thought of being left behind and had run from the wreckage in panic. She stopped outside the overhead arc of spinning rotor blades, hesitant about what to do, staring at the men grouped together beside the helicopter.

Before Donna could make a decision, Susan and Marla ran up to her from behind. They tried grabbing her, but she shook free and rushed forward. Her tousled hair slapped at her tear-stained face as she ran for the helicopter.

Thompson saw the running woman and shouted a warning over the intercom. Connor had his head turned and didn't notice her approach.

Sanders and Steiner were blocked from seeing what was going on by the open cockpit door and the men on the opposite side could do nothing to stop her.

Donna was determined. The collision wasn't deliberate, but in her haste she stumbled and brushed against the open cockpit door, knocking Steiner into Connor's seat. Sanders saw her at the last moment, barely able to grab her with one hand. He tripped and fell, pulling both of them to the ground.

Connor recoiled reflexively as Steiner bumped into him. His knee hit the control stick and his foot jarred the left pedal, causing an immediate change in the helicopter's stability.

Thompson responded automatically, but even with his quick reaction, the helicopter yawed and the fuselage rolled right, tilting the blades and swinging the tail dangerously close to the rocks. Just as quickly, the helicopter was stable again. At least as much as it could be, with only the front of the skids on the ground and fierce gusts still rolling over the ridge.

Connor yelled at Steiner, who was closing the door. "Get the litter back to the airplane. Call me on your radio when you get there. And take that crazy woman with you!"

The pain in Connor's back was intense. The added strain of twisting away from Steiner had aggravated the muscles. His temples pulsated with stress. A building migraine only added to the severe discomfort.

Sanders lay on the ground, gritting his teeth. Donna had grabbed his injured limb when they fell. The arm throbbed so much he almost screamed. He slapped her hard with his good hand, twice, and she seemed to come to her senses.

Steiner reached down and pulled Sanders and Donna off the ground, their clothes smudged with dirt. Sanders held his broken arm in obvious agony. Donna touched her scarlet cheek where she had been slapped and apologized meekly between sobs.

"Take her to the airplane, Captain, and make sure you don't let go. We're taking the litter back, too. I'll meet you there."

Time was critical. They had already wasted several minutes moving the heavy patient. Now they would waste several more taking him back.

The four men and Steiner hurried in spite of their fatigue. The comfort of the obnoxious man was the least of their concern. They reached the wreckage on the heels of Sanders. He held Donna securely around the waist. Susan was on the other side, talking to her, and Marla walked behind them in case she tried getting away again.

Donna was placid after Sanders slapped her. The shock made her stop and regain her composure. She was embarrassed and let them lead her away without a struggle. "I'm sorry. I'm so sorry." She started crying again.

The litter smacked the floor of the wreckage harder than anyone intended before being pushed against the side of the aisle. The ordeal of carrying the weight was over.

"What the hell are you doing?" The fat man mumbled for the sixth time since leaving the helicopter. The backboard and metal floor were uncomfortable, only partially offset by the muscle relaxer and pain medicine he'd received to diminish the pain. "Why am I here? I'll sue everyone . . ."

"Harold, Shut up!" Marla's voice was strong. She had finally had enough of his bickering. "You're staying here with me. We'll be fine until the next helicopter arrives. Now be quiet. Please! The medic will give you more medication before he leaves."

Everyone seemed surprised by Marla's outburst, especially Harold. He stared at her with drowsy, bloodshot eyes. No one saw him mouth the word "bitch" and sneer in anger.

"We're back at the wreckage," Steiner announced over the hand-held radio. "Bril's staying here. I'm sending another passenger in his place. We're almost on the way."

CHAPTER THIRTY-EIGHT

Steiner made a quick decision. Another passenger could go, and he had to decide who the person would be. Kwapich, Bidwell, and Simms were too heavy. All three volunteered to stay anyway. Both Susan and Sanders were also adamant about staying, leaving Marla and Donna. Donna was the lightest by twenty pounds, but because of her state of mind, Marla was a better choice.

"No. I'll stay with Harold," Marla decided. "I can give him his medicine and keep him quiet." She had an unwavering tone of voice that surprised them all, for less than an hour before she had argued differently. Her timid personality had gained some resolve.

"Donna? How are you feeling?" Steiner wanted to ensure she was okay before letting her on the helicopter.

Donna sat in a row of seats with Susan beside her, holding her hand. "I'm all right," she sniffled. "I'm so sorry. I just wanted to stay with the girls. They're my responsibility. I panicked."

Steiner wasn't sure of her sincerity, but she had relaxed enough he decided to trust her. "Okay. I'm going to give you something for your nerves. If you stay calm and do what you're told, you can leave on the helicopter."

The radio barked as Connor tried flexing his back again. "We're almost there. I've got the same woman as before. She's calmed down and I've given her a sedative. She'll be all right."

Connor recognized Steiner's voice through the background static. "Roger. In that case we have room for two. One will take my place up front in the cockpit."

A surprised look came over Thompson. "What do you think you're doing?"

"What I have to." Connor pushed painfully against the door, moving gingerly while struggling to step down. "You can do this. You're a damn good pilot. Remember your training. You'll be fine. Stay focused and get them home safe."

Thompson was going to argue further, but stopped. Connor's words were etched with finality. His illness had finally caught up with him. Having his mentor in the cockpit, if only for reassurance, was a luxury he would have to do without. Before he could say anything further, Connor stepped outside, his helmet left behind on the seat.

Donna stayed close to Steiner—afraid he would change his mind and leave her. They hurried as quickly as they could. He carried his remaining medical kit over his shoulder. His other kit and the trauma bags had already been loaded. Sanders and Bril accompanied them from the wreckage.

In less than a minute Steiner stood beside the right cargo door and helped Donna board. She looked frightened and relieved at the same time, trembling as she joined the others on the floor. They all sat tightly together, three against the bulkhead and three others directly in front, resting against their knees.

Three of the girls appeared anxious, wrapped in wool blankets and glancing at the cockpit with concerned expressions after each jostle of wind. Lisa had a more reserved look. She stayed fixated outside, staring at Connor.

The older, traumatized woman was partially slumped over, resting her head on Lisa's shoulder. The woman with the dislocated hip appeared calm. She smiled at no one in particular with a glazed expression. Illiamin remained comatose and the man with the puncture wound hadn't moved since being placed on the floor.

"Hurry," Thompson yelled from the cockpit. His voice was stern. "Get another passenger up front so we can get out of here."

Steiner ran to the front of the helicopter where Connor stood leaning hunched over against a boulder. His bent frame looked exhausted and beaten. Bril and Sanders were standing nearby.

While the men were distracted, Lisa saw an opportunity to get out of the helicopter and approach Connor. He was the reason she was here. She knew it the moment she saw him.

Lisa gently nudged the frail woman away from her shoulder and into Mary Lou, sitting on the opposite side. The woman looked at her somberly but didn't say anything.

Mary Lou tried shifting away from the woman. "Lisa, what are you doing?" Her voice was barely heard over the drone of the engine.

Lisa leaned closer. "It's okay. She needs someone to comfort her, is all. I need to get out of the helicopter."

Before Mary Lou could protest further, Lisa turned and crouched beside Illiamin, reaching carefully across him to open the cargo door. The door was heavy, but she managed to pull forcefully until the frame slid back on the rail. In a flash she was outside and running toward the front of the helicopter.

Connor saw her jump down, too surprised to say anything. Steiner and Sanders noticed the questioning look on his face, both turning at the same time to see what he was looking at.

Thompson felt the shift in weight before he saw Lisa moving away from the helicopter. "What now?" He mumbled to himself. *We need to get the hell out of here.*

Steiner caught Lisa as she approached, holding an arm around her shoulders so she couldn't get away. "Where are you going? You need to get back aboard so we can take off." His voice was firm, loud enough to carry over the wind and engine noise, but he controlled his frustration so he wouldn't frighten her.

"I want to stay." Lisa didn't fight his grasp. She stared into his eyes with strong determination, turned and looked intently at Connor.

Steiner was unsure if he should let her go and glanced at Sanders for help. He shrugged and knelt beside her. Bril stood watching the helicopter, unsure of what to do.

"Lisa, there isn't time. You need to get back on the helicopter. Everyone is waiting."

Connor watched the spectacle, uncertain what the young girl intended but was somehow drawn to her. He knelt in front of Lisa, mesmerized by her gaze. "What is it, honey?"

"I want to stay. I can help you."

The men assumed she was speaking in general terms, not specifically about Connor.

Lisa reached for him, leaning forward to touch his cheek. A soothing feeling of warmth immediately spread across Connor's face. Suddenly, his headache was gone. She reached with the other hand, wanting to embrace him, but Steiner held her from moving closer, unsure if she was trying to run away.

Sanders shifted between her and Connor, gently grasping her hand without realizing her intent. "Lisa, it's okay. Please get back into the helicopter. There's no reason to be afraid."

Tears moistened the corners of her eyes. "I'm not afraid. I just want to help."

"Okay, honey. We'll be fine here by ourselves. You go with the other girls. Steiner will take you back now. He'll be on the helicopter with you."

She ignored his comment and looked directly at Connor. "You're going to be all right. Don't give up."

Steiner gently prodded Lisa away. She turned with him, his arm tenderly around her shoulder, knowing he was only doing what he thought was necessary. Steiner sympathized with her, despite her age, wanting to stay himself.

She glanced back at Connor before climbing inside the helicopter and seating herself next to Donna. She hoped her effort was enough.

Connor watched her go, a strange feeling of remorse overcoming him. For the moment the pain in his back was forgotten. Her voice was familiar somehow, a flicker of remembrance or soft whisper of guidance from long ago he couldn't place. *Am I imagining things, or is there a reason she's here?*

"Mister Connor, you okay?" Bril had a concerned expression on his face. "You look like you've seen a ghost."

Connor snapped out of his daze. "What? No, I was just thinking." He stared at the helicopter a moment longer before refocusing on Bril.

Steiner made sure Lisa was seated before joining the others by the rocks. Connor motioned the men closer. Shouting above the noise, his eyes moved from one to the other. "I'm staying. I need someone lighter than me in the cockpit. Anyone volunteer?"

"Captain Sanders is injured, but he wants to stay," Steiner answered.

The captain nodded his head in confirmation. Steiner's expression showed he didn't agree.

There was no time for debate. Connor made the decision for them. "We don't have time to argue. Captain, you're going." Sanders shook his head no before Connor finished speaking.

"Listen to me. I need you up front to help Thompson with the radios. I'm in too bad of shape. I know you want to stay, but with your injury you won't be much help on the ground. Steiner is already going and Bril can help here until another helicopter arrives."

There was a moment of indecision from Sanders. The comment surprised him. *You're in too bad of shape to fly? I'm the one with the broken arm!*

"You're more valuable in the helicopter," Connor stated more forcefully. "You're the only one who can do this."

Sanders thought the statement was an exaggeration to get him aboard, but before he could think of an adequate reply, Steiner guided him toward the helicopter. After a brief thought of struggle, he relented, allowing himself to be helped into the seat and buckled in. A helmet was placed loosely over his head. He felt something behind his back, and as a last gesture he handed over a rolled up jacket left on the seat.

Before there was time to reconsider, the door closed and was latched shut from the outside. Sanders watched Steiner pass the jacket and a small item he hurriedly retrieved from his medical kit to the older pilot. Seconds later, the men dispersed and a much younger voice barked over the intercom.

"You have a floor switch by your right foot so you can talk." Thompson directed his comments at Sanders. "Have you ever been in a helicopter before?"

Sanders shook his head no, as he tried finding the floor switch.

"I need you to keep your hands on your lap and your feet away from the pedals. Watch out your side and keep me advised of any obstructions as we lift off. If I need anything further, I'll let you know. Understand?"

The instruction was direct and to the point. Sanders did as he was told. He found the floor switch and answered. Thompson seemed more at ease in the cockpit than on the ground. *I hope his flying skills are as cool as his demeanor.*

As Thompson talked, Steiner entered the back and pulled the cargo door shut. He rearranged one of the litters into position beside the door, moving his bags out of the way before settling in a corner behind the co-pilot's seat. There was barely enough room to move and monitor the patients. The woman with the injured hip was lying next to him and the remaining litter was positioned beside the opposite door. He could only reach the farthest one by stepping between or leaning across the other passengers. The layout would have to do.

"We're ready in back," Steiner spoke through his helmet microphone while still adjusting the chin strap. He caught himself before saying they were all secure, which was far from the truth.

There were no seat belts for the passengers and no restraints to hold the litters in place. They were violating several regulations. Safety requirements didn't matter at this point. The situation dictated what needed to be done. If they crashed now, their lives were over anyway.

"We're coming up." Thompson glanced at the clock in the corner of the instrument panel. Sixteen minutes had passed since they landed.

Already light on the skids, only a slight increase in power was needed to ascend. Keeping his eyes moving between the torque gauge and outside references, he held the collective control at maximum power, compensating for the changing airflow as they lifted above the ground. Constant pedal corrections kept the helicopter aligned between the rocks.

His feet and hands were quick, responding instantly with corrective inputs. He had the advantage of youth and stamina, but the wind was deceptive and changed velocity in a succession of jabs and heavy punches like a champion boxer. Twice, he almost let the mountain air get the better of him but recovered before allowing the tail to swing too far sideways.

At five feet above the ground, the helicopter stopped. Maximum power wouldn't provide more lift. The fuselage and the tail rotor still hung below the height of the surrounding rocks, caught in a downward flow of air.

Thompson swore silently. He knew pulling in more power could over torque the engine and cause a loss of lift, crashing them onto the ridge. He couldn't land either. The slope prevented a safe touchdown and hovering any longer would only delay the inevitable. He needed more power from the engine and prayed Connor was right.

An inch more was all he needed. He brought the collective up slowly. The torque increased above the red line and held. The engine was strong and didn't hesitate. They were at five feet, then ten, and finally they were clear of the rocks.

As the fuselage rose above the height of the surrounding obstructions, the swirling vortices changed to a more horizontal vector through the rotor blades. The additional lift was sudden, raising the helicopter even further. The change was all he needed.

Thompson reduced power as they entered the clouds a second later, sliding right simultaneously away from the ridge. As the edge of the pinnacle disappeared through the chin bubble, he nosed over and accelerated in a shallow dive, gaining airspeed through the milky nothingness above the valley.

Visibility was non-existent as he tracked a direct course over the glacier. He leveled and kept the helicopter steady, concentrating on the instruments. Their destination was an invisible point in space marked on the GPS screen. Colored indications for heading and distance were the only guide. Without them they would be flying blind in a maze of towering mountains.

Thick accumulations of moisture-laden clouds had already pushed into the valley, obscuring the landscape from above and below. Icing was a definite possibility. The temperature was near freezing, and Thompson turned the pitot heat and de-ice switches on before concentrating his full attention back on the instruments.

Instrument navigation is a delicate procedure. When done correctly, pilots must disregard their own sense of motion and trust the mechanical information shown on the instruments. If Thompson deviated from the course, turned too late or too early, descended too much, or tracked to the wrong point, they would impact the unseen granite pinnacles lurking in the clouds. Turbulence and vertical air currents throwing the helicopter in multiple directions only made the situation more difficult.

Sanders thought the worst when they first entered the clouds. His fears were compounded by sudden, seemingly unintentional helicopter movements. The pilot offered no assurance and remained fixated on the instruments. After everything that had already transpired, he sat in stone-faced silence, convinced he was going to die in a situation he had absolutely no control over. He fully expected to crash at any second and searched the instrument panel for some indication of clarity.

"Are you familiar with this model of GPS?"

The unexpected question caught Sanders by surprise. He glanced at the young pilot, who appeared much more composed and focused than he was. He ignored the question and darted his eyes across the different indicators until recognizing the basic flight instruments all pilots were familiar with. The descent had stopped. They were in level flight.

Still concerned about being in a helicopter in the clouds, below the height of the mountains, Sanders wanted to yell to start climbing. At first he didn't understand what Thompson was doing and then realized he was tracking a course on the GPS. The discovery only partly relieved his anxiety. He preferred flying on instruments thousands of feet above the ground, not within the terrain itself.

"It's the box mounted on the dash."

Sanders located the sage-green electronic device in the bottom of the windshield. The type was different from the one he was used to. "No. The screen and control knobs are different. What do you need?"

Thompson would have to operate the GPS by himself. "Familiarize yourself with the four radios and navigation receivers on the center console. If you have any questions, ask. Don't change anything. I'll let you know when."

The first waypoint approached quickly. Thompson timed the turn short of the position, compensating for the change in direction so they didn't overshoot the desired track. At the same time he selected the second waypoint from the menu screen. The move worked as planned.

With the wind blowing directly off the tail, the helicopter moved rapidly through the thick cloud cover. Thompson maintained the same, precise heading, using the instruments for guidance to match the GPS track. He verified the heading on the note pad, written earlier by Connor, was the same. There was no margin for error.

On course and at a safe altitude above the glacier, Thompson felt more at ease but not enough to relax. Even though his outward demeanor appeared calm, inside he was as worried as anyone. They were far from being out of danger. The weather and terrain were a continuing challenge. Factoring in their reduced fuel, his limited experience, the worn-out airframe, and the stressed engine, he knew there were too many opportunities for something to go wrong.

CHAPTER THIRTY-NINE

Connor leaned in a bent posture against an outcropping of rock, watching while Bril positioned himself in front of the helicopter. The full force of the rotor wash slapped at Bril's face, but he kept his eyes on the tail as the fuselage lifted higher above the ground.

The helicopter rocked and wobbled in a dangerous dance for position in the turbulent air, fighting for every foot of altitude as the gusts tried pushing the tail sideways. The margin of error between obstacles was slim and keeping the tail boom aligned was critical. All Bril could do was signal with his hands, but the gesture provided Thompson with another reference he desperately needed.

Bril squinted against the swirling wind with his arms extended sideways, providing corrections when the tail shifted left or right. He wasn't sure of the effectiveness, since Thompson seemingly compensated for any movement of the helicopter immediately on his own. At least doing something made him feel better.

The concentration on Thompson's face was intense. His gaze flashed between Bril, the ground, and the torque gauge in rapid succession, processing the information in milliseconds of thought and motion. The changing wind was quick and deceptive, but he was faster and more determined. Youth won over strength, this time. There was only a brief moment of hesitation before the helicopter was above the rocks and clear, sliding into the abyss above the glacier.

Bril gave a final wave before turning and approaching Connor. The senior warrant officer was hunched over for support, staring into the clouds where the sound of the helicopter still reverberated through the mountain air. He appeared pale and beaten but managed a smile through the pain, feeling more at ease once the helicopter safely cleared the ridge.

Connor knew Thompson could handle the takeoff. He was a good pilot. There was a deep feeling of satisfaction knowing he played a direct part in refining his skills. A heavy burden slowly lifted from Connor's shoulders. Now he could complete what he originally intended. The rescue only delayed his ultimate goal.

"Damn, sir. You all right? You look terrible."

Silence was the only answer as Connor stared into the distance. He cocked his head slightly to hear.

Bril realized what he was doing and turned to listen as well. The rhythmic sound was barely discernible, then increased in tone briefly before disappearing completely. In a few seconds only the din of the rushing wind reached their ears. The beat of the helicopter was gone.

"Help me sit down, will you?" Connor's voice was steady in spite of the pain. He was relieved the helicopter made it off the mountain and acted as if being hunched forward with his hand pushing against his lower back was perfectly normal.

Bril supported Connor by the arm and slowly let him slide to the ground so his back rested against a mound of rock. "Are you going to be okay, sir?"

"I think so. Just give me a couple minutes." He exhaled noticeably in relief.

"I'm guessing this isn't the first time your back has given you trouble. You still did a great job flying, sir."

"Thanks, Bril." Connor leaned backward, trying to stretch the taut muscles. "Helicopter pilots and bad backs seem to go together. The discomfort only gets worse with age."

"Yes, sir. I've noticed." Bril didn't mention Connor's condition was the worst he'd seen.

"Hand me your hand-held radio, will you? I want to see how Thompson is doing and give Shultz an update if they haven't been talking to each other already."

Bril made sure the dial was on the correct frequency before handing the radio over. Connor hoped the reception was adequate. At least the surrounding rocks shielded the radio from the wind.

"One-one-four, this is Connor. Shultz, you read me, over?"

"Go ahead. I'm receiving you scratchy but readable."

Shultz had become more concerned about the rescue attempt with each passing minute. Not knowing what was transpiring on the mountain made him edgy. He wanted to call several times for an update but held off, knowing Connor was busy enough without unnecessary interruptions. From the change in radio reception, he knew something was different, suddenly realizing the transmission was being sent not from the helicopter but from a portable survival radio.

"Everything okay there? What's the status of the survivors, over?"

"The helicopter departed with Thompson and Steiner a few minutes ago. Ten survivors aboard, including three litter patients. Six other survivors remain behind."

Connor exhaled slowly before continuing. "Bril and I decided to stay with the remaining survivors at the crash site. We gave up our seats on the helicopter. Thompson should be talking to you shortly. He's probably monitoring the conversation now."

Shultz shook his head in irritation. He was the one who allowed Bril to go along on the rescue and now he was stuck on the mountain. He didn't like the outcome one bit. Even more troubling was Connor allowing the younger and less experienced pilot to fly off the mountain with a full load of passengers. Not an easy mission for even the most capable aviator.

Shultz was pissed and wanted to cuss in frustration but held his tongue. Stepping away from responsibility was something Connor didn't do. There had to be a good reason. He could see Ferguson watching him and saw equal concern etched on his face.

Neither of them noticed Hovan hang his head. He already guessed why Connor had stayed behind. His physical condition had to be an issue. He hoped there wasn't some darker reason as well.

Before Shultz could think of a response, Thompson's clearer voice broke over the radio.

"Eight-three-zero monitors you both. I'm nearing the second waypoint at the turn in the valley. I'm in the clouds on instruments. Keep on talking to each other. I'll call after I make the turn."

Damn if the kid didn't sound cool, considering the circumstances. Shultz's pulse quickened at the thought of what he was going through. Flying on instruments in bad weather was demanding for two pilots. Thompson was doing everything himself. At least he was smart enough to mark a route through the valley on the way in. Always plan ahead and give yourself another option, Connor had instructed Shultz years ago. There was no doubt in his mind, Thompson had learned the same lesson.

Once Connor heard Thompson's transmission, he started second-guessing his decision to remain on the ground. With the helicopter in the clouds, he knew his presence would have been an asset even if he couldn't fly himself. He miscalculated the extent of the cloud cover in the lower valley and placed too much responsibility on Thompson. He only hoped the kid was a good as he thought he was.

"Gil? How's the weather up there? You and the others going to be okay?" Shultz knew there was nothing he could do for assistance but hoped for an explanation from Connor on his reason for staying behind.

"We'll be fine for the night. The ridge is engulfed in clouds now and the temperature is dropping. The wreckage will provide enough shelter. Most of us are in good condition, except for myself and one of the remaining passengers. I'm completely worn out. My medical condition finally caught up with me. I wasn't much use in the helicopter. That's why I gave up my seat. Lieutenant Hovan can fill you in on the details."

Ferguson saw Shultz and Hovan exchange a knowing look. They were keeping something from him. Something Hovan had already shared with Shultz. He realized there must have been more to Connor being in the area earlier than a simple training flight and was suspicious but held judgment until they could tell him the truth.

The wind had increased in intensity. The tops of the trees were swaying noticeably against the backdrop of shrouded mountains. Dark clouds were spreading into the lower foothills. Tentacles of vapor hung below the solid mass like strips of clothing, moving and changing shape and clarity with the currents of air.

Shultz watched, glad for the moment he was still on the ground and hopeful Thompson was as good as Connor thought. Those left on the ridge were probably thinking the same thing.

"Okay, Gil. How are you set on food and water?"

Connor was unsure of the answer. The thought hadn't occurred to him until now. He took his finger off the transmit button and looked at Bril for an explanation.

"Enough bottled water and MREs for a day or two. We can melt snow and ration food if we have to. There are enough blankets for the eight of us. Might be a cold night, but we'll manage."

Shultz knew they were in for a miserable night. On the mountain the temperature would be below freezing. Shelter and warmth were critical. If the weather trapped them for longer than a day, the next helicopter might only be needed for collecting bodies.

"We'll have rescue helicopters on the way as soon as the weather breaks, hopefully by tomorrow. We still haven't heard from the second medevac. We'll fly out of here in the other Huey if we have to. You and Bril stay safe."

"You, too. We'll be waiting."

There was nothing else to say. Connor handed the radio back to Bril.

"Leave the radio on awhile longer. I want to know when Thompson and the survivors are safely out of the mountains. I'll rest easier then."

Bril felt the same way and nodded his head in reply. He placed the radio back in his vest with the volume on and antenna extended.

"You need a hand getting up?"

"Yeah, that would be great." Connor extended his arm so Bril could pull him off the ground. He grunted as the back muscles flexed painfully in opposition. Balancing carefully on his feet, he carried the flight jacket Shultz loaned him. The bundle would've been forgotten on the seat if Sanders hadn't found it.

Bril grabbed Connor's arm above the elbow. "We should have put you on one of the stretchers in the back of the helicopter. You're in no shape to be spending a night on this mountain."

"I'll be better once I lie down and relax." He appreciated Bril's concern but was determined to walk on his own. "Let me try to walk to the wreckage."

"You sure, sir? You look a little unstable."

"Yeah, I'm sure, Bril. Thanks." Connor pushed against the damaged tissue in his lower back again. The pressure reduced the stinging muscle spasm but did nothing for his posture. He remained hunched over and bent at the waist, gingerly holding Shultz's jacket in his arm as he started walking carefully toward the wreckage. The small bottle of pills Steiner gave him rattled inside the pocket.

Bril walked beside Connor at an equally slow pace, staying close so he could catch him if he stumbled. "If you don't mind me asking, is there something else wrong with you? I mean besides the usual back problems most helicopter pilots experience."

Connor stopped and looked at Bril before answering. Two survivors were approaching from the wreckage as he hurried an explanation.

"I guess I owe you the truth. I've got cancer. I'm dealing with the symptoms the best I can." His explanation was true enough without being specific. Elaborating on the terminal details was not something he wanted to share.

Bril saw the others approaching and figured Connor didn't want them to hear. Cutting the conversation short was fine with him. He was uncomfortable listening to people's medical problems as much as they did in expressing them. He felt sympathy, but words always seemed hollow and insincere when all he could offer were condolences.

"They give you anything for the pain?" He couldn't think of anything else to say.

Connor was in just as much of a hurry to end the dialogue. "Steiner gave me some pain pills. I'll be fine. One other thing, Bril."

"Sir?"

"As far as anyone else is concerned, I pulled my back out, nothing more. Okay?"

"Yes, sir." He wondered if Connor's cancer was terminal and quickly dismissed the thought. *Would he have been flying if it was?*

CHAPTER FORTY

Thompson turned over the second waypoint at the curve in the valley. There were no breaks in the overcast and visibility was only a few feet as he stayed focused on the flight instruments, keeping the helicopter on course with the GPS track.

"We're picking up some moisture." Sanders' voice was calmer than before. Once he understood what Thompson was doing, he was more comfortable. Sitting in a strange aircraft at the mercy of another pilot was particularly hard for an airline captain. Trusting an unfamiliar person's judgment was never easy. In this case, he didn't have a choice.

Thompson glanced at the windshield where the drizzle peppered the outside glass. Icing was a strong possibility, and he wanted to be free of the clouds as soon as possible. They still had over ten miles to cover before clearing the outer foothills, and he had no intention of descending unless they found a break in the weather.

Only after safely passing the second waypoint and turning on a new bearing to the north did Thompson call Shultz.

"One-one-four, this is eight-three-zero. We're out of the valley and nearing your location. Should be a few miles south of you now, over."

The response was immediate. "Roger that, eight-three-zero. The cloud cover is a solid layer above us. Maybe a thousand feet from the ground. We started picking up some light drizzle a few minutes ago."

"Same here, one-one-four." Thompson had only met Shultz once and felt more comfortable using the aircraft call sign. "No icing yet. Fuel is tight. We're heading straight for Fairbanks. Can you see the foothills?"

Shultz opened his door to look behind the helicopter. His voice was reserved. "The weather doesn't look good. The clouds appear to be hanging near the top of the hills. I can see a higher gap above the canyon where the river cuts through but no breaks in the overcast."

"Roger. We'll continue at our present altitude. Any information on the second medevac?"

"Negative, eight-three-zero. The terrain is blocking reception. No contact with Flight Operations since you departed our location over a half hour ago, either."

Shultz figured the operations sergeant was getting antsy for an update. "When you get a chance, can you contact them?"

"Roger. I'll relay when I can."

"I copy, eight-three-zero. Good luck. We're standing by."

Shultz was concerned about the second Black Hawk arriving before the ceiling dropped and being trapped at the airstrip. They couldn't afford to wait any longer.

"Lieutenant, I think we need to leave in the Huey. If we wait much longer, we'll be stuck here. I'll tell Mildred what we're doing."

Hovan had been looking outside, thinking the same thing. He nodded his head reluctantly. He was concerned about flying the helicopter, but as long as Shultz rode up front with him, he knew he could get them back to base.

"Okay. I'll get the blades untied. You and Ferguson carry Mildred's husband."

Thompson continued on a course northwest away from the mountains, while Sanders kept busy referencing the chart and navigation

319

receivers for a position fix. They were too far from Fairbanks to monitor any of the navigational aids, but by using the coordinates displayed on the GPS, he was able to confirm their approximate location on the chart.

"I show us about a mile south of the foothills. We're still too far out to pick up the navigational beacon at Fairbanks."

After departing the mountain, Thompson was skeptical of the airline pilot riding in the copilot's seat. He was burdened enough without Connor along and thought Sanders would try to either take charge or be useless with his injury. Only after they were safely off the ridge and in the clouds did he realize Sanders' flight experience could be a benefit. The tension became less noticeable once they accepted each other's position.

"Okay, thanks. Glad to have you along, Captain."

"To tell you the truth, I was reluctant to leave." He touched the bandage on his forehead, having forgotten about the injury during the loading and tumble with Donna. His head ached when he touched the injury. He was surprised the bandage was still in place. "Just glad I can help."

The passengers in the back had remained relatively silent since boarding the helicopter. The engine noise drowned out any normal conversation. There were no headsets and Steiner was the only one wearing a helmet. He kept busy shifting position among the patients, checking vital signs and reassuring everyone.

Most of the passengers stared outside or closed their eyes in an attempt to rest. Once they were off the mountain, they assumed everything was all right. They had no way of knowing how dangerous the flight through the valley had been.

"How are things going back there, Sergeant Steiner?"

"No change, sir." He answered Thompson after sitting back on the floor, thankful for the brief interruption. He was as alarmed as Sanders after realizing they were flying blind in the clouds. There was nothing he could do except trust in the young warrant officer's ability.

"I'm concerned about the older patient with the puncture wound. His pulse is weak. The other two seem stable for now. How much longer do you figure until we arrive at the hospital?"

"Thirty, thirty-five minutes. I can't coax any more airspeed out of this old bird, but we've got a tail wind helping us."

"Yes, sir." Steiner rubbed his eyes. The physical exertion and mental stress of moving and caring for the patients was catching up with him. He fought back a yawn.

"When you get a chance, sir, have Flight Operations contact the hospital and give them a heads up. Ambulances and medical personnel will take at least ten minutes to reposition to the helipad. They'll be in for a busy day."

"I'll give them a try now." Thompson switched the selector to the FM radio.

Rays of sunlight began filtering through a thinning layer above them. They were in and out of the clouds for a minute and then, in an instant, were out of them completely. Visibility suddenly increased to twenty miles, with patchy powder-blue sky and a blanket of clouds covering the ground a thousand feet below. Both pilots smiled at the change in weather. Things were looking better.

"Operations, Army eight-three-zero, over?"

After a short break, a strong voice answered with a hint of static in the background. "Army eight-three-zero, this is Medevac Operations. Go ahead, over."

"Roger, Ops. We're inbound with survivors from the Northern Mountain Air flight. Ten passengers total. Two in critical condition and one serious. ETA thirty minutes. Request you advise Fairbanks Memorial, over."

"Roger, roger, eight-three-zero. I copy ten survivors, two critical, one serious." His voice changed to a higher pitch as he repeated the information. "Do you have names of the survivors and medical stats on the injured, over?"

"Standby, Ops. Steiner, you want to talk to them direct?"

"Can do, sir. I'm switching over now."

A separate communication panel was mounted in the rear ceiling. Steiner switched his selector to the appropriate setting and began transmitting direct. He passed each patient's vital signs and a brief explanation of their injury, allowing the medical staff on the ground to prepare for their arrival.

While Steiner continued sending information, Sanders directed Thompson's attention. The lower overcast appeared to open in the distance, dissipating into a scattered layer with pockets of heavier stratus. They should have an easy descent into Fairbanks.

Once the patient information was acknowledged, a different voice called over the frequency. The raspy tone was strained and hurried.

"Army eight-three-zero, this is Evac two-three-nine on Fox Mike. You copy?"

"Sounds like your standby crew is finally on the way," Thompson announced over the intercom to Steiner. "Go ahead, two-three-nine. What's your position?"

"We're approximately five miles southeast of Blair Lakes, approaching the Little Delta River at a thousand feet. I monitored your transmission with Flight Operations. Understand there are still survivors at the crash site. What's the situation, over."

Lou Maxwell looked over at his copilot and then at the thickening clouds lying on the foothills ahead of their flight path. His female counterpart seemed unconcerned with the worsening weather, and he wasn't sure if her demeanor was false bravado or a lack of awareness. With minimal Alaska flying experience of his own, he was having doubts about the mission. Maintenance delays at Fort Wainwright and a lack of information before they departed only added to his frustration.

Amy Lorell was an experienced helicopter pilot. A former warrant officer in the 101st Airborne Division, she joined the National Guard after her active duty commitment. She'd been flying Black Hawks with the Alaska Guard out of Point Barrow for the previous three years, commuting from her home in Fairbanks for monthly drills and any additional flights she could coax out of the detachment commander.

For the last two weeks Lorell had been flying as a copilot with the 95th Air Medical Company at Fort Wainwright. When the unit's regular copilot was hospitalized for an appendectomy, the Alaska Guard was asked if they had a pilot who would volunteer, rather than request another pilot from overseas.

Since Lorell already lived in Fairbanks and was looking for additional flight time, she jumped at the chance. Her wishful thinking had her believe she would be flying as a pilot-in-command, but the regular Army thought differently.

Regulations and the chain-of-command, at least from what she was told, wouldn't allow a National Guard pilot to fly as more than a copilot. Experienced or not, she was delegated to the left seat, frustrated by her less than enthusiastic counterpart on almost every occasion. He was cautious to an extreme. Too cautious, as far as Lorell was concerned.

The voice of the medevac pilot sounded unfamiliar to Thompson, which was no surprise. He had yet to meet all the medevac crews, who were rotating in and out of Alaska at a faster rate than his unit.

"We're well above you, two-three-nine. Descending out of fifty-five hundred. The weather closed in around the crash site when we departed. Clouds were still dropping with high winds and turbulence. Stay low over the river and you should reach one-one-four's position without a problem. Their location is on the east side of the drainage, about four miles past the foothills. They're monitoring this frequency and VHF guard. Two survivors are with them. One has broken legs and the other is uninjured."

Before two-three-nine could answer, Thompson tried Shultz on the same frequency. "Break, break. One-one-four, did you copy two-three-nine, over?"

The prompt reply was loud and clear. "Negative, eight-three-zero. I'm hearing you okay but not receiving two-three-nine. Weather is still deteriorating. How far out is the second medevac, over?"

"About ten minutes." Thompson calculated the Black Hawk's faster airspeed for an ETA.

Shultz's voice had a sense of urgency. "They're cutting it close. The canyon through the hills is open if they stay low over the river. No chance of a further rescue attempt at the crash site. Nothing but solid clouds to the south of us. Looks like we'll be the only passengers going out, over."

"Copy that, one-one-four. Standby." Thompson relayed the information to 239 and passed the coordinates for Shultz's position. The pilot sounded relieved the rescue mission was being cut short.

"Good luck, guys." The comment was directed by Thompson at both aircraft. "Sounds like we'll be trying again tomorrow if the weather breaks. Eight-three-zero clear."

The GPS showed thirty miles from Fairbanks when Flight Operations passed another update. Appropriate agencies had been notified of the situation. An Alaska Air Guard C-130 out of Anchorage was finally en route and would remain over the crash site, as fuel permitted. Two Air Guard rescue helicopters were also scheduled to arrive later in the afternoon. They would attempt a rescue the following day if the weather allowed.

According to the operations sergeant, the local media had also become aware of the rescue and were congregating at Fairbanks Memorial Hospital, awaiting eight-three-zero's arrival. He sounded happy to have deflected the media's attention away from Flight Operations.

There was also a message from the acting battalion commander. Thompson needed to see him after repositioning back to Fort Wainwright. From the implication, the message was more than a request.

CHAPTER FORTY-ONE

Walking the last fifty feet was the worst. The uneven ground caused Connor to stumble and nearly fall. Bril caught him by the arm, unintentionally straining his back further. A gasp of air was the only response, but the increased pain was obvious by his expression.

"Sorry about that, sir. You better let me help you the rest of the way."

Connor pressed a hand heavily over his eyes as he let the intensity subside. He leaned hard into Bril, nodding in acceptance, afraid of sounding weak and emasculated.

The two men from the crash site reached them a moment later. With their unshaven faces, Kwapich and Bidwell looked as if they had been on the mountain for days, but they didn't seem discouraged. Other than the disturbing method of arrival, they would have been content staying in a tent.

"We were getting worried." Both of them look surprised at seeing the middle-aged helicopter pilot and wondered why he remained behind.

Kwapich looked over Bril's shoulder as if expecting Sanders to emerge from the outcropping of rocks behind them. "After the helicopter left we wondered what was keeping you. Did Sanders go with the other survivors?"

"Yeah, there was a change of plan." Connor forced an explanation between shallow breaths of air. "I twisted my back... thought it better to give up the seat."

Bidwell's eyebrows raised and Kwapich remained expressionless, both pondering the explanation. Connor could tell they were skeptical and offered more details, bending the truth slightly.

"I was in no condition to fly after my back flared up. Sitting made the pain worse, and I was basically useless in the cockpit. Being a pilot, Sanders could help with the radios, and his injured arm made him the next priority anyway. He was as reluctant to go as I was to stay, believe me."

They accepted the explanation. Kwapich stepped forward, helping support Connor by the opposite arm. "We better get you inside where you can lay down. A flat surface might help."

"No objections here." Connor had lost his hard-headedness about accepting assistance. He doubted he could walk more than a few feet on his own.

Hurried introductions were offered as they proceeded. They were all in a hurry to get inside away from the cold.

"I'll get a spot cleared on the floor in the cabin. There are eight of us, including you two. Should be plenty of room." Bidwell hurried away at a fast walk.

The thick overcast completely covered the ridge. Only a few yards of visibility remained in some areas, slightly more in others. Pushed by the wind, the clouds danced over the terrain, mixing with other layers riding the slopes and swirling over the glacier. At times, the lower clouds dissipated, only to return with equal vigor. Heavy with moisture, a light drizzle began to fall and soon intensified, dampening the rough ground.

Nearer the wreckage, the damage from the crash was more apparent. Connor could judge the force of impact by the amount of distortion in the fuselage. The cabin section was bent and wrinkled along the outer skin, yet somehow retained a general cylindrical shape. Only the reinforced bulkheads had stopped the frame from collapsing completely.

The tail section and mangled wings sustained heavy damage, either from the primary impact or from secondary collisions with other obstacles. Overall, Connor judged the damage to be barely survivable. He didn't say anything but wondered how there were only three fatalities.

Bidwell waited in the forward entry door as they approached. He helped the men inside. Connor felt foolish being handled like a cripple but was grateful for the assistance.

The interior looked only marginally better than the outside. The large man they had been unable to transport rested against the starboard wall. He was on his side, still laying on the rigid spine board with a seat cushion pushed against his back for support. A blanket covered his midsection. He appeared to be asleep.

A young man he recognized as one of the litter bearers stood in the back with a tall, stylishly dressed woman, stuffing pieces of clothing from a suitcase into an open crack of the fuselage wall. Despite the stained outfit and smudged makeup, her mannerisms and clothing denoted wealth. Her appearance reflected a middle-aged woman fighting a never-ending battle with age. A battle she was slowly losing. She stood in stark contrast to the young man wearing torn jeans and a faded jacket.

Further forward, another woman stood alone, holding a malamute dog by the collar. Even with disheveled hair, a cheap airline blanket around her shoulders, and scuffed pants and shoes, she seemed out of place amid the post-crash chaos. She was fit and attractive. Her bright eyes and warm smile provided a comforting welcome.

Connor tried ignoring his injury and nodded to the woman politely. The gesture was returned as they locked eyes for several seconds. She seemed to blush slightly and brushed a strand of hair away from her cheek.

There was a space available near the center of the cabin. Getting there and onto the floor without aggravating the pain wasn't easy. With the women watching he suddenly felt ashamed at his inability to move on his own. Bidwell helped him into a kneeling position, then onto his back. The pressure brought immediate relief.

"That's better. Thanks for giving me a hand."

Slowly extending his legs, he was able to stretch the taut muscles and ease the tension. For the first time in hours, he felt only a minimal amount of pain and closed his eyes. The sensation wouldn't last, and he thought about the pills Steiner gave him. He could feel the small bottle in his pocket.

"Rest easy for a while. We still have to prepare the cabin for the night." Bidwell's voice sounded calm, without emotion. He forced a smile before joining Bril and Kwapich by the cockpit.

"Would you like a pillow for your head?" The pretty woman he noticed upon entering the fuselage knelt beside him, holding a small pillow she had retrieved from one of the overhead bins. A sincere expression of concern was evident in her eyes.

Connor was taken off guard. She seemed to be reading his emotions. "Oh, sure. That would be great. Thank you."

"I'm Susan Douglas. Looks like we'll be roommates." An innocent smile crossed her lips. She gently lifted his neck just enough to slide the pillow in place.

"I guess so. Sorry to crash your slumber party. I'm Gil Connor."

"Nice to meet you, Gil. Is giving up your seat on the helicopter something you normally do?"

"Not usually. But I heard a good-looking woman was still here and in need of rescue. The other pilot refused to wait for me, so here I am."

"I see. And the back? Did you hurt yourself in a quest to rescue this woman or after running for the helicopter when it lifted off?"

Connor enjoyed the flirtatious banter. It was only a temporary disruption from his intended plan. "Injury? I'm actually faking. I just wanted you to come over and talk with me."

328

"Really? Does that mean I can have my pillow back?"

"I'm afraid not. You see the other men think I'm actually injured. If you take your pillow and leave, they'll know I'm only trying to get out of work and will throw me outside for the night."

They smiled at each other and chuckled. The laughter caused a small spasm in Connor's tender back. He grimaced slightly and looked away, trying to hide the discomfort, but she noticed immediately.

She rested a hand on his chest. "Okay, Mister Faker, how about something for the pain? There are some aspirin around here somewhere if you'd like?"

"Actually, I've got other pills. Sergeant Steiner left them with me. I could use some now. Can you get them from my jacket pocket?"

She did as asked, then disappeared from his line of sight to retrieve a half-empty water bottle from somewhere close by. "Do you need to sit up?"

"Probably." He leaned forward carefully on his elbows, straining with effort.

Susan placed a pill in his mouth and tipped enough liquid from the water bottle for him to swallow.

"Thank you. You're an angel. Do I get a sponge bath with the medicine?"

"Easy, big boy. In your condition you should be happy with a conversation and a warm smile. Now lean back on the floor."

She supported his shoulders as he relaxed into the pillow. "There, that should help. Relax for a bit and let the medicine take effect. I'll get you a blanket."

"I'm fine, really." Connor wanted her to stay. He wasn't used to expressing himself easily with people but felt comfortable in her presence. He was surprised at his own reaction. Later on, when no one was looking, he could take all the pills and finish his misery.

"Pull up a chair. I'll tell you my life story if you tell me yours."

She smiled her perfect smile again. "All on the first date? You could be bored to sleep."

"In the absence of dinner and a movie, I'll take what I can get."

"I'll tell you what. I need to check on the others to see if they need any help. If you're not already asleep from the pain medication when I get back, I'll talk the night away."

Connor smiled, then became serious. Even though he wanted to end his misery, he couldn't force himself to give in, not yet. "I can get up if someone needs help." He started to move. "I feel better . . ."

"Oh no, you don't. You stay put." Susan placed a hand on his arm. "You can barely take a breath without hurting yourself. I can see the pain in your face. You relax or I'll sic the dogs on you."

Connor reluctantly rested his head back on the pillow. She was right. "It's a deal. But I have to warn you. Dogs usually like me."

"Oh, because of a shared pedigree?"

"Something like that. But only if they're mongrels."

Susan patted his arm before leaving. She didn't know quite what to think of him. There was an unexpected attraction between them. On initial appearance she assumed he would be less approachable. The lines around his eyes and mouth curled in a partial scowl, giving a false impression of his personality. Instead, he was ruggedly handsome and charming.

After looking deep into his eyes, she could see a gentleness hidden by his outward demeanor. A reflection of terrible sorrow was also lurking within. Not from physical pain, she sensed, but emotional scarring from some haunting memory in his past.

When she looked back, he was watching her. There was an ache in his eyes she understood. Not sexual but more of a personal and spiritual void. She smiled and stepped out into the cold air.

Connor lay for a minute staring at the plastic liner on the ceiling. He found himself thinking of her and tried focusing on something else. There was an alluring quality about the woman that distracted him. In one sense, he wanted to develop a relationship but in another, knew time was against him. The reality of his illness prevented any worthwhile pursuit. Even so, he couldn't push the thought entirely away.

As he lay there contemplating his limited options, he reached the same conclusion that drove him to take the helicopter in the first place. His desire to be on the mountain was more than a reprieve from the pain. He knew the disease would inevitably destroy him, yet he was unwilling to accept the terms of surrender. He only needed to take advantage of being stuck on the mountain, while there was still an opportunity for vindication.

In the wreckage, the sound of the racing wind mixed with the protesting groans of metal. The rain, too, had intensified, falling harder and amplifying against the metal skin.

Connor could hear the heavy drops hitting the roof between the gusts pushing and pulling at the fuselage. He closed his eyes, feeling each variation of movement and sound. Combined with the medicine, the subtle motion was intoxicating, like being rocked by gentle ocean swells. In a short time he was fast asleep.

CHAPTER FORTY-TWO

Maxwell was having doubts about continuing. Clouds obscured the hilltops on either side of the canyon, and a steady rain was falling, decreasing the visibility to less than a mile. Winds were buffeting the helicopter with increasing intensity. He slowed to sixty knots, keeping his eyes on the terrain.

"This doesn't look good. I think we should head back before the weather gets any worse."

Maxwell glanced at Lorell, hoping for confirmation. Instead, she maintained a calm demeanor, concerned about the weather as well but not sharing his pessimism. "We'll be all right, Lou. We're almost through the hills. The terrain flattens out ahead before reaching the mountains. Let's keep going for a few more minutes. We can turn around if we need to."

She knew in a few minutes they would be at the airstrip where Shultz and the others were waiting. Loading them aboard wouldn't take but another minute or two. Abandoning them now seemed foolish. The weather was lousy but still flyable. She felt comfortable continuing.

Specialist Damian Prosky, the flight medic, watched the trees passing out the left side of the helicopter. His mind was on helping the survivors stranded with the damaged Black Hawk. He was disappointed they couldn't help the others on the mountain.

The crew chief, Sergeant Chris Nickels, sat in the right crew seat. He, too, watched the terrain, wondering if they could reach Shultz's location. The weather was a concern, but he had confidence in the pilots, more so in Lorell than Maxwell. Her Alaska experience gave her an edge as far as he was concerned.

The helicopter was loaded with extra sleeping bags, rations, and medical gear, stacked out of the way in the corners of the cargo compartment or on the shelves of the carousel. Since they could no longer reach the crash site, the gear was taking up space. There was barely room for the five people waiting at the airstrip.

"I don't see any change in the weather." Maxwell fidgeted in his seat, glancing left and right between the wiper blades moving across the windshield. "How's the visibility behind us, guys? Any change? I don't want to get stuck here."

Nickels leaned sideways, tilting his head into the gunner's window so he had a better angle. "No, sir. No change. Visibility is still about three-quarters of a mile, maybe a little more to the west."

"Same here, sir," Prosky announced from the opposite side. "I don't see any change. Sure wouldn't want to spend a night in this weather."

"Okay." Maxwell sounded disappointed. He looked at the GPS display, then back through the windshield. "Amy, you want to fly? I'm going to double check the coordinates the other helicopter gave us."

Lorell shot a quick glance at Maxwell before moving her hands and feet onto the flight controls. "I've got the controls."

She had already verified the coordinates and checked them against the navigation chart beside her seat, but kept silent, grateful he relinquished the controls. She kept a steady heading and slowly inched their airspeed higher.

The steep walls of the canyon disappeared, changing to rolling hills on either side of the river drainage spitting out of the mountains. The rise of the terrain was deceptive and began increasing at a steeper angle toward the high peaks ahead. The difference was barely perceptible from the helicopter. Only the clouds narrowing the distance above the ground provided any indication.

"You want me to give Shultz a call? We're about four minutes out." Lorell could see Maxwell had placed the notepad with the coordinates aside and was studying the weather with a concerned look on his face.

"Ah . . . no, I'll do it. Watch your airspeed. If the ceiling gets any lower, we'll have to turn around."

"I think we'll be okay, Lou. We still have about three hundred feet."

Maxwell ignored her and pressed the transmit button. "One-one-four, this is two-three-nine on Fox Mike, over."

"Two-three-nine, this is one-one-four. We've been waiting for you. How far you out?" Shultz's voice sounded relieved.

"Four minutes, Joe, if we can make it. The ceiling and visibility are dropping. The canyon behind us is almost socked in. What does the weather look like from your location, over?"

There was a brief pause before Shultz answered. "Visibility is a half mile looking in your direction. We're getting a mixture of rain and snow. It's intensified in the last ten minutes. The ceiling is about two hundred feet and the winds are gusting to thirty knots from the south-west. When you get here, land behind us on the strip. The winds will be at an angle off your right front. As soon as you touch down, we'll hurry as fast as we can with the litter."

"Roger, Joe. After we land, Prosky and Nickels will give you a hand."

Shultz had been wondering if the standby crew was still en route. There was no chance of communication until they flew through the canyon. He had been watching the weather, becoming increasingly worried after losing sight of the foothills. He also knew Maxwell wouldn't fly very long in bad weather.

After Thompson relayed Maxwell was inbound, Shultz told Hovan to hold off on getting the Huey ready. Instead, he kept the Black Hawk's APU running so he could continue monitoring the radios. Once the ten-minute ETA passed, they switched plans again.

Shultz was just about to shut down the APU when Maxwell called. Hovan was already outside with Ferguson, getting ready to move the injured patient over to the Huey.

Mildred was visibly uncomfortable with the delay and even more so by the worsening weather. Her husband had remained mostly silent. The morphine was effective in dulling the pain.

"Don't move him yet," Shultz shouted and waved at Ferguson, who was standing beside Hovan in the open door. They were preoccupied and didn't hear him talking on the radio over the hum of the APU.

Ferguson looked up. "What?"

Shultz motioned for him to plug into the intercom. He nodded and climbed into the nearest crew seat. Hovan jumped in the back corner so he was out of the rain while they talked.

"Maxwell is a few minutes out. Tell Lieutenant Hovan to secure the Huey, and I'll shut off the APU. Grab our tie-downs and the inlet covers. We need to button everything up tight before we leave. The winds could be worse tonight."

"Will do, Joe." Ferguson reached for his cord. He stopped before unplugging and feigned disappointment. "I was looking forward to flying in a Huey again. But I'm not turning down a ride, not in this weather."

By the time Shultz turned off the radios and shut down the APU and battery, Hovan and Ferguson were busy outside. Mildred was wrapping another blanket around her husband for protection against the wind.

Shultz kept his helmet on as a barrier against the rain before climbing out of the pilot's seat. He helped Ferguson secure each blade with ropes attached to the skids. They then protected the engine inlets and exhaust stacks with padded inserts and canvas covers.

Hovan did the same with the Huey. He was running back when the sound of the approaching Black Hawk was heard over the wind.

Lorell searched through the rain-streaked windshield for the landing site. The GPS showed the location a quarter mile to their front, but damn if she could see it. They were flying a hundred feet above the terrain and the dark spruce trees bordering the drainage masked the narrow strip of dirt.

"Five hundred yards! Where the hell is it?" Maxwell searched intently ahead of the helicopter. "I should've verified the coordinates with Shultz."

"I see it," Lorell stated. She had begun doubting the accuracy of the coordinates herself. "The GPS never lies. I'm slowing for the approach."

"You sure? I don't have it in sight." Maxwell stared a few seconds longer. "Okay, I see the opening. Nice and easy, Amy. Keep the nose in the wind."

Lorell knew exactly what she was doing. She flared the helicopter and slowed to a fast walk over the center of the airstrip. Shultz's Black Hawk and the Huey were visible at the far end. They could see a figure running between the helicopters.

Nickels slid the right cargo door open and leaned partway outside. The rain stung his eyes. "Right side is clear as long as you stay over the center of the strip. Keep the tail aligned with the runway."

"Left side is clear," Prosky added a moment later. "The ground has some wheel ruts but no slope I can see."

"Thank you." Lorell continued forward until they were fifty feet behind Shultz's Black Hawk.

"I don't like these winds." Maxwell was uncomfortable, but content in letting his more experienced copilot handle the controls.

"Me either, Lou. I'm coming down."

A strong gust hit the helicopter, instantly pushing the tail to the left. Lorell corrected immediately, aligning the nose before the tail could swing into the brush.

Maxwell's eyes widened. "Shit, that was a strong gust."

She smiled and slowly descended until the tail wheel touched the ground. The main wheels followed as the fuselage settled perfectly in the middle of the strip. She let the helicopter coast another ten feet before stopping.

"Going to idle. Lock the brakes."

"Roger." Maxwell pulled up on the locking handle as Lorell pushed heavily on the control pedals. "Brakes are locked. Nice job, Amy."

"Thanks. Let's get everyone aboard."

Prosky and Nickels were quickly outside and hurrying toward the other helicopter. They met Hovan and Ferguson at the cargo door, already in the process of lifting the injured man from the carousel.

"How is he?" Prosky addressed Ferguson as Shultz and Mildred came around from the other side. He could see the man was wrapped snuggly in a blanket and secured on the litter.

"Ralph is stable," Mildred answered with a frown on her face. "Now, can we get him into the helicopter and get out of here. We've had enough excitement for one day."

"Uh . . . of course. I'm the flight medic, Specialist Prosky."

"This is Mildred, Prosky," Shultz added in a hurry. "She can brief you while we're moving him. She's a retired nurse and Ralph's wife."

Nickels and Shultz took a front corner of the litter, with Hovan and Ferguson positioned at the rear. Mildred followed with the flight medic, bringing him up to date on Ralph's condition. She was thorough and Prosky was impressed.

Less than four minutes later, everyone was aboard and strapped in. Lorell was already rolling the throttle up by the time the doors were pulled shut. She glanced at the engine torque indications, but the added weight wasn't a concern at this altitude.

"Secure in back," Nickels announced.

Prosky was busy checking Ralph's vital signs. Shultz occupied the flight medic's crew seat behind the pilots, and Hovan and Ferguson sat against the rear bulkhead.

Mildred sat next to her husband, trying to ignore the vibration of the helicopter and the abrupt shudders during each strong gust. The last thing she wanted to think about was another malfunction, but as they lifted off the ground, she couldn't think about anything else.

"Tail wheel is off the ground. Ten feet . . . twenty. You're looking good." Nickels stayed focused outside as he passed information through the intercom. "We're above the trees. Clear on my side."

"Right front is clear," Maxwell added. "Damn, the clouds have dropped. Visibility too. This could get dicey. You okay flying, Amy?"

"I'm fine, Lou. I'll stay low over the trees."

Lorell accelerated until the airspeed showed sixty knots before banking over the gravel riverbed. The fuselage yawed with the sudden change in wind direction. In an instant the groundspeed shot up dramatically with the strong tail wind. She adjusted the controls, maintaining the same low altitude.

Visibility was at a quarter mile and the ceiling a hundred feet. The rain had turned mostly to wet snow, obscuring the terrain on either side of the drainage.

Lorell kept the airspeed as fast as she dared, allowing enough reaction time if they needed to come to a hover or turn around to avoid entering the tightening overcast.

Shultz was plugged into the intercom. He remained silent, letting Lorell and Maxwell do their job. His comments would only be a distraction.

Short of the canyon, the ceiling and visibility began lifting. The change wasn't much, but it at least equaled what the conditions were when they passed through before. No one noticed as Lorell and Maxwell breathed a sigh of relief.

A moment later they were on the other side. The helicopter banked on a direct course for Fort Wainwright, staying low over the Tanana Flats.

Shultz's thoughts were already on what he would be doing tomorrow. He would make sure he was involved in the rescue of the remaining survivors. Bril and Connor were counting on him.

CHAPTER FORTY-THREE

Twenty miles south of Fairbanks, Thompson's heavily loaded helicopter leveled above the flat terrain, flying a few hundred feet below the scattered layer he had descended through only moments before. In the distance, large buildings and bright structures of the city were becoming recognizable against the dark landscape. With each passing mile, the shades and colors became sharper and more distinct.

Thompson felt a shift in the balance of the helicopter as Steiner changed position. The movement was more hurried than before and Thompson immediately sensed something was wrong. Steiner crouched over the patient lying against the right door and quickly pulled the blankets and clothing away from his chest.

The girls and women packed against the bulkhead sensed the urgency and slid further to the side, allowing more room for him to work. Steiner pulled a bright red, canvas bag, the size of a briefcase, from the corner. Inside was a portable defibrillator he needed for shocking the patient's heart back to life.

Steiner's voice broke over the intercom. The words cracked with urgency. "I've lost a pulse. No heartbeat. I'm starting CPR."

Donna saw Steiner's reaction and knew something was wrong. She hesitated, frozen by indecision. The terror of being left behind had passed, yet the girl's coach waited for someone else, anyone else, to volunteer. No one did. She was the closest.

Steiner looked at her, then away. She was the only adult who could help, but could he trust her? Another pair of hands could be the difference between life and death.

After her embarrassing spectacle on the mountain, Donna needed to set a positive example. The girls would tell everyone about her panicked reaction, and she would be humiliated. Redeeming herself was the only way.

She took a deep breath and swallowed hard. Her body moved, surprising her. She slid in close beside Steiner, locking eyes with him, silently wishing he would decline assistance. Instead, he nodded his head in thanks.

"How can I help?" She had to yell over the sound of the engine. Her voice faltered with uncertainty.

He leaned sideways, talking directly into her ear. "I already turned the defibrillator on. Attach the chest pads while I start artificial breathing. The instructions are written on the bag, there." He handed her the pads and pointed to the laminated plastic sheet with large print.

She was scared, afraid of what would happen, yet for the first time didn't let the fear overwhelm her. She looked at him, then the patient and began reading.

The instructions were simple. Taking another deep breath she bent forward, plugging the cables into the monitor. A series of bright lights illuminated and an electronic voice explained the next step in a sequence of short commands. The words were impossible to hear over the engine, and she didn't try. She only had to follow the diagram on the inside cover.

Steiner pulled a plastic mouthpiece with an attached air bag from another case and placed the cup over the man's airway. He squeezed the bag several times, forcing air into his lungs.

Once Donna had the chest pads in place, he stopped air compressions and motioned her hands away from the patient. They watched as the man's chest jerked from repeated bursts of electric shock. The machine paused, automatically checking for a heartbeat before repeating the procedure. On the third try, the machine stopped. His heart rhythm was restored.

Steiner slid in closer. The man's pulse was weak and his breathing barely distinguishable. The defibrillator pads were left attached, allowing the device to continue monitoring the patient for signs of distress.

Gentle squeezes of the air bag forced more air into his lungs. His chest expanded with the compressions, providing oxygen to the blood stream. In seconds, the man's pulse was stronger. He began breathing on his own and for the moment at least, he appeared out of danger.

"We've got a pulse." Steiner's voice was noticeably relieved. "How much longer, sir?"

"Ten minutes, tops. I was just about to call Fairbanks tower."

"Have them notify the hospital one of the patients went into cardiac arrest. They need to be standing by with a crash cart."

"Will do. Good job bringing him back, Sergeant Steiner."

Leaning into Donna, Steiner spoke into her ear again over the noise. "Thank you. Help me bundle him back up. He needs to keep warm." Silently he wondered what had caused her change in personality.

Donna nodded her head and smiled before pulling the blankets over the man's exposed torso. With Steiner's help she had saved a person from the brink of death. For Donna, it was a life changing moment.

Lisa first noticed the commotion when Steiner moved and hurriedly checked the injured man's pulse. She was stuck between her friend Becka and Donna. They were leaning against her and afraid to move. She tried sliding closer to help Steiner, but she was trapped by the weight of their bodies. She became frustrated. There was a reason she had been on the airplane. Her chance to save the helicopter pilot had passed and now she couldn't help the man in cardiac arrest, either.

When Donna finally overcame her fear and slid closer to the man, Lisa prayed. Her faith gave her strength. She reached out, almost touching her coach's leg, willing the energy to pass through her fingers to Donna and into the man's lifeless body. She relaxed. No one noticed the powerful force flowing through her. The man's heartbeat suddenly returned-his life restored.

Sanders became more comfortable after leaving the mountains behind. Out of the bad weather and almost on the ground, he didn't mind being the kid's copilot. He set the tower frequency on the radio and turned Thompson's selector without being asked.

"You're on tower frequency."

Glancing at the console out of habit, Thompson confirmed the correct setting before keying the transmit button.

"Fairbanks tower, Army eight-three-zero. Ten miles southeast for landing at Fairbanks Memorial, over."

The tower response was immediate. Apparently, the controller was already aware of the situation. "Roger, Army eight-three-zero. You're cleared into the surface area to Fairbanks Memorial. Winds are one-four-zero degrees at eight knots. Altimeter is two-nine-eight-four. Advise when you're on the ground."

Thompson acknowledged before asking the controller to advise the hospital of the cardiac arrest. The chatter from other aircraft on the radio lessened, as if their talking might somehow interfere with the patient's outcome.

As the helicopter passed Clear Creek Buttes, the man-made structures of the city were easily distinguishable. Blue metal storage buildings near the Tanana River served as a reference for the approach. The warehouses were visible from miles away, contrasting against the white exterior of the main medical complex. From there, the course was a straight line to a soccer field across the street, where the last turn into the helipad would begin.

The landing area was painted with a large red and white cross and could handle the biggest of helicopters. The concrete pad lay situated in a field between a busy street and the hospital parking lot. A steep approach was necessary to avoid the nearby buildings and power lines.

Children stared up from the soccer field and waved as Thompson began slowing the helicopter. Several ambulances could be seen waiting adjacent to the helipad, along with three local television vans and a group of reporters and medical staff. News of the rescue had traveled quickly.

A grimace of opposition etched Sanders' face. "This is going to be a circus."

"The rescue is big news, Captain. You might as well talk to them before they make up the facts." The tone of Thompson's voice inferred he had no intention of shutting down the helicopter. A quick exit after unloading the survivors seemed a better option. He was more than content to let Sanders handle the media.

Thompson slowed the approach over the power lines, flaring the helicopter to touch down smoothly in the center of the pad. He lowered the collective control so the weight was fully distributed on the skids and rolled the throttle to idle.

A segment light on the caution panel flickered for a moment when they touched down. Thompson wasn't surprised. He didn't say anything. He had been monitoring the fuel since leaving the mountains and expected the Low Fuel light to illuminate. Enough fuel remained for the short flight back to Fort Wainwright.

"Watch the passengers when you get out, Sergeant Steiner. Make sure they don't walk back toward the tail rotor."

"Roger, I'm climbing out." The cargo door slid back, followed by Steiner's loud voice giving instructions.

"Everyone remain seated until the injured patients by the doors are unloaded. When I wave you out, walk toward the ambulances and stay together." He made eye contact with each of the passengers to ensure they understood.

A sigh of relief escaped Steiner. He watched the first ambulance back in toward the helicopter with the rear doors open, stopping just outside the span of spinning rotor blades. Orderlies and a doctor immediately wheeled a gurney from the vehicle while a second ambulance backed in beside it. He motioned them toward the closest cargo door before directing the next gurney to the opposite side. He quickly briefed the medical team on each patient's condition.

"I guess I better go face the music." Sanders extended his arm across the console to shake Thompson's hand in farewell. "I'm sure the accident board will have lots of questions."

"You'll do just fine. From what I saw on the mountain, you did a hell of a job getting the plane on the ground."

"Maybe, but I still have three fatalities to answer for. I suspect the injured and traumatized passengers will see the situation differently. Someone has to take the blame."

Thompson knew he was right. Still, he wasn't sure how to respond. Any reassurance he offered was hollow at best. He realized the accident board would eventually get around to interviewing him as well. "Take care, Captain, and good luck."

Sanders backed out of the helicopter using his good arm for leverage. He thought of something else and stopped, meeting Thompson's eyes.

"I've never been in a helicopter before, but I've been a pilot for a long time. What you and your crew did today was amazing. You guys are real professionals. We're all thankful you showed up when you did."

A slight smile creased Thompson's face. The comment was all the thanks he needed. He wondered if Sanders knew Connor was the real driving force behind the rescue. Without Connor, the flight would never have been attempted, and it would certainly never have succeeded. Even getting off the mountain safely was a direct result of Connor's influence.

Connor's and his chain of command would view the incident differently, of course. Regulations had been violated, a lot of them. Hopefully, because of the outcome, their conduct wouldn't be judged too harshly, although Connor's reason for being there in the first place might be looked at with a different perspective. Even so, he wasn't about to let Connor take the heat on his own.

Thompson suspected the zealous media would overemphasize the rescue and only hoped his mentor would be around to share in the coverage. Their sensationalized reporting might be Connor's only chance of staying away from disciplinary action. Of course, the outcome didn't matter to Connor. With his terminal cancer the repercussions weren't important. If they were, he wouldn't have stolen the helicopter in the first place. *Perhaps there was a darker motive. Would he be returning at all?*

Reporters swarmed around the survivors as medical personnel tried hurrying them into the hospital. The scene was chaotic until Sanders approached, distracting their attention while the others continued inside.

The first ambulance began pulling away from the helicopter. Another immediately took its place. Steiner repeated the briefing procedure with the new medical team and waited until the last patient was safely loaded.

"Don't wait for me, Mister Thompson." Steiner plugged back into the intercom. "I'll be here for a while. I've got plenty of paperwork to fill out before I leave. I'll catch a ride back to base later."

"You sure? The reporters will be hounding you as soon as they figure out your involvement. Besides, I was hoping for some backup while I brief the commander."

Steiner could tell he was only partially joking. "I'll be there in another hour."

He broke eye contact for a second before continuing. "For what my opinion's worth, I think you and Connor are damn good pilots. I'll fly with you anytime. What you guys accomplished with this old helicopter was a hell of a feat. No other pilots could have done better."

"Thanks, Sergeant. I appreciate it." Thompson was just thankful they made the flight back. Expressing more than a light compliment was something neither of them was used to, but this day was certainly an exception. His reply was equally heartfelt.

"You did all the hard work. You're one hell of a medic. Without your expertise, more people would've died. You saved a lot of lives today. Nothing is more important than that. I had the easy part. All I did was fly the helicopter."

Steiner searched for an answer. "Yes, sir. We're a good team. See you back at base."

He was suddenly gone, walking quickly toward the hospital. Thompson rolled the throttle full open and pulled in collective, smoothly climbing away from the helipad. Five minutes later he was on the ground beside the hangar, letting the engine cool as he thought about how he would explain everything to his commander.

CHAPTER FORTY-FOUR

A sense of something out of place caused Connor to stir. Moist pressure against his chin didn't match the events in his dream. He opened his eyes. Only inches away, a strange face was staring at him. The playful eyes and cocked head held a curious look as if wondering why someone would be sleeping at this time of day. The dog's muzzle bumped his chin again, prodding Connor for a response.

Only after Connor recovered from surprise and began stroking behind the animal's furry ears, did the dog seem satisfied. The malamute lay on all fours, resting its head comfortably on Connor's chest. The amber eyes studied him with a satisfied expression.

Voices in the rear of the fuselage drew Connor's attention. They sounded surprisingly jovial. He heard a woman speaking and could smell the odor of food. A sudden wave of hunger overcame him as he realized he hadn't eaten anything since early in the morning.

The thought of something else alarmed him. He remembered he was in a wrecked plane and knew leaking fuel was an almost certainty. Cooking over an open flame could ignite the fuel vapor. He was about to yell a warning when he realized there was no danger. The smell was from an Army ready-to-eat ration, heated by adding water to a chemical mix in a protective pouch around the food. There was no flame. The process was completely safe.

From his position on the floor, Connor could see the heavy man still lying on the spine board. He was in a deep sleep, causing the wool blanket around his chest to rise and fall with each breath. The shoes he had been wearing earlier were off to the side and an extra cushion had been placed against the wall as a buffer. His appearance suggested he had been moved during Connor's slumber.

Maneuvering himself carefully to a sitting position, Connor felt his muscles flex in mild protest. A dull ache had replaced the stabbing pain. The sharp spasms and burning intensity were gone for the time being. Lying on the hard surface in combination with the muscle relaxers eased the worst of the tension. He could move with only minor discomfort.

Connor recognized the four people in the rear of the cabin. Susan and the other woman were sitting across from Kwapich and Simms. Open MRE packets were beside them. They seemed to be enjoying the military rations. They talked freely. Each of them sat cross-legged on a cushion from the passenger seats.

The dog repositioned its head on Connor's chest, then sat up and looked at him for continued attention. Connor obliged by stroking under his chin. Satisfied, the malamute lay back down with a soft moan.

Other than conversation, there was only silence. The noise from the howling wind and creaking fuselage were gone. The worst of the storm seemed to have passed. Connor wondered how long he had been asleep. Checking his watch, the dial showed a little after seven-thirty in the evening. Could he really have been out that long? Glancing through the small windows for confirmation, he saw only shades of gray. The ridge was still enveloped in clouds.

Connor looked around the interior. Most of the seats were missing. Cushions and extra clothing were in a pile by the forward bulkhead. The temperature felt surprisingly comfortable. Only a slight chill was present where his body rested against the wall. The access doors and cracks had been sealed from the outside. The accommodations weren't perfect but were adequate for protection from the freezing air.

A creak from the forward entryway drew Connor's attention. A draft of cold air filtered through as Bril and Bidwell entered. They were carrying sleeping bags and some camping gear retrieved from the aft baggage compartment.

The sleeping man didn't stir. His heavy breathing subsided into a low rumble. They gave him a brief glance before continuing.

"How you feeling, Mister Connor?" Bril set the items out of the way before kneeling beside him.

"Lots better. Are we set for the night, Bril? Anything I can do?"

Bril knew he was being sincere but didn't bite at the offer. "No, sir. Everything is taken care of. There wasn't much to do. We managed to wrench the rear door closed and seal the cracks with some clothing from the suitcases. The front access still works fine for entry and exit."

"Good. What about food and water? Anything other than MREs?" Connor wanted to take charge but realized he had no authority over the survivors. Bril was different of course and understood the situation. At this point Connor just wanted to contribute something and thought he might be able to offer some suggestions.

The dog looked on with indifference as Bril patted his side. "Water is limited, but there should be enough for tomorrow. There's some run-off from an ice overhang if we run out. The survivors salvaged several water bottles and a few candy bars and crackers after the crash. With the case of MREs Steiner brought, there should be enough food for a day or two, as long as we eat sparingly."

After pulling the door closed, Bidwell joined them in the center of the fuselage. He nodded to Connor politely and remained standing. "You're looking better. You were out for a long time. How do you feel?"

"Much better, thanks. Sorry I wasn't any help."

"No need to apologize. I've pulled my back out a few times, myself. I know the feeling. There isn't anything you can do except stay off your feet and let the sore muscles recover."

"It's true," Kwapich added. He approached from the rear. "I can vouch for Hank's condition. His back usually goes out about the time we start hauling loads of meat back to camp."

Bidwell was used to the ribbing but didn't let the banter pass without comment. "Only because I usually have the game quartered and bagged by the time you arrive. A process of several hours and great physical exertion, I might add."

"Ouch!" Kwapich feigned insult. "One time I wasn't there to help and you never let me forget. I guess being several miles away at the time shouldn't be a factor."

The two hunters grinned good-naturedly even though fatigue was evident on their faces. Connor could tell they were good friends. "Sounds like you guys were scheduled for a hunting trip when the plane crashed."

"Yeah, we were meeting our guide in Fairbanks. We had an eight-day moose and sheep hunt planned." Kwapich sounded disappointed. "We've been planning this for years. Looks like the hunt will be delayed, but we still might have a few days, depending on when we get out of here."

"In the meantime we'll consider this a camping trip." Bidwell shifted his feet. "Glad you Army guys could join us."

There was a relaxed atmosphere to the conversation. Connor guessed they were seasoned hunters who knew how to handle themselves. He envied their adventure. Spending time in the wilderness was something he always appreciated. The outdoors somehow provided a calming atmosphere to his inner turmoil.

Throughout his life, he hadn't been very religious. He believed in God, but attending church was something he usually avoided. To him, nature seemed a more appropriate cathedral. Solitude gave him a personal connection he was more comfortable with. Flying had the same effect on him, being alone with only his thoughts for company. The bond was something he never felt anywhere else, something special he couldn't identify.

Those private moments changed after his daughter's death. An angry rejection of faith took their place. But as much as he wanted to deny a presence, Connor knew he was never alone in his grief. Maybe it was the reason he resented religion so much. His prayers had been ignored. His beliefs had failed him. He wasn't alone, but he wanted to be.

Bril stopped petting the dog and stood between the two men. "I was just explaining our situation to Mister Connor. I think we're set for the night."

Kwapich answered first. "Right, nothing more we can do. I even have a deck of cards if anyone's interested?"

Bidwell saw Connor's questioning look and explained. "Our hunting gear was part of our baggage on the plane. In addition to the typical outdoor clothing and sleeping bags, we always carry a deck of cards and some reading material, for those long days when we're stuck in camp."

"Good idea." Connor wondered if they realized how valuable their sleeping bags would be. He turned his attention back to Bril. "Everyone set for sleeping arrangements? Steiner brought a case of blankets, right?"

"Yes, sir. A dozen in the case and two more they unpacked from their gear." He motioned to Kwapich and Bidwell. "Should be enough we don't freeze to death. The cushions from the seats will help insulate the floor."

"The ladies can use the sleeping bags." Kwapich was serious, not just being polite. "Hank and I both have fleece underwear and warm jackets."

There was a nod of agreement from Bidwell. "With the blankets we'll be nice and toasty."

"That's nice of you guys. I'm sure they'll appreciate the offer." Connor wasn't surprised. Their gesture was more than politeness. It was how real men acted.

"We wouldn't consider anything else." Kwapich nodded at Bril as he continued.

"By the way, this young man has been a real help. Getting things organized would have been much harder without him. He saved us a bunch of time and energy."

Bril blushed slightly. "Just glad I could help out. From what I've seen, you had everything well in hand."

"Not hardly. Anyway, you two finish talking while we get something to eat. It's been a long day." They moved toward the back with a tired stride.

CHAPTER FORTY-FIVE

B ril squatted beside Connor and the dog again, lowering his
voice. "Things would be a real mess without those two." He
motioned in the direction of Kwapich and Bidwell. "They
know what they're doing. Good thing we didn't end up with a couple
of city slickers."

Connor had been thinking the same thing. He nodded as Bril
continued.

"We did a survey of the wreckage while you were sleeping. The
battery was already disconnected from the electrical system and we
plugged an oil line in the broken wing Sanders must have missed.
The other lines and fuel tanks were okay. Most of the leaked fuel
already seeped into the ground or was diluted by the rain. There's
not much chance of a fire, but the survivors were briefed on the
hazard. No matches, lighters, or any open flame. No one here
smokes."

"You did good, Bril."

"There wasn't much left to do. Captain Sanders and our friends
took charge after the crash."

"I suspect they're used to that sort of thing. They seem like the take-charge type. The situation would have been far worse without them."

Bril glanced at the survivors gathered in the back. "Nice of them to offer their sleeping bags. The women will sleep comfortably. Hopefully, we don't have to spend more than a night on the mountain."

A wool Army blanket and a couple of thin airline blankets apiece would suffice for the men. Combined with their regular clothing and seat cushions for padding, they would be warm enough.

Connor collected his thoughts. "I sure would like to know if Thompson made the flight back okay and what the weather is going to do."

"Funny you should mention it." Bril pulled the survival radio from his vest. "While you were sleeping one of the Air Guard rescue C-130s contacted us. The pilot said they would stay on station until later tonight. Said he would call in three hours with an update. He should be contacting us at eight o'clock."

They both checked their watches. The time was a quarter before the hour. Connor took the radio from Bril, confirming the battery was on so they didn't miss the call.

He placed the radio against his hip, searching Bril's expression for more information. For some reason, he was holding back on the status of the helicopter. Connor was concerned until he saw his mouth turn upward in a smile.

"What did the C-130 pilot say? Since you have a grin on your face, I assume Thompson and Steiner made it back safely?"

Bril's smile widened. "Yes, sir, they sure did. From what the C-130 pilot said, their return was a big media event. Even the national networks picked up the story. About time the military got some positive coverage."

"Yeah, sure is. Thompson, Steiner, and you deserve all the credit you can get. Shultz and Ferguson, too. Did they get picked up?"

"The second medevac got them out okay. The two survivors with Mister Shultz were dropped at the hospital. Both were doing fine. A maintenance team will probably be flown in to repair my helicopter tomorrow. And another crew to retrieve yours, weather permitting."

Connor welcomed the news. He was never a fan of the media but, in this case, was grateful for their presence. The coverage would likely ensure the others didn't receive any serious repercussions for violating Army regulations. On the other hand, he knew his own selfish actions would never be forgiven. He couldn't care less. The important thing was saving lives. The rescue was a good way to end his career.

"Did they pass a weather forecast?"

"Yes, sir. We should be out of here by tomorrow."

"I noticed the winds have slacked off. When exactly did they say the weather was going to clear?"

"According to the forecast, the clouds are expected to lift by late afternoon tomorrow. The Air Guard pilot said we could expect more snow tonight and light winds after midnight. Should be a partial clearing by late morning, with increased winds and broken high clouds in the afternoon. He also said two Air Guard helicopters and one of our medevac helicopters will be waiting on base for the weather to break."

"Good. Looks like everyone will be home by tomorrow evening." Connor imagined the families of the remaining survivors would be worried. Those who had families, anyway. "You have a wife, Bril? Kids?"

"No, sir. Not yet. Haven't met the right girl to even start thinking about marriage or kids. You?"

"Only ex-wives." He didn't mention his son and daughter. "Make sure you find the right one and hang on to her. Spoil her and enjoy your life together. Time passes all too quickly."

The comment seemed out of place. Bril thought Connor must have more than a few regrets. "Yes, sir. I will."

He was about to inquire about kids when the two women approached. His and Connor's attention shifted in their direction at the same time.

Bril noticed his eyes lock on Susan and immediately light up. She was a pretty woman, and he could see why Connor was attracted to her. The hair hanging out of place on her forehead and smudged cheeks didn't diminish her good looks. She appeared tired but still carried a warm smile.

The other woman seemed less at ease. Her appearance and mannerisms were more formal from being in higher-end social circles. In spite of her background though, she was not snobbish and seemed generally concerned. If anything, she was trying to compensate for the previous behavior of her husband.

"You look better." Susan was the first to talk. "I take it the medication helped?"

"Sure did. I was out longer than I intended though." Connor locked eyes with her for a moment, as if reading her thoughts. She returned his gaze for a moment before turning to introduce the other woman.

"This is Marla. Her husband Harold is the man asleep on the floor. He suffered a back injury in the crash. Your medic must have dispensed some wonder drug because he's stirred only once since you arrived."

"The medicine seemed effective on both of us." Connor introduced himself to Marla and then glanced at Harold. "I never heard him get up or anyone else for that matter."

"The pills dull the pain and make him groggy. The guys managed to walk him outside and back in without disturbing you." Marla stared in her husband's direction with an unconcerned expression. "He needed a bathroom break before another dose of medicine."

"Is his condition serious?" Connor wondered if Steiner gave him the same pills.

"Your medic didn't think the injury was more than a pinched nerve."

The corners of Marla's mouth curved into a brief smile, then vanished. Two packaged Army rations were offered to Bril and Connor. "We thought you might like something to eat."

"Only one apiece," Susan added. "They'll have to last until we're rescued, I'm afraid."

Bril placed the ration under his arm while Connor set his on the floor by the pillow. The motion got the dog's attention, and he sniffed the package curiously.

"Mine was lasagna. Very tasty for a packaged meal." Marla seemed pleased with her assessment. "I saved the crackers and dessert until tomorrow."

"They're much better than they used to be." Connor tried making small talk but wished he could be alone with Susan.

Susan coughed and handed them each a bottle of water, letting her hand linger when Connor reached forward. "The water is being rationed until we can refill the bottles."

They chatted for a few more minutes until Marla politely excused herself to check on her husband. Bril could tell Connor and Susan wanted to be alone and made a pretext to go outside. The dog followed him, tired of the interruptions.

"I see you found a new friend." Susan pointed toward the door as the malamute left.

"I told you animals like me."

She moved to his side of the aisle, and he moved the packaged ration so she could sit next to him.

"Would you like to share some crackers and cheese? They're not bad."

"Only if you share your water. I held off eating until you were awake. Thought you might like some company." Her voice sounded appealing.

"I never turn down an offer from a beautiful woman."

"Really?" She was teasing him now. "And do you receive many of those?"

Connor played along while opening the plastic package, trying to sound distraught. "Hardly ever. My shy, boyish personality usually works against me."

She responded with light laughter. "I doubt it. You seem very capable of handling yourself around women."

"Only the ones I'm interested in." He smiled in slight embarrassment.

Susan was attracted to him. She saw through his cover of self-assuredness to a child-like vulnerability. At the same time, he possessed a subtle inner strength that was reassuring.

They changed the subject, discussing the weather until Marla finished. She checked Harold's pulse and adjusted his blanket before standing. His condition was not what she expected. She forced a smile as she passed, leaving them in conversation.

"So what's your story? You join the military out of patriotic duty, the thrill of adventure, or are you hiding from someone? I bet you have a girl in every port?"

Connor could see the humor in her eyes. He squeezed some processed cheese onto a cracker. She didn't realize how pointed the one question was, except he was hiding from himself, not the law. Hiding inside a liquor bottle certainly hadn't worked. A girl in every port was a stretch, but he did have three former wives. A girl in every port would have been easier.

He sensed the questions were more than a playful exchange of words. "Guilty on the first two. The third I can't speak about. The facts are ultra top secret. The fourth, well it goes with being part of number three."

Susan returned his subtle grin. "Ultra top secret? That does sound serious. So you're sort of like James Bond, only older and more . . ."

"Dashing?" He feigned a serious expression.

"I was going to say injury prone."

Connor laughed. "You've got me pegged."

The more they talked, the more connected she felt. "Any family?" She asked in a friendly manner, curious about his personal life.

Her eyes sparkled. Trusting her was easy. Connor wanted to confide completely even though there was no point in doing so. A mixture of sadness and joy overcame him as he thought about the two laminated photos in his wallet, one each of his daughter and son. He hadn't shown them to anyone for years. Now wasn't the time, either. He couldn't lose focus on what he needed to do.

"A couple kids. Boy and girl from the first marriage." He didn't offer any more information.

"First marriage?" Susan asked. She noticed earlier he wasn't wearing a ring. A previous wife was no surprise. The military was hard on marriages.

"Yeah. I guess I was a glutton for punishment after the first and made some bad decisions. But I suppose they could say the same thing."

He squeezed a dollop of cheese on another cracker before looking at her for a reaction. There was no judgment in her eyes, only interest.

"They? How many bad decisions did you make?" She pursued the question with casual amusement.

"Three. But I've learned from my mistakes, believe me. The last was almost a decade ago."

Before she could inquire further, he asked his own. "And you? Any ex-husbands or broken hearts?"

Susan swallowed before answering. "Just one. I'm widowed. My husband died years ago. He left me four wonderful kids and a bunch of happy memories."

Connor could see the emotional attachment. He was instantly jealous and felt foolish. "I'm sorry. Your kids all grown?"

Her face lit up with pride. "They're out of the house and on their own. My two oldest boys and daughter are married. Six beautiful grandchildren between them. My youngest boy is in the Air Force, stationed in Germany."

"I envy you, all those grandkids running around. Must be fun spoiling them?"

"Of course, spoiling grandbabies is revenge for all the anguish our kids put us through."

They shared a laugh. "I don't see them nearly as much as I'd like. Two of the kids live in Anchorage, so I can't visit as often."

Before he could respond, an unfamiliar voice sounded through the handheld radio. "Lonesome Dove, this is Air Guard rescue. Do you copy, over?"

"Lonesome Dove?" Connor directed the comment at Susan. "He obviously doesn't know who I'm spending my time with."

She touched his arm playfully. "Sounds like he has a sense of humor."

"Air Guard Rescue, good to hear you're still in the area. Sorry you had to miss happy hour at the officer's club."

The pilot took the comment in stride. "Not a problem. We'll make up for the absence tomorrow. By the way, you guys are buying."

Connor smirked good-naturedly. "It would help if we could get off this mountain first."

"Roger that. The weather just might cooperate. I don't want to get your hopes up too much, but the weather guru revised the forecast. Looks like you all might be home a couple hours sooner, maybe by early afternoon."

Bril returned from outside, having expected the call, and listened in. The other survivors either didn't hear the radio or were reluctant to divert attention from their own conversation. Their faces showed little emotion.

"We'll be waiting. Any chance of a hot breakfast being dropped off in the morning?"

The Air Guard pilot laughed over the radio. "I'll see what we can do. How you holding up down there?"

"We're comfortable." Connor glanced at Bril and Susan who smiled through tired expressions.

"Okay, Lonesome Dove. Stay warm. The temperature at your elevation is forecast in the twenties tonight. We'll remain on station monitoring this frequency for the next few hours. Get some rest. Another aircraft will make contact at eight in the morning. They should have a better perspective on the weather by then."

"We appreciate the concern down here. Thanks for the update, Air Guard."

The C-130 pilot ended the call and Connor shut off the power switch to preserve the battery. Setting the radio aside, he flexed his neck and back, relaxing the tight muscles.

"It's snowing outside. The rain turned to snow while you were sleeping." Bril made the statement with little emotion. Even his youthful stamina showed signs of fatigue. "We're still in the clouds. Visibility is only about twenty feet, so don't stray far if you have to go outside."

Connor wondered why the dog wasn't with him. "What happened to your companion, Bril?"

"Muck? He's with the other dog. They were with me for a while, but the older one has an injured leg and doesn't walk very far. She seemed content to stay with her owner. He's one of the deceased in the cargo compartment."

"The dog's probably traumatized, too. You better pick a sleeping spot and get situated for the night, Bril."

"I will, sir. Let me tell the others what the Air Guard pilot said. With the overcast, the sky will be dark soon. I've got some chem lights in my survival vest. I'll hang one by the forward door for the night. Then I'm ready to call it quits."

Bril was gone for a few minutes before returning with a heavy blanket, which he set on the floor along with a few of the seat cushions for padding. He hung one of the amber, plastic chemical lights near the door and then unfurled the blankets. Curling up inside, he yawned and turned his head toward the wall.

CHAPTER FORTY-SIX

Connor and Susan talked with lowered voices into the evening. He was a good listener, keeping most of his past to himself as she condensed her life into short clips of interest. The content was not as important as being near her. For the first time in a long time, he felt a void in his life being filled.

Eventually, she questioned his past. Not out of suspicion, but curiosity, for she was as interested in him as he was in her.

"You haven't mentioned much about your life, Gil. I bet you've had an interesting career. And after three marriages, only two children? Any grandkids?"

Once she asked the question, he opened up more than intended. At first he glossed over his youth and the painful memories of Vietnam, but when he talked about his children the emotional scars became obvious. Explaining the circumstances of his infant daughter's death was the hardest. The loss of his son added even more regret.

Susan could only imagine the terrible weight of guilt and sorrow he carried. The emotions were far deeper than most people understood and something no parent should ever have to endure.

Talking about his past weakened Connor, but at the same time he felt less encumbered by emotional baggage. Carrying out his plan would be harder now. Meeting Susan made his choice more complicated. His feelings for her were genuine, but he knew a relationship was only wishful thinking. His cancer had paved a different path, leaving him no choice in the matter. Soon, he would see his kids again. That was all he cared about.

They talked awhile longer before gathering some items for the night. One by one, the others did the same, bored with small talk and no longer resisting the temptation of sleep. Each of them made a short trip outside before arranging cushions on either side of the aisle. One by one, they settled in for the night, the women in warm sleeping bags and the men wrapped in a layer of blankets.

Connor and Susan lay across from each other. The soft glow of the chemical light was the only illumination. Grasping his hand for a moment, she looked softly into his eyes. "Good night, fly boy."

He smiled and squeezed her hand in response. In minutes, she was asleep.

Connor tossed and turned before eventually nodding off. Sleep was a fitful rest. Every half hour or so he would awaken and reposition, adjusting the blankets tightly around his body. The heavy fabric and Shultz's borrowed jacket blocked most of the cold, but his joints were stiff from the thin cushions and hard floor. Even worse, his back muscles were flaring up again, shooting jolts of pain along his spine.

Reluctant to take another pill for fear of being incapacitated before he could carry out his plan, he finally relented and took one when the pain became unbearable. Waiting for the medicine to take effect and listening to the sounds of breathing, he was surprised when someone slid silently past him. They knelt beside the large man further forward on the floor.

In the pale light, he recognized Marla and saw a glint of what looked like a hypodermic needle in her hand. She moved, blocking his view, and after a long pause returned to the back of the cabin. The man remained motionless. His breathing was slower, almost indiscernible.

Connor was unsure of Marla's intention but assumed she administered another dose of pain medication. Her husband was obviously given more than just pain pills. The medicine was certainly effective.

After waiting several minutes, Connor slowly stood and moved toward the door, trying to be quiet. The effort pulled sharply at his stiff muscles, causing minor spasms of opposition, but he managed to step outside without causing further grief. The access door latched with a dull thud as he turned the handle. If the cold draft of air entering the cabin hadn't disturbed anyone, the sound of the door closing probably did.

There was at least two inches of fresh snow on the ground. Indentations from his boots left a clear trail toward the cargo compartment. Even with the thick overcast, the summer twilight and white terrain provided enough illumination to see where he was going. He guessed the time was around midnight or early morning, for the sun was still hidden.

The weather was better than Bril described earlier. The snow had stopped, and the clouds had dispersed off the ridge. Visibility was at least a hundred yards, for he could see the slope where the flatter ground extended from the mountain.

The door to the cargo compartment was left slightly ajar for the dogs to go in and out. Connor glanced inside and saw two pairs of eyes staring back. The young malamute rose to greet him. The other dog nestled against a covered body and lifted her head dejectedly.

The three fatalities were lying beside each other on the metal floor. Open luggage and other cargo were strewn around the interior. The appearance was more chaotic than the cabin section.

Connor stroked the dog named Muck behind the ears. "How you doing, buddy? You need to go the bathroom, too?"

The malamute accompanied him along the ridge, staying close by. A short time later the other dog joined them, limping slightly as she struggled to keep up. Connor stopped and knelt beside her, feeling his own muscles flare in protest. "Seems we're both hurting, old girl."

He patted the dog on the head and under the chin, letting her smell his hand. "Let me take a look." He spoke softly and felt along her injured hind leg. There were no bulges he could feel, but she yelped when he tried flexing the hip.

"Sorry about that." Connor massaged her back and hindquarter, thinking the injury was just a sprain. "I'll walk slower. No hurry where we're going."

When they were at the end of the ridge, Connor stopped to relieve himself. The dogs wandered off nearby, sniffing the ground before conducting their own business.

The medicine started taking effect. Connor could feel his eyes becoming heavy. His back still ached. He swallowed three more pills, far more than he needed, but the extras wouldn't make a difference. He rested on a narrow patch of soft lichen, underneath an overhang of rock where the ground was shielded from the wet snow. Carefully kneeling and lowering himself to a prone position, he lay on his back, gazing up at the sky.

The cold air made him shiver. Thoughts of his daughter and son overwhelmed him. He missed them. His eyes moistened as stars appeared above, sparkling in the night sky through a break in the overcast. In his medicated state he imagined they looked like airport beacons, guiding him home.

CHAPTER FORTY-SEVEN

Sounds of laughter drifted through the still air. There was a fragrance of fresh flowers and warm pastry. The sky was tinted a perfect shade of indigo-blue, and the forest of birch and poplar was ripe with the vibrant colors of fall.

A spacious lodge filled with guests sat nestled on a hill nearby, surrounded by lush lawns and a stained cedar deck. Rocking chairs sat empty on the porch and a column of thin smoke curled from the tall chimney. Heavy timbered beams and thick pine logs gave an appearance of reserved strength and exceptional craftsmanship.

In the distance, the sun was rising above the pillared mountains, casting a warm glow over the valley. Snowcapped peaks rose above the lower slopes, still bare from the summer heat. Above the tree line, a waterfall cascaded off a high basin into a deep gorge, joining a larger drainage through a carved path toward the sea.

The setting was peaceful and welcoming, but Connor couldn't remember being there before. He breathed in deeply, tasting the clean alpine air.

Turning slowly to capture the entire landscape, he could see he was near a small inlet of a calm, clear lake, stretching for miles along a pristine shoreline. His eyes caught a ripple of movement on the water. A fish flipped and then another as a pair of loons glided effortlessly over the glassy surface.

Off to the side, a gravel walkway extended down from the lodge to a small, floating pier. A single, wooden boat was tied alongside and someone was loading fishing gear into the bow. The reflection of sunlight off the water shielded the man's features, but his outline and the way he moved looked familiar.

The pain and tension in Connor's back was missing. There was no soreness or stiffness in his limbs. He felt young and healthy, in his prime again. An overwhelming sense of peacefulness engulfed him. He wondered where he was.

He stepped onto the wooden planked dock with an easy stride. As he approached the figure in the small boat, he could distinguish an athletic body with short, blond hair, wearing faded denim jeans and a flannel shirt. The man was kneeling and facing away, leaning over an open tackle box in search of something inside.

"Good morning. I seem to be lost. Can you help me out?"

The young man turned and stood facing him with a welcoming smile. "Hi, Dad. I was just getting the boat ready. Thought you might want to go fishing later."

Connor stared in shock, unsure of what he was seeing, then recovered and met his son with a strong embrace. They hugged warmly, enjoying the moment before pulling away and holding each other by the shoulders. He mirrored his son's smile, looking him over with disbelief.

"Where did you come from? Where is this place, son?"

"You'll see, Dad. Everything is fine. We've been waiting for you."

Slowly, understanding spread across Connor's face. He thought for a moment and then his eyes brightened. "We? Is she with you?"

"Of course. They're all here. Grandma, Grandpa, your Army buddies. And someone who has been very excited to see you."

"Tara? She's here? Where is she?"

His son grinned wider and chuckled. "I guess she couldn't wait any longer."

He turned to where his son pointed and saw a little girl running down the walkway. Her tiny legs were a blur of motion. Her lemon-colored chinos and embroidered top bounced in harmony with her raven hair. "Daddy, Daddy!" she called, giggling excitedly at the same time.

He moved quickly to meet her, falling to his knees as she ran into his arms. They held each other tightly for a long time, relishing the moment. The wait had been such a long time. Tears of joy ran down his cheeks.

She kept her hands around his neck as he stood and carried her, studying his face the way she always did. He kissed her and brushed the hair from her forehead.

"I missed you, cutie pie. I missed you so much."

"Daddy, my daddy." The sound of her voice filled the air with joyful innocence. Her small hands clasped his cheeks, and she pressed her nose against his, swimming in the color of his eyes. They smiled and laughed, together again at last.

CHAPTER FORTY-EIGHT

By mid-morning of the following day, the weather gave little indication of improvement. Low, dense clouds hung over the city of Fairbanks and the nearby military bases as rescue crews waited impatiently. Three helicopters were fueled and ready, sitting with their blades untied and doors open in anticipation of a quick departure. The window of opportunity for rescue might be short, and no one wanted unnecessary delays.

An Air Guard C-130 out of Anchorage was the first to arrive over the crash site. The crew maintained a high orbit above the jagged summits, circling at twenty thousand feet. The pilot reported a broken layer around the peaks, with heavy fog in the valleys and lower approaches. Winds were light, causing little change in the cloud cover.

At the top of the hour, the C-130 commander attempted contact with the survivors on the emergency band frequency. There was no response initially and Colonel Patrick "Paddy" Hannesy tried several times before a broken transmission was heard in reply.

"This is Air Guard Rescue, good morning. I'm receiving you broken and barely readable. We are currently overhead your position. How is everyone holding up, over?"

"Rog . . . guard . . . Any chang . . . forecas . . . ver?"

Enough of the fractured, static transmission was decipherable for Hannesy to understand. He passed the latest weather and what he was seeing from his perspective to the survivors, leaving out the likelihood of another storm arriving within the next twenty-four hours.

"The rescue helicopters are waiting for the clouds to lift. We're hoping for a late morning or early afternoon rescue. How was the night on the mountain? Any problems?"

There was a delay and a change in pitch to the voice. "Affirm. One . . . dittion . . . fatalit . . . uring . . . night . . . ver."

Colonel Hannesy looked at his first officer for confirmation. "Did he say one of the survivors died during the night?"

The first officer nodded before speaking. "Sure sounded that way."

Hannesy was no stranger to aviation tragedies, having flown military and civilian aircraft for almost forty years. Any loss of life reflected on the actions of the rescuers, whether circumstantial or not.

"Say again. Understand one fatality during the night. Is that correct?"

The response took longer this time. Each transmission became weaker and more garbled from the depleted battery in the portable radio. "firmative . . . one . . . ditional . . . tality. . . . name . . . Con . . . er."

Hannesy and the first officer exchanged a look of regret. "The news won't go over very well. I better pass on the information. Looks like one more body for the morgue."

Bril had been fiddling with the radio since the Air Guard aircraft contacted them. Sometime during the night, the power switch had been turned on, draining the battery.

He cursed himself for leaving the radio in a location where the power could be inadvertently activated. At the same time he was upset at Connor. Bril couldn't understand his decision for leaving.

Susan was the one who found Connor in the early morning, at the end of the ridge. She went looking for him after realizing he was gone. The dogs were curled close against his unmoving body and the youngest seemed reluctant to leave. A feeling of helplessness overcame her. The stress and emotional trauma of the crash, combined with the deaths of her fellow passengers and now Connor, pushed her to the limit. She sat down and cried, holding his hand to her cheek.

In Fairbanks, word of another fatality on the mountain reached the waiting helicopter crews. A somber atmosphere replaced the optimism they felt when the day first began. The pilots spent their time between the aircraft and the hangar, checking the weather between conversations and reading about the previous day's rescue in the morning paper. The crew chiefs and medics checked and rechecked their equipment or worked on menial tasks to keep them busy.

Shultz was the most affected by the news. He went inside to make a phone call, wanting to verify the name of the fatality, but there was little doubt. He'd been told about Connor's conversation with Sergeant Mayo and his reference to suicide.

Shultz couldn't possibly fathom everything going through Connor's mind, but the prospect of suffering through months of hopeless pain explained his behavior. The extent and eventual outcome of the disease provided him with limited hope. He just never figured Connor would go out without a fight.

He tried evaluating Connor's thought process, wondering what his own actions would be in a similar situation. He couldn't hold any resentment. Suicide was a way out, a simple choice of how and when to die. Shultz managed a smile. *Connor had done it again. He lived by his own rules. He might as well die by them, too.*

Shultz checked the weather for the third time. There was some new data, and he received another briefing on the latest outlook. The forecast was better but not great. Waiting made him antsy. He needed to do something, if only to verify what the forecaster said, and decided to launch ahead of the others. Once in the air, he would have a better perspective if the weather changed.

Shultz was airborne in a matter of minutes, soon after informing the other crews of his intention. Ferguson again accompanied him. A different medic and crew chief were in the back. Steiner had been tasked by the chain of command with writing a report on the rescue. A task he was very unhappy about.

Thompson was supposed to be doing the same, but he had talked his way out of the assignment due to a shortage of pilots. Instead, he would accompany the unit's maintenance officer and Lieutenant Hovan to pick up the UH-1 helicopter left at the airstrip. A maintenance team and the standby medevac pilots from Shultz's unit would also be riding along. They intended to repair the damaged engine before flying the Black Hawk home.

South of Fairbanks, the cloud layer was lifting. Shultz had no trouble flying along the river drainage into the foothills of the Alaska Range. He reached the face of the glacier before a solid ceiling prevented them from going further. Frustrated, he passed the information to the orbiting C-130 and repositioned to wait at the airstrip from the day before.

"Evac two-three-nine, message has been relayed." Hannesy and his crew had been circling for almost three hours and were frustrated as much as the Army crew. The tops of the peaks and upper slopes were clear, leaving a thick overcast in the valleys and partial accumulations hanging on the ridges. The morning sun reflected brightly off the snow-capped mountains jutting through the clouds.

A light wind was blowing, slowly pushing the wide, pillowed overcast northeast between the expanse of towering rocks and ice. The crash site would be visible for a few minutes, then masked again by the upper limit of clouds. The layer was gradually thinning and lifting from the heat of the sun but not quickly enough to suit them.

"Air Guard Rescue, Evac two-three-nine is on the ground. We'll be running on auxiliary power to save fuel. I'll be monitoring the radios. Let us know if anything changes."

"I copy, Evac. We just got a message from base. An Army Huey just launched with recovery crews for the two stranded helicopters at your location. They're estimating thirty-minutes en route. Both Air Guard helicopters will be departing in the next few minutes. If the weather doesn't improve by the time they arrive, they plan on waiting at the field site with you."

"Roger that. We're standing by."

Ferguson looked at Shultz, who had a thousand-mile stare on his face. He imagined he was thinking about Connor. No one back at the base mentioned the word suicide, but when news of his terminal cancer and unauthorized flight spread, speculation on his motives leaned in the obvious direction. Once word of Connor's conversation with Sergeant Mayo leaked out, the rumors intensified. Ferguson didn't know what to believe, but he could see the situation weighed heavily on Shultz's mind.

"Space is going to be crowded in here with three more helicopters."

The statement broke Shultz's concentration. He looked around outside as if noticing the size of the airstrip for the first time. "Yeah, some might have to land on the riverbed."

CHAPTER FORTY-NINE

Ferguson could tell Shultz wasn't interested in a conversation and left him alone, watching the gentle breeze rustle the willow bushes instead. The medic and crew chief could be heard discussing a recently released movie, but neither pilot paid attention.

By the time the Air Guard HH-60 Pave Hawk helicopters neared the mountains, the C-130 was reporting occasional breaks in the lower overcast over the glacier. The crash site was visible above the thicker cumulus in the valley. Hannesy informed Shultz he thought an approach was possible if they could find a hole through the clouds and followed a mountain ridge in from the foothills.

Shultz restarted the engines immediately. The helicopter was still at idle when the two Air Guard Pave Hawks arrived. They passed the slower Huey in flight a few miles out from the foothills. Deciding not to land, they instead circled over the nearby river drainage, formulating a plan over the radio.

"Evac two-three-nine, this is Helo Six. I can see sunlight filtering through a break in the cloud base a few miles south. I'll climb through first and see how the weather looks."

Shultz searched the skyline before answering. "Roger, Helo Six. I have all three helicopters in sight. Holding position until the Huey is on the ground."

Once the helicopter touched down, Shultz made a smooth take-off, keeping the nearest Air Guard Pave Hawk in sight. "Evac two-three-nine is lifting off. We'll stay east of the drainage until you advise, Helo Six."

He mirrored the holding pattern of the second Air Guard helicopter, maintaining a mile separation on the opposite side of the drainage. Shultz noticed the clouds had lifted several hundred feet since they arrived. He kept the helicopter in a low orbit, watching the valley and distant glacier for obvious breaks in the overcast.

Several minutes passed before the C-130 sent another update. "Helo Six, the crash site is clear. Winds are six knots out of the southwest at my altitude. Do not have you in sight."

Colonel Hannesy kept his focus outside the aircraft while transmitting, searching the clouds below the crash site for a visual sighting of the helicopter.

The first officer was flying. He kept the aircraft in a continuous, high orbit over the mountains, waiting for Hannesy to take the controls so he could get another cup of coffee. Since arriving on station earlier in the morning, they had been alternating on the controls every hour and both were getting bored with the repetitive routine.

"I don't see a damn thing except mountains and clouds," Hannesy stated. He kept his eyes glued outside. "The helicopter must be blending in with the terrain. What say we take a closer look?"

"How low you want to go?"

Hannesy wanted to stay above the height of the tallest mountains, but low enough for a view of the helicopter. He directed the first officer to descend another four thousand feet, glancing at the instrument panel before refocusing his eyes on the terrain.

There had been no contact with the survivors since the first broken transmission earlier in the morning. Hannesy wasn't worried. He figured their portable survival radio was out of power, leaving them with no means of contact. They wouldn't know the rescue was under way until a helicopter arrived. He was more worried about the next weather system and the likelihood of a helicopter arriving at all.

Shultz was about to call the Air Guard Pave Hawk for a situation report when a strong voice interrupted the radio silence. "Helo Six is at six thousand, above the cloud base and climbing. Nothing but clear blue sky on top."

Shultz managed a slight smile. "Helo Six, Evac two-three-nine copies. Any problems getting through?"

"Negative, Evac. There's a wide hole over the valley, just north of the glacier. We can see the crash site ahead of us. I'll make the first lift. Since we have three helos, we might as well spread the load. You still want the second lift, Evac?"

"Roger, Helo Six. I'll pick up three survivors and the deceased helicopter pilot. He was a friend of mine."

"Fine with us, Evac. You might as well take the dogs, too, if you don't mind. Helo Five can pick up the remaining survivors on the last lift. I'll advise when I'm departing the crash site."

Shultz didn't bother explaining further. He wanted to be the one transporting Connor's body. It was the least he could do for his mentor. An Army helicopter seemed more fitting than one from the Air Guard. Flying him off the mountain was a simple way of paying his respect. He was sure Connor would've done the same if the situation were reversed.

Before leaving the airfield, Shultz grabbed a black body bag from the supply office. The zippered, heavy-duty enclosure was big enough for a large adult, designed to protect the body during transport. The flight medic would carry the bag with him when he hoisted down to the crash site. The Air Guard helicopter carried additional bags for the other deceased.

At the lower altitude, Hannesy could see the Pave Hawk reach a stable hover over the ridge. The basket with the flight medic lowered easily in the light winds and the first fatality was loaded a short time later. Two more followed in succession, then one of the survivors.

The deceased were taken first since the medic needed the assistance of the other men at the crash site in moving the bodies. He was hoisted up last, preceded by one of the women survivors. The entire sequence took less than fifteen minutes.

"Helo Six is departing with three fatalities and one survivor on board. You're clear to climb, Evac. I'll stay on the eastern side at seven thousand. Advise once you're through, over."

Colonel Hannesy contacted the airbase with news of the successful lift. He was content letting his first officer fly and watched the second helicopter ascend over the glacier.

Unlike the day before, there was no turbulence or swirling winds to worry about. Keeping the helicopter stable over the ridge was easy in comparison. Shultz had no trouble holding position as they repeated the procedure of the first helicopter. His steadiness masked his inner feeling of grief.

The surrounding mountains towered brightly into the blue sky. Sunlight sparkled off the white peaks and cornices of ice. The landscape was peaceful and welcoming, in stark contrast to the dreary conditions of the day before.

The crew chief lowered the medic on the hoist and waited patiently while the first passenger was loaded. He maintained eye contact with the ground for any change in the helicopter's position. Radio transmissions were kept to a minimum.

Ferguson watched the people on the ground. A woman with her hair in disarray from the rotor wash was the first in the lift basket. She held on tightly to the attaching straps, staring at the helicopter during the ascent. In a minute she was inside and looking around with a wide-eyed expression on her face. Assisted by the crew chief, she quickly found a seat and fastened herself in, glancing at the cockpit with a cheerful smile.

The second person was already in the basket when Ferguson returned his attention outside. He could see Bril wearing his olive-gray flight jacket and holding a dog between his legs. He thought it was unusual. The medic must have sent Bril with the dogs, instead of having him help load Connor's body.

As the basket left the ground, he glanced at the instrument panel. All indications were normal as Shultz held their position over the ground with little effort. Control inputs were minimal in the light breeze, requiring only slight variations to compensate for the swaying of the basket.

A shifting in the balance of the helicopter indicated the basket was inside. Ferguson turned around as the occupants were unloaded. He could see Bril holding the dog by the collar while he found a seat. Then he realized the person wasn't Bril at all, but Connor, who was grinning affectionately at the woman.

A confused stare was all Ferguson could muster for a few seconds. He thought at first Connor and Shultz must have been playing a practical joke, and then he realized the perceived death was all a misunderstanding. The name of the deceased survivor must have been wrong. They could sort the truth out later.

He recovered and smiled, placing his hands on the flight controls. "I've got the controls. Take a break."

Shultz turned with a questioning look. "I'm good. I'd rather wait until his body is aboard."

"He already is." Nodding his head toward the back, Ferguson smiled even wider. "I've got the controls. Go ahead and say hello."

Relinquishing the controls with a questioning look, Shultz twisted in his seat toward the back. He gawked, unable to speak for a few seconds before realizing what must have happened. Connor met his gaze and wondered why a puzzled look was evident on Shultz's face. He retrieved a headset from a nearby seat and placed the cups over his ears.

"Hello, Joe." The dog licked his face, happy to be out of the rotor wash. "I was hoping you would be flying today. Thanks for picking us up."

Shultz's voice stumbled with suppressed emotion before explaining they thought he had died during the night. "The rescue C-130 relayed the name of the last fatality as Con something. After learning of your cancer and the theft of the helicopter . . . well, the possibility of suicide seemed a likely option. Everyone assumed the worst. Sorry for doubting you. Welcome back."

"Thanks." Connor looked down in embarrassment. The truth was far more accurate than Shultz realized. Later, he would explain what really happened. At this point, he wasn't entirely sure himself.

"Did one of the original survivors die last night?"

Connor nodded as he spoke. "Yeah, unfortunately. The man's name was Connover so I can understand the confusion. He sustained a back injury in the crash and was too heavy for transport yesterday. He died sometime during the night. His wife is pretty upset. The coroner will figure out what happened."

As Danny Simms, the remaining dog, and then the medic was hoisted aboard, Connor gave a condensed version of events since they last spoke. When he reached the part about wandering away from the wreckage, he left out his true motive.

In a deliberate voice he explained how he had gone outside and fallen asleep from the effects of the pain medication, only to be protected from the cold by the dogs huddled beside him. The survivors searched for him in the morning when they realized he was gone. Susan found him and at first thought he was dead. Only after blinking his eyes open, uncertain of his surroundings, did she calm down.

No one was pleased knowing he spent six hours on the frozen ground. Finding out Mister Connover had passed away while everyone slept made the situation worse. Considering what everyone had already been through, the added trauma was especially hard.

The confusion over the loss of life was a result of a weak radio signal. A garbled transmission about the death of Connover must have been mistaken for his own.

Shultz took the explanation in stride. Connor seemed different now as if the physical pain and weight of old memories were gone. They talked for a few more minutes until the hoist was brought inside and secured.

The helicopter departed in a smooth acceleration over the glacier. Shultz established a slow climb, turning northward on a course away from the mountains. He grinned, thinking of everything that had transpired. The freshness of a new day, after the passing storm, befitted the moment. Connor was alive and well. The darkness had passed.

The last Air Guard helicopter hovered into position above the ridge. Bril, Kwapich, and Bidwell waited on the ground for the medic, helping him load the remaining body in the basket. Bidwell and Kwapich went next, followed by Bril and the medic. No one remained. The rescue was over.

CHAPTER FIFTY

Marla kept her gaze fixed outside the helicopter. Tears of sorrow had been replaced by a blank stare. What little composure she possessed after the crash, faded upon finding her husband had died during the night. The others offered comfort the best they could, but the ensuing rescue diverted their attention. Their condolences didn't matter to her. She was a good actor. A façade of grief was easy. No one would guess the truth.

Harold was many things, but a good husband wasn't one of them. He was a swindler, a pathological liar, abusive, and an adulterer. His desire for wealth was the driving force in his life, providing the power and prestige he perceived as entitlement for his existence. People meant nothing to him, other than those with a high society pedigree who could enhance his ego.

His intensity for climbing the corporate ladder drove a wedge in their relationship. He made millions during the tech boom as a fund manager investing other people's money. Even after the market crashed, he continued to prosper. He was smart, if nothing else, and saw the downturn before anyone else, coercing investors to continue buying. Thousands of people lost their money. He wasn't one of them.

Harold became more abusive with power and increased wealth. He took out his anger on Marla, openly ridiculing her or anyone who dared challenge his authority. The cheating was bad enough—the emotional trauma of him flaunting the affairs was even worse. She thought about a divorce but decided to give their marriage another try. Besides, he would never let her walk away with anything substantial. Giving up the social status and luxurious lifestyle Harold provided wasn't a real consideration.

Along with his arrogance, Harold's weight increased dramatically. A sharp decline in physical appearance didn't stop his many infidelities, which he made little effort to hide. Money could buy anything, including beautiful and exotic women. Only after being diagnosed with chronic, type-two diabetes did his lifestyle change—or so Marla thought. Impotence was one of the symptoms of the disease and one she truly believed he was suffering from.

She had hoped there was still some good inside him. The trip to Alaska was intended as a vacation, an attempt to rekindle their marriage. He went along reluctantly, swearing he still loved her and would never be with another woman. Once the vacation was over, he planned to attend a business meeting in Anchorage before returning home. Then, he promised her, things would be different.

Harold's true personality returned after the crash. She realized he would never change. Initially, she just wanted to get away, determined to be on the helicopter. When that wasn't possible, she decided to make the best of the situation. The pain medication and muscle relaxers the medic provided would at least keep him quiet. Once they were rescued, she would let someone else care for him. Maybe a change is what they both needed—her most of all.

Harold never mentioned his diabetes to the medic. His ego wouldn't allow the disclosure. Besides, he was being evacuated on the helicopter. Marla could take care of the injections. She knew any medication he was given wouldn't interfere with the insulin. The muscle relaxers had already taken effect by the time he realized he would be left on the mountain. He was too groggy to say much of anything.

Following the helicopter's departure, while everyone was busy, Marla tested her husband's blood sugar. The level was high but not particularly surprising considering the crash and ensuing trauma. Giving him an injection was easy enough. She'd done the procedure many times before. In spite of Harold's arrogance, he was actually afraid of needles and preferred Marla doing the procedure for him.

Harold's diabetes was treated with a rapid-acting type of insulin. His daily activities and the consumption of food and beverages determined the frequency and amount. Periodic testing was critical because the blood glucose level needed to remain within a certain range. Too high or too low could be fatal, a fact Marla was very aware of.

The insulin for Harold was kept in a small collapsible cooler brought aboard the aircraft and tucked inside a tan leather duffel bag in an overhead compartment. Harold hated the injections but was smart enough to keep the medication close by in case of an emergency. He was particular about no one getting inside the bag and disturbing the contents, even Marla. He usually did everything, short of actually injecting the needle into his abdomen.

The duffel was still in the compartment, undamaged after the crash. She was careful. No one noticed what she was really doing. While everyone was busy, she pulled the bag down and set it out of the way on the floor. The thick zipper opened easily. In addition to the cooler, there was a shaving kit, change of clothes, cell phone, and digital camera, all belonging to Harold. She pushed the smaller items to the side and removed the cooler, exposing a pocket sewn inside the liner of the duffel bag. The enclosure was partially open with some papers tucked inside. Curious, she pulled out the contents.

The folded papers were credit card receipts. There was also a small plastic prescription bottle she'd never seen before. Harold was meticulous about keeping receipts, but she didn't recognize the credit card as one for their joint account. One receipt confirmed a hotel reservation for his business meeting when she would fly home ahead of him. The other receipt was for a round trip airline ticket from Boston to Anchorage. The purchase didn't make sense. They lived in New York and traveled to Alaska on a cruise ship. The flight home was one-way.

Marla studied the receipts, anger building inside her. She set them aside and read the label on the half-empty bottle of blue pills. The name *Viagra* stood out, and she knew the trip was all a lie.

Harold had been uninterested in sex with her for over a year. He blamed the impotence. The bottle of *Viagra* told a different story. The receipts confirmed her suspicion. He was having another affair. His mistress, high-end escort or whatever he wanted to call her, would be meeting him for a lover's tryst. He had been lying all along.

His cell phone was next. All the messages had been deleted, except one. The text was from the same morning. A woman named Eva wrote she had received the itinerary and would be waiting at the hotel in three days. She signed off with XOXO.

His reply was curt. "Can't wait. I need you."

One by one, she placed the items back inside the bag. Her eyes were moist. She thought about her life and what a sham her marriage had been. Her expression suddenly changed. She leaned back, a flicker of a smile crossing her lips. The medic and other survivors didn't know Harold was diabetic. The medication he'd been given would keep him silent. *Killing him would be easy.*

His death would be a simple mistake, if the coroner even suspected. She'd claim his glucose levels were high, at least she'd thought so. Maybe she misread the numbers. Injecting him with too much insulin was an accident. In her confused state following the crash, perhaps she misread the dosage, too.

Harold never had a chance. The extra large doses of insulin, one in the evening and another before midnight, did the trick. She was very careful. It was the perfect crime. The resulting hypoglycemia went unnoticed due to his already lethargic condition. He lapsed into shock, then coma and death, unaware of what was happening. Everyone thought he was sleeping comfortably. All except Marla.

EPILOGUE

Connor remembered his dream. The events seemed so real. Every aspect was still vivid in his mind. He was certain his daughter and son were together with him, if only for a short while. After the joyful reunion by the lake, they walked together toward the lodge. He carried Tara in one arm, the other around Eric's shoulders.

There was a faint whisper in the air. Tara and Eric seemed to understand what the voice said and stopped at the bottom of the walkway. Tara kissed him and asked to be let down, hugging him tightly as he kneeled, then placed her hands on his cheeks. Her voice sounded more mature as she spoke, but there was only love in her eyes.

"Daddy, this isn't your time. You still have more to do."

"What do you mean, honey?" He asked, looking at Eric for confirmation, then back into her eyes. "I thought we would be together now."

"I know, Daddy. Me, too. We'll all be waiting for you. They decided to send you back for a while."

"No, honey. You and Eric are here. I want to stay with you."

His son grasped him gently by the shoulder as he knelt beside them. "Everything will be okay, Dad."

Tara touched her nose to his and kissed him. "I love you, Daddy."

Eric repeated the words. Connor grabbed both of them in a bear hug. "I don't understand. I want to stay."

"We know, Dad. We'll see you soon. We promise."

They stepped away into a halo of light, leaving him with open arms in a nothingness of space. And then they were gone. His eyes closed, and he was asleep again. He wasn't sure for how long, only the next memory of something pushing at his arm.

A hand shook him awake, causing him to open his eyes, and when he did he was back on the ridge. Susan nudged him again, startled but relieved he was alive. She immediately fell forward, embracing him tightly. He felt suddenly different. His reason for being there was clear.

Soon after Susan found him, he told her about the cancer and how the events in his dream—if it really was a dream—had changed him. The physical pain was completely gone. He felt a renewed enthusiasm for life. Everything would be different now, of that he was certain.

She cried of course, but they knew they had found something real in each other, something that had been missing from their lives for far too long. Together, they decided, they would live life to the fullest.

He tried to explain the reason for his staying on the mountain and walking away from the wreckage, how Vietnam had changed him and how he lost faith after his daughter died. Those experiences showed him the dark side of life, how evil can be so prevalent, how the innocent are taken so easily. He stopped believing in himself and in God.

Susan told him she felt the same way after her husband died. People have faith in different ways, for different reasons. She realized you can't believe in evil without believing in good. If true evil exists in the world, then kindness and love and faith must exist as well. Her husband was in a better place. She believed the truth with all her heart. Connor's son and daughter were there, too.

Connor and Susan thought about the future, resting against each other on the flight home. A peacefulness neither had felt before surrounded them. There were no worries. Life was too precious. They smiled warmly between glances outside.

The air smelled fresh after the storm. The mountains were as picturesque as a postcard. High overhead, the sky was clear and calm, beckoning a new beginning. Rays of sunlight reached down from the heavens, reflecting brightly in Connor's deep blue eyes.

****

Once the last helicopter departed off the ridge and was safely out of the mountains, Colonel Hannesy radioed a farewell. It was time to head home. In a few weeks the wreckage would be buried in snow, invisible until the next summer thaw. Over time, what remained would be crushed under the repeated weight of ice or swept away by an avalanche, eventually broken into pieces and dispersed on the creviced glacier below. All evidence of the crash would be gone.

Colonel Hannesy ran a hand through his thinning silver hair. The rescue was another successful mission under his belt. He lost count of exactly how many, years ago. Maybe he should retire. Flying wasn't the seductive mistress she used to be. He was getting old. A day of fishing and an ice-cold beer sounded just as good.

"How about a break? You want to fly for a while?" The first officer yawned with boredom. "I could use a fresh cup of coffee."

"Sure. Hang on a second."

Reaching behind his seat, Colonel Hannesy pulled out a worn helmet bag and retrieved a tootsie pop. He had long since given up chewing tobacco. The wrapper was peeled away and the candy placed in his mouth with the stem extending from his lips. He crumpled the paper and tossed the wad at the bag, missing the open pocket where it bounced and lay on the floor.

The sides of the helmet bag were adorned with patches from a dozen different units, some old and frayed and some in better condition. The various insignia ranged in shape and color, but one, in particular, stood out among the rest. The word *Guardians* was stitched in white above contrasting colors of green, gold, and maroon, and the name 56th Support Squadron framed the bottom. In the center was a depiction of a small airplane flying above a jungle landscape and the apparition of an angel with open wings.

"All right, I've got the controls. Time to put the horse in the barn."

BECAUSE I FLY

Because I fly
I laugh more than other men,
I look up and see more than they.
I know how the clouds feel,
What it's like to have the blue in my lap,
To look down on birds,
To feel the freedom in a thing called a stick.
Who but I can slice between God's billowed legs,
And feel them laugh and crash with his every step.
Who else but I have seen the unclimbed peaks?
The rainbow's secret?
The real reason birds sing?
Because I Fly,
I envy no man on earth.

—Grover C. Norwood, USAF (Retired)